ALEXANDER GRIGORENKO

ILGET

THE THREE NAMES OF A LIFE

ИНСТИТУТ ПЕРЕВОДА

AD VERBUM

ILGET: THE THREE NAMES OF A LIFE

by Alexander Grigorenko

First published in Russian as *Ильгет. Три имени судьбы* in 2013

Translated from the Russian by Christopher Culver

Published with the support
of the Institute for Literary Translation, Russia

Proofreading by Stephen Dalziel

Agreement via Wiedling Literary Agency

Book cover and interior book design by Max Mendor

© Glagoslav Publications 2024

www.glagoslav.com

ISBN: 978-1-80484-125-9
ISBN: 978-1-80484-126-6

First published in English by Glagoslav Publications in March 2024

A catalogue record for this book is available from the British Library.

ALEXANDER GRIGORENKO

ILGET

THE THREE NAMES OF A LIFE

TRANSLATED FROM THE RUSSIAN
BY CHRISTOPHER CULVER

GLAGOSLAV PUBLICATIONS

CONTENTS

MAN OF THE EARTH (THE SECOND NAME)

Find that which has been lost,
Pursue that which has fled,
Crush that which has crushed,
Slay that which has slain.

Sodeni the Hero, Evenki epic

And seeing all the Hellespont covered over with the ships, and all the shores and the plains of Abydos full of men, then Xerxes pronounced himself a happy man, and after that he fell to weeping. Artabanos his uncle… asked as follows: "O king, how far different from one another are the things which thou hast done now and a short while before now! For having pronounced thyself a happy man, thou art now shedding tears." He said: "Yea, for after I had reckoned up, it came into my mind to feel pity at the thought how brief was the whole life of man, seeing that of these multitudes not one will be alive when a hundred years have gone by."

Herodotus, *History*, Book VII "Polyhymnia",
trans. G. C. Macaulay

THE TREE OF THE YENISEI

I was born on the banks of the river that my people call the Khug, the steppe-dwellers the Khem-Sug, and the Tungus – and many peoples after them – the Yenisei.

Each of those names means the same, "the Great Water", and one might even say that river has no name. To give something a name is to become master over it, but that river is its own master.

The Yenisei is the Tree on which the world stands.

The tree's crown is the Sayan Mountains, which conceals from men the abode of the luminous spirits and the souls of those not yet born. The tree's roots extend to the northern sea, where the Icy Crone shakes her hair and sends into the world snowstorms and death. The life of any person proceeds along this very path from crown to roots.

The branches of the Tree consist of a countless multitude of rivers: large rivers and small, even tiny ones. Each of them means life for a particular tribe, clan, or family, for thus was the world created: no one can exist without his own river. It is assigned to him as his birthright. If it happened that the population of the taiga swelled, then the number of rivers, too, would grow larger. It could be no other way.

The nest of a man on the Tree is where his mother buried his umbilical cord.

His mother wipes her hands, and then the people and spirits who witnessed his coming into the world, will say, "Look, a person was born and will dwell among us." No need to part from your kin and native spirits, because what falls there right next to you onto a bed of green grass is your fate, and no one knows what it will be.

It sometimes happens that along with one's fate, some mysterious talent is also sent: a keen intelligence, musical gifts, the ability to see the unseen and hear what cannot be heard. Why this is so, is not for us to know. But those who are left without such gifts should not consider themselves deprived, for our world situated on the Tree of the Yenisei was made such that no living soul can be lost on it. Even one who falls out of his nest and is tormented by alien spirits and foreigners, knows that there is a way back, and he is comforted by this fact...

This same thought has warmed my heart, like the warm dust with which I cover my feet. My life was divided into three lives, and two of them I lived alongside the Yenisei. The third life told me that the Tree of the Yenisei is a lie, and I had to accept that fact just like everything that I had accepted before. But I cannot do so...

To do so and go on living would be an even greater lie.

My life lies like a tangled net on my knees. I desperately try to find the initial thread in it, in order to draw out everything that I saw myself, everything that I heard from other people, what came in my dreams and visions, so that I might understand what shaped it and why I came into this world.

DOG'S EAR (THE FIRST NAME)

Catching the wind

They ran through the fir-wood, trampling trees like grass. The earth shook before their eyes. Their young feet and their fear drove them and they ultimately reached a gently sloping riverbank. They were two.

When they reached the riverbank, they stopped, recovered from their frantic flight, and looked around. Then, though they stood only half a pace apart, one cried to the other, "I'll go down, you go up there..."

The second said nothing in reply. Without a word and no longer so franticly, they went off each in his own direction, but they were no more than a dozen paces from one another when a third appeared from a thicket, with heavy but swift steps. He was a thickset man, nearly as wide as the two of them put together. In his hand he gripped a short stick with a lash attached to the end.

When they caught sight of the stout man behind them, they stopped. He went down to the water without even a glance at them. There he examined deep prints made by human feet, as well as the furrow that the bottom of a large boat had carved into the wet sand. There had been a boat there waiting for its owner to take it out today for some burbot fishing.

"Were you headed off on a long journey?" the man, without even looking up head, shouted harshly.

With the toe of his light reindeer-skin boot he rolled a few pebbles into the furrow, but the other two paid that no heed. They stood rooted to the same spot where the appearance of the stout man had caught them, and they waited to hear what he would say next.

"Do you think that he is as stupid as you? That he stole the boat, sailed along for a bit, and abandoned it?"

Without speaking, the two plodded over to where the older man was. They were tall, big-boned young men, with the kind of shining black hair found in those who are strong and have never known hunger or disease. They had just reached the age when youth transitions into manhood. They were the stout man's sons. They possessed nearly the strength of an adult, but even stronger was a childish fear that their tender young souls had not yet overcome. Now their thoughts buzzed, like horseflies around a hunk of rotten meat, around the stick in their father's hand and the lash attached to it.

One of the boys finally spoke. "If he left at night, then he's already far away by now."

Their father said nothing. He put his hands, with the lash still in his grip, behind his back – his two hands barely met, so wide was he. He looked somewhere above the forested hill, where the sky was pink with dawn.

"Last night was a big moon," the second boy said after a silence. "He was afraid to go when you could see anything like during the day. He probably ran off towards morning, when it was completely dark."

After these words, the stout man turned his head towards them, though his short neck barely allowed him to do so. He was waiting for the boy to go on.

"It hasn't been so long now, we can catch up with him from the other side."

Their father brought his hands out from behind his back. "You missed him, you dog turd, you fish shit," he said quietly, almost peaceably, and then suddenly he took two steps backwards and beat the air with the whip he held. "Alright now, run!"

The two youths came to their senses and rushed into the fir-wood, where they beat through the clearing. The stout man ran after them.

Their encampment was located almost directly on the Bountiful River, separated from it by a few thickets one could get through in a few breaths. But as they all knew, if one followed the flow of the river, then it made a sharp bend and approached their encampment from the other side – not so close, but a frantic person would have to run only for a short time in order to reach the water.

The three of them burst into their encampment. There, next to four summer chums, a woman and an old man sat. They said nothing. Aghast at what had happened the previous night, the woman had abandoned her work. An empty pot lay in the grass. No smoke appeared over the chums. Only a few firebrands still smoldered in the fireplace. They huddled around it out of habit, in order to avoid the mosquitoes that were now, at the beginning of autumn, not so fierce – their season had passed.

The two youths dashed into their chum.

"Grab your bows, and as many arrows as you can!" their father shouted. "Grab everything that you've got!"

The stout man did not enter his own abode, the largest of them all. He heard a creak, like that made by the branch of a tree that was battered and nearly dead:

"Where is your bow?"

It was the old man, known as Man-Effigy, who said this. He had lived his life to the very last dregs of it and already his real name was lost, though strangely he never died. He spoke up so rarely that when he did, people started at his voice as at a strange sound. He was the uncle of the stout man's wife. She fed him, and sometimes – like on that morning when the old man was unwilling or unable to walk on his own – she would carry his light body over the threshold. But Man-Effigy almost never engaged in any conversation with his niece, and therefore, as soon as she heard the old man's croak, she shuddered. So did the stout man.

"Where is your bow?" came the voice again. "And your spear? And your mail coat?"

The stout man turned scarlet. The hand with the lash appeared from behind his back and crept upwards, though it soon stopped. "Shut up," he said quietly.

But the croak came all the more clearly. "You sleep soundly, Yabto," said Man-Effigy, "soundly like when you were a young'un."

"Shut up!"

The old man laughed. "Now watch out for your pants, be sure to tighten them. If you sleep so soundly you might even lose them…"

The hand holding the lash again rose, and it seemed that in a flash the old man might laugh again, but the stout man's sons came out of the chum with their weapons and called out to their father.

They quickly reached the bend in the Bountiful River and, gasping for breath, stood by the water. For the first time, they seemed to reflect on the fact that what they were doing was like trying to catch the wind.

Each of them realized that the stolen boat could have already passed this way. And also that the person who had stolen it might stop at any spot along the river's long, sinuous banks.

Yet a sixth sense told them that the fugitive chose precisely the way that they expected him to take. All of them – especially the stout man's sons – trusted that the fugitive was yearning for open space, and therefore he would try with all his might to head downstream, towards where the Bountiful River flows into the boundless Yenisei. The idea that there might be a shorter way, namely to cross to the other bank and head into the taiga, was something they did not even consider, because from that bank the lands of the Nga people stretched…

Yabto's fury at his sons had passed, though he tried to hide the fact. He still glared like a wolf and spoke to them brusquely. His sons were the least to blame for what had happened the night before, and as the stout man realized that, he gasped more out of the shame he felt than the running, too fast and too far for his heavy bulk. But the pain, as always happened, only sharpened Yabto's mind.

"We don't need to wait for him here, we'll go further downstream," he said, and the three of them walked on.

His sons knew what their father was thinking: to catch the boat, they needed to spread themselves out. Moreover, at that spot there was too wide a water between the banks, the fugitive might easily escape their arrows. Worst of all was that on a wide river, it was nearly impossible for them to reach the victim after they had hit him. But no matter what, they had to get ahold of him, for only that would cure the disaster that had come upon their camp late on the night before.

Not far off was a place where the river narrowed, the water flowed faster and, if they slew the fugitive on his approach, they could dash through the current and catch the boat. The stout man's sons undoubtedly possessed the strength for this.

At the spot where the riverbanks came closest together, their father ordered them to lie in ambush. They hid among dense willows, thirty paces from one another. Yabto would fire off a shot first. His sons were to finish their foe off if their father had only wounded him – the possibility of him missing was something no one even entertained. The stout man ordered them to hide better, as he feared that the fugitive in the boat might spot their ambush and immediately run away on the other bank. He was smart, this big man... But Yabto realized that what he was doing involved little smarts and a whole lot of blind faith that the one who had brought him such shame was bound to meet his death.

He recalled the fugitive who, just like his sons, was akin to him in that he had dwelt in the taiga. As he thought about the fugitive, he no longer hoped, he *knew* that things would turn out just as he now believed...

The stout man's faith was rewarded.

A boat appeared far off. When one of the sons saw it, he howled like a dog – Yabto regretted that he had left his lash in their camp... The boat was moving surprisingly equidistantly between the two banks, though no oar could be seen.

"He dropped down, he's hiding!" shouted that same son, forgetting all about their ambush. "I saw him myself! Father, shoot him!"

"You dummy!" the other son cried.

The stout man shot off an arrow – the black plume whistled over the river and came to a stop in the middle of the boat. Other arrows followed and fell next to Yabto's.

The boat turned sideways, then spun towards the bank, as if someone had been steering it and then dropped his oar. Fortune was with the stout man. He groaned with satisfaction as his sons dropped their weapons on the bank, rushed into the water, and grabbed ahold of the boat. Yabto ran up to them as fast as he could.

The entire bottom of the boat, its half-rotted wood, was studded with the black-feathered arrows that the stout man and his sons had shot. There was nothing else in the boat.

Yabto stared silently at their catch. Finally, he muttered, "I will go back now and kill the old man."

***

That night some weapons had disappeared from their encampment: a horned bow, a quiver with three dozen arrows, a spear, a leather tunic sewn with light iron plates, and a knife with a white handle made of reindeer bone.

His sons were right: the fugitive had committed his theft towards morning, when the full moon was behind the rocks and the sun had not yet appeared. That person had got past the small bells they had set as guard and escaped unnoticed.

He seemed much too small to plunder so much heavy gear, but he got away with everything. He even stole the bells attached to the spear and bow. He had anticipated what his pursuers would do.

I was that person.

I only needed the boat to get to the other bank of the river from their camp. That morning I hid behind some rocks and watched the stout man's sons flee, like pale little insects, from their father's lash.

That was unwise – I should have realized that I had committed an unjustifiable act, and immediately got as far away as possible. But I was young and I yearned so much to watch it – maybe it was for that very spectacle that I had decided to do it. I had to hold myself back from what would have been another rash action, namely to jump up, shout, cast off my parka, and lower my pants in order to show them my backside.

A vengeful thought warmed my heart: Yabto was running about now and totally furious, but the worst still lay ahead of him. Some time would pass, and the news of his incredible shame would make its way from one camp to another. People know that anyone who allows a mere boy to steal his weapons is a nobody.

***

The three of them returned to their encampment at sunset, hauling the boat behind them. While Yabto and his sons had tried in vain to catch the wind, the people of his household had got over the initial shock of that morning and life had returned to its ordinary rhythm. Food was ready and waiting for the men, smoke wafted over the tops of the chums as usual. Their father, without showing that he had come back with the same shame he felt in the morning, sat down next to his sons in the large chum. The three of them rushed to grab some of the meat.

The stout man tore at his reindeer with short, strong teeth. There was not even the hint of sorrow on his face – he appeared to be merely content that that cursed morning and cursed day had now passed into evening. Moreover, despondency would never grab hold of him for more than part of the day; his family knew this, so they did not wonder at him, but they said nothing.

When Yabto had eaten his fill, he wiped his hands on his hair, then he collapsed, his stomach full, onto the furs set on the floor behind him. The boys' mother said something silly, she asked, "Where is that person now, do you know?"

The sons froze, but their father, who lay there still on his back and stared vaguely at the smoke-hole, quietly replied, "Somewhere in the taiga, just as he should be. He came to us, then he went back. If only I hadn't lost the spear, it was brand new."

The boys' mother sighed and again said something silly. "How could he haul so much back with him? He was so small…"

But the stout man paid no heed to his wife's words. He lay there for a while longer, belched contentedly, and then started and abruptly got up. "Come here," he ordered his sons. He turned to his wife and added, "You go lie down, I will be back shortly."

He stepped out of the chum, stretched and gave a satisfied sigh, and then walked to the edge of the encampment, to where Man-Effigy lived. The stout man barely fitted into that chum, half the size of his own. Man-Effigy was sitting at the hearth, as straight as a stake hammered into the earth. His eyes were closed.

"Are you sleeping, old man?" Yabto asked, his voice raised.

"No," the old man replied at once. "I haven't sleep in a long time. Years."

"Amazing," the stout man feigned astonishment. "To me it seems like you are always sleeping. You never speak, never open your eyes. Why is that? Don't you want to see what's going on in the world?"

"I've already seen it all."

Here, by the light of the hearth, Yabto could clearly see just how transparent Man-Effigy was, like a fallen autumn leaf that retained only its thin network of veins that once held the flesh.

"Your niece says that you can see the future. Is that true?" he finally asked.

"Do you want me to foretell something?"

"I do… If, of course, my wife wasn't fooling."

"She's a silly thing, but look," Man-Effigy said. "Why should I tell the future when you yourself can? You never come into my chum, but here you are. It must be because you want to tell me about…"

Yabto burst out laughing. "You're right." He suppressed his laughter and went on, "You ought to die already, old man. Now is the time. I've had enough of you."

"You had enough of me today?" the old man asked, his eyes still closed. His laughter was suggested only by a twitch of the wrinkles on his lips, that were closed over his toothless mouth.

When the stout man saw that, he cast off his initial affability like a burden that was no longer needed. "Why did that scoundrel get away?" Yabto hissed. "Why did he leave last night? Did you tell him everything?"

The network of lines on the old man's lips moved like it was alive, and this drove Yabto into a fury, though he still managed to contain it.

"This morning you wanted to give me a beating," Man-Effigy said. "Why didn't you?"

"If you hadn't opened your stinking mouth…"

As if he had not heard that, the old man went on. "If you had just swung that stick of yours, there would be no need for this conversation. You're a fool, Yabto, because you lied to your slaves that they are your sons. Slaves and sons are separate things. Sooner or later each of them is going to find out who he really is. They already know. Did Lar not teach you anything?"

Suddenly the stout man lost his fury. "He could kill every one of us here. Don't you know that yourself?"

The old man swayed back slightly. "Your own son, you can beat him with a strap or that favorite lash of yours. You can beat your son for any infraction without driving him away from you. But you cast Lar aside, like something shameful. You hid him so far off that no one could ever return him to you. Maybe Lar knows nothing, but do you really think that he doesn't realize that he's not your son? He does realize, if, of course, he's alive… The little guy was already right on the edge, I just helped him take that step. What would have happened if I hadn't? Do you know?"

The stout man said nothing.

"Listen, Yabto," the old man nearly implored him. "Listen to me. After all, I've never asked you for anything. Show some wisdom here, don't go looking for the little guy. He's weak, he'll perish in the taiga before you could find him."

"What about my weapons?!" Yabto cried. "Who will return them to me? And when other people find out…"

"Forget about the weapons," the old man continued. "You're a fortunate fellow, you'll find a better spear, and an iron cap and mail, and you'll make a great new bow. And don't talk about shame. After all, you're a brave man, you've never feared shame. All the misfortune, dear fellow, comes down to the fact that you can't distinguish between sons and slaves…"

After these words, Yabto leapt up as if someone had kicked him in the rear from under the earth – he nearly collapsed the old man's tent.

Goose

The stout man came from the Nenets tribe of the Nenyang, the Mosquito People. He was born when the migrations of birds went south, towards the Sayan Mountains, which once were named the Mountains of Paradise. His father himself dreamed of traveling beyond those mountains, which served as a barrier between them and a land where it was always warm. One time he got quite close to the mountains and saw their white tips, but he lacked the boldness to go any further. On that same day, watching jealously as a reindeer caravan went by, he hoped that his son's dreams would range afar as easily as those birds, and he said, "He shall be called Yabto," which in Nenets means "Goose".

Yabto's father was not a rich man, in fact he was a poor one, but life then was easy: hostilities between men had quieted down, the local river gave abundant catch, the lords of the forest were generous and drove animals into traps or arrow range, and his son grew up, and even more quickly grew outwards.

He was four years old when a distant relative came to visit his father's camp and, seeing little Yabto, shook his hand. "What's your name, big guy?"

"Goose," his father answered for him.

"Goose?" the relative beamed. "Where is your neck?"

Yabto had no neck at all; his big head with its jutting hair sat between his shoulders.

The relative laughed, and in turn so did his father and Yabto himself. He did not remember why exactly they laughed, but he remembered that laughter forever.

Then, when he began to hunt, catch fish, and take after his father's example, even taking part in some raiding, he never quite grew a neck. Yabto finally realized that his father had named him that in order to amuse other people.

He grew strong and could chastise any man for laughing at him, but clearly he had developed a personality like his body and it was like a rock among the flowing stream. When anyone laughed at him, he too begin to laugh, and ultimately they were both laughing at his silly father.

Such an approach had been suggested to Yabto by a kindly demon who settled between his shoulder blades when he was fifteen or sixteen years old. On ordinary days, the demon was silent, but it awoke whenever the stout man felt pain and resentment. The demon uttered a few soothing words to its master and never erred.

Time passed, people grew tired of the joke and the stout man himself stopped thinking of it, but the hurt he had suffered as a child remained and turned into contempt for his father – a languid contempt for a man who was kind to all, but could never manage to hold on to good fortune. Even though good fortune came to him readily, it nevertheless evaded him like a school of fish passing through a thin, poorly made net without stopping.

Yabto's father never grieved at this, however. He was an easygoing man and lived dissolutely. As his son looked at him, he longed to grow up quickly and become a man completely unlike his father. That is precisely what happened.

Yabto's mother had died of hunger long before, when they were migrating to their winter camp. His father took the loss easily. But when his two sisters left for other clans in exchange for a meager bride-price, and the third – the most beautiful – was abducted by her suitor, his father seemed like one uprooted, he turned into an old man in an instant, and then he went blind. Yabto set him up in a separate hut that was kept warm and ensured that the old man was fed to his heart's content.

He waited a year after his sister's abduction, then went to his unwanted in-laws and castigated them for not appearing at the set time to ask forgiveness and make peace, as custom dictated. He went there unarmed and everyone could see that young Yabto alone was incapable of extracting revenge for the insult. The stout man's words, however, were of such truth and confidence that shame came over his new relatives. The abductor got a thrashing from his father, while Yabto received a small iron pot, two knives, and a new fishing net. This was a meager peace offering, but the stout man said nothing, he simply left and brought the items back to his household.

He became the best of patriarchs, different in all ways from his father. When his father went blind, a new storehouse appeared in their camp, the chums got strong new reindeer skins on them, and then his father's boat made out of a patchwork of skins was replaced by a new dugout made from a single pine trunk.

Most important, the demon inside him suggested something unprecedented in these parts: to attach in the middle of the boat a tall pole with crossbars on it, and to stretch between them several reindeer skins sewn together. The boat then seemed to fly along, and under the demon's tutelage Yabto learned to sail against the current. Deftly handling the oars, he went up the river nearly as swiftly as down it. People were amazed by his cleverness, and some tried to emulate him, but to lesser effect or none at all. Clearly their demons were nothing compared to the one that lived between the stout man's shoulder blades.

When his father died, Yabto invited his relatives. But also many people from outside his family came uninvited to commemorate the man who had lived so carefree. All of them, both the Nenyang clan and those outside it, upon seeing the storehouse, the new skins on the chums, and the boat, said that the deceased should have traded his carefree attitude for the skill of his son. People told Yabto that he should always stay the same man he was then, and then there would be no better man in the taiga than he.

Soon the stout man married and acquired several reindeer for their migrations. The good demon between his shoulder blades fell blessedly silent, and through that silence told Yabto that he would walk his own true path where no danger lay. Yabto was righteous and thus happy.

He knew that not all men were kindly disposed to him, that some considered him a coward. But those who said such things knew something else, too: Yabto was saving up his courage like food for a long journey, and if there were any need to do so, he could smash any man's head. Therefore, no one called him a coward to his face.

He knew, too, the other name he had been given: Scavenger. Several times he had been spotted among deserted chums that had been ravaged by raiding. No one knew what he was looking for there. But Yabto knew that any old lost item had, like any person or animal, its own place in the world and anyone who thought differently was a mere fool. He told his relatives this and they admitted that he was right.

Having lived a great many years now, the stout man could find nothing to reproach himself for. Perhaps only for the fact that, after burying his father, he did not perform the customary action of carving a wooden effigy to represent his deceased parent and feeding it. But his father, even having gone blind, had been fed well to the end of his days and never heard a word of reproach from his son. Not only his father – everything around Yabto relied on his strength and goodheartedness.

It was to Yabto that Man-Effigy, that evil old man, owed the fact that he was still alive. He had arrived six months after Yabto's marriage, when a plague struck his wife's family and took all her relatives except for that old man. All these years Yabto had served the old man food and accepted his ungrateful silence, and even rare words of reproach. Yabto was never neglectful. But he listened to the demon within him and would take no advice from anyone else.

Now the old man expected the demon to tell him that the old man's words, laughter, and mockery were no more than the baying of dogs. Yet the demon said nothing…

It said nothing on this shameful day when, it seemed to Yabto, the river of his life had not only made a bend but changed course completely, and was now flowing who knows where.

Finally, he said to the old man, "Soon we'll migrate downriver. On the other bank I know a good place, a peaceful one. I'll abandon you there. I hope that the Nga will spot you and finally remember that you exist. Get ready." He then turned to leave.

"Hey," the old man exclaimed, "Aren't you afraid that I'll escape, like Dog's Ear?"

As Yabto spat and walked out of the chum, he clearly heard behind him the familiar creaking of a dead tree.

He walked over to where his bed and his quiet wife awaited, and then suddenly he heard something: the demon between his shoulder blades struck him in the back so hard that his sight momentarily dimmed.

A merciless thought came into the stout man's mind like fire raining down from the sky. He fell to his knees and put his head in his hands. "The slave… the weakling… how could I not have guessed, how did I not realize it? Where could he run to? That fish shit…"

Sounds erupted from inside him, the stout man was either laughing or crying. "Yabto!" he heard his wife's joyful cry, "You've got an empty pot where your head should be!"

Children

He could not sleep. He only went over in his mind that day on which his life had changed course.

The stout man stared at the now-empty part of the chum: just last night his weapons had gleamed there in the light of the hearth, but thoughts of that accursed night now slipped from his mind. He involuntarily recalled something else: a day that shone with autumn flowers and the sun in the water.

Yabto shuddered at the thought of how that day had so resembled this one. It had been sixteen years before.

He had named his elder son Yabtonga, which meant "Goose Foot", for he considered the boy part of himself and he knew that, when the time came, the boy would follow after him. These were the days when Yabtonga took his first steps. The younger son Yawire was still lying in his cradle – his name meant "Radiant One" and he had been called that for his bright-black hair and glowing cheeks.

The stout man's wife Uma – whose name meant "Kiss Woman" and who came from the Tyor clan, known as the People of the Scream – was again with child, and she annoyed her husband with her wailing that she would lose the baby if she did not get some fat fish from the big river to eat – taimen and sturgeon, which one could rarely catch in their nearby Bountiful River. So insistent was she that Goose, who ordinarily heeded no one but himself, came to have a greater hankering for fat fish than his wife. At that time, people were making long journeys not so much to stock up on fat fish but to downright gorge on them. People believed that the power of their juicy flesh would last them all year, until the next spring came.

After a day-long journey, the stout man's boat passed the river mouth. Then, for seven days, Yabto eagerly rowed his boat against the current, under the reindeer skins sewn together, over the blade-smooth waters of the Yenisei. Kiss Woman marveled at his stubbornness and strength.

The stout man sought a place to make an encampment and, by accident, he found one.

Something gently impacted the hull of the boat and Yabto, who was seated at the stern, saw that it was the body of a man. The body rolled and went under, the stout man saw it only for an instant and managed to make out its bare feet from which the river had stripped off the boots.

Neither the woman nor the old man paid any attention to the impact on the boat, perhaps they did not even hear it. Yabto was about to say something about the dead man, but then he looked towards the shore and, without saying a word, he directed his boat towards a place he should not have: the mouth of an unfamiliar little river, which might represent land belonging to others and therefore one could expect a run-in with its owners. From far off, Yabto could discern traces of fighting.

"Why are you going this way?" Uma asked, anxious.

"I want to take a look..." He then fell silent.

They had no idea to whom the encampment here belonged and what people they represented. It was an even meadow overgrown with short grass, surrounded by a neat semicircle of forest with a single rock and three boulders by the water.

The hearths were still smoking. The enemy had turned human presence here into barrenness and left no trace of the quiet life that had once gone on.

Yabto walked among the destroyed abodes and tried to find something, anything, in the grass – not because it might come in useful but out of mere curiosity. He found no traces of the battle except a stone with a reindeer's head that was covered in dark blood – sticky blood, which had flowed not long before in a human being's veins. He supposed that when the strangers arrived, there were no men in the encampment at all, and the starving foes took everything without a fight. But the blood – it might have well been at the hands of women they kidnapped, for women carried knifes for their handicrafts.

Yabto's frisky, curly-tailed dogs were searching for something for themselves. The stout man had completely forgotten about them and only remembered when he heard a bark: his young, black-furred bitch, which he found indispensable when hunting squirrels, was rummaging in the woods. Yabto ran towards the sound, nearly tripping on the wet, mossy boulders. It took him a long time to find the dog, and he suddenly thought that the bitch had noticed some creature among the branches and began hunting without her master's command. But when he saw her, he realized that it was not up in the trees that the dog's quarry lay: as the bitch barked, she hunched her front paws and brought her muzzle low to the ground, as if she was forcing some animal out of its burrow.

The appearance of this prey so struck Yabto that, at first, he was unable to make sense of what exactly lay before him.

In a shallow gully, among three tall larches, sat two children. They sat there straight, frozen to the spot, like two stakes that had been hammered into the earth. One of them was clearly bigger than the other. They said nothing. The children's faces were covered with wet, filthy patches, they had dirt stuck to their cheeks, as if they had just crawled out from under the earth. The black dog was already hoarse with barking, and even a sharp shout from the stout man could not stop her – her master finally threw a stone at her. The barking subsided to a slight whine and then ceased entirely.

A silence fell that seemed endless to Yabto, then the smaller of those two hammered stakes fell sideways into the dull-green moss and sobbed. The sound of crying floated through the taiga like a thin, swaying cobweb. Then the other hammered stake spoke up – he stood up and moaned with his mouth open like a fish, while tears flowed from his eyes and carved channels on his dirty cheeks. Now the crying of both of them seemed to fill the taiga, intertwined – it would have been impossible for anyone not to hear it in the vicinity of that encampment bereft of its people and animals.

Upon hearing the crying, the people of Yabto's household walked over from the riverbank. Kiss Woman, pregnant and carrying her younger son on her back, came first. Then Man-Effigy, already then so old that even his very name was lost, came leading Yabto's elder son by the hand.

The stout man had been with his wife for not a long time, hardly more than three years, and everyday he found that she fully merited both her own name and that of her clan, Tyor, the People of the Scream.

The woman had been named Kiss for her habit, as a little girl, of clinging to and embracing loved ones and strangers alike, even dogs. When she got married, she demanded affection every free moment, and during lovemaking she screamed so loud that it scared away the birds around their encampment.

For this young lady, juicy like sturgeon flesh, Yabto had paid several dozen fox and sable skins and a stone pot – nearly a third of his inheritance from his father. He was seriously worried that even he, a young and strong man, lacked the stamina to satisfy such a demanding wife, and this expensive catch might one day betray him.

But as soon as Uma gave birth to their first child, and in short order their second, Yabto realized that he had been worried for naught: Kiss Woman's true passion was not for love and affection but for children. Moreover, bearing children seemed to be no torment for her, but rather a delight: Uma herself said that she wished she were a fish, so that children would issue from her one after another like roe. Now, when they had two children, she screamed at them constantly and found therein the same satisfaction as she had found in lovemaking.

From the beginning of their life together, Yabto promised to himself that he would tame Uma, and with time he managed to do so. But now she, leading the way, stood there in the destroyed encampment – the weight she carried on her back and in her belly only lent firmness to her legs. She was the first to dash into the gully, where she swept up the smaller of the two children and began to wipe his face with her hands. She then picked up the other child and did the same.

Then Yabto realized that she had already made her decision, and doubt came over his heart. "Stop," he said.

The stout man sensed that his wife was about to scream, but he was wrong. Uma set the little child on the ground, then plunged her hand into the soft ground and tore off a chunk of moss like a blanket. Then she turned to her husband and said in a firm and even tone, "Someone hid them here, under the moss, that is why they are still alive." Then she added, "I don't need that fat fish any more."

That last remark was a mere silliness that Goose, with his ability to ignore anything inconsequential, immediately forgot. He began to think about what mattered here: he was now faced with a find like nothing he had ever found before. These two children, the bigger and smaller alike, were approximately the same age as his own sons. Suddenly Yabto had a vision of himself surrounded by four warriors, fine, stately, and as devoted to him as his dogs. This vision was so clear that a wide smile broke out on his face. Uma saw that and realized that her husband had made his decision as quickly and firmly as she had made hers.

The stout man picked up both of the children and carried them to the riverbank, where their boat awaited. The children were no longer crying. They only made a sound when Uma scooped up water from the river with her hands and began to wash their faces.

The water revealed something amazing: the boys had the same face. Though Uma peered closely at them, she could not find the slightest difference. There in the forest, Kiss Woman and the stout man, without exchanging a word, both took the boys to be two brothers born in quick succession, just like their own sons, and that is why one was slightly stronger and half a head taller than the other.

Uma called to her husband, "They apparently came from the same womb."

Yabto looked at them and said, "Don't be silly, now. Rather think about the fact that we'll have to feed them. How?"

With a motion she was well used to making, Uma took from her back the leather cradle where four-month-old Yawire was staring wide-eyed, set it on the grass in front of her, and began to undo her summer parka. "Tell my uncle not to look!" she cried, and then she was naked to the waist before Yabto knew it. Her breasts with their greenish veins were plopped over the round mass of her belly.

"There's enough for everyone here," she whispered loudly and smiled. "Enough for the whole taiga. Give me both of them."

Yabto handed the children over.

"Go on," Uma said. "If you're hungry, then go ahead and eat. Come on."

The children lay there motionless. Uma forced them towards her. The older boy snuffled and began to breathe heavily, but his lips would not open. The younger boy jerked his head away, turning his neck as much as he possibly could, and seemed about to scream.

But instead it was Yawire, lying in the baby carrier at his mother's feet, who cried out. Yabtonga, standing some distance away with the old man, wailed. In their wake the woman from the Tyor clan was about to pipe up with a loud song as she usually did, but she stopped before she could fully draw breath for it: as soon as her own children had cried out, the foundlings began to suck. They did so greedily, like puppies who were never sated. They squealed and nearly choked on her milk.

"Go away," Uma told her husband, and then loudly called her elder son over. Yabtonga ran towards his mother, though he tripped as he did so and several times fell face-first down into the pebbles along the shore, after which his wailing grew ever louder and more furious.

Yabto went down to their boat. The old man sat next to it on the trunk of a tree that the river had cast ashore. From behind the stout man came a sound like that of fighting, and he made out the familiar words, "Don't shout… You poor little things… There's enough for everyone…"

A conversation now passed between Yabto and Man-Effigy, one of the few that had ever happened in their lives.

"What do you need them for?" the old man asked.

"They will be men," Yabto replied.

"You don't have your own men?"

"They will grow up and be my strength."

"While they're growing up, you'll have to feed them – and when they're grown up, marry them off. Are you a rich man? Where are you going to find such wealth to pay four times the bride-price? If they all survive, that is."

The stout man turned, came face to face with the old man, and smiled enigmatically. "As long as they don't die, they will be with me. And during that time, we will amass such wealth that they can marry every bride in the taiga. Then let them live as they wish."

For some time they only stared at one another. Then Man-Effigy broke the silence. "Do you remember the covenant?"

"What covenant?"

"That memory does not lie in one's mind but in one's blood. It is blood that makes people remember."

"What are you talking about, old man?"

"As if you don't know. They will grow up and then they'll get their revenge on you."

Yabto was dumbfounded and nearly leapt up. "What are you thinking, saying such things? I saved them from certain death. They would have died the very next day from the cold at night, if the wolves hadn't got them first."

But now the old man stood up and showed such wrath as no one had ever seen before. "Do you know what people they come from? What gods they honor, what spirits protect them – do you know that? Who are you to tread like that on the tail of fate?"

"I am their fate," Yabto quietly said and then walked away.

It was impossible to tell what tribe these children had belonged to. They were still so young that they could only mumble vaguely, and only a close relative could have made out any of the words.

On the great river they nevertheless enjoyed some fat fish and then returned to their own encampment after a few days. Yabto did not even put his coat on and barely touched the oars.

Three months after their return from the Yenisei, Uma gave birth to a daughter. Her name was Nara, which meant "Springtime Girl".

***

That the boys had come from the same womb was something that her woman's intuition told Uma. She trusted in it more than the truth that she could never know, and she decided that one of the children had first sipped the life-giving juice of that womb and therefore came into the world twice as big as his brother.

The new sons confirmed that Uma had been right.

Not only did the foundlings share the same face, they also would fall ill at the same times, cry, or ask for food, they began to walk and utter their first clear words simultaneously, and start to play with her own children, and all in all they lived as a single person.

Uma made no difference between them and her own sons, they all got the same portions of meat, the same slaps, or the same gifts. She had enough screaming in her, where it was hard to tell scolding from doting, for everyone.

But a year passed, and something else came to light. The children had the same face, and the same life beat within them, but their temperaments were as alike as a bear's and a ground squirrel's.

When the larger boy's teeth came in, he immediately put them to work by biting his father's finger. Yabto, who was normally sparing in his affection, had wanted to amuse his newfound son and patted the latter on the nose – the child struck with the speed of a serpent and bit into the doting hand. Yabto burst out laughing and again brought his finger close to the child's face, but the latter grabbed it with both of his tiny hands, put it into his mouth, and then bit down with all his might. Yabto, still laughing, jerked his hand away; it really had hurt. On the same day, the stout man named the foundling child after a little fish that was impossible to catch without getting pricked: Lar, that is, "Ruff".

The smaller child was quiet and nearly escaped notice. So much so that even Uma, surrounded by children and occupied by her tasks, sometimes forgot about his very existence. Nevertheless, he was the first of the children to learn to talk – these were clear words that more people than just Kiss Woman could understand. Only one day the inconspicuous child amazed everyone. In spring, when the snow was already gone, the still nameless child walked up to the fire that his mother and father sat by and, jutting a finger up at the sky, said:

"Bud... Ku-a, ku-a..."

"What is he saying?" Yabto asked.

"'A bird,'" Uma replied. "He's showing how geese make sounds."

The stout man turned to look at the sky, but there was nothing there except thick, shining clouds. He laughed. "Where do you see any birds, you whelp?"

They each went to see to their own tasks and by noon, when the sun had risen as far as it would in spring, they paid the child no mind – the inconspicuous boy himself grabbed their attention. He ran up to the fire by which his father and mother were again seated, pointed at the same place in the sky, and cried, "Ku-a… Ku-a… Bud!"

A smile began to appear on Yabto's lips, but then stopped: he heard a familiar sound, leapt up from his seat, and looked up: in the blue sky a swaying line like a broken branch came into view. It was the first migration of that spring.

"He guessed it," the stout man said with satisfaction as he lowered himself back onto a plank of wood next to the fire.

This episode would probably have faded from the adults' memory, but the next morning the still unnamed boy again came up to his parents. He pointed at the sky and again muttered "Bud" – and after a considerable time had passed, at least half the day, another flock came flying from the same place where the boy had pointed with his tiny hand. This repeated several times, and the foundling boy was never mistaken: flocks appeared as if at his command.

Yabto began to suspect that something was wrong, but Uma, after she returned one day from the tiny chum in which her uncle lived, told her husband, "He must be able to hear the birds from half a day's flight away."

"You've got it wrong," replied Yabto, unable to believe her.

"No, I don't. It's like another story I heard: a blind old man led his tribe from place to place, and at each potential stop he would taste the soil first, and that never failed him. For that he was called Clever Tongue."

"Then he's like a Dog's Ear," the stout man said.

That is how I got my first name, Wenga.

Lar

Lar began to fight nearly as soon as he learned to stand upright.

In those days, and a long time thereafter, too, mothers paid little mind to who bloodied whose nose, and Uma was the same. She would pull the fighting boys apart, whether it was two of them or three, or all at once – and generously dispense slaps. Only later did Kiss Woman began to notice that while the melee might include any of the children, one of them was always Lar. She tried pointing that out to her husband, but he told her to be quiet, because a man ought to learn how to fight, just like a woman should know how to sew and chop wood. Such was the eternal law...

Yabto himself would stand at a distance with his arms across his chest and observe these fights, noting the worth of each boy. Yabtonga was good, Yawire fairly decent, Dog's Ear good for nothing, but only Lar would make a fine bear hunter and an even better warrior. It did not bother Yabto at all that the foundling was superior to his own sons.

This went on for several years. When the fights began to result in real blood, the stout man allowed that, too. But he missed what really mattered: the reason why his sons fought. Their fights nearly always came down to the same thing: Lar was defending his brother. Due to my scrawniness, Yabto's own sons tried to push me out of their games or assign me some role that was insignificant or even embarrassing. Lar would feel the offense even before I did, and clench his fists.

But the stout man did not distinguish between us. Time passed, and he fashioned bows for his sons, each according to his strength, and began taking them hunting. I remember bringing my first catch, a black grouse, back to the encampment.

Those were peaceful times. Life was following the course that the stout man had outlined, and then it suddenly went awry: Lar broke Yabtonga's skull.

It was not a fracas but a duel fought according to all the rules. There had been several brief fights in which my brother had the upper hand. But Yabtonga was stubborn and insisted on another bout. Ultimately Lar got angry at his persistence and knocked him to the ground, grabbed him by his hair, and bashed his face repeatedly against the stones.

After that, Yabtonga no longer asked for another round – dark blood was pouring down his face. He got up from the ground shakily and slowly, like an old man, walked towards his parents' chum, and fell down midway. He then shook with vomiting. Everyone, even Lar himself, were speechless from fright. I immediately left my brothers and ran to find my mother.

Uma wailed over her son like a dead person.

Father took Lar away from the encampment, ordered him to take his jumper off, and then beat him with a belt until blood flowed just as abundantly as it had down Yabtonga's face. Both were then ailing, but their young bodies quickly recovered from their wounds. Soon both were back on their feet and staring at one another like two unacquainted dogs, ready at any moment to attack and rip each other's throats open, but aware that their fearsome master was watching them.

Yabto knew that he had been harsh, but it did not bother him – he believed from his own experience that youthful rage passes as quickly as it appears. He was wrong in this – a month later, his elder son came out of the forest leaning on Yawire's shoulder: there was no blood on Yabtonga's face, but he walked like one wounded in the stomach.

This time the stout man did not beat Lar, instead he locked him in the storehouse. Yabtonga felt that something had happened that was more serious than an ordinary boys' fight, even one with real venom. He thought about what he should do this time. He was right to have this feeling, though he did not see the main thing.

I witnessed this fight.

Father ordered Yabtonga, Lar, and me to go to the riverbank and cut willows in order to weave traps. As soon as the chums vanished behind the trees, Yabtonga and Lar stopped, stared at one another, and then without a word they dropped their knives to the ground and grappled.

It was a long fight and it ended when Lar kneed Yabtonga several times in the stomach. The latter fell and then writhed like a worm.

Yawire came running from the encampment as if he had heard about everything. We were struck dumb with fear, and for some time we only stood and watched Yabtonga's agony. When he managed to take his first breath, which resembled a reindeer's snort, Lar grabbed his arm to help him up.

Yabtonga however got to his feet on his own and, through his gasps, said, "You just wait. Time will pass, and I will drive over your bones." Then he looked at me. "And yours. We will all drive over your bones."

After Yabtonga said that, he started to drop, but his younger brother deftly supported him with his shoulder.

They walked into the encampment. Lar remained behind on the riverbank and I stayed with him. We had been so struck by Yabtonga's words that we were not even conscious of any fear of punishment: we looked at one another as if asking what he had meant. Lar and Yabtonga had never uttered anything mean to one another, but this had been something special, and we sensed that in those words there was something else besides simple meanness.

We were fifteen years old, just like Yabtonga. The stout man had ordered that our origin be kept secret, so we knew nothing of it: we believed that Yabto and Uma were our real parents.

All this time, the adults had lived tranquil lives. They watched their sons gradually turning into men and were contented thereby, but they forgot that those boys' minds, too, were also growing sharper.

In early childhood, Yabto's children paid no mind to the fact that Wenga and Lar shared the same face. Now they could see it. Moreover, Yabtonga had started to grow big like his father, and Yawire was soft in body and had the same puffy cheeks as his mother. Yet the other two boys, though different in build, remained thin, with straight reindeer-like faces, and their hair was of a dull gray color, unlike the bright black hair of the encampment's other inhabitants.

From birth to this day, they treated all their children the same. But now doubts began to swirl in the heads of the stout man's sons.

One day Yabtonga asked his mother when she had given birth to Wenga and Lar. Was it earlier than him, or did it happen between him and Yawire? This question took Uma by surprise: she was busy with some demanding chores – she was scraping a skin – and was unable to provide any immediate and clear answer.

She hesitated and then said, "That's right. You're the eldest. Yawire is the youngest."

Yabtonga would have liked to ask by how much he was older than the identically faced brothers, but his mother sent him away – it was clear that she found her son's curiosity more difficult to deal with than the task of scraping the skin.

The doubts swirling in their heads grew stronger, and finally Yabtonga dared to go straight to his father and ask, "Why don't Lar and Wenga resemble you or us? Perhaps our mother..."

He did not even manage to finish the sentence, because the stout man's hand flashed across his face. The blow left him staggering. He said no more, and from then on he did not ask any more questions.

He had no need to ask any questions, and at such risk, when it was obvious now. Yabtonga did not really know anything, but the truth was as clear as day: Wenga and Lar came from somewhere else. His mother had confirmed this by remaining silent, while his father had done so by striking him.

He shared this welcome secret with Yawire. From that day on, the brothers were even closer to one another, and they talked privately about the strangers. Those words about driving over Wenga and Lar's bones had come into Yabtonga's mind of their own accord, and his lips readily uttered them, for he knew for certain that he was fighting with an outsider.

And now the defeated Yabtonga knew for certain that it could be no other way. Sooner or later his father would put the reindeer-faced brothers in their place. It was simply a matter of time; though that time, unfortunately, passed like a reindeer convoy that had already grown fatigued.

***

Yabto did not beat Lar, he locked him in an empty storehouse and forbid any food from being brought to him. In the stout man's view, this was the most reasonable thing to do: while hunger went to work on breaking the little animal's spirit, he had time to figure things out, to tear apart the entwined serpents and scatter them across the grass.

In this he was again mistaken: Uma undermined his plan. All day she nursed her ailing son with herbal concoctions, and in the evening she went into the large chum and fell at the stout man's feet, disheveled and her eyes full of tears. "Get Lar out of there, get him out," she wailed.

Yabto tried to calm his wife, and it might have seemed that he managed to do so on this evening: Uma turned away from him and fell asleep. But the same thing happened on the next day, and again on the third. Uma's moaning was stubborn and intimidating, all in the hope of shattering the stout man's will, but instead it only stoked his wrath. Just as fire starts water boiling at the bottom of a pot and the tempest rises to the surface, so Yabto seethed inside. And when Kiss Woman cried, "You broke the commandment, you brought foreign blood, foreign spirits into our home! Uncle was right," Yabto struck his wife and walked away.

He soon erected his own small tent away from the encampment and settled into it.

The demon told him a sad thing, something Yabto would have realized regardless: he had to give up his dream of four warriors who would respond readily to his command, even to the very movement of his lips. All that he had paid in effort, patience, and kindness was now crumbling into dust. He recalled the little children's fingers that he had set himself on the feather of arrows.

With that part of his mind that did not turn into words or actions, but existed nevertheless, he realized that everyone else had been right: the old man, his wife, his son, and even Lar. They had acted in accordance with something innate within them.

Uma, for whom children and the torments of childbirth had come as a joy, would never be the same again. It was not her who chose who her true children were but something in her blood.

The same spirit apparently dwelt inside the violent foundling child and whispered words of its own.

The people of the stout man's household did not come looking for him, though they knew that the last moments of the fat autumn before the long winter were going by quickly. They remained quiet, like an old, lame dog.

But one morning – a bright and clear morning, that washed over one's heart with a cool breeze that was not yet fiercely cold – Yabto came out of his tent in hale spirits. His strength had returned to him.

His family was coming apart, which meant that he had to gather them back together just as shepherds on the tundra gather their herds, with sticks, dogs, and terror, driving every reindeer back into their corral without entreating them. Yabto knew what he had to do.

Once, long ago when he was still an adolescent, his father took him on a campaign organized by the united families of several Yurak and Tungus clans. They traveled for a great distance, farther than Yabto had ever gone in his life, to the upper waters of the Yenisei, where there lived peoples that subsisted by keeping animals unseen in the taiga: horses and sheep.

They went as far as the places where the taiga first gives way to empty spaces, smooth hills dotted with standing stones, and then resumes at the foot of mountains covered with eternal snow.

It was war then, a good war. Yabto recalled a slain foe who held in his hands a short stick that ended in a long braid of thin belts woven together. His father's comrades crowded around the deceased: by all appearances he had been a man of high rank.

"What is that for?" young Yabto asked, pointing at the stick. "For herding reindeer?"

His father laughed. "No, that stick is too short for reindeer. That is for beating people. Just for beating people and nothing else."

Yabto's family subsisted on game and fish. They had few reindeer, only enough for their migrations. Such a thing was unnecessary in their parts. But now Yabto remembered it and, sitting in his separate tent, he spent a few days thinking about how he ought to do something similar.

That lashed stick had proven to be a remarkable thing. It revealed to Yabto a secret: it matters to a person what he is being beaten with. Each kind of beating produces its distinct result. It is one thing when it is a person's hand, or whatever comes into it in a moment of anger – a person, Yabto realized, can bear and even forgive those beatings. But it is something else when a thing comes along that is made solely for inflicting pain – especially if it was made well. The very sight of such a weapon would break anyone's stubbornness and make their will as soft and pliable as clay.

Finally, the lash transforms the man who holds it, too.

As Yabto gripped the handle of his new weapon, he banished what the old man had said about memory living in the blood. He shrugged off the shame he had felt at his error – that he had immediately decided to make the foundlings his heirs and not his slaves. A slave is a troublesome thing: he has to be guarded, and one must always remember that even a broken and docile slave is like a pit with stakes in the bottom that lies forgotten in the forest… Let him no longer see himself surrounded by four warriors. Let there be instead two warriors – that is not bad, other men do not even have that. Now the stout man knew how to go about things, and he felt at ease.

"If they didn't obey me when I was good to them," Yabto said aloud, "they will obey me with the lash." He then quickly folded up his tent and walked back towards the encampment.

***

During the four or five days that father was gone from the encampment, no one could resolve to go to the storehouse in which Lar was locked.

It pained me, but I lacked the courage.

One thing was clear: what Lar had done was no longer something that would be punished by beatings, there was only death. But the people of the encampment were unable to believe that the head of their household would slay a person whom he had regarded as a son, like some reindeer at a feast.

Yabto returned to the encampment with something new attached to his belt. The stout man's sons and wife had nev-

44

er seen such a weapon, but they did not ask what it portended – they had neither the courage nor even the need to do so.

When the stout man's wife saw the lash, she saw that her husband had changed and would never be the same again, and she shied away from him.

After his return, however, Yabto did not show any rage, indeed he even seemed kind – he immediately went into his large chum, sat by the hot cauldron, and asked his wife for a small knife to cut meat. "As you know, I love eating with that small knife," he said in an almost affable tone.

Uma jumped up, ran numbly to the far side of the chum, and returned with what her husband had asked for. "I know," she said dully as she sat down opposite him.

The stout man ate leisurely and with relish. Once he had eaten his fill, he wiped his fingers on his hair as was his habit, and then he lay on his back. Uma wondered about those first words that her husband had spoken. Yabto sensed this and spent a long time blissfully licking his greasy lips. Uma had already opened her mouth to ask whether she should call their sons in, but her husband himself spoke up, still lying on his back:

"Go to Yabtonga and Yawire, have them open the storehouse and bring him out."

"Bring him here?"

"Why? No one needs him here. Back to his own chum."

Kiss Woman quickly rose to leave, she was suddenly feeling energetic.

"But…"

Uma froze on the threshold.

"Give him some food. Not too much at once, pour him a small bowl of warm fish soup. Go."

***

Yabtonga and Yawire climbed the ladder up to the storehouse, which stood on larch piles the height of a man.

Together they pulled away the heavy pole that barred the door.

Lar was lying in the corner, face down and with his hands under his chest.

"Get up," Yabto's elder son shouted.

Lar did not move. The brothers felt unable to come any closer to him.

"Is he dead?" Yawire timidly asked. "Go look…"

Yabtonga had built the storehouse not long before – in many places the fresh pine logs were covered with marks similar to those which bears made on the edges of their territory.

More than hunger, Lar had been suffering from thirst. He had even licked at what moisture remained in the wood and, to get to it, he bloodied his fingers and mouth. There was a small crack in the storehouse to let light and air in, through which he might stick his hand out and catch at least a few drops of rain – but to Lar's great misfortune, those days had all been clear and dry.

"He ate the wood," the younger of the brothers said, almost in a tone of compassion. "You see?"

Yabtonga was silent. He took a deep breath, resolutely walked up to Lar and, grabbing him by the shoulders, began to roll him over on his back. He was apparently convinced that Lar had already perished, because when the latter came to and sat up on the floor on his own, Yabtonga leapt away, all the way back to the door, while Yawire retreated into the corner.

Lar stared at the brothers and smiled, revealing teeth pink with blood.

"Get up," Yabtonga cried. "Father has ordered us to take you to our chum. Get up, they say."

"Calm down… I'll get up." Lar wanted to show good spirits and tried to leap straight to his feet, just like he might jump out of bed in the morning, but he immediately collapsed back to the floor. His vision was clouded by a darkness in which strange, incomprehensible patterns flickered. His brothers took him by his arms and hauled him towards the exit.

"How are we going to bring him down?" Yawire asked his brother. Lar, so weakened, could hardly get down the ladder on his own two legs.

"We'll drop him down," Yabtonga replied in a loud voice.

"Why? If that kills him, father will kill us."

"We'll say that he killed himself, alright? Shall we?"

"Come on."

"We'll tell him that. Hey, fish face, maybe you want to kill yourself? You're not long for this world anyway. That's right, brother, not at all. Father has made a stick with a lash on it, you hear me? Something like no one else has ever had. He spent a long time making it, all that time while you were here chowing down on the wood. He was making all that effort for you, brother." Yabtonga spoke these words slowly and with great relish, bringing his face so close to Lar's that their noses nearly touched. "So maybe you want to kill yourself?" he repeated with a smile.

Instead of a reply, Lar closed his eyes as if acquiescing, and then suddenly with all the strength he had left he butted his head into Yabtonga's face.

Yabtonga recoiled. Blood gushed from his nose. When he regained his composure, he got back up and stepped towards Lar with his hands straight out and tense, like two crossbows. Yawire flung himself at his brother's feet and cried, "Don't! Father will…"

But it was too late for Yabtonga to do what he had in mind, for Lar had turned and crawled to the exit, and in the blink of an eye he was gone from the storehouse.

When the brothers, stunned, got ahold of themselves and ran to the door, Lar was on his hands and knees and licking up water from a hollow in a rock, like a dog. He drank all the water there, then licked the rock dry, then slowly got to his feet and stood there like a stunted tree. Without waiting for his brothers to descend, he walked towards the encampment.

But in short order Lar no longer had anything to boast about, for he tripped and fell facedown into the moss. His brothers again grabbed him by the arms and tried to drag his limp body to their chum. They did not see that Lar was smiling.

They threw him down on some furs and, panting, walked away. Father had told them that from now on, Lar would live alone until his fate was decided. The brothers moved into their father's abode, while Uma and Nara moved into the impure women's chum. Obviously, burdened with their own affairs and due to my own scrawniness, the people in the encampment had forgotten about me. I lay at the far side of the chum, hidden among furs, and I clenched my lips as tightly as I could, lest I burst out crying.

When Yabtonga and Yawire went out, I emerged from my hiding place and went to find Lar.

He saw me and smiled, revealing teeth dark with blood.

"Runt... Brother... I hit him again, Yabtonga. I hit him again, that wolverine, that scavenger." Then he told me everything that had happened in the storehouse.

"Why did you do that?"

Lar sat up and, perplexed, said, "You dummy. If I didn't hit him, he would have taken it out on you."

"Then father would get you for it."

"He wouldn't... Father – if he is our father – should be happy to have a strong son. He should be happy even if I beat him bloody. I will bear it, it will only make me stronger... Bring me some food, brother. Steal some, so that nothing happens to you."

"I'll steal some."

I did not manage to fulfill this promise. The curtain moved, and I barely slipped under the furs in time.

***

Kiss Woman entered. In her hands was a steaming bowl of fish soup. She set the bowl next to the prone Lar.

"Can you eat on your own?"

Lar said nothing. Uma repeated her question and held out a spoon, but Lar did not make the slightest movement in reply – he lay there like a log, his gaze fixed on the patch of sky visible through the smoke-hole. Uma waited for a bit, then pulled the bowl towards her, spooned some soup from it, and carefully brought it towards Lar's face.

Lar had become insensate from hunger and that last fight, but the aroma of the broth reawakened his appetite. He slowly began to sit up – he trembled and pursed his lips as best as he could. Uma gave him several spoonfuls of the broth. Lar swallowed these down, shuddering as he did so, and after each spoonful he begged, "More… more…"

"That's enough," Uma suddenly announced. She took the bowl with the remains of the food away.

"More," Lar insisted.

"You can't," she said firmly. "It would kill you."

Lar froze. Uma saw how he was tormented inside and expected that, any second now, curses would come flying from his mouth towards her. But that is not what happened.

Lar burst into tears.

Kiss Woman had last heard such crying when Lar had been very small indeed. She took his head in her hands, stroked his wet cheeks with her palms, and said again and again, "You poor thing… You poor thing…"

Lar kept crying with no shame at all.

"You poor thing…" Uma repeated. "Why did you do it?"

He suppressed his crying and asked, "Do what?"

"Hit my son. You nearly killed my son Yabtonga."

"What about me?" Lar said. "Am I not your son?"

Uma shuddered and fell as silent as a person struck over the head.

"Am I not your son?"

After those words, the bowl went flying into the darkness of the chum. Uma jumped up.

"Bastard!"

After she shouted this, Kiss Woman vanished behind the curtain. But the word did not offend Lar, it simply fell like a stone into an empty pot – clearly he already lacked the strength to get offended. Lar felt within him a nearly forgotten warmth. He rolled onto his side and seemed about to fall asleep. But he was prevented from doing so.

***

Yabto's face, like a round stone, appeared in the chum.

"So, you're a strong guy, son," the stout man said as he sat down next to Lar's bed. "How many days did you go without food, and yet you're still alive, and even have the strength to eat. A strong guy."

Lar sat up.

"What am I to do with you? Kill you?"

Lar said nothing.

"Otherwise you'll kill everyone here. First Yabtonga, then Yawire, and then, when you are a bit older, me. Wenga and the old man I don't even think about..."

"We fought," the foundling child finally spoke, "according to the rules."

"Well, sure," Yabto nodded. "By the rules, indeed. Be honest, do you hate Yabtonga, your brother?"

Lar was silent.

The stout man answered for him. "You hate him."

"He said that he would drive over my bones. Mine and Wenga's," Lar finally said. Then he added, "Not now. Eventually."

Yabto smiled broadly. "Well now," he said, "what a smart son I have."

"Tell me, who am I?" the foundling asked bluntly.

"You're a bastard," Yabto calmly replied.

"Mother said the same. All of you have been hostile to me. Tell me, did I come from somewhere else?"

Yabto took the lashed stick from his belt and lifted Lar's chin with it.

"Who is my own and who is not, is something I decide, and I don't need your input. Anyone who lives in my encampment can be deemed so. You had better ask about something else: how much meat am I going to feed you, and what do I get in return?" The stout man fell silent and then, after a brief pause, he said, "Is it really such a bad life, boy?"

Lar raised his eyes – anger flashed in them. "If you want to kill me, then kill me."

Yabto withdrew the lashed stick from under Lar's chin.

"I could do that, too."

He stood up and walked away. He turned on the threshold. "Tell me, are you already hankering after a wife?"

Lar turned away.

"You are," Yabto chuckled. "I already wanted one at your age. Now you listen to me. I will marry you off. To a beautiful girl from a good family. If you value your life, don't leave this chum until I come to you first."

"I want food," Lar said.

But the stout man paid that no heed, as he had noticed movement at the far side of the chum. He walked over and pulled me out from under the furs. With one arm, like handling a puppy, he flung me outside and then stepped out himself. I cowered against the ground in fear, but Yabto walked past without saying a word.

***

That day, Lar was not given the slightest morsel of food.

I was nearby, but I could not go to him. I felt for him and suffered. I thought of how he was lying there, hearing people talking, hearing the dull chopping of an ax and the rare cracking of branches – mother was at work by the hearth, he must have heard the resonant thud of the large kettle on something hard, probably a stone, and the swearing that followed it…

Lar could not make out any words, but he did not need to in order to understand that over there, quite close, life was going on that shortly before had been his life, too. He looked at his hands, wiggled his fingers, stared blankly at the interior of the chum, and realized his present situation, one which no longer had anything to do with the present situation of those other people.

No one came to him.

Lar probably hoped that they were at least talking about him, but the autumn wind made their speech too indistinct to make out. The hunger that had been slightly appeased by the little food which Uma had brought, returned, but now it was no longer that dull sensation that it had been while he was confined to the storehouse. His hunger reawoke raging and brought Lar to the brink of despair.

At a certain point, a sort of indifferent courage welled up within him. He rolled over onto his stomach, got up on all fours, and then slowly rose to his feet…

But when he was fully erect, that courage vanished as if it had never been. Weakness overcame him, he broke out in a sweat, his knees trembled, and his last strength gave way to fear.

That was the great insight of the stout man. He understood that if he fed the founding child at least a little bit, the latter would forget about any dangers and leave. His young innards would quickly digest any disease that had settled in it – unless, of course, that was death – and then nothing would stop Lar. But Yabto knew the magical power of hunger, for he himself had once gone hungry…

Lar collapsed to the furs and feel asleep. Sleep was his sole escape. When he woke up that night – the bright black circle of the sky through the smoke-hole hung above his face – he felt something strange next to him: it was a wet stick. His fingers grasped it and he realized that it was a reindeer bone that still had some scraps of meat on it – he dug his teeth into it, gnawed at it, sucked at it, and picked it clean with his hands and tongue.

For a moment, he thought of me, and it warmed his heart and he smiled.

Thus, once a day or every other day, he would awake to find a scrap of food next to him. The same bone, or a bowl that contained a fish head and some scrapings from the pot. This saved him from death and aroused within him an unbearable desire to live, and therefore it fed his fear of Yabto.

Lar had already begun to forget everything except his own hunger, and he was ready to display any docility if, when he awoke, it would only bring another bone or bowl.

His thoughts turned to me, but he was wrong: it was Kiss Woman who threw him those scraps, and it was Yabto who determined how much could be brought to him.

***

One morning Lar found the bowl nearby – it had been filled with a thick broth. He crawled towards this food and, grabbing the rim with his lips, he drank in the warm, meaty goo. Then, gathering the first strength he had felt, he sat up on the furs, grabbed the slippery pieces of reindeer offal with fingers that could hardly obey him, and shoved them into his mouth.

"Chew it," came a voice from somewhere above. "Otherwise you'll choke."

It was Yabto who said this. The stout man towered above Lar, who was now reduced to a quiet, shrunken child.

"Don't be greedy. Today we'll give you some more food to eat, and then tomorrow we're off."

"To where?"

"I'm taking you to get yourself a wife. Or did you forget?"

Lar was dumbstruck. He thought back to what the stout man had said, but he had taken it then for mockery.

Lar pondered the stout man's words, as if they were a river pebble placed into his mouth and he senselessly rolled with his tongue some needless, incomprehensible thing that had no taste or smell. He knew what getting married was all about, he had seen a wedding before, yet he could not understand what Yabto was talking about.

But his dumbness lasted only a brief time. The mention of more food later that day and, Lar was probably hoping, just as generous a portion as now, pushed any thought of Yabto's strange intentions out of his dulled, slack mind. He lacked the strength to feel hurt or anger, he was already unable to feel what any person in his position ought to have felt: hatred towards the stout man. The boy stared at his torturer with grateful, teary eyes like those of an old dog. He looked forward to the evening.

****

The next day, my brother vanished from the lives of the people in the encampment. He disappeared without anyone even noticing it, like an item that had been carelessly tied to one's belt.

Since that time when Yabto got the clever idea of eradicating his adopted son's obstinacy with hunger, a great many days passed.

The dry autumn went by in the blink of an eye.

One night, as Lar was picking the last bits of meat off the bone which Kiss Woman, no longer trying to keep her attentions furtive, had brought with a sudden rustling of the flap over the chum's entrance, the cruel pre-winter wind was blowing through the taiga.

The wind howled and flung up heavy clumps of snow. That snow came into the chum through the smoke-hole, it covered the hearth, and in the same way the cold crept in and assailed Lar.

He crept under the skins, shivered and, warmed by those shivers, fell asleep.

In the morning, the road awaited.

He was still asleep when Yabto came into the chum and, without saying a word, grabbed him with his iron-strong hands by the tunic – at the collar and below it – and flung him outside. After Lar's face hit the cruel snow, he came to. He had not been out of his prison for a long time, and from the first gulp of cold air his head spun. His ears were overwhelmed by all the myriad sounds that inhabited that open space. It seemed that he lay in the snow for a long time, but in reality it was merely for an instant. Yabto grabbed him by the collar and jerked him up onto his feet.

"Can you walk?"

Indeed, Lar could walk and was surprised himself by it – the weakness that he had once felt in his knees was gone. Yabto held him by his sleeve and pointed him where they needed to go. The wind had died down after it had generously covered the earth in snow. None of the people came out to meet him. The encampment seemed dead.

Yabto had ordered everyone to stay in their dwellings and not even stick their noses out. They wondered what Lar's fate would be.

The stout man himself had revealed it the night before:

"Tomorrow I am taking Lar off to be married. I know a family."

Everyone was silent.

Finally, the stout man's wife asked shyly, "What about the bride-price?"

"He'll work it off. In three years or so, if he doesn't run away."

"What family is that?" Uma asked, her curiosity overpowering her fear.

"A family from the other bank."

I saw Yabtonga look down – he was hiding a smile he could not control.

With these few words exchanged and that smile, the people of the encampment said farewell to Lar.

Yabto seemed to be acting rashly in crossing the river without waiting for the ice first. But just as people prepare jerky, so he had prepared Lar for this journey, one that he had spent a long time thinking over, and not without satisfaction. For this he was prepared to ford the river – Yabto knew just where – though the swirling water mixed with snow would be up to his waist, and he would be traveling with loaded reindeer and with Lar, whom the stout man considered mere cargo, too.

Yabto stared intently at Lar – the latter was shivering from cold and looking off somewhere to the side.

"What am I to do with you?" Yabto asked him, as if speaking to himself. "If I give you some food to eat, you'll run away, and if I don't, you'll fall from the reindeer…"

"I won't run away," Lar said.

"Then get on."

The foundling boy hesitated. Now he was not looking off to the side but straight at the man who had been his father, and for a brief moment Yabto could see in this gaze, through the dullness of hunger, Lar as he had used to be.

"Give me some food…"

"Get on the reindeer. You'll get some food once we're crossing the river." Yabto laughed and added, "Very soon now. A big chunk."

Lar sighed with annoyance and got on the back of an old, white-headed reindeer bull. As he climbed up, he realized that he had grown taller, albeit by the slightest bit, for a reindeer is a very slight creature. He turned to look for the last time at the encampment, and he reeled and covered his face with his hand, as if the sight sickened him – a dull, tearless anguish rolled over his face.

Lar understood that he was leaving the encampment for a reason. But he knew no other home, and the people living here had been Lar's only kin. Now, hungry and subdued, he was leaving his home all alone, vanishing from it, like an unlucky hunter who has accidentally stumbled into a swamp in the middle of nowhere in the taiga.

Yabto drove up, took the reindeer by its antlers, and pulled it towards him. When the small caravan had made its first steps towards the riverbank, Lar cried out, "Wenga! Wenga, you runt! Brother…"

Yabto said nothing, he only pulled up on the reins. He came close to Lar, pulled him to the ground, and kneed him in the stomach. Then he put the youth's limp body back on the reindeer and, taking the harness, mounted, looked around, and whistled. A spotted, sharp-eared dog came flying from among the chums – the son of the black bitch that, fifteen years before, had come upon the two foundlings near the dead encampment of the people from some nameless race.

The caravan got under way.

The runt

Silence reined in the chum. Yabtonga was first to speak – in his father's absence he considered himself the man in charge.

"Lar called to you," he said to me. "Why didn't you answer him? Are you deaf? Maybe you aren't a Dog's Ear any more."

I said nothing and simply stared into space.

"Were you offended at being called a runt?" Yabtonga stood up, walked to the entrance, and opened the flap: father had forbidden him from leaving the chum until the faintest trace of the departing caravan could no longer be heard. "There is a lot to do today, and it all falls on us," he told his mother and brother. Then he turned to me and said, "Go on out, don't be afraid. Do you think that since Lar's gone, I'm going to hurt you?"

I stood up and went out.

I understood that, just like Lar, I was stepping across the threshold into a whole different life. I was torn by thoughts that I could hardly understand myself, by memories and sounds, and my whole being was like a forest buzzing with gadflies and midges.

Lar's virtue lay in his incredible impudence.

My virtue was a sense of hearing that allowed me to detect birds half a day's flight away. The people in the encampment had already forgotten about this wondrous thing that they had witnessed years before. But such keen hearing never went away: like any talent that the gods endow a person with, it had a will of its own. It could catch faint, far-off sounds that, it seemed to me, were insignificant: the whistling of a bird's wings as it dropped from a far-off cliff, the crackling sound of a growing root piercing the stony ground, the sighs or weeping of some people I did not know. But few words came clear to me, though I longed to know what the people around me were talking about, especially when I grew wise enough to know what was going on, or could go on, between people.

It sometimes happened that I heard Yabtonga boasting – he had gone into the forest with Yawire and they talked about the happy futures they would have someday, something that, out of fear of Lar, they dared not speak of inside the chum. But this was no wonder, I heard this not as a Dog's Ear but as anyone who was eavesdropping.

When I began to have doubts about where I came from, I lacked the courage to ask questions, and I hoped that my gift would help. But the people who knew the truth did not even speak of it among themselves. Yabto kept his thoughts to himself and trusted no one else, while mother was so plunged into fear she had lost not only any ability to talk about it, but also to scream as she had once loved to do, while Man-Effigy lived quietly and saw no need to open his mouth.

But one day, my innate talent manifested its will in a remarkable way: I could hear what people were thinking about. This was like some kind of vague buzzing, or a thin, faint whistling – I could not make out the sounds exactly or understand their meaning. But my hearing could embrace the sound like a physical object, it could sense therein the hardness of stone, the sharpness of iron, the lightness of a conifer cone that a crossbill had pecked clean. And over those last days, as Lar's fate plummeted, the sound grew heavy, oppressive, unbearable.

The sounds wore me down. When Lar shouted my name from the back of that reindeer, I could only look down and from then on I was utterly silent.

***

Yabtonga loved to play man of the house: until Yabto returned, the man's elder son lorded over everything. He would order his mother to do the things that she always did anyway: chop wood, carry water, cook food. Together with Yawire he repaired the old, ramshackle cargo sleds and, clad in his father's hooded jumper, he would set off hunting. He ordered me to go somewhere away from the camp and dispose of the heads of wild reindeer that he had recently slaughtered.

"Those stink," he said, and then he drove off.

I hauled the heads, which were frozen and did not actually give off any smell, into the forest, and then I went to help mother. Kiss Woman – alone out of everyone – felt sorry for me, only her pity was furtive. One day, when no one was nearby, she looked around, went up to me, took my hand, and placed thereon a delicacy: a chunk of reindeer fat that had frozen solid. She stroked my head and said, "Oh, you…"

Several days later, when the stout man had returned, everyone learned of Lar's fate.

It was a happy one. Yabto himself recounted it as he sat by the hearth in the big chum, once he had already slept and eaten after his wearying journey. The first thing he said was to remind us that he belonged to the glorious Nenyang clan, the Mosquito People.

"We never took wives or wooed suitors from the other side of the river," he said. "But now I did so. Lar, my son…"

The others looked up.

"My son Lar," Yabto went on, "proved to be a bad son. An angry, insolent, lazy one. That is how he repaid me for feeding him since the day he was born, clothing him, giving him weapons, teaching him everything a man should know. How should a father respond when faced with such an ungrateful son?"

The others were silent.

"By killing him," Yabtonga said in a whisper.

His father heard that. "I could have done that. But I decided to repay the bad done to me with some good. I gave him the chance to be born again. For three years he'll be tending the herds of Kheno, who keeps reindeer – that will serve as the bride-price for his daughter. Kheno has the biggest family in the whole taiga. Lar will help his people manage with their reindeer, and they'll help him shake off his insolent and arrogant ways. The old man was happy to have him, and we should be happy, too. Lar will remember my kindness."

Yabto cast his gaze over his family and now talked about what they were wanting to hear from him. "It's just that the Nga people that Kheno's family belongs to, understand how a person is made up, which of the five spirits is chief within him. Only the Nga people can make someone into a different person. That is why I crossed to that side of the river."

"Everyone fears them," Yawire said.

"Out of foolishness. I have long known that all those stories about the Nga, about the terrible sacrifice they offer the gods and spirits, are spread by ignorant folk. People wonder what the gods and spirits want – meat, fat, other food, or perhaps the blood of their best dog – and they are often wrong about that. Only the Nga people know it for sure. That is why they are always so fortunate. On this side of the river, Lar would have died at the hands of his angry parents, or he would become a vagabond that does not live by his own hearth – he could have looked forward to death either way. That is the only outcome that he could expect with his insolent attitude. But on the other side of the river, he will stay alive. Let him remember the mercy I showed him. And you all remember it, too."

Yabto stood up, he needed to step outside. His sons stood up with him.

"Go back to your own chum," the stout man said.

From the other side of the river, he had brought a wondrous horned bow, as well as a knife of shining iron with a white handle, the likes of which no one had ever seen before.

***

That night I could not sleep, I waited for Yabtonga and Yawire to talk among themselves about Lar's fate. However, the brothers made no sound and, lulled by their even breathing, I fell asleep, too.

My sleep was interrupted by something warm and stinking: it hit my forehead and streamed down my face. I opened my eyes and saw how the stream came from Yabtonga, who stood right above my head. His younger brother was giggling, somewhat afraid, over on his own bed.

When my sleepy mind finally realized what was happening, Yabtonga had finished his business and was pulling his pants back up.

"Are you going to go complaining about me to father?" he asked.

Yawire's giggling grew louder.

"Or maybe you want to get revenge?"

I ran from the chum.

The predawn moon, along with a lonely star that seemed inseparable from it, were just about to disappear behind the wooded hill. I walked deep into the forest, pulled my jumper off, and fell to my knees to wipe my face and hair with snow. I washed the filth away until my head had become like a conifer branch, so covered was it now with long, hard needles. Then I turned the hood of my jumper inside out, collected snow in it, and then I wiped my hands and fingernails with the white clumps that had stuck to the fur. I was untouched by either resentment or anger.

My empty soul was silent, it prepared for something bigger.

Yabtonga had realized his longtime dream, he had destroyed his enemy, though this was not actually that enemy himself but a little person with the same face. He was troubled by fear that I would run complaining to his father, but not for long.

Yabtonga was ultimately prepared to pay for that happy moment with some welts on his back. Deep in his heart he was ready for trials, as he considered himself to be a real warrior. No such displays of bravery were even needed – everything had worked out perfectly. The runt Wenga said nothing to anyone – who would admit to such a shameful thing? – and Yabto did not have it in him to beat his elder son.

But mainly, after he returned from the other side of the river, father stopped even noticing me.

Things had already been like this before. The stout man found more worthwhile things to think about, and the taciturn boy that had stopped somewhere on the transition into manhood, meant little compared to them.

Yabtonga, for his part, became happier and more high-spirited by the day, and this rubbed off on his younger brother. Yabtonga's soul was like a fish that had miraculously found its way out of a net – he seemed to become twice as quick-witted as before, he could handle anything: he could throw the lariat accurately, he learned to hunt with a blind and a decoy reindeer. The stout man rejoiced to see this and entrusted more and more adult tasks to his son. One day Yabtonga bagged an elk all by himself, and it took four sledges to bring his catch back to the encampment. The task of hauling off the elk's head later fell to me...

Yabtonga dreamed of marrying, of war, and of earning his new adult name that is secretly conferred on any man when he grows out of his mocking childhood name. The greater Yabtonga's fortune waxed, the more my own life waned.

Yabtonga weighed on me as Lar had once done in our mother's womb.

I was slowly pushed away from the common pot. Every time the males of the family sat down to eat, Yabtonga – not father – told me, "Go fetch some wood, we don't have much left" or "Go feed the dogs." Finally, instead of mother it was I who started bringing food to Man-Effigy, who almost never emerged from his chum and would eat only there. The old man never exchanged a single word with me, he only opened his eyes to indicate where I should set the food, and then he would again fall back into his usual dozing.

Eventually I started sitting down to eat with the women, with Uma and Nara. This was only fair, since I had been doing women's work – preparing wood, carrying water – and I did not say a word in my own defense.

Just as Lar's words of farewell had augured, Yabtonga began to oppress me.

***

The next autumn came a day that changed my life.

I was bringing food to Man-Effigy. As usual, I had not even glanced at the old man and I turned to go, but I heard a voice:

"It's good that you are so demure," the old man said. "That's how it should be. An orphan should be demure."

I froze. "Who's an orphan, old man?"

"You are, my dear. And your brother Lar, too. You are both orphans. Children that came from other people."

"But I've got a father and a mother…"

"Even you don't believe that," Man-Effigy retorted. "Don't have anything to say for yourself?"

I bowed my head and said, "Lar fought. But Yabto is hard on me…"

"Hush now, clever one, and listen. Yabto is not your father. Nor is Uma your mother, though she fed you and your brother with her breast. Do you want to know who you are, where you came from?"

"Who am I?"

"I don't know. A long time ago, many years ago, Yabto and I traveled by boat to the Yenisei to get some fish. We found you there. Your encampment was right on the riverbank and there had been a battle. Someone hid you under moss and so you survived. Yabto and Uma saved your life, remember that."

"Why did they do that?"

"He wanted more men in the family," the old man said and then laughed out loud. "And he got you: Lar who he dumped on the Nga people, and you the runt."

Man-Effigy then bent forward and whispered. "Come closer, I'll tell you one more secret. You'll find it interesting." The voice of the old man was like rustling snow. "I tried to talk Yabto out of saving you. That's right, I tried to talk him out of it."

"Why"

"Figure it out yourself. You don't know?"

"No, I don't..."

Man-Effigy closed his eyes and pronounced, "You can't take in strangers. Not everything you find along the way belongs to you. Now, you remember that as time goes by – if you are still alive, of course. Judge for yourself what happened: Yabto wanted to fashion some warrior sons out of you, and now he's angry that it didn't work out. Ultimately he might make you into his slaves, but a person is a slave from the very beginning, as soon as one of the gods decides to assign him such a fate. He couldn't even make slaves out of you. What slave could you make out of Lar, for example, if there is a great leader growing inside him? Though you might be fit for that – you're small, someone can get away with pissing in your face..."

I shuddered.

"And you're too weak, you're like a woman."

"What am I to do?"

The old man replied at once, "Run away."

"Run away where?"

"Wherever, just run. It will only get worse. You have nothing to look forward to here, no inheritance, no wife. Only leftover scraps of food, beatings, and the heaviest hand-drawn sledges. You're a nobody, I don't even know what kind of people would see you as their own. When you were found, you were so little that you could not utter a single word in your own language. What kind of Yurak are you? But if you run away, perhaps you will find some meaning for your life? Perhaps one has been prepared for you up there," the old man jabbed his finger towards the smoke-hole, "or there," he pointed at his shoes.

"Tell me, where is that riverbank we were found by?"

"How could I say? I'm almost blind. A whole lot of rivers flow into the Yenisei." Man-Effigy leaned slightly and grinned. "Yabto knows. Go ask him." There was no kindness in his eyes.

"Then I will go to the Nga people and look for Lar."

"In your case, the Nga won't be any different than any other people – you are a stranger to everyone." Suddenly his voice changed and became warm, unusually so. "Run away," Man-Effigy whispered. "You're got strong, youthful legs. And strength… Strength is a gift that is given and taken away when higher powers wish it. No man can make himself strong, even if he can carry a whole elk on his shoulders. Lar was strong, but where is he now? Do you understand me, boy?"

"Yes."

"Then run away. You've got strong legs…"

I went out of the small chum. From the very moment that I crossed the threshold, the old man's words entered into my heart: run away, run away, run away, my heart said.

In an instant everything had changed and my turbulent life became clear.

None of the people there knew what life-saving secret Dog's Ear carried within him.

Nara

From that moment I had something to do: prepare for my escape. Every object, every word I adapted in pursuit of this aim. I had my bow, one of the three that the stout man had once fashioned for his sons, each according to his strength. The one I received was enough to hunt capercaillie or hares, but I knew that this was already half the battle. I only needed to get ahold of more arrows, repair my skis, and stockpile some initial food.

I tried to make arrows myself – I went to the river, used my small knife to cut osier in the frozen thickets on the riverbank, and I set some hollow, tubular bones aside so that I could later carve arrowheads from them. This was a laborious task: I had almost never been taken along hunting – it was Yabtonga who had grown up to be a fine hunter, his luck and the stout man's were enough to ensure that the family never went hungry.

Yawire followed on his brother's heels, but with enough of a gap that he could not become hunters like them overnight.

But I, Dog's Ear, would stay behind in the encampment to help Uma and Nara. The women never sought to insult or offend me, but they also would never let me out of their sight. Springtime Girl – she was then fourteen years old – must have considered me one of her dolls and demanded that I always stick around her.

"You're a weakling, we can't let you wander off," she said.

"I'm a man."

"What kind of man are you?" Nara laughed. "Go down to the river, there's some ice there: brush the snow off and take a look at your reflection."

I would grab an ax and a hand-drawn sledge, and tell mother that I was going to fetch wood, but I really went down to my secret stash of materials for making arrows and arrowheads. If I managed to make at least one arrow each day, then by winter's end I would have a quiverful and could depart into the taiga without fear – or so I thought. But my hands still found this work challenging, my arrowheads ended up crooked and clumsy, like a raven's beak, or the wood would splinter. Worse of all, I wasn't aware that arrows from osier were only made for children's toys. To make real arrows, I needed a carefully chosen larch trunk, one out of a hundred, a sharp adze, strong arms, and several years of practice. I had none of those things, I had never seen it done. My stubbornness made up for my lack of knowledge, however.

Many days passed before I got my first arrow as I had pictured it: straight, sharp, with a colorful owl feather. The second arrow came after a shorter time, and then the third within a day.

One day, when I had set off to get wood, I tossed my small bow onto the sledge. When I reached my hiding place, I carefully brushed the snow from the large chunk of birch bark that covered the stash and drew my first arrow out of it. To avoid losing my precious jewel somewhere among the branches, or breaking the arrowhead on a hard tree, I shot the arrow up into the sky. It soared up and turned into a gleaming black speck, hung for an instant in the sky, and then began to fall back down. Without hitting a single branch, it eagerly plunged into the snow a dozen paces away. But I was prevented from picking it up, for Springtime Girl was already holding it in her hands and smiling at me. She had followed me there and hid between the thick trunks of a dead pine. Nara smiled.

"So, this is going to chop wood," she said.

"Give it to me."

With one hand Nara gripped the arrow by its tip, and with the other at its feather. "Shall I break it?"

"Give it to me."

Springtime Girl could hear the trembling in my voice.

"What do you need arrows for?"

"For hunting. I want to bag an animal."

"Don't you already get enough meat here?"

"I want to hunt for myself."

"Hunt for yourself? What kind of hunter are you? Go down to the river, there's some ice there. Brush off the…"

"I have already been down to the river."

"Maybe you want to run your own household?" Nara asked, laughing.

"I do," I retorted, and surprised even myself.

"You're silly to say that. You're a small guy, you're shorter than I am."

"So what?"

"You don't have the strength for a bow big enough to kill a reindeer or elk. How are you going to feed your wife? With partridges and fish?"

"I don't need any wife."

"It's you no one needs. I would hang myself before I married a runt like you. If you want to survive, then go on living here. Stay here forever."

I took a step towards Nara. The arrow in her hands bent. "I'll break it…"

The realization left me staggering: one more word, and this evil creature would learn my secret. She knew almost everything. I roared in despair and rushed forward…

Nara squealed, the wood in her hands cracked, and together we collapsed into the snow like ensnared animals beating against their trap.

I got ahold of myself when I saw a pink stain on the snow: it was blood. The bone arrowhead had left a gash in Nara's cheek, she was sitting opposite me and pressing her palm to the wound – red trails appeared between her fingers and flowed down the sleeve of her parka.

"Show me…"

"You wolverine, you fish shit," she blurted, then jumped up and rushed back towards the encampment.

My first thought was to run away now, right away. I had my bow, a few arrows, a hand-drawn sledge, my small knife, and the ax.

The stout man, Uma, and my brothers would see the gash in Nara's cheek and ask who had assaulted her. Springtime Girl would tell them the runt's secret, about how he was making arrows, and moreover wanted to go hunting for himself and live on his own. Yabtonga would be the most astonished of all, he had already grown used to the fact that the boy on whose face he had pissed, had already stopped speaking almost entirely. Yabto's elder son would think of what more he might do than he had already done, to this boy who had the same face as Lar, whom he despised. Yawire might have some suggestions, too…

After I had thought this over, I decided to take my arrows from their hiding place, put them on the sledge where the arrow and ax already were, take the reins, and go.

I did not know where I should go, my mind was gripped by only one thought: that everything had been decided suddenly and against my will. As I walked, my blood surged through my body, I was already thinking about how to hunt for food…

But a sudden gust of wind brought with it a remarkable sound, and for the first time I could distinguish the words: two female voices. One was scolding while the other, crying, spoke the words, "I fell and a willow scraped my face…"

My feet now halted. I returned to the stash, hid my arrows there, and then went back to the encampment.

***

Nara had not betrayed me and I was grateful to her for it. But my gratitude was mixed with the fear that my secret was hanging by the thread of her whims. Worst of all, she seemed to understand her power. Those first days after she had got that wound, she did not speak a word to me, she would not even glance in my direction, and that sapped the very strength from my arms and legs.

But one day I realized what I should do: the gratitude had to be repaid.

I owned nothing besides my clothes, my child's bow, the secret stash, and a small blade for handiwork that women carry. For several days I ran into the forest, picked up birch bark powered with snow, and intently went to work on it. I was no longer thinking about arrows – from the bones intended for arrowheads I carved beads in the shape of small birds. I presented Nara with the resulting flock, on a string I had made from a piece of old suede, on a morning when the stout man and his sons had left on a long trip and Uma was sitting in her chum preparing skins.

Springtime Girl did not show any surprise: she accepted the gift, held it in her outstretched hand, and watched the white flock flutter in the wind.

"Do you like it?" I asked, hopeful.

Nara said nothing for a time, as if she wanted to first admire the beads to her heart's content. Then a sly laugh escaped her lips and she looked at me askance. "Are you afraid I'll tell father?"

Springtime Girl's words hit me like a blow. "No," I replied dully, and then I went to see to my own chores.

That same night I decided to escape and I cursed myself for the weakness that I had shown.

Iron Horn

Everything fell apart when the sun had risen above the hill, which meant midday. Not three but four draught reindeer were approaching the encampment.

Yabto led the way, and next to him on a huge, black-headed reindeer bull was a stranger. He looked like the very twin brother of the man of our encampment, for he too lacked a neck, and was the same height and build.

But Yabto did not have any brothers.

The man was a Tungus and bore the name Iron Horn. Deer leapt on his cheeks, arrows fell from his eyelids, a snake crawled along the bridge of his nose, and his mouth was square: of all the Tungus who covered themselves in tattoos, he was the first to hide his true face.

Yabto and Iron Horn had known each other for many years, from the time when the men of several Nenets and Tungus families joined together on the expedition to the upper waters of the Yenisei. They had both been mere youths then, the same age as the stout man's sons were now.

Yabto had run into the Tungus halfway along his journey from the encampment, and this chance meeting had led the stout man to forget all about hunting.

"You've got fine boys," Iron Horn said. "Strong ones. I'd like sons like that, but I am all alone, pal."

"Why don't you marry?"

"I don't want to." The shield-faced man threw back his head and laughed, and the reindeer on his cheeks leapt away from the snake. "But your boys are fine ones," he repeated. "They are probably looking forward to some inheritance from their father, armor or a mail shirt. Hey you," the Tungus now turned his reindeer towards where Yabtonga stood, "do you have a mail shirt?"

While the elder son hesitated about whether to answer the man's question, his father did it for him: "Good iron is expensive. You haven't earned it yet…"

"He will eventually, he's trying. Why should a big and strong young man have to rely on anyone else for it?" Yabto realized what the Tungus meant. He himself had not received any good weapons among his inheritance – his father had generally preferred hunting to war. The armor of shining iron, a yellow bird at the chest, and the pointy iron hat that had been won on the expedition to the upper Yenisei – his father had traded all that for a herd of a hundred head of reindeer – he wanted to become a reindeer herder and leave for the tundra forever. But that same year, plague killed all the reindeer.

In his youth the stout man had longed to own such armor, he would take it out and look at the yellow bird on it.

When his father died, Yabto did not offer the wooden effigy in his memory a drop of blood after hunting, nor a morsel of food – his father's spirit would pay for his foolishness he had shown as a mortal man and for his son's humiliation. After what the Tungus man had said, Yabto suddenly wondered if he himself would receive enough in the afterlife.

When one does have anything to pay for a good weapon, one can obtain it through war. But the gods never sent the stout man a good war; the people living in the vicinity were either too strong or poor. These thoughts briefly blew through his mind like the wind.

"Maybe you know where a person could obtain good iron as easily as he could bag a capercaillie in the forest?" he asked, with a slight sneer.

The Tungus laughed again but then suddenly stopped. Now he said in a voice in which Yabto could not detect a hint of laughter, "I do."

They stared at one another for a moment.

"Let's go home," Yabto finally said. "There's a lot of meat in the storehouse. You'll be our guest, Iron Horn."

***

The visit of an old acquaintance called for celebration. Pots were boiling and a rich aroma hung over the taiga.

Over a meal in the large chum, the Tungus told the stout man how back in the month of burbot, he had come upon an elk and pursued it into territory that belonged to other people. The catch was too good to simply let go, and Iron Horn ran after it through that territory without any fear for himself. The animal eventually ended up where the hills grew taller and a river ran through. The elk had little strength left: the arrow that had fallen in its flight into the animal's hind leg, barely broke the skin, but its tip stuck in the flesh, and slowly the life drained out of the animal like water from a tiny hole in a pot. The Tungus man, on the other hand, moved along smoothly on his skis, he slowed to a measured paced and followed the elk's trail, waiting for one last, sure shot.

Iron Horn possessed greater endurance than any animal – he could pursue any catch or foe for days on end without food or sleep. He was the sole hunter living wherever his heart chose to dwell. He came from the clan of the Kondogir, he had his own territory, but if Iron Horn ever visited his native places, it was like a thief in the night. His kinsmen had long cursed him.

His greatest satisfaction came in finding a companion to go on a brief raid with – the Tungus man lacked a force for waging a good war.

In the years following the death of his father and mother, he had made so many sworn enemies that he could expect an ambush around any corner. But he was content with his vagabond life. Iron Horn loved danger, he loved pursuing animals, tracking them, and lying in wait. And therefore the Tungus did not ever have to worry about hauling home the huge amount of meat he obtained, for home was wherever he had shot his last arrow. The Tungus man would dig a hole in the snow, build a shelter from three sticks, a small piece of reindeer skin he carried on his bag, some birch bark and stones, and he would live there all on his own next to a fire, eating the meat cooked on skewers or even raw…

The elk had not yet come into sight, but from its tracks Iron Horn could see that the animal was frequently falling on its forelegs. Its prints were accompanied by red stains. The path was leading upward, and the Tungus man approached the top of a round hill with the same measured pace – he knew nearly for certain that the elk would give up on the other side. He caught sight of the animal on the flat hilltop: the elk was standing with its side to him, leaving its entire massive body exposed to his arrow, and with his great hunter's intuition Iron Horn knew that it would give up its life without any final struggle. The Tungus man drew a large, forked arrow and set it on his bowstring.

The elk looked one last time at the man – and disappeared. The hunter was taken aback, for he had only looked down for a second. He dashed onward, and what he saw left him even more stunned.

***

After the huge beast had drilled through the thick snow, it rolled down the steep slope, already almost dead. Men were running towards it, shouting. They had bows, and as the Tungus man peered more closely, he saw arrows in the body of the elk, many arrows…

The men – there were four – stood around their unexpected catch. One of them walked up to the immobile creature and, with his big knife, cut its throat to finish it off.

The four men were speaking a language that Iron Horn knew as well as his own: the men were Ostyaks, who used the term "ket" among each other and for transportation preferred dogs to reindeer.

With his keen hearing the Tungus man caught their expressions of amazement. He hesitated for some time about whether he should descend and argue over the catch, but he soon understood that it was not worth it.

From the lower ground rose a thick smoke, such as would be produced by myriad chums, and apparently these men were a tiny portion compared to those who had remained in their encampment. But on this day the Tungus man was again amazed, and not for the last time.

A fifth man walked up to those four. He was an old man, bow-legged, short, and still hale. His voice was like the cracking of a falling tree and he spoke loudly, as if intentionally addressing also the Tungus man hiding behind the hilltop:

"Someone was driving it and then just let it go. That's not good. God will punish that. Go bring the sledges…"

"It was Togot who said that!" the Tungus man now told Yabto, nearly shouting into the latter's face. "Togot, can you imagine?"

"Oh…" the stout man muttered.

Every people forges iron as they know how, but the Ostyaks surpassed everyone else in skill, and Togot surpassed every other Ostyak. He could talk to iron like to a cherished dog, and the iron would obey him. Rumors flew that Togot's roots went back to hunters for earthly reindeer who had moved into the underworld, due to which he, like those people, was bow-legged and short in stature, but most importantly he could see the lower parts of the earth better than its surface.

Togot wandered in search of the red stone just as other men wandered with their herds, or in search of rich game. Therefore, no one knew where the old man lived. It was he who clad in iron the Ar, the Assan, the Yug – all the peoples who spoke the Ostyak tongue, and he only asked that his work never fall into the hands of foreigners.

Nevertheless, the people who venerated Togot like a shaman, were tempted by the high price that other peoples would pay for knives, spears, armor, and mail shirts. More-over, Ostyaks sometimes perished in battle, and the old man's creations would fall to the victor – everyone knew about it, and throughout the taiga Ostyak weapons forged from the shiny metal were a sign of a rich inheritance, while an Ostyak scraper was regarded as the finest gift for a bride.

"That smoke was not coming from chums," Iron Horn said. "He has found iron – a lot of iron – and for that he was burn-ing massive trees. You understand?" The Tungus fell silent and stared inquiringly at Yabto.

The stout man had already guessed what his guest was getting at. "Where there many men with him? Only those four?" he finally asked.

"I don't think there were more than the men I saw. Those snot-noses were his sons. Perhaps he had brought slaves there with him. Togot has always had slaves… But weapons weren't needed for dealing with them. That item there would suffice." The Tungus man smiled and pointed to the lashed stick that lay next to Yabto.

The stout man smiled in response.

That day they did not talk any further about the old man. Iron Horn was clever and knew that he had to wait for Yab-to's careful mind to work.

In the morning, as soon as they woke up, they again ate together – long before dawn Uma had cooked meat. Yabto was the first to speak:

"There are only two of us."

"Your elder son is nearly a man. What do you call him?"

"Goose Foot. The other is called Shining One."

"I saw that you have one more son, a small guy…"

"He doesn't count. The runt, though he is the same age as Yabtonga. He is more suited for things here, women's work. His name is Dog's Ear. In his childhood he could hear birds from half a day's flight away. Whether he can do that now, I don't know."

This surprised Iron Horn. "Well, there you go," he said. "Can you call him?"

The stout man gave a full-throated shout, and soon thereafter Yabtonga and Yawire – they were practicing shooting their arrows into scraps of reindeer skins hung from a pine branch – grabbed me and pushed me into the big chum.

"Your father says that you can hear birds from half a day's flight away. Is that true?"

The voice I heard was friendly, but I hesitated in answering. Every time I found myself in the stout man's chum, I felt danger and froze within, and now I saw that danger in the big reindeer bone that Yabto was pounding with a stone in order to get at the marrow inside. My suspicions were confirmed: the bone came flying towards my face, but I managed to duck in time.

"He's a nimble one," the Tungus said with praise.

"Answer him," Yabto said.

"I used to be able to hear like that. Now, I don't know."

"Leave," Yabto ordered.

Once I jumped out of the chum, I was unaware that my fate was decided while I had not even taken more than a few steps away.

"He's got eyes like a sable in a snare," Iron Horn said. "You can't let eyes like that go to waste."

"I can and I don't care," the stout man said and, after a silence, he added, "Alright, then, we'll take him along."

Yabto went to clad himself and his sons in the taiga's best iron, so that Yabtonga and Yawire could get a taste of war. The Tungus, on the other hand, lived by brigandry, but the only thing iron about him was in his name.

To appease the spirits, the stout man decided to do something unheard of: he offered as a sacrifice the decoy reindeer with which he had bagged up to a dozen wild reindeer in a single hunt. He then left the encampment with peace of mind, trusting in his own great generosity. To those remaining behind, he said nothing about where he was going and why – it was not their concern, especially if the storehouse was already full.

Their caravan, which consisted of a dozen reindeer and five sleighs, left at dawn, and after nine days and nights it reached the place where Iron Horn had lost the elk.

Togot

The Tungus man was skilled at raiding.

During the journey, at their stops for the night, he would discuss something with Yabto at a distance, so that none of the youths could hear a word of it. Yabtonga and Yawire were allowed to go and practice their shooting. My task was to look after the reindeer, pitch the tent, make the fire, and cook meat. Yabtonga was like a puppy, all excited about going on his first big hunt, and this kindled joy in his younger brother, too.

Once near to the Ostyaks' secret camp, Iron Horn assigned everyone their position in the fighting. I was ordered to stay with the reindeer and sleighs in a ravine among the hills. The stout man's sons lay in ambush along the edges of Togot's camp, which abutted a small lake with a hole cut into the ice, so that he could draw water and cool his iron.

It was as if the red stone had been waiting for the Ostyak, for a whole multitude of dead larches were already at hand. Some of the smith's men, working furiously with axes, chopped up the logs that bore within them a tarry, fierce heat, and dragged them to the furnace, the black maws of which gaped at the taiga. Other men, standing in pairs, were using huge pestles to pound the red stone in flat, shallow pits. From that distance it was impossible to tell who among them were the smith's sons and who were his slaves – they all wore the same dirty shirts, and all had faces where stone dust and soot were mixed with the sweat of many days.

The old man himself was walking through the camp and swearing at everyone with angry Ostyak words. That morning, his work had still not got started. Togot was angry that the evening before, those lazy wolverines, those shit-eaters and lumps of offal, had laid down to sleep right after eating, without preparing all the necessary wood and red stone, and the day was short. The man's slaves and his sons had probably heard such words so often that no one was spurred to work any faster by the old man's shouting, and Togot himself only waved his stick…

Just as a lynx pounces on the head of a hunter taken utterly unawares, so two strangers fell upon the camp. They rolled down the steep, almost sheer hill and, after a few steps, found themselves in the middle of the camp, near the furnace.

"May you live to ripe old age, Togot," the Tungus said in a loud voice.

The old man's astonishment left him speechless, and his men shrank as at a blow and stopped working. Only one sound could still be heard in the stillness: Iron Horn's cheery voice.

"You have chosen a lucky spot, old man. Wealth has fallen from heaven all by itself – a whole heap of meat, and nice guests. Have you eaten my elk?"

Togot looked at the Tungus for a long time and finally he muttered, reluctantly and solely out of a desire to break the silence, "Why did you drive it on but then abandon it? God will punish you… You'll die of hunger."

"I am Iron Horn. Have you heard about me?"

"Perhaps I have, but then forgot. Should I remember every vagabond? I've got my own people."

The old man was regaining his composure, his voice grew steadier, and that spread to the other men there. Four of them left the larch logs and, axes in hand, surrounded the men speaking on four sides. These were the old man's sons.

"You don't seem very nice."

"Are you very nice, you with covered face?" Togot then raised his stick and pointed it at Yabto. "Did that Yurak, with the neck of a fox, come with the nicest of intentions?"

The old man was bringing up a sore subject, because every member of his people knew that the Yuraks and Tungus had been their foes since the beginning of time. The Yuraks and Tungus felt the same about the Ostyaks and Selkups.

"That's all unnecessary, old man," Iron Horn said, trying to speak as peaceably as he possibly could. "We just wanted to have a look at your work. After all, you are said to be a great master smith…"

"Why have you come?" Togot barked.

His sons took a step closer.

"Sell us some of your iron."

"I won't."

"I'll pay generously for it."

"No, I told you…"

"Why not? Perhaps we can strike a bargain?"

"This is Ostyak iron. I don't bargain with it, especially not with tattoo-faces like you."

"Look, if you still haven't managed to forge enough armor, knives, or blades, we'll wait. Your work is worth enduring some insults. Why don't you invite us in?"

Togot said nothing, he only looked down. When he lifted his head, the outsiders saw his open mouth and yellow teeth, from which frequent bursts of soundless laughter emerged. "All your head is good for, Tungus, is a home for lice," he said between bursts of laughter. "Otherwise you would realize that you need to get out of here while you're still alive, and not ask to visit."

After this was said, the whole encampment shook with laughter – his sons laughed at the brilliant retort, the slaves laughed, leaning on their pestles, and Iron Horn himself laughed…

Only Yabto did not laugh – he walked up and sunk his knife into the old man's belly.

He did this without saying anything, and as casually as if he were spearing a chunk of meat in a pot. Togot's sons, unable to immediately leap the gap from laughter to death, hesitated for a moment, and that cost them their lives.

Two arrows came flying from somewhere – one came to a stop in the head of a young Ostyak, the other struck his brother in the shoulder several yards away. The other two Ostyaks stared wide-eyed in amazement and frantically looked for the shooters – this confusion lasted long enough for Yabto and Iron Horn to rush upon them and do them in with their knives.

The life of that secret camp was cut short, just like that of the pale insect that the smith had spoken of when he mocked the tattoo-faced Tungus.

Togot was still alive when the Tungus walked up to him and said, "Pity that you did not invite us in, old man. Where is your weapon?"

"Ostyak iron will bring you grief one day," the old man muttered through pale lips. "You and that Yurak of yours. You carrion-eaters…"

The stout man's sons emerged from where they lay in wait and rushed into the camp. Yabtonga seemed slightly deranged and did not whoop, he whined – he was downcast that victory had come all too easily. He shot arrows into the dead bodies of the Ostyaks and stopped only when his father picked up a chunk of red stone and flung it at his head. Yawire, dancing with glee, was looking for his own arrow which had struck one of Togot's sons in the shoulder.

Yabtonga rushed up to his father and pointed to a hole in the nearby hill; the smith's people had brought red stone forth from it. "Father, there are *khabi* there, they are still alive. They're hiding. Let me go kill them, father. Please let me…" Yabtonga was nearly crying.

"You like war, son?"

Yabtonga was shivering as if he had just emerged from ice-cold water. He did not answer.

"You probably think war always goes like this?"

"Father, let me…"

Yawire ran up, with the same entreating look in his eyes. Yabto's thoughts turned to the old man's slaves, but this was interrupted by Iron Horn, who was pointing at the ravine.

"Look…"

Only now did Yabto notice two faint stripes left in the snow: the ski marks went off into lower ground and then disappeared between the hills.

"I took a closer look, there is already some snow over the tracks," the Tungus said. "He got away already some time go, probably as soon as we got here."

Without exchanging another word, they rushed towards the shelter fashioned in the hillside where, like puppies in a snowstorm, Togot's slaves lay in a big ball. All were still alive.

The tattoo-faced Tungus grabbed one of them by the scruff of his coat. "How many of you are there?" he roared. "Go on, talk!"

The slave gasped for air with his wide, toothless mouth and tried to say something, but he could not find his voice.

"How many?"

Iron Horn brought his knife to the slave's throat. The latter froze, stopped breathing, and raised his hand where two of his five fingers were cut off. The Tungus withdrew his knife and the slave immediately darted back into the hole and merged into a single filthy clump with his fellows.

"He went towards the place where our reindeer are," he said to Yabto. "Can that boy of yours stop him?"

The stout man was silent for a moment, then answered, "I don't think he has even got a bow."

"Then more Ostyaks will be here soon," the Tungus said. "They will come with their iron and see our tracks."

"We need to gather up our booty."

"Wait a moment…" The Tungus got on his skis and hurried after the trail in the snow.

***

The man was the most pathetic of Togot's five slaves. He was not fit for preparing the larch trunks, or for pounding the red stone with a pestle. Like me, he cooked the food and took care of the chums.

No one – neither the old man nor his sons – remembered which people this man had come from. He attracted less notice than even the most unnoticed of dogs. But he was the meekest, most hardworking, and most loyal of the slaves. Togot, who always had a rod in his hands, never beat him, for this slave completed jobs even before his master could ask for them.

When the strangers came, the slave was hacking apart some frozen meat on a chopping block behind a distant chum, on the margins of the camp. The invaders had not noticed this slave, but the slave saw everything. He got on his skis as soon as Iron Horn began to speak.

No one knows how he anticipated the great disaster of which Togot's other men had no inkling. He had only made it a short way from the camp when he caught sight of a small caravan ahead. The reindeer were tearing through the snow, still shallow for that time of year, in search of lichen to eat. Not far from a loaded sleigh stood a figure with a bow at the ready.

It was me.

The heart of a *soning*

When Yabto set off on the raid, he had not asked me if I had a bow, so insignificant did the stout man consider me.

I found Yabto's doings as strange and repugnant as he himself, but I was young, and the news that we would make war got me fired up inside. When I learned what tasks would fall to me, ones that did not require handling any weapons, I was offended. I remembered the warm, foul wetness on my face, and I hid my whole secret stash, the bow and the arrows with bone tips, on the sledge. Then, during one of our stops for the night, I stole a real, iron-tipped arrow from Yabtonga's quiver.

At the raid, I wanted to prove myself just as worthy as the others, though I realized I was only fooling myself.

When they set off, Iron Horn ordered me to stay by the reindeer no matter what. Just like the stout man, he did not ask anything about weapons, for he could hardly imagine a man setting off into the taiga without his bow; the Tungus did not think I was crazy.

"You watch out, boy," he said as he left and lightly nudged me on my forehead. "If you see the enemy, shoot. Don't even think twice about it."

When the four of them had disappeared from sight, I strung my bow – I had hidden the bowstring under my coat – and took the stolen arrow out. With the giddy joy of youth, I thought that now my hands were not empty and I was just as worthy as the Tungus man, Yabto, and his sons. To relish the feeling, I lifted my weapon and pulled the bowstring at the very instance when a tiny figure appeared under the arrowhead.

It took time for that man to spot our caravan, but when he did, he stopped. He was probably thinking about which direction to flee, but he could not think for long – steep forested hills rose on both sides, leaving only one way to go. We stood staring at one another, unmoving, and both of us realized that we could not escape from the other.

The man saw my weapon, but took a step towards me nonetheless. My heart detected that he was a foe and began to beat madly. I shouted out. "Hey, you, stop!"

The man stopped.

"Who are you?"

No answer came. Something drove me to speak again. "Lie down in the snow and don't move."

The man in front of me did not move: now I could clearly see that he had no bow or other weapons, unless he was concealing a small knife. Along with my blood pounding at the sight of the enemy, I was overcome with fear at having to kill him, and my heart felt relief when I thought that the man was perhaps moving so slowly because he would obey my order, and lie down on the snow.

I scrutinized his small, pockmarked face, dull eyes, and tattered coat – he was similar to me in build and appearance. I let the bowstring fall slack and shouted once more. "Lie down!"

But the man did not lie down – he started forward and, without stopping, he walked towards me swinging his arms, like someone who knew just the right way to go. His eyes remained fixed on me, as if he was aware of my fear and scoffed at it.

I let my arrow fly…

At that instant, all sounds seemed to stop, but my sight became as clear as day: I did not hear the bowstring buzz and slap against my sleeve, nor did I hear the whistle of the arrow, I only saw the arrow soundlessly fly towards the man and come to a stop in the middle of his forehead.

The man stood there for a moment and then fell face first into the snow.

From the lower ground came the Tungus, striding like the god Manga. He went up to the slain man and turned him over, and I could see from far off the half-broken shaft jutting from his head. Suddenly my hearing returned and fresh sounds came flooding in:

"Come here," Iron Horn shouted.

I ran up to him. The dead man was staring up at the sky with dull eyes wide – he had slipped out of this life like a fledging bird from the nest. The snow under the body was soaked with blood down to the very earth.

The even pattern tattooed around the Tungus man's mouth barely moved as he said, "Take a good look."

Iron Horn drew his large, curved knife from its sheath and cut open the dead man's filthy, shabby coat to expose his body: it was pale and covered in scabs, the trace of some disease. In a flash the knife tore through the skin at the ribs and the Tungus man was reaching into the body with his wide arm, as if into a sack, and feeling for something. The reindeer began dancing against their harnesses when he jerked his hand out, and I saw a uneven ball in his blackened palm.

"Eat it."

The Tungus did not shout, he was speaking in a voice that I had never heard a person use before.

"Eat it," he repeated. "You are no runt any more, you are a warrior. Just like me or your father. No matter how many foes you go on to kill, your first slain foe should live inside you. This is the beginning."

But I was unable to reach out and take it. The Tungus man cut the heart in half.

"If you're afraid, we'll eat it together."

Yabto came walking up from the lower ground in no particular hurry. He stood at a distance and watched what was happening. I saw a barely detectable smile appear on the stout man's face, and some force overcame my numbness and pushed me to reach out and accept what the Tungus was offering.

When Yabto saw this, he stopped smiling, turned, and set off back down.

Iron Horn followed him with his eyes and after a brief silence, he said, "Have you ever heard about the *soning?*"

"No."

"They are heroes, each of them is worth a whole army. When a *soning* gets old, he asks others to slay him and eat his heart, so that he can pass his strength on to his people. You are one of those people."

"That man didn't even have a knife."

"You're smart," the tattoo-faced man smiled. "Remember this: a man who walks unarmed towards an armed enemy is a *soning.* Even if he is a slave. You'll understand when the *soning*'s heart awakens within you."

After the Tungus said this, he smiled broadly, lightly tapped my forehead, and went off to find Yabto.

***

Iron Horn was joking when he said that he and his companions could wait until the smith had forged a lot of good iron.

His joke prophesied disaster: the plunder proved terribly small, only enough to fully equip a single warrior. One shirt of shining plate-mail, a big spear with a blade wider and longer than usual, a piece of armor in two halves, and an iron hat. In the earthen shelter dug into the hill lay formless chunks of iron that Togot had not yet worked with.

The Tungus did not complain for long. He told Yabto that, though the booty was small, it was easy to divide up, and he offered the stout man the armor and blade, while he would get the mail shirt and iron hat. Yabto was unsatisfied, however. Iron Horn said that he could settle for a smaller share, but this did not appease Yabto. Then the Tungus said that he knew a place where the plunder could be traded for pots, furs, and herds.

"I don't need any reindeer," the stout man said.

The Tungus clapped him on his shoulder. "Still, you've got your own army, small as it is. You'll get more iron."

"We're leaving," Yabto said, and he picked up his share and carried it towards the sledges.

Yabtonga ran up to him. "Father, there are *khabi* there. I told you, remember? What are we going to do with them?"

"Whatever you want."

Yabtonga squeaked and, after shouting to Yawire, he rushed to the earthen shelter, drawing an arrow forth as he went. As the stout man walked on, he heard the twang of a bowstring and cries. The human voices quickly fell silent, but the sound of the weapon continued.

On the road back, Yabto seemed to cheer up, and he spoke amicably with the eternally cheery Tungus. But during one of our overnight stops – halfway back to our encampment – Iron Horn never woke up.

I saw the Tungus man… He was lying in the tent face up, the snake on his nose was now frozen, the deer on his plump cheeks and the pattern around his mouth sagged towards his short neck, across which a bloody gash ran.

Yabto put the Tungus man's share of the booty and weapons on his own sledge.

Togot lived off on his own and even his clan did not know where the master smith roamed. Therefore, news of the slayings at the camp reached the Ostyaks only when the springtime thaw exposed the men's bones. Only a great shaman could search for whoever had extinguished this hearth. Once Togot and all his heirs were gone, the Ostyaks felt that they no longer boasted the best weapons. They swore to find the killers, whether they were many or just a single person.

A slave's heart

After the raid Yabto and his sons slept and ate to their hearts' content for several days. This leisure assuaged the last traces of annoyance that had hung over the stout man the whole way back.

But then he spoke to me for the first time in those days. I was hauling a sledge full of wood from the forest when Yabto stepped out of the big chum.

"Come here."

I let go of the sledge and ran at his call. I stopped several steps away as deference demanded.

The master of our encampment squatted. His eyes were at the same level as my own. "I have never had any bone-tipped arrows. Where did they come from? I saw you packed them." There was no threat apparent in the stout man's tone, he spoke only as someone who wanted to keep things in order, and Yabto knew every one of his possessions like the palm of his hand.

"You stole an iron-tipped arrow, from those I gave to Yabtonga. Didn't you?"

"Yes."

"I think you wanted to say, 'Yes, father.'"

"Yes, father."

Yabto smiled. "Why did you steal only one? Is one good arrow really all a warrior needs? Why aren't you answering? Are you scared that Yabtonga will notice that an arrow is missing?"

I was happy at that ready-made answer that saved me from needing to search for words, and I simply answered, "Yes, father."

"After all, you wanted to wage war like everyone else, so you could have asked me for an arrow. Why didn't you?"

The stout man got up – he realized that the words came to this runt only with effort. "You're a good shooter. You can shoot more than just capercaillie. Where did you get the bone-tipped arrows from?"

"I made them myself."

"What for?"

"For capercaillie…"

Yabto said nothing for a moment, then suddenly asked, "Remember the Tungus man? No need to answer, I can see that you do. You probably hoped he would cut my throat? After all, I'm harsh, but the tattoo-face was nice to you. He was the only adult that would talk to you, and even teach you how to take an enemy's heart. What did it taste like? Like fresh reindeer liver? Come on, tell me what it was like to consume a man's heart."

"I don't know."

"That man was Togot's slave. You ate a slave's heart, and now you might become a slave yourself. Do you realize that? Do you realize what a kindness Iron Horn did to you?"

I looked down.

Yabto had had enough of this conversation, he knew that he could not expect any answer from this boy with the same face as Lar.

"You already are a slave," he said. "From now on, no bow for you, not even such a pathetic one, nor arrows, not even bone-tipped ones. Only sledges and that ax for chopping wood and hauling it in. I don't need a son who ate a slave's heart."

Yabto turned and went back into his chum, and as he did, he heard the sledge's runners meekly rustle on behind him. But suddenly, he felt a strange pang: it was shame. The stout man had referred to Wenga as his son, and now he was ashamed at his lie. "What made you say that falsehood?" came the mocking voice of his demon.

He twice heaved a heavy sigh and the pang vanished as quickly as it had come. The demon was silent. Yabto smiled and thought with pleasure that it all came down to his great generosity, which some mischievous spirit had taken advantage of and made him speak with that pathetic creature.

Shortly thereafter, Yabtonga and Yawire were giggling and playing with my weapons. They shot the arrows at an old deer skin; the bone tips would barely penetrate the target.

By evening, the broken bow and arrow shafts were crackling in the fire.

***

"Now you don't have any arrows. What are you going to hunt with, big guy?"

It was Nara. She stood opposite me and chuckled. "Do you still intend to go and live on your own?"

I tried to avoid looking at her – her laughter whipped my face like a slender vine. I desperately wanted to cry, and when the torment had grown too great and the wood was already unloaded, I straightened, grabbed my ax, and said dully, "Go away."

Nara's laughter stopped. "Go on, hit me," she said, as if she were whispering it in my ear.

I put the ax down and set to breaking some branches over my knee. The crack of the dry wood gave me some sense of relief.

I thought that it would be nice to tell this creature that I had already slain my first enemy and eaten his heart – after all, she probably had no idea. My brothers considered themselves grown men and, following the example of my father, did not talk about their doings with the women.

But before I could even open my mouth, Nara spoke: "Are you afraid to hit me? You have already killed someone, after all."

I shuddered within. After a brief silence I replied, as severely as I could muster, "Yes, I have. An enemy. And I ate half of his heart."

"Oh!" Springtime Girl squealed as if someone had presented her with a gift of large pearls. "A real warrior!"

"Yes, a real one." I nearly shouted this, as again I felt a hot shame come over me.

"Yet this real warrior is doing women's work."

Nara had not even managed to close her mouth before a pine branch whistled past her face. In the long silence that followed, I saw her black eyes, like two little bows, open wide as if someone had drawn the bowstring.

Finally she spoke. "Well, you won't kill me, like... like the man you killed."

"No, I won't."

I grabbed the ax from the snow and placed it on the sledge. "Go away. Don't you have your own work to do?"

Yet Nara did not go away.

"You want to watch a real warrior do women's work? Then watch."

Springtime Girl did not budge, nor say a word. Suddenly she spoke as if she were pulling her greatest possession from its treasure chest. "A man came to see father. They ate a lot of meat and went on for days. They spent a lot of time talking loudly and laughing."

"Yeah, I heard."

"No, you didn't. That man came from the other side of the river, the land of the Nga people," Nara went on, and after these words I froze. "I overheard that man. I was next to the chum, mother had ordered me to bring them some fish..."

"Say it!"

"The man said that he had seen Lar. That he was alive and well, and he ate well with everyone else. Old man Kheno had made a fine reindeer herder out of him, and soon, even sooner than in three years, he would give Lar his daughter, the prettiest one..."

Nara's speech came more and more slowly, she rolled the words like pebbles from along the riverbank in her hand. Tears flowed down her cheeks.

Just like they had flowed when her father took Lar away from their encampment, only no one else had seen those tears. She hid them like the greatest of secrets and shed them only at the rare moments when she was alone.

And I, runt Wenga, a person with a slight body and Lar's face, had become Springtime Girl's treasure alongside those tears. I had no inkling that Nara had already developed that great skill of woman to lie, conceal, and hide – and thus tell the truth about herself better than with the finest of words. I became her doll, the most precious of all, and when she laughed at me she was revealing a secret that I figured out only many years later.

Now that she realized that her tears had given her away but she was not angry at herself for it, she only felt a quiet, tender pain.

She undid the collar of her parka and took out the string of white birds. "Look, your birds are here with me," she said. "For ever."

She turned and walked away.

***

Only half of my spirit was left. Lar, the other half, had been taken away by the stout man and sent across the river, to the land of the Nga people.

What kept me going were the words that Man-Effigy had told me: "Run away." I continued to bring food to the old man in his chum and I hoped that this man who had revealed to me the greatest secret, would at least repeat those words, or call me a coward.

The old man never said anything, however. He refused to even open his eyes and look at anything that was happening around him. Yet the cherished words remained inside me. I began to believe the stout man's claim that I had been poisoned by that slave's heart.

But when Wenga saw Springtime Girl's tears, he suddenly understood that he really could go on. He had no idea what kind of life it might be, but he was no longer afraid of it.

And thus – without any fear – I saw the winter through. Then spring gave way to sultry, glaring summer. I was waiting for something that I could not even put into words, and this waiting gave me not anxiety but strength. In my thoughts, Nara had taken the place of those cherished words.

Springtime Girl was beautiful – father, mother, and especially my brothers had commented on it. I realized that they were speaking the truth.

But Nara's beauty was like the northern lights: one might admire them, but even in one's wildest dreams one could not hope to possess them. After she had shed those tears, Nara no longer laughed at me, she uttered no words of mockery, rather she completely avoided seeing me. But this did not hurt me in the slightest, I could watch her from afar, and when she was not to be seen I knew that Springtime Girl was nevertheless somewhere nearby, helping mother prepare skins or sew clothing or boots.

Nara brought my brother back to me: when I looked at her, I felt like Lar's heart was beating there, too. The three of us became one.

Since that time, I had not heard any news of Lar. The man from the other side of the river did not visit again.

In early autumn, draught reindeer from the Tungus Kondogir clan arrived at our camp. The old man who led the way, Molkon, asked esteemed Yabto for his daughter, to marry his son Altaney, which in Tungus means "Strong Man".

Molkon offered Yabto the bride-price, exactly one hundred reindeer, and if a forest-dweller did not need such a big herd, it could be traded for fine goods and weapons.

Yabto gave his consent and they drank to it.

Nara was set atop a white-headed female reindeer and taken away north, to where the Middle Katanga flows into the Yenisei.

The night after Springtime Girl departed, my wondrous sense of hearing reawakened. Through the howling wind I could hear the huffing of reindeer and a quiet weeping that sounded like laughing.

The escape

Strength and wits do not reside permanently inside a person, they come to him as if merely visiting, when fortune invites them. The same happened with me.

My wits reawoke like a man who has slept well and left all trace of fatigue behind on the bed.

My wits told me that I already had everything necessary to leave. Weapons were stored in Yabto's chum, and the boat readied for tomorrow's fishing awaited on the riverbank.

My wits told me that thinking too much about the future and fearing failure makes for cowardice, which is also a messenger sent by fortune. If fortune tells cowardice to go away, it does so and abandons the hearts of even the humblest of men.

Towards daybreak, when the sky had turned pale and the huge whitish moon had descended to the hilltops, where it hid during the day, I went out of the chum I shared with Yabtonga and Yawire. They heard nothing. I walked up to where the stout man and his wife dwelt. In my hands was the small ax.

My heart was calm, as if it sensed that the long-awaited day had come. The night before, something astonishing had happened: Man-Effigy spoke to me for the first time in many months.

"Get rid of the bells," the old man said without even opening his eyes.

I sat a dish with me before him. "What bells?"

"Long, long ago a woman betrayed her husband. There was a war, and the men would sleep in their armor. One woman caressed her husband and asked him to take off his armor and make love to her. The husband did that, but that night the woman's lover came and killed him as he slept. The woman and her lover ran off and lived a long life, to the envy of many. From then on, killing a sleeping man was no longer a sin. But if a man wants to sleep without armor like in peacetime, he ties bells to his weapons. They would ring when someone else tries to grab hold of the weapons."

The old man said nothing more after that.

I had rarely been in my parents' chum, but I knew that Yabto kept the plunder from Togot's camp next to him. My freshly awakened wits said that the surest approach would be to slay the stout man in his sleep, with a single blow of my ax, and, if necessary, to do the same to Kiss Woman. I would have been ready to do this, yet I felt there was no need for it.

But on that day I could feel fortune with every fiber of my being, and fortune did its work: it had plunged people and dogs alike into a sweet predawn sleep, it sent a pale light through the smoke-hole of the chum so that my eyes could get used to the darkness, and it gave me a sure hand.

I saw a dim iron point along the middle of a bow – I held the bell quiet, took the big bow from the chum, and laid it outside. In the same place I soon found a spear, a quiver full of long arrows, a mail shirt of leather and iron, armor, and a pale-blue, curved knife.

On the threshold I unfolded a large piece of old suede – this was something I had thought of in advance, so that the sound of metal would not wake anyone as I hauled it towards the riverbank – and I placed on it everything I had stolen. The iron did not let me down and remained silent as the suede slid over the wet grass.

I remember that I was seriously worried about only one thing: that I would not have the strength to push the huge boat into the water. The boat had no mast then, the stout man would install one only when he intended on sailing up the Yenisei.

But fortune sent me strength, too, though my feet seemed to plunge into the sand up to my knees.

The dark, gentle water took hold of the boat and quietly bore it away. The taiga was silent, waiting for the imminent dawn, and this blessed silence washed over my heart. I gripped the oar but did not dare to stir the water, and I watched as the riverbank I had left slowly dwindled in the distance. I thought of how the road from unhappiness to happiness was short indeed, it lay in a man's own hands, and I cried at the happiness being so near. The tears burned my cheeks. I cried silently and clenched my jaw shut with all my might, as if I was afraid to let this precious crying run loose and thereby lose it.

From out of the sky somewhere came a weak, fluctuating sound. It grew louder and encroached on the surrounding stillness: the first cranes were leaving the taiga. I felt then that there would be no more tears. I looked up and saw the even wedge shape which they made as they flew, which resembled the tip of an arrow. The sky was growing brighter.

I took the oar and directed the boat towards the other shore.

***

Yabto was not accustomed to being angry at himself.

His mind was as if clouded – he remembered this as he recalled waking up and seeing the place empty where his weapons had lain. He had wasted a day in trying to catch the boat, and he had given the runt time to get far away into the taiga. Only some trickery sent by an entity hostile to Yabto and his demon, diverted the stout man's mind from the only thought that mattered: that there was only one way for the runt to run, namely to the other bank and the land of the Nga people, where Lar was.

Yabto sought some reason for the cloudiness of his mind and he found it in Man-Effigy. The old man ate little, but he undoubtedly stirred up as much trouble as a powerful enemy. The old man's life, a life so long that it seemed to be an insult, had to end, and Yabto would do what the gods had apparently forgotten to do. He would return things to the way they should be and get back what he had lost.

But now, when his delirium had subsided somewhat, Yabto realized that that puny young man could hardly carry so many weapons. Catching up with him, tracking him down there in the taiga, would not be so hard for an experienced hunter. He only needed to follow his reason, keep his demon happy, and not make any mistakes.

The next morning, the day after the boat had come back, the stout man and his sons sailed across the Bountiful River.

Midway along their walk from the shore was a small lake into which a stream flowed. Yabto ordered his sons to split up and search for any human tracks, while he walked along the winding stream.

He scanned the terrain carefully, as if sweeping the river with a fine net, so as to not leave the slightest possibility of making another mistake.

The stout man knew that after only a short journey, the mountains would begin: the flat-topped ridges arranged in a row, like furrows made by the claws of a great beast that scraped the earth when it was young and soft. As the stream approached the mountains, its serpentine winding grew straighter and then passed into a gorge where the current was deeper and louder.

Yabtonga walked a dozen paces away to his father's right, and Yawire to Yabto's left at about the same distance. Yabto led the way. On his back he carried the strong bow, nearly an adult one, that he had once fashioned for Lar.

Along the way they came across a three-month-old bear. The young creature had recently separated from its mother and, with a plaintive growl, it was trying to catch fish on the rapids – the stream was rich in grayling. When the bear saw the humans, it roared and began to scamper away – Yabto's sons saw its rear first, before they even had time to get scared. They raised a cry and then laughed at the fleeing bear.

With a brief, menacing grunt Yabto bade his sons be silent. "Keep looking down at the ground, you silly wolverines."

When the little river entered the gorge, it gained strength and began to burble loudly, drowning out their voices. The autumn sun, which was unusually generous for that time of year, rose to its highest point and froze between the mountains and their bright-yellow and scarlet patches of dying foliage. In some places midges had been reawakened by the warm weather. This was a season for good pre-winter hunting and fishing. The taiga was calling to them like a generous host invites guests, and a feeling of annoyance buzzed around Yabto's heart like a horsefly.

But he, a man who had seen a great deal, knew that it was not worth paying any attention to that horsefly, for the other half of his heart was hearing something different: the demon that dwelt between his shoulder blades whispered that it would pave the way for him, lead him to success, and that he was stronger, much stronger, than that other spirit that was casting its favor on the runt.

The good demon soon proved itself. At the place where the mountain ended and the river became wider and less turbulent, Yabto caught sight of a hole on the shore. At the bottom of this hole lay a fish, half rotten. The stout man smiled broadly, and motioned to his sons that they come to him.

"That's him! That's him!" Yabtonga whispered rapturously.

"You two walk along the shore," the stout man said curtly.

The sons wandered off, each trying to detect other signs of a human being, and soon Yawire whistled and rushed back to his father: he had found, hidden in the grass along the bank, a fish snare woven from a vine.

"The runt," said Yabtonga, trembling. "It's him. It must be. He's somewhere nearby. What should we do, father?"

Yabto did not reply but only examined the fish-trap. It had been skillfully woven, and apparently a long time ago – it was already broken in several places. "Have you ever seen the runt make traps?"

"We would cut vines together, we used to…"

"If you can't be sensible, then shut up. This is not him."

"Then who?" his sons immediately asked.

"I don't know," Yabto replied and flung the trap back into the grass. He walked off from his sons and sat on a rock right next to the water. For a time he was deep in thought.

"So, father, should we move on?" Yabtonga asked meekly.

"No," the stout man replied and got up from the rock. "We'll stop here. The day is almost gone. You," he pointed to Yawire, "prepare camp. And you," he ordered his elder son, "catch some food for tomorrow. Don't wander off too far, the hunting is plentiful right here."

"But father, he'll get away," Yabtonga cried. "The sun is still high…"

"Maybe you know where to look for him?" Yabto asked with a wry smile, and then firmly said, "He won't get away. Now do what I told you to do."

His sons went into the forest to cut wood for their camp and catch some food. The stout man chose a place that was relatively dry and laid down in the grass. He looked up at the sky, smooth as iron, and enjoyed the peacefulness of the place. He was not worried about anything and trusted in his demon, which had brought him to this place as an adult leads a baby by the hand.

The fact that the runt had nothing to do with the fish-trap meant nothing to the stout man. He knew that this spot, where three gorges met, would be passed by anyone – or nearly anyone – bound for the land of the Nga people. Wenga might go by whatever path appealed to him, but sooner or later he would end up here, and in several days' time the river would lead straight to Kheno's encampment.

Here the demon that dwelt between the stout man's shoulder blades told him that the runt had his own demon, but it was no match for him, Yabto's demon.

***

Apparently, that demon was right.

The way that led to the encampment where my brother awaited, was unfamiliar to me, like any other path across this earth. I heard no voice behind me. My demon was merely faith in my good fortune that allowed me to do what I had been unable to commit to for so long. This faith, in a way I found inexplicable, approved some thoughts and rejected others.

I knew only one thing, something I had picked up from the adults' conversations: I needed to walk towards where a star pointed, the one we called the Hole in the Universe and the Tungus man called Buga Sangarin. That star would lead me north, to the dwelling place of Nga, lord of cold and evil, and thus the place of his people, too, and there I would find Lar. Our souls, ripped asunder, would become one again. So I thought.

On that morning when I reached the other bank, thoughts began to enter my mind that brought me an inexplicable happiness. I obeyed one of them and took some thick, half-rotten wood lying on the bank and placed in the boat, and then I let the boat drift with the current. The boat departed from shore, slowly spun as it hit a few whirlpools, and as it dwindled I thought that I had done well by weighing it down: it was moving so smoothly that, from a distance, there really seemed to be someone inside it, someone who had put his oar down and fallen sleep.

Not far from shore I found a burrow that some animal had dug. I expanded it with my spear and placed there the iron shirt, the helmet, and the armor, and then I used my knife to cut a big chunk of moss to cover this stash. So that I would not forget where it was, I stuck some dead wood into the moss. I kept my horned bow, the quiver with iron-tipped arrows, the spear, and my old ax that I had used to chop firewood when I was a slave. I gathered myself, breathed in deeply, and ran.

I ran as fast as I could, but suddenly some invisible and impassable barrier brought me to a stop and drove me back to the riverbank. As I ducked down among the willows, I watched Yabto rage on the other side of the river. This sight took some weight off my soul, and it lent my legs twice again as much strength. I flew along without even being aware of my body, my legs deftly found their way among the wet, mossy rocks, and I felt that I could run forever with no consideration for danger. A single thought had pushed out all others: a new life was on the way, and whatever it was like, it would be better than my old life.

Without breaking my run, I climbed a mountain and stopped only at the top, so that I could take a look around me. But the mountains had nothing to tell me: the lowlands were covered by white, downy fog, and only the occasional bird, like a black, barely discernible speck, circled above the peaks.

There on the peak, the first concern that came to mind was Yabto's bow. It was a powerful bow made of horn and wood, the only fine weapon that the stout man had owned before the raid on the Ostyak's secret camp. The bow was so tall it nearly came up to my eyes, and to my great joy Yabto had strung it the night before, as he had been planning to catch burbot.

Just like with the boat, I had been worried that this weapon would require greater strength than I possessed. I thought that was the time to test my luck. I drew an arrow from the quiver. The feather at its end touched the bowstring and, when my hand began to draw back, the bow did not want to yield to me right away. My hand froze halfway and my chest involuntarily let out such a cry of despair that the bow shook and yielded to me: the arrow disappeared into the sky. I did not catch any glimpse of it and did not bother to look for it.

Elated and feeling all-powerful, I descended into the lowlands.

That day I walked as if the gods had paved a way for me. Every step convinced me of it. When the sun began to set, I felt hunger for the first time that day. It was a young, spiteful hunger that hindered my steps, and it had pounced on me like a lynx lying in ambush. I had not brought the slightest morsel of food along, but wonders never ceased: on a large branch, like a giant hand reaching towards me, a black capercaillie sat as if waiting. It had fallen into my grasp like a present. I ate my catch without even building a fire, and as soon as I reached the foothill of a mountain, I laid down and slept. The next morning I walked along a dry gorge, drank water from a stream, and before sunset made a fire to roast a fat rabbit with faded and ragged fur that I had caught the previous day.

Thus, it was along this path that I spent the day which Yabto's mistake had afforded me. Before I fell asleep, I looked up at the sky to see where the Hole in the Universe was shining.

The good fortune which had given me weapons and freedom protected me until the first star. It protected me as a I slept, so that the next day I would reach the bank of the small river where the stout man was waiting for his good fortune to manifest itself.

***

Yabto was the first to wake up. He went to urinate, and then he nudged his sleeping sons with his foot. He ordered them to demolish the shelter made from spruce branches, throw grass over the long-extinguished fire, and then hide among the willows.

I fell into the trap before I even had time to wonder at the demon's betrayal.

At midday, a river appeared in front of me. I looked at the water and thought about this meeting. The body of the river pointed like an arrow towards the north, to where my star had twinkled the night before. That river, I thought, was too small for the smallest boat, but ample enough that it could provide people with food. That meant that if I walked along its bank, sooner or later I would reach some kind of encampment, whether large or small.

Then I walked up to a place where a fire had burned not long before. I saw the dead coals covered with clumps of grass – Yawire was too hasty in doing what his father had ordered and made a bad job of it. The thought that here, there had been people who needed to cover their tracks in such a remote place, struck me like a blow and shook me out of my complacency.

I set the spear down at my feet, looked around, and then suddenly saw Yabtonga.

Yabtonga emerged from the willows and calmly walked towards me with his bow ready to shoot. He smiled, as if eating a delicious piece of fat. I turned then and saw Yawire, he was standing still also with his bow drawn.

As I looked at them I felt only a howling void inside my head. This did not last long, however. Suddenly I began to suffocate and fell to the earth, where darkness came over my eyes. The stout man and his lariat had joined in.

***

Yabto made a temporary camp by the river.

The sons built a little hut from thin spruce trunks and several pieces of hide, which they always took on any short journey. Then they gathered firewood and brought it in.

Not far from the fire was a tree, a pine that was not very thick. I had been nearly asphyxiated and the stout man shook me out of my clothes, like some little item from a sack, and then tied me naked to the trunk. I came too when Yabto was tightening a knot over my chest. The rope barely left me room to breathe.

I expected to hear shouting and cursing, and to feel pain. But nothing happened.

When Yabtonga and Yawire went off into the forest to catch some birds, Yabto spoke for the first time. He was sitting by the fire and looking at the weak, flickering flames. He did not add any more fuel to it, though some dry branches lay right next to him.

"It's like autumn forgot to come," he said, looking off somewhere to the side. "The sun is shining like in summertime. Best time to hunt. Elks are fat, reindeer are fat. They can barely move, they are so fat. That's how generous the taiga is, isn't it?"

Yabto stood and walked towards me. He stopped a yard away and stared into my face for a long time.

"Where is the iron?"

No answer came.

"Did you hide it? No use staying silent."

The stout man walked away and sat down again by the fire. The flames had almost died out, smoke from the coals rose in clumps and melted away.

"You're not the runt that you seemed. No one could have hoodwinked me like that, even Iron Horn, but you did. Clearly some great spirit helped you in that. Do you know the spirit's name? Ha, how could you know? You're no shaman. What would you be worth without that spirit? Less than the most pathetic person. And now that damnable spirit helped you. Where did he lead you and what did he get you into? Don't you have anything to say? Do you still trust in that spirit? You shouldn't boy, it'll abandon you, I know that for sure..."

Yabto stood up and again walked towards the pine – the runt's refusal to speak had obviously left him angry. "I'll find the iron all the same. My sons and I will follow your path back. I know these parts and I know which way you came."

He spoke the truth, and the stout man's truth aroused despair inside me, which in turn untied my mute tongue. "If you know where it is, then kill me. What are you waiting for? You said yourself you don't need a son that has eaten a slave's heart. Why don't you kill me, are you afraid to shed the blood of kin?"

The stout man laughed. "Those dimwitted old bones told you everything. Well, he was right when he told me that if I brought you to our encampment, I was bringing foreign spirits, too. You two were so small, and you didn't have much time left at all – any wolf cub could have torn you apart, a wolverine would have been bigger to you than an elk. If they hadn't got you, you would have died of hunger. But me, a kind soul, I saved your lousy lives, I fed you along with my own sons and wanted to make the finest of warriors out of you. But the old man was right – foreign spirits will never truly become part of a man's own family, and foreign gods won't lend any help. They didn't even help you."

Yabto brought his face near to mine and whispered, "Just think, who are you now, huh? A body with no soul in it. Your life belongs to me like the clothes I'm wearing. You're alive, but you're already gone. A shaman can wander through the worlds and never find a slave's soul, because it just goes up in smoke. A man becomes a slave when his own spirits abandon him. Just like your spirits abandoned you. Who fed them? Who made sacrifices to them? They were angry at you since the day you were born, and that is why you live a life that is more miserable than an old dog's. And not just you, but your brother, too."

"Lar is alive," I whispered angrily.

Yabto laughed and drew from his belt a knife of pale iron with a white bone handle – it was the first time I had ever seen it.

"Look," Yabto raised the knife up to my eyes, "this is Lar. The horn bow you stole from me is Lar, too. Kheno bought Lar off me with those, and he tore his hair at the thought of giving up things so precious. Your brother's spirit is weak. I squashed it like a bug."

There was no longer any menacing tone in Yabto's voice, rather he spoke like he was admonishing some totally hopeless person.

"I could let you live, bring you back to the Bountiful River where you could go on living the same life you did before, only I don't have to lie to you any more. Remember, Dog's Ear, you don't have any other life, and never will. If you had made to Kheno's encampment, he would have got another slave for free."

He drew his face back and added after a brief silence, "Soon Yabtonga and Yawire will be here, they're bringing meat. I'll untie you. We'll eat and then go to wherever you hid what you stole."

As he spoke, every word hit me like a deftly shot arrow and sapped my strength. My vision was turning blurry and I dropped my head down, but Yabto walked up and lifted it back up by the chin.

"Don't want to talk?" he said. "Say nothing, then. Don't you want to live, huh? Open and close your eyes to show me that you want to live."

I still found the strength within me to open my eyes, and then not to close them again. I stared the stout man in the face, a red and flat face on which sweat was streaming down. I did not close my eyes until my lids began to involuntarily sag.

The stout man had understood everything. He took his hand from my chin and returned to the fire, where he began to blow the coals that had already gone out. He hoped to awaken in them whatever remained of the recent fire. But the fire did not respond. Yabto stood up, spat, and began to break twigs to start a new fire. The crack of the wood assaulted my ears, I looked and saw that the stout man was deeply annoyed, and his movements had become sharp and deliberate.

I guessed why he was making a fire on such a warm day. He would jab a stick into the flames, it would catch fire and turn into a lance with a red-hot tip that would serve to brand my body. But like someone who has spent a long time sitting on furs and can no longer feel his legs, though he sees them, and cannot stand up, and thinks that that they are something foreign tied to his body, thus I felt no fear, nor alarm, nor anguish. I clearly saw what was happening before my very eyes, but everything – Yabto, the pine, the fire, the river – seemed so very far away. The only thing I felt then was anger, like a dull ache.

***

The stout man's efforts, it seemed, had worked only too well: they had driven the very soul from his now tamed opponent. Yabto realized that himself and decided to revive his foe with fire, but fire, which had always obeyed him, did not answer his call: the sparks only bounced off the thin stick. The wind was still. Birds sang gaily among the quiet, content taiga. Yabto abandoned what he was doing and violently slapped himself on the cheek – his cheek burned with a tingling pain.

Yabto understood now why fire did not want to help him in this case: he looked up at the sky and was blinded for a moment. The morning was turning into midday and the sun was growing brighter, incredibly so for autumn. The earth was steaming like in summertime, and all the life that lurked in the grass and branches, ready to hibernate or die, suddenly felt the unexpected change and now chirped, buzzed, fluttered in a myriad of tiny bodies, almost too small to see. Among the things that awakened were biting insects, the chief horror and torment of the summertime, which robbed man and beast alike of any opportunity to enjoy the brief warm season. Yabto however found these insects a welcome sight.

He went to the river, scooped up water with his hands, and washed his sticky face. On a day like this, the stout man thought, gadflies would come rising up from the river, and through the burbling of the waters he heard the familiar buzz which every person in the taiga cursed. Mosquitoes and gadflies drive reindeer mad, and they can even drive an elk into a swamp.

"Heh," the stout man said, "do you hear that buzzing? Things are looking bad for you, boy. Bad indeed. The demon which brought you here won't give me your blood, it wants it for itself. That spirit of yours is lousy, it's a wolverine, not a spirit."

Yabto laughed, as if he truly felt happy then. "But how can you withstand those insects?" he shouted merrily. "How could anyone, when even the sun is against him?"

The sun was now between the mountains and its rays fell like fierce arrows on my head. Soon my whole body began to burn.

***

Yabto's sons returned empty-handed.

"You want to throw down your mittens there on the threshold?" Yabto asked, no trace of anger in his voice. He still felt the same cheerfulness as before.

"There are just no animals around," Yabtonga said guiltily and stared at the ground.

Yawire, standing as always a step behind his brother, sniffed loudly.

"We saw a musk-deer, but it got away…" Yabtonga said, then fell silent.

He was not, however, thinking of how to come up with an excuse for his father, for he had caught sight of my naked body covered in mosquitoes; all my remaining strength now went to not screaming out. This spectacle left Yabtonga enraptured.

The stout man even seemed happy to hear of his sons' shameful lack of success in hunting. It was a reason to leave, and come back later when the mosquitoes' feast was in full swing. He put the quiver full of arrows on his back, then grabbed the horned bow and brandished it before me. "Alright if I go hunting?" he shouted and, without waiting for an answer – he hardly expected any – he curtly ordered his sons to make a fire from some overlapping logs on a meadow two dozen yards from the river, so that the smoke would protect only them and not hinder the mosquitoes from feasting on the runt.

"Sure, father," Yabto said eagerly. He understood his father's aim. "We'll take care of everything."

His elder son was about to run off, but Yabto grabbed him by the hood of his parka and said sternly, "I know you, so listen carefully: when I get back I don't want to see a single scratch or bruise on him. You understand me?"

"I do, father."

"And don't you dare speak to him."

The stout man let go of his son and, without a backward glance, walked toward the forest.

***

He walked on and greedily took in all the sounds of the forest, hoping to find within them the one he was particularly waiting for. He even slowed his pace so that he would not be too far away and miss it. The forest was alive with the twittering of birds and the wind caressed the mountaintops. Yabto stopped…

His expectations were met. Soon a long, drawn-out howl reached his ears, it was similar to the distant cry of a marsh bird. The howl broke off and turned into a barely audible laugh. Yabto smiled and walked on.

He heard right. It was my body that had howled and laughed. The only thing I remember about that torture is that my spirit caved in just as my eyes had failed. I was ready to do anything that the stout man said. Then oblivion came over me.

Among the great many ways of tormenting an enemy – scalping him alive, cutting his body up into little bits like meat at dinner, burning him with fiery brands, or impaling him on a tree cleaned of its branches – leaving him exposed to the mosquitoes was considered the most exquisite. It required time and patience. On a hot summer day, the mosquitoes would drive a man insane by sundown, and he would howl and laugh like a man of feeble mind. By the middle of the following day, the mosquitoes would have left only a white, exsanguinated body – the clouds of insects would have carried the enemy's life off into the taiga.

But Yabto knew that I would not perish, and he did not intend that himself. The unusual autumn heat had come as a gift, but the gift of a spirit, of the incorporeal demon that guides a man, cannot be harmful. In these days the demon had been so close that the stout man felt he could hear not only its words but its very breathing.

He quickly found what he had gone into the forest for.

Yabto came back down the hill. Two fat capercaillies tied to his belt beat against his legs. One more was lying in a sack on his back – the taiga had sent him these birds as if on a plate. As the stout man walked back, he looked back over his life, which suddenly took shape in his mind with unusual clarity. He had lived under a strong protection, though many times he might have perished at the hands of others, or from cold or starvation, but also from his own mistakes. Perhaps that is what they call fate, Yabto thought. He forgot all about his sorrow and knew that the anxiety which had sometimes visited him would no longer return. He had no fear of his fate.

When he reached the lower ground again, he saw the smoke from the fire and quickened his step. The sun was about to set. Yabto no longer heard any cries and assumed that the mosquitoes had taken so much out of the runt that he lacked the strength even to cry out. He walked towards the overlapping logs where he could get his first glimpse of the temporary camp on the river.

The first thing that the stout man saw was the bare pine tree, and bits of rope lying at its base. The runt's clothes were gone, too.

"Oh!" Yabto said to himself. He was still at a total loss. "Yabtonga! Yawire!"

No answer came. He now rushed along the riverbank, without even knowing why, and soon found Yabtonga.

His elder son was lying face down on the rocks in the middle of the river, half an arrow's flight from their camp – his body rocked in the current, and so did the arrow that stuck out of his back.

Yabto found his other son later, half a day's journey away, where the river becomes winding and narrows to almost nothing.

The land of the Nga people

The land of the Nga people begins on the right bank of Yabto's native river and extends north all the way to the frozen sea. This was the greatest of territories, and the people themselves were immense, beyond number. No one knew how many families numbered themselves among the Nga people. Just as vast was the fear that others felt towards this tribe.

The Mosquito People, the Beaver People, the Cape People, the Willow People, the Brook People, the Birch People, the Fox People, the Squirrel People – all those tribes whose own names were easy to explain, could not tell where the Nga people had come from.

Who the ancestor was who had concluded an eternal pact with the supreme evil being, the lord of cold and ruler of hell, or even if that spirit had instead chosen that people for himself, no one knew. The Nga people themselves kept it secret, and that secret gave rise to a fear passed down within other tribes, father to son like a legacy.

Shamans could make sense of it: Nga, the son of Num the supreme god, maker of the earth and all within it, tricked his father. He secretly covered in impurity the first human beings, whom Num had made, and therefore they became mortal and lost their sense of disgust against impure things, which Num had endowed them with. Num was wroth and wanted to reduce his son to a vagabond among the heavens, but Nga's false repentance assuaged his father and Num did not exile him. Nga said that his contrition was so great that he would not dare ask his father for his share of the heavens, and instead he asked for some inheritance down on the earth, the most humiliating thing that one could imagine.

"Let the land I receive fit on the tip of a staff," Nga said, "just don't disown me, father."

Num saw his son's contrition and urged him to accept more, but his son cried, tore his hair, and shed tears that fell onto the earth and caused floods in which many perished. Finally Num agreed to give him a plot of land that fitted onto the tip of a staff. Nga wiped his tears, set the staff over the surface of the earth, and then pushed the staff right through.

"You did promise to give me everything that the staff picked up. Everything that lies under the earth is mine. Be true to your word, my god."

Nga laughed as he said this, but Num's heart sank, for he had lost not only men as he had created them – immortal and knowing nothing of impurity – he had also lost his son, whose godlike mind had led him to betray his father.

"It shall be as you say," Num said.

These were the last words that that god uttered within the visible universe. After he said them, he departed for the very end of the farthest heaven, and no longer showed himself.

Long ago there were shamans who ascended into the heavens, but none of them could ever reach the far limits of his abode. When people asked them, "Where is our god? What is he up to?", the shamans could only avoid their glance and reply, "He is sleeping. Don't bother him. Just live your lives."

When Num became a recluse, the earth was the territory of innumerable gods and spirits. They were just like people, neither evil nor good, strong at times and weak at others, brave and cowardly alike. Only there were no simpletons among them, for all possessed a keen mind and knew their domains.

Something prevented people from being able to believe the shamans, however. Their lives were difficult and hard to make sense of.

"Did that god leave us something before he went to sleep?" they would optimistically ask. "It's not possible that such a benevolent god went to sleep just like that. Would a great lord really lie down to sleep and leave his flock unattended? Who did that god assign in his stead?"

"Us," the shamans replied.

"And what can you do?"

"We can communicate with the supernatural world. With some of its representatives we can reach agreement, with others we can bargain, and the weak ones we can drive away."

"What about that god? Will he ever wake up?"

"He does his own thing, and that could happen at any moment. But that might make things worse…"

"How so?"

"Who knows what that god might think when he wakes up. That's why you should offer sacrifices. Each year, at the start of spring, sacrifice a white reindeer and sprinkle its blood at sunrise, so that Num will see that you remember him, and you won't suffer the consequences when he reawakens. Then he will reward those who did not forget him. But sacrifice to Nga, too, sprinkle the blood of a black reindeer on the ground at sunset. Don't forget Nga. After all, unlike his father, he isn't sleeping and he won't forgive any offense."

People did what they were told. At first they often asked the shamans whether Num had woken up. The shamans told them to be patient. Thus, many generations passed and people grew weary. Then there were no longer shamans capable of ascending into the higher heavens. But every spring people would sprinkle the blood of a white reindeer on the earth at sunrise, since their ancestors had done the same for many generations now. They did not perform this sacrifice out of hope for anything, but rather out of fear at breaching the proper order of things. Although many people, especially the smartest, realized that sacrificing to a sleeping god did not make much sense, no one wanted to be first to violate something that had been laid down from the beginning of time. Plus, one reindeer was not all that much, even for a poor family.

Nga, however, was right at hand, so they slew their black reindeer with bated breath. Some truly managed to avoid any great misfortune for the whole year after they performed the sacrifice. But others who could see farther than their own noses, understood that a correctly performed sacrifice, while it could save some, would not save many others, and death would sooner or later take what was coming to it. People felt deeply anxious.

But one day a man came along who had come up with a simple and life-changing idea. He thought that one reindeer was too little for the god who had shown the greatest sympathy to human beings. It was virtually nothing. In fact it was worse than nothing, it was like spitting in that god's face. The man belonged to some ordinary tribe, like the Willow People, Brook People, or Cape People. He told his kinsmen about his idea, and he probably laughed that no one had ever thought about this before.

"So how many reindeer should we sacrifice to Nga at one time?" his kinsmen asked.

"None whatsoever," the man answered, to the amazement of everyone. To avoid getting a beating, he quickly clarified what he meant. "Such a powerful god doesn't need any reindeer. They are no sacrifice."

"What do you mean, no sacrifice?"

"A proper sacrifice is like ripping out a piece of your own heart," the man said. "If the whole taiga turned barren, and this reindeer was the last one on earth and we would subsequently all die of starvation, that would be a sacrifice."

"We don't follow."

"You'll understand in a moment." He was a brave man, he went up to one of the warriors and said, "You've got a young wife. Do you love her? Really love her?"

"I do," the warrior replied.

"Then give her to Nga. Sprinkle her blood at sunset. That would be a real sacrifice."

While the warrior was gasping and trying to make sense of such brazenness, the man went to the clan's chief. "And you, sacrifice your son. How old is he? A month? Give your son to Nga, it will not insult him. In fact, he would be overjoyed and he'll remember that no one honored him as much as you. Then Nga will ward any misfortune away from your next son and all of us."

"And you," the man shouted to the warrior, "get yourself three wives, and each will be better than the one you have now. Now do you understand what a real sacrifice is?"

The warrior wanted to kill the man, but the chief put a hand up to block his weapon. "What are you yourself going to offer Nga as a sacrifice, then?"

"For the moment, just my mind. Nga sees all and knows who gave you all this advice. When I raise a family and acquire wealth like all of you, then we'll see."

"What sacrifice would Num want, then?" the chief asked.

"Num?" The man smiled. "Does he really exist?"

They wanted to tear the man apart, but they changed their minds and simply beat him up and left him in some waste ground.

The man assumed that what had saved his life, was his remark that Nga sees it when someone gives people good advice. He was not wrong in this.

His legs and ribs broken, he might have died of hunger, or wild animals and mosquitoes might have got to him, but within several days he was found by a young woman, the wife of that same warrior. She brought him a little food, a bow, arrows, and an ax, and moreover a potion made of bear bile to dress the man's wounds. The woman said that she had left her husband for him because she had never seen a braver warrior, as unassuming as the man was physically.

They managed to survive together: they dug a shelter in the earth, covered it with trees, birch bark, and the hides of elk which that man hunted in late autumn. They waited out the great cold, and in late spring the woman bore a child – a daughter – and gave it to her husband, so that he could consecrate it to the god of the underworld. Then she bore a new child every year, and her sons – and they were only sons – proved impervious to pain and cold.

That man and his wife were the ancestors of the Nga people.

Their progeny spread throughout the taiga and then beyond, all the way to the sea. They fragmented into small clans and families, each of which maintained the common rite: each year they would offer a firstborn to their patron god, and whoever did not have such would offer they most precious thing they had. People remembered the key tenet: there is nothing worse than insulting the gods with meager sacrifices.

Other Yurak clans, and even other peoples, knew what the Nga people held to. They tried to win wars against them, but victory was always on the side of the Nga people. Then, after many generations had passed, and no one was sure whether the descendants of those two brave ancestors still followed that custom, fear of that great family persisted through rumors. Fear painted vivid pictures in people's minds, though those who dealt with the Nga people found them no different on the outside than any other inhabitants of the taiga – Yabto, for example, had spent several pleasant days in the company of Kheno, the herder at the latter's encampment.

***

Kheno was the head of a sizeable family that might even be called a clan of its own, but the old man said that in any event, his roots went back to that same brave male and female ancestor.

A large host of sons lived, hunted, and herded with him, and each had his own wife and child. A special branch of the family were the old man's three younger brothers, who had recognized Kheno's great strength and intelligence and remained with him in a single encampment. Those brothers had their own families and grown sons, who in turn had their own wives, and grown daughters who had married husbands of their own.

Kheno could raise up a force of forty armored warriors, but he tried to avoid unnecessary conflict. He lived in peace with his kinsmen and was generous with gifts. He was revered as the greatest patriarch among all the Nga clans and renowned as all-powerful, though in fact the old man was so weak that he could hardly walk.

Nevertheless, through one of Kheno's cousins disaster came upon his big family. That cousin, who would eventually be dubbed Tusyada, "Lacking Fire", after all that happened, was a dissolute man. His original name was something else that is now forgotten and cursed.

That man, of powerful build and feeble mind, considered himself equal to Kheno, or at least close. For a time he had been the senior shepherd and constantly lost reindeer, and while this hardly mattered, considering Kheno's immense wealth, one day he lost almost a third of a herd to the wolves. The wolves proved smarter than the shepherds: they performed an intricate ambush and separated some hundred reindeer from the herd, and while some wolves attacked the remaining herd and thereby distracted the men, the others drove their prey to a cliff over a lake – the reindeer fell from the great height onto the rocks along the water's edge.

The shepherds thought it best to move their herd away and not seek revenge on the wolves. The senior shepherd then justified himself to Kheno by loudly cursing the people under him as stupid and cowardly, and saying that he had instructed them well but then they had botched everything. Kheno listened to his brother patiently, and then said that such disaster could happen to anyone, plus wolves are smarter than humans, so it was no wonder. The next day, however, the old man told the shepherds to take their orders from one of his brothers-in-law instead.

The man whom Kheno demoted responded to this insult by beating his wife. Then he tried to give the chief all kinds of advice, for example, damming the river in several places so they would always have fish; going to war against the Sitts (a race of smiths who dwelt underground and were only the size of a dog) and compelling them to forge weapons only for the Nga people; separating the herds into white, black, and spotted reindeer so that the shepherds' eyes wouldn't tire, and so forth.

Kheno would listen to his cousin's advice without ever taking it seriously, and he never chastised the man for his foolishness. He was too appreciative of his own blood to chastise close relatives as he might everyone else – to the latter he was very severe. But the old man's kindness eventually brought disaster.

Ultimately the cousin realized that Kheno had no need for his dazzling mind. The old man had come to hate his kinsman's very voice and would not forbid others from mocking his cousin. The cousin felt truly despondent, he would spend whole days in bed in his chum without speaking to anyone. But then he suddenly realized that there was no need to despair, for he had two grown sons for whom he fulfilled the same role as Kheno to everyone else. He then went hunting with them, caught birds on the lakes, fished with nets, and eagerly taught them everything that they, in fact, already knew, having learned it from other men. The sons quietly endured this humiliation, but their father boasted of the catch to the members of his household, "Look how well I feed you. I feed you so well." The man's wife secretly wept. Yet the man continued to boast, and one day, those same words he had spoken to his family he said to the fire:

"Look how well I feed you. I feed you so well," he muttered as he tossed some twigs into the hearth.

At once Mother Fire appeared from the flames and hissed, "You fool. It is I who feed you."

If the man had simply fallen face first to the ground, the spirit might have forgotten the insult, but instead he began to argue with her. "No, I feed you. What are you without me?"

Mother Fire froze, stared at the fool and, without bothering to argue she vanished. The man threw some dry logs on. The fire flared up almost to the very smoke-hole of the chum, and then it burned nicely all night long.

The next morning, Kheno's cousin began to lay a new fire, but the wood would not catch. He assumed that the wood was still slightly wet, so he brought some dry pine twigs, but there was still no fire. Then the man decided that his flint must be bad, so he rushed to his neighbor to get another one. The very moment he stepped into the neighboring chum, however, the fire there went out. His neighbors set about making a new fire, but it refused to burn. The man then went to other chums, but wherever he appeared, the fire would go out.

People began to get scared. "What have you done," they cried to Kheno's brother, "to make fire hate you? It doesn't want to burn whenever you're around."

In reply, the man could only open and close his mouth like a fish; he was clearly afraid to tell people that, the night before, he had argued with Mother Fire.

People ran after him through the big encampment in order to give him a beating, and they probably would have done so, but the man threw himself into Kheno's chum to seek protection.

The old man was seated by the fire.

"He has brought disaster," people shouted.

Kheno was about to ask them why they were so angry, but he was interrupted by Mother Fire, who appeared from the flames at his feet and spoke loudly enough for everyone to hear:

"So, do you finally understand who feeds whom? Now all your fires will go out."

After the spirit said this, it stretched like a slender snake up into the sky and vanished. The fireplace at the old man's feet immediately began to hiss as if water had been poured on it.

The old man realized everything that had happened. "This is not like those reindeer you fed to the wolves," he slowly said, his eyes fixed on his hopeless relative. "This is not like those reindeer, cousin…"

People rushed upon the man, longing to tear him apart. Kheno forbid them from doing so. "If we kill him, how will we find out how to propitiate Mother Fire?"

The man fell to his knees and cried, "Kill me! It's all my fault!"

"Shut up," the old man interrupted him. "Is the life of a guilty man worth all that much, especially one as stupid as you? Mother Fire is a great spirit, and to obtain her forgiveness, we need something more than a man's life."

Kheno remembered the legacy of his ancestors: do not insult the spirits with false sacrifices.

They sent for a shaman and told him everything that had happened. The shaman performed his ritual in the dark chum, he roamed through the worlds in search of the offended Mother Fire, to learn how they might atone for the sin that had impacted the whole family. Towards morning he returned with an answer.

"What have you done, you evil man?" croaked the shaman, exhausted after his journey. "To satisfy the Mother, you must sacrifice your son and feed his blood to the fire. Then the spirit will be satisfied."

The man was ready to do so. "Which son? I have two."

"The elder son," the shaman replied, then he dropped his drum and collapsed, overcome with sleep.

The elder son bore the name Serkhasawa, "White Head". He was in his twentieth spring. Serkhasawa was short but stocky, quick and taciturn, unlike his father who only shut his mouth when he slept. Kheno had been thinking about finding a suitable wife for him.

Serkhasawa was aware of the crime that his father had committed. He sat by the entrance to his chum and awaited his fate.

"Get up," people told White Head. "If you don't come willingly, we'll tie you up."

When the hopeless cousin heard this, he fell to the grass and burst into tears. Serkhasawa got up, took his father's limp arm and threw it around his shoulder, and then carried the hopeless man to the hearth in the middle of the camp, where Kheno's chum stood. When he reached that spot, he dropped his sobbing father and began to smack him.

"Get up," he said quietly. "Come on, get up, don't flood my path with your tears."

He helped his father up and waited for a kinsman to arrange the tinder and get the first, thin smoke. He then took his parka off and knelt by the hearth. The hopeless man stood behind his son, his face was red and wet and a long moaning sound came from his mouth.

"Come on!" cried one of the people there, and so angrily that the man stopped moaning. He then went up to Serkhasawa and lay a hand on his shoulder. "Forgive me, son..."

"Do you have a knife?" Serkhasawa asked.

Kheno did not. He took his own knife from his belt and handed it to his cousin. The latter muttered something through his teeth, cringed, and slashed with the blade.

Blood gushed over the smoldering wood. Instantly a hungry flame erupted and consumed what had been fed in – the old man threw dry wood into the fireplace, twigs from deciduous trees, and the fire crackled as if relishing the sacrifice. When the people recovered from their astonishment, someone said that Serkhasawa should be seen off to the lower world with honors, like a great leader. They had already forgotten about the hopeless man and only remembered when Kheno addressed them:

"Forget the name he bore before. From now on his name shall be Tusyada, and nothing else." He turned to the man, "Go and live your life however you can."

Everyone went off to see to their own tasks. The summer sun was at its height.

Tusyada got to his chum, fell onto the furs, and closed his eyes. He wanted to fall into oblivion, but it would not come. He felt as if he should summon death to him, and he pondered how he might do that, but as he turned these thoughts over in his mind, he fell asleep, like any tired person falls asleep after making a great effort.

Tusyada's wife was not around – Kheno's cousin had forgotten all about her. She was a small, spry woman with a lovely face that seemed carved out of ivory. Her name was Mayana, "Misery", and she considered it an apt one, for her coming into the world had been difficult – her mother nearly died in childbirth – and she lived with no especial hope of happiness.

Mayana went into the forest to pray for her son in the lower world – in accordance with custom, others gathered, too. Mayana did not think about what would come tomorrow. She never thought about that...

***

The next day, all fires in the entire encampment were out.

People rubbed the tinder until it took the skin on their palms off, they rained tears on their flints, but they could not produce even the slightest smoke.

The shaman was called in.

"Perform the rite," they told him. "Ask Mother Fire what was wrong with the sacrifice."

The shaman did not even bother to take up his drum, he simply replied, "The Mother wanted Tusyada's son. So, Serkhasawa must not have been his son. We deceived the Mother."

Tusyada shuddered. "How could I have deceived the spirit if I did what you told me? I killed my own son with my own two hands and fed his blood to the fire."

"Your blood did not flow in him, otherwise the spirit would have accepted the sacrifice."

"How could he not be my son?" Tusyada cried. "My wife bore him, I saw it myself."

But the people were so angry that they did not believe the man who had now been forever named "Without Fire". They went to find Mayana and detained her as if she were a thief.

"Tell us who the father of your firstborn was."

Mayana wept, she was so overcome by fear that she could not say anything. The people around her began to reach for their spears.

"He's my son, my son!" Tusyada's wife cried.

Kheno drew her to himself and said quietly, almost affectionately, "No need to cry, Mayana. Here's a string. Go into your chum, still until the evening comes, and tie a knot for every time you have lain with a man besides your husband. Then give it to me."

Mayana went into her chum and cried all day, but in the evening she emerged and gave Kheno the string. There was only a single knot on it.

Thus the deception was revealed. The people rushed to Tusyada's chum to bring out the boy considered his younger son, but the chum was empty. Kheno ordered them to quickly search the forest, but they returned empty-handed.

That boy was called Nokho, "Arctic Fox".

Nokho

He was eighteen years old then.

When Serkhasawa's blood was poured out, he ran into the forest so that no one could see the shame and grief he felt. When he returned the next morning, he discovered that the disaster his hopeless father had brought continued. Nokho went into his chum, grabbed his weapons, and ran away into the forest. When Mayana showed old Kheno the string with the single knot on it, her younger son was already far away in the taiga.

He anticipated that they would run after him, so he hid in a cave along a forested hill – only he and his brother Serkhasawa had known of this shelter. In childhood they would come here and play games quite unlike the games of other children. Then, when the brothers were at an age to hunt on their own, they would take shelter here from blizzards and thunderstorms.

Nokho waited out the initial danger there. He remained vigilant, he knew that his family might chase him, just like wolves chase an elk until their quarry's strength is depleted and it allows itself to be killed. Mother Fire's curse lay upon every one of Kheno's people, their hearths would be dead, and so would the hearths of any other people whom they came in contact with. If word spread of the curse, they would become for all other clans and tribes of the taiga the same as Nokho, mere fat flicked off the scraper.

Perhaps it was by the grace of some supernatural force that the disaster had fallen upon them in early summer, when the sun could cook their food just as well as their fires could. But the warm season was short, and if Nokho's family could not find him and sprinkle the hearth with his blood, they would all perish with the coming of the cold. The old man wanted to solve this quickly, and he made every effort to ensure that news of the curse did not travel further than his own family. Nokho knew that he could survive if he could only hold on until winter, when the great cold would show no mercy to his kin and thereby save him from his life as a fugitive.

Tusyada's son slept with one eye open and never spent more than half a day in any one place. He regularly kept watch, always from a different place, and several times he caught a glimpse of armed men. He wandered far from his native territory, then back almost to the encampment, in order to leave confusing tracks for his kinsmen. The greatest danger might have been the dogs, and not the people, but obviously some protecting spirit prevented the wind from taking up Nokho's scent and bringing it to the dogs' keen noses.

The taiga was generous to a fugitive, it sent him small but sure game. Nokho first caught forest birds and then, after a month of wandering, he grew bolder and laid traps and caught fish. Incredibly, Mother Fire's curse did not affect Tusyada's younger son; the fire at his feet always burned amply.

Thus he wandered until the autumn, until the very day when he came to a riverbank where he had once laid a trap, and there saw a naked person tied to a tree and two clothed individuals who were shouting and waving their arms.

Nokho ducked down and hurried into a clump of willows from which he could see the riverbank perfectly. He drew from his quiver three arrows and set them before him, so that no more time would pass between each shot than the cracking of a twig.

Nokho shot twice; the third arrow, which he had prepared in case he missed, proved unnecessary...

***

When Nokho cut the rope around the naked youth (something he later regretted – the rope could have come in handy), the latter collapsed to the ground as if all his bones had just been removed. Dark streams of dried blood ran along his swollen body, from the top of his head to the tips of his toes, as if he had been doused with water from a boiling pot. His chest, belly, and legs were crisscrossed with dark-blue indentations from the rope. Yet there was still life in his eyes – they told Nokho that this young man was worth trying to save. And these eyes did not deceive Nokho, for the runt found within him strength to sit up.

That is how I met Nokho.

My summer parka, trousers, and boots were laying in the grass nearby and he brought them to me.

"Get dressed," he told me. "Can you manage?"

I reached for the clothing, but I was unable to stand up.

"A third man left, but he'll be back soon," I told my rescuer.

"Let him," Nokho said calmly. The easy victory had quenched in him any awareness of danger.

"He'll squash you like a bug. He's their father Yabto. I can't get dressed. You go on, get out of here."

When Nokho heard the stout man's name, he froze for an instant, as if he were rummaging in his memory for something.

"Yabto, that scavenger?" he asked and, without waiting for any reply, he ran to the riverbank where Yabtonga and Yawire lay.

Nokho dragged the bodies into the middle of the stream, where the water was up to his waist, and let them drift with the current. He then told me to lie still while he put the trousers and boots on me. The parka he told me to put on by myself, while he was gathering the weapons that the stout man's sons had left behind.

"Why did you call Yabto a scavenger?" I asked.

"That's what people call him," Nokho replied automatically and without interrupting his efforts.

He put the two bows and a quiver on me, then lifted me onto his back and ran into the forest. Nokho was unusually strong for his age, while I was tiny for mine, and so he could run on without stopping.

***

Nokho brought his unexpected find into his cave.

He knew no spells, and he had no potions, but he rubbed my body with cooled ashes. He did this with total confidence, and it worked: the heat that came over my body reduced the raging.

Thus several days passed. Nokho would bring his catch and we ate in the evenings and recounted our respective lives.

"Why did you save me?"

"I was bored here alone. Now there's two of us."

"Three."

"Do you see any third person here?"

"I mean Lar, my brother. We shared the same womb. I have to free him, he's being kept a slave by the old man of your encampment."

"Lar," Nokho muttered. He felt silent as he tried to remember. "The tall, thin boy that Yabto brought?"

"Yeah."

"He's no slave."

I started. "Yabto said that he had sold him for a knife of pale iron and a horned bow…"

"Kheno doesn't keep any slaves."

"So Yabto lied to me. What for?"

"For the same reason he tied you to that tree. He wanted to grind you down. Kheno gave him the bow and knife as a gift. The old man always showers gifts on his guests, especially those whom he likes."

His words were like a gust of warm wind. "So Lar's alive?" I said. "I heard from another man, one of your people, that Lar was doing well, eating fat, and soon the old man would give him a wife. Is that true? Tell me. If I don't find Lar, it's like I'm only half a person."

Nokho got up and went to the distant corner of the cave, where there were some dry branches that he had stockpiled long ago, back when Serkhasawa was still alive. He set the pile down next to the fire and began breaking the twigs and feeding them in. He said nothing as he did so.

Finally, he spoke up: "It's true. You want to see him?"

"Is he nearby?"

"Quite. If you feel strong enough, then let's go."

"Right now, at night?"

"For us it's the best time."

Nokho led the way, he found it perfectly through the autumn darkness, while I could barely keep up. I was gasping for breath, but Nokho, who had been tranquil and even cheery a short time before, rushed on like he was tracking a foe. Things had turned brighter for me, but now from this endless running a shadow fell over my soul, which I assumed was fatigue.

***

We arrived in a birch forest. "We're here," Nokho said. He placed his weapons on the ground and removed from his belt a suede bag with his flint inside.

"I thought you were leading me to your encampment. Where are we?"

Nokho did not reply. He took from his quiver something that looked like a large stick – it was a torch made from wood that had been boiled and tightly twisted together – handed it to me, and then took his flint. The pitch with which the wood had been soaked caught fire at the very first spark, and I soon saw planks of wood in front of me.

It was the cemetery of Kheno's large family. The wooden biers creaked and swung in the wind that blew above our heads. In those days, it was the custom to bury everyone in the same way that today only shamans are buried: in trees, so that the soul, which, for some reason, remained in the body, would not touch the earth and reach the underworld earlier than the spirits decided its fate. If that was not done, then a departed soul could become an evil spirit and begin to get revenge on those who treated it so disrespectfully.

"These," Nokho illuminated some planks in the middle of the grove with his touch, "were placed here long ago. Old people indeed. And here is the old man's wife. Over there is one more wife. They died as soon as they bore children. But that was long ago. Here, come with me."

We reached the end of the grove. Nokho took the torch for me in order to search for something in the grass, and finally he lifted a long ladder made out of two thin pieces of unhewn wood.

Nokho set the ladder against one of the trunks, which had around it a rope that held one such bier, and then he handed the torch back to me. "Go up and take a look."

***

I slowly climbed up as if I were afraid to fall. The pitch-covered wood in my hands hissed and burned even brighter, and the harsh white light revealed everything before me: an old winter parka, torn reindeer-skin boots, long hair of ashen color, and a gray mask in which I recognized my own features.

It was Lar. He had ended up here, among the birch trunks, not long before, at a time when it was warm even at night and people were switching from their winter clothes. He was untouched by insects or the small creatures that lived in the trees. The sun had dried his face but left thereon the traces of his last suffering: tense lips, stripes on his forehead, and empty eyes that had sprung open after he had died.

Lar resembled a man totally unable to fall asleep.

Grief was slow to come over me – I had only the strange feeling that, when I descended from the ladder, I was setting foot onto a totally different earth.

"The old man really did want to get him a wife," Nokho said. "He found him a bride, only it wasn't his daughter. He doesn't have any. It was the daughter of his eldest nephew. He has a whole lot of nephews… The girl's brothers said, 'They say you're a big fighter. Come on, show us how strong you are,' and he readily agreed. He liked a fight, though he was not so strong himself. The fight was three against one. They threw him to the ground so hard that he died. They said that they didn't mean to kill him, it just turned out like that. They said your brother was weak and came at them, and that's how he died. Now he's eating fat among the smoke in the sky. They'll find him a wife up there, too."

I sat down on the grass and repeated after him, unable to understand what he had said: "Among the smoke in the sky?"

"Your brother's bier was light," Nokho said. "As light as down feathers. He must have had little sin in him. That's what people say. An evil man is heavy, sometimes too heavy for six men to lift, and the tree won't bear the weight. Such a man did a lot of bad things, and so he had a lot of sin upon him. He killed a kinsman, or disrespected fire, or he stopped tracking an animal after he wounded it, and just abandoned it to die in the taiga. The spirits turn away from such a man and no longer serve him. The spirits drag him down towards the underworld, that's why the bier feels so heavy. But your brother obviously never sinned. That's why it will be easy for you to get revenge, too."

Thus the word "revenge" was uttered for the first time, but at that moment it simply slipped past my ears. My heart still wasn't ready to hear it.

Mourning

In the cave my soul spoke words that my mouth would never utter.

My brother's body flew up into the black sky like an arrow, my slain brother rushed towards the nighttime stars – but he did not make it, he fell back into the branches, on his bier... My heart groaned. I cursed the Yuraks, I cursed every member of the human race for lacking any goodness or compassion among them, only malice twice over.

The taiga is vast and many are the people in it. The smoke of innumerable chums rises up into the sky, there are immense and wealthy encampments, well-trodden paths and nomads. The bird awaits its arrow, the fish its net, so that the basket of catch would seethe like pots over the hearth; the wild beast seeks its fate among the trees, kindly *kaygus* help men so that their lineage shall not die out, but my brother Lar, my brother, got no encampment, no chum, no fortune, no affection, not even kind words...

What was his strength for? His prowess? Why was he endowed with that youthful heart and strong legs, his eyes that could spot a creature far off, powerful arms and a keen sense of smell, if there was no place for him in the taiga? No chum, hearth, reindeer, harnessed sleighs, or kindhearted wife was allotted to him – the only things that Lar, my brother, got were anger, reproach, and violent death. He was found among moss in the forest, where he had been hidden to save his life. He was adopted with no memory of his own tribe, no awareness of his own blood – and thus he ended up on the branches of others.

I was left all alone, the only one left in the whole taiga, alone under the sky, alone between worlds, alone among men – I had no chum, no hearth, no tribe. Let my arms grow stronger by waging war, by extracting revenge; let any feeling of pity fly from my mouth like the last smoke from an extinguished fire flies out through the hole atop a chum. Let the names of my enemies erupt from my mouth like flocks of jays, the names of those who took my brother's life and took from me my brother: the names of those who took our tribe from us, robbed us of our blood and extinguished our blood memory like a fire in the hearth. Let war be waged on those who had ravaged my memory, let vengeance be extracted.

I did not weep. The words that my mouth spoke existed in some other realm where there were no longer tears, nor any grief or joy or laughter. My soul was reduced to an abode that had long been abandoned and even any trace of former inhabitation was gone. I rocked back and forth like one insane and I spoke dully, with my eyes closed. Then I fell silent.

***

A long time passed before Nokho broke the silence. "Do you want revenge?"

I did not reply. I felt that my mind was gradually returning to reason.

"How are you going to get revenge?" he went on, his eyes fixed on mine. "Kheno's family is a whole clan of its own. Just the young men alone amount to forty individuals. You would be finished before you even had time to raise your spear."

"As long as I'm not the only one who goes up in smoke."

"You asked me why I rescued you…"

"You told me."

"No. That wasn't really an answer. Listen to what I'm going to tell you. A hunter goes into the forest and tells his household that he'll return after seven days and nights. They tell him, 'Go and come back,' and they start to wait. But the hunter does not return after seven days and nights, not even after ten. One month passes, then another, and still no sign of him. Snow comes creeping down from the mountains, but he is still gone. And then his family asks a shaman to search for his soul, but the shaman can't find him among either the living or the dead. 'He must have been separated from the world of men, he disappeared, fell into some hole leading to the underworld... The taiga or some creature got him. He went into the lower world just as he was, with no one to pray for him, no last rites, and now he suffers there. Such was his fate. Don't expect him back.' The hunter's family wept and then forgot him. But the hunter was alive. He was a captive, enslaved by another people, but he escaped and returned home. But when the women saw him, they screamed and hid in their chums, the children threw stones at him, and the men said, 'You're a spirit. Why have you come back to the world of the living? Go away.' The hunter shouts, 'What is with you people? I'm your kinsman!' 'Our kinsman promised to return after seven days and nights, but he didn't. The taiga took our kinsman, and you are a spirit with his face.' The man steps closer to them. 'No,' he cries, 'I'm a living person! Come here, feel my arms, my face, they are still warm.' But the men don't want to hear it, they reach for their bows and shoot off some arrows. He runs to save his life and again winds up in the taiga. Now any person who meets the hunter can kill him and be praised for it, because that person would be saving the family from the wily spirit that was fooling the family; he had warm arms only to embrace another person and then grab ahold of that person's neck... The hunter thus lived a vagabond life. He really did have warm arms. Like everyone else he wanted to eat, he felt the cold, he suffered pain, but he was no longer a human being. He was alive and dead at the same time, he existed and yet he did not. His name was forgotten, like fat flung off the scraper. An animal without its hide, that is what a man bereft of a name and a clan is like. He was dead to his own people, but to strangers he could only be a slave. Where did he belong? Where could he go? Who would take him in?"

"I don't know," I said. "Why are you telling me all this?"

"Because this happened to us, my own family. I was little when I heard the story, but I remember it well. And now I see that I have become that hunter. And you, too. So listen. The hunter needed to find someone in the same position he was. I found you. Don't go looking for your own people, because now I am your people, and you are mine. Your brother is dead, now I'm your brother. We will manage to survive, we'll raid camps, get ourselves wives, reindeer, and dogs, and we won't need any clan or tribe, because we will make a tribe for ourselves. Trust me, brother, that is how it's going to be, you hear me? As long as we can make it to the middle of the winter, when the great cold comes and starts to kill Kheno's people."

I hesitated to reply, but then said, looking my rescuer right in the eye, "You are indeed my brother. But Lar was my brother, too, and they killed him. How can I let the cold have revenge for him? Is he really happy where he is now?"

"You aren't giving up your revenge," Nokho replied calmly. "You are simply sharing it. Though you were a slave, you probably don't know what it is like to live without fire at a time when even the birds freeze solid and drop from the sky. Don't we need an ally to aid us? Wait a moment..."

Nokho got up, took an arrow from his quiver, and began to sharpen the iron tip on a stone. When he judged that this was done, he slashed the iron across his palm. The drops of his blood fell into the fire and produced tiny sparks.

"Now you do the same," he said and handed me the arrow.

In short order both of us had a bloody palm.

"Give me your hand..."

We shook hands for a long time. The blood flowed from our wounds, mixed, hardened, and finally joined our hands together like fish glue bonds the parts of a bow.

Nokho smiled. "Now your revenge is my revenge, too. Just listen to me. I'm your older brother, and I know how things should be done…"

We embraced and I said, "Lar was my older brother, too, though we were born on the same day. He was bigger than me. You're bigger than me, too. Only, I wanted to ask you…"

"Go ahead, ask."

"Two people is not much of an army."

Nokho beamed when he saw that I had finally got my wits about me again, and shared the same thoughts which he had mused over since the day we ran from Yabto's encampment. "You don't think we can beat them?" he asked.

"I don't know how. If you know, then say it. Kheno has forty warriors, you said so yourself."

Nokho leapt away from me. "You see that fire?" he whispered angrily. "Take a closer look, see how bright it's burning. Remember that the curse didn't fall on me. Only on them! My brain-dead father, my whore mother, Kheno, his sons, brothers, cousins, their brides – all are cursed. The shaman is either a fool, a swindler, or a traitor. He claimed that Mother Fire wanted my blood specifically, and now they are searching under every stone for me, like a thief that stole their most beautiful and wealthy maiden, but they won't find me. They don't realize that they are all cursed, from the old man down to any wet newborn baby, and my blood won't help, just like Serkhasawa's blood didn't help. That's how Mother Fire wants it to be, and why is not my concern. If you hadn't come alone, I would spend every day coming a bit closer to the encampment and watching from my hiding place how they started gnawing on each other from the cold, then turned into sluggish worms, and finally into solid wood. I would watch and it would bring joy to two hearts, mine and Serkhasawa's. He despised them and gave them his life like one flings a bone with a bit of meat on it to a worthless relative. Kheno is a wolverine, he is wasting time in this stupid, shameful panic instead of accepting fate like my brother did. If you don't believe me, then tell me, who is going to help a cursed man? Who will save him? Can a man who has been cursed ever win?"

Some time went by as I gathered my thoughts, but then I spoke in a fast torrent. "I lived with Yabto and always thought that I was born in his encampment. That Uma was my mother and Lar's. That Nara was my sister, Yabtonga and Yawire my brothers. First I lived as their son, then their slave. I wanted to leave when they took Lar away. I made arrows, with bone tips. A lot of time went by, a long time. I thought that I had ended up in that position for good, that I would be doing the women's work until I died. That I could escape is something that came to me suddenly, in a single day, a single instant, and everything, from the first move I made to the last, worked. Even fear dared not come over me. I've heard that behind every single person's back is a demon that guides him or her from birth. It comes up out of the earth, from the same hole that your mother buries your umbilical cord in. I was small and shy, and I believed that, I believed that I wasn't capable of running away or using weapons. It was the demon that did it, it was! It put the people in the encampment and the dogs to sleep, it breathed determination into my heart, gave me the boat and good weather..."

I stopped to compose myself, then went on, "And then it delivered me up to Yabto and the biting insects. Then you came. Tell me, was all this still that demon? If so, where is it bringing me this time? Tell me, if you know, what does it want from me?"

Nokho suddenly laughed, "From you? Nothing." Then he stopped laughing and added, "Maybe it wants to see what sort of man you will become on your own?"

The tracks

The autumn turned into winter, rivers' courses began to narrow, clear ice covered the backwaters, and Kheno realized that his life and that of his family were dripping away like water from a poorly made birch-bark container.

The hearths in the big encampment had lain inert for a long time now, but the people there did not dare reach for a flint, for fear of coming across as beggars and thereby offending Mother Fire. They still hoped that they would manage to undo the curse. Their stores of meat jerky were still ample, they ate raw reindeer meat and liver, but without cooked food their stomachs ached, mothers stopped producing milk, and men lost their strength.

Kheno made a desperate attempt to save them.

The people of that family knew their territory like the back of their hand, and their failure to hunt Nokho down was thought to be related to the same curse. In order to ensure that the offended deity knew how sincere they were in their contrition, the people responsible for the whole mess were sacrificed: Tusyada and Mayana. On the day of the first snowfall they were brought into the clan's sanctuary and impaled on the trunks of two young pines cleared of their branches. The trunks were wide enough to prolong the agony and, if a person were strong, death would come from that endless pain and not from the tree piercing their body itself.

The man and his wife cried, then fell silent and their faces became blank.

The old man sent a few young people into the sanctuary on some minor errand, so that they could see once more the fate that the witless man and his unfaithful wife had suffered.

After the sacrifice, no one hurried to find out whether Mother Fire's wrath had been assuaged. Kheno forbade anyone from picking up a flint. He had something else in mind.

The approaching winter augured death, but its approach was slow, and that gave people hope. Other people represented a much greater danger. The Mother's curse was like a plague, where even an accidental meeting of two men out in the taiga could lead to the deaths of many. Any member of Kheno's family that came near to the hearth of others could put their fire out for ever. The old man prayed to every god and spirit he knew to prevent the curse from impacting other people. But the old man's reason told him only one thing: only the people who dwelt in the innumerable chums of the great Nga clan were capable of helping his family escape the terrible trap into which one silly man's stupidity had driven them.

One evening the old man was sitting in his chum, wrapped in furs and turning various thoughts over in his mind. They were heavy thoughts, like huge boulders, and dangerous as a swamp. The old man called on his memory and his knowledge of human beings in order to choose from a variety of options, each of which might either save them or produce an even greater disaster.

The next morning, he learned that a traitor lurked within his family: someone had sneaked into the sanctuary and stabbed the still-living Mayana and Tusyada in the heart.

"An evil fool is worse than a good one, at least from him you know what to expect," he said when he heard the news.

Under any other circumstances, Kheno would have tracked down whoever dared commit such audacity. But this time, he saw in this betrayal a sign that there was no time left for deliberation, for there was not even the slightest hope that Mother Fire's anger would abate.

Kheno allowed himself to hesitate no longer and he made his choice. He called his best men, his sons and brothers, and said to them:

"Tusyada's son is a glorious young man. That's why we haven't been able to catch him so far. I don't believe that he is dead, that some animal got him, or that he fell into a pit or met some stronger opponent – he is too intelligent and crafty for that. If we have to scour the whole taiga to find him, turn it over like we would a blanket, then that is what we must do. But we can't search the whole taiga all by ourselves. Our wider relatives would have to help us. Today each of you will take your finest reindeer and gifts, and go to the senior in each family and ask them to help. Now listen up, this is what you are going to say to them. You'll say that in our family, in spite of the zealous veneration we show to the spirits of the forest, waters, and herds, as well as the gods and our lord Nga, something terrible happened. Through a mistake made long ago, a man came into our family, the son of poor parents, and he quarreled with Mother Fire and got cursed for it. He extinguishes any flame that he comes near. He ran away in order to escape just punishment, and he's hiding out in the taiga. He is the carrier of a disease that can wipe out each and every one of us. He must be tracked down, no matter what it takes. The whole clan has to scour the taiga like a fine-toothed comb goes through thick hair to pick out a dangerous insect. That is what you'll say. You see, you don't have to lie at all. Save your cunning for something else. But I implore you, whatever happens, do not get close to those people's hearths."

"Where are we supposed to speak with their elders, then?" asked one of the old man's brothers. "In the forest on a fallen log?"

"That is where you will need your cunning. You can get close to the encampment and watch for one of the men to come along, then have him summon the elders. You can send a loud arrow flying, and they will come to you. Then tell them you are messengers from Kheno's family – my name would save any one of you. Most importantly, tell them that your news is so important than only the elders can hear it. Show them your gifts, that'll speed things up. And if they insistently invite you in, tell them this: as a sign of how truly sorry they are, Kheno's whole family, from him all the way down to the children, have forbidden themselves to eat cooked food and warm themselves by the hearth until that godless Nokho is found."

The old man finished his speech and waited to hear what the best men of his family would say. But the men were silent. Finally, one of the old man's younger brothers, whose name was Lidyang, which meant "Beaver", spoke.

"As long as I live, your wisdom will never cease to amaze me."

"What do you want to say? Say it."

"One person walking through the taiga and putting out fires is no more than a tiny animal, a squirrel, ant, or worm for the innumerable Nga people. Are you sure that our glorious relatives will immediately reach for their weapons and set off to turn the whole taiga inside out, in order to help you?"

"If you have something in mind better than the words you just said, then out with it." A hint of a smile appeared over the old man's dry lips, but then suddenly, with the lightning-fast motion of a serpent, he grabbed his brother by the latter's thin beard. "When you go where I tell you and say the words that I order you to say, you had better be thinking about how you are going to die. Imagine our wives and children turning into stiff wood covered in hoarfrost. Then maybe the spirit behind your shoulders will suggest the necessary words and get some sense into your head."

Kheno released his grip. Lidyang straightened up like a branch that someone had been holding back. The other men said nothing.

"All of you ought to be thinking of that. We have almost no time left before the cold comes." The patriarch rose, and the others did so after him. They headed for the reindeer paddock. Kheno provided each of his emissaries with a caravan loaded with gifts, and he indicated the name of the respective authorities and the river or lake where their encampment could be found.

***

The emissaries returned one by one, after three or four days and nights had passed. They arrived back with empty sledges, which meant that their gifts had been accepted. Kheno's best men all reported the same thing: bonds of kinship obliged the Nga people to help such a respected man as Kheno in a time of need. They would scour the taiga and find the scoundrel who had offended Mother Fire.

"They also asked us to relay that Kheno shouldn't wear himself and his family down with such a severe penance," said the last of the emissaries to arrive. "Everyone knows how zealous you are in showing reverence to the spirits. So, eat, drink, and don't be hard on yourself."

The old man listened to this, and without saying a word, he hobbled off to his chum. No one dared approach him. He sat on the furs, stared at the stones of his hearth that were now shining with damp, and thought of how grief was a leveler, it made the minds of an old man and a child equal. In the words of his last emissary, the true price of his overhasty plan was revealed. Lidyang was right: his distant relatives would always ensure that a few men in their encampments kept guard over the hearths and not let any outsiders near, especially a young man with long hair and green eyes who would ultimately perish from the cold himself, having been cursed by the Mother. And they would talk to one another about how hardly anyone could compare to old man Kheno in his piety…

Kheno heard anxious voices: people were waiting for his answer. The old man realized that if he continued to give his legs a rest and remained in the chum for the slightest bit longer, it would be a mistake worse than the one he had already made. What he had now realized would become clear to everyone else. As long as death had not yet crossed the threshold, his people could not be left without faith that they would be saved.

Faith was their only ally, it would stand in for the complacent hearts of their distant relatives.

Kheno rose and stepped out of his chum. A dozen faces – old and young alike – were staring at him with searching eyes.

"What are we going to do, father?" came a voice from among them.

Their father spoke. "As you know, I sent to the most respected families of our vast clan for help. All of them agreed as one to help get us out of this trouble. They have already equipped their warriors, and those warriors have set out across the taiga – they will shake the taiga like a reindeer hide to find that vile insect that is somewhere between the strands of fur and trembling for his life. He won't get the satisfaction of watching us perish. Maybe, as I stand here talking to you, he is already on some sledge, tied up and squirming like a snake with its head cut off. If that hasn't happened yet, it will soon. But our kinsmen asked to relay that we shouldn't be sitting back and watching. The sky has sent us a savior: the first snow. It's shallow, soft, and it will reveal the tracks of any man or animal. Nokho has been walking over leaves and stones, he has been careful, and that's why he is still alive. Now the only choice he has left is to hide away in some fox den and die of hunger, because the snow will show every step he makes, and he won't have anywhere to go when all those good people rise against him. So, listen up, my children. Gather your strength, equip yourselves, and go. Breathe in the air and look carefully at the ground! It will show us how we can be saved. Go!"

The old man ended his speech and then relished the reverent silence that it provoked. Then the first shout came, followed by the shouts of everyone else: the tribe was shouting with all their might, as if a mighty effort had only just begun.

The men went to their respective chums, grabbed their weapons, and returned to the middle of the encampment.

***

They were led by a tall, stern man with a face like unhewn wood. This was Khungal, whose name meant "Forepaw", one of Kheno's older nephews. The old man had often entrusted him with matters of war and big hunting after he himself was no longer so sprightly, and his younger brothers had got old and lost their strength.

They went out along the established path that they usually used for their migrations, and when half a day later they reached Fish Lake, Forepaw divided the men into bands of three or four each. These were each assigned their own route: their commander indicated places rich in game or fish where it would be easiest for someone to subsist.

"Tomorrow we will meet here," he said. "If someone fails to show up, I'll assume that they found some tracks, or died, and I will go after them."

"Without a chum and furs, we'll freeze," said Yando, the youngest of the men, who was known for reindeer racing.

"Your dog will stand in for your wife: hug it as you sleep and you'll stay warm."

The commander's reply produced general laughter, but Yando paid no attention to it. "And if everyone comes back?" he asked.

"That meant that we weren't looking in the right places, and we'll have to search elsewhere. Now shut your mouth and don't open it again until you're far from here."

The way Khungal had made this last joke, no one dared laugh.

The night was bright and the snow barely covered the ground. People believed that at this time, the spirits were on their side. Nokho had run away during the summer in a light parka made from thin skins, and he was surely more afraid of the cold than his foes. That thought lent them strength.

***

Fortune smiled on the reindeer racer and his two brothers who walked with him. Footprints left by a grown man descended from a rocky height into a valley where a sleepy river burbled. All three of the men – Yando, Mydwano ("Liver", a swarthy young man with big, wet eyes), and Khetanzi ("Long-Legged Spider", dubbed such due to his tree-climbing skills) exchanged glances.

"It's him," Yando whispered.

They all knew Nokho well, he had been their childhood playmate.

"It's him indeed," Mydwano said. "His feet are a whole span longer than mine."

"Poor guy," Khetanzi said and then sneezed. "But clearly that's his fate. Maut, Mitten!"

Khetanzi's dogs, a snow-white, broad-chested male named Maut and the smaller Mitten, who had a sharp snout like a fox and light-red spots, surpassed all other dogs at Kheno's encampment in intelligence. They now ran up at their master's call.

Mitten carefully sniffed the tracks and then looked at Khetanzi. He patted the dog on her neck and, exchanging a gleeful look with his brothers, he whispered into the dog's ear:

"Go on, find him. And you," he grabbed Maut by the scruff of his neck, "bring him here, to us."

Mitten quietly whined and then rushed towards the lower ground, and the other dog ran after it. The three men hastened after them in turn.

They ran with no concern for their legs, and each of them could see that they were getting closer to Nokho's lair. But then something happened that they did not expect. They saw the dogs ahead of them in the distance come to a stop.

"The trail went into the water," Khetanzi said as he tried to catch his breath.

But the trail continued unbroken along the riverbank, and only at the spot where Mitten sat quietly and the strong, simple-minded Maut danced did the men notice another line of footprints: they descended from a hill, crossed the track along the riverbank, and then followed it side by side. This second series of footprints was nearly only half the size of Nokho's. When the brothers saw that, they were dumbfounded.

"So, he's alive," Yando said slowly. "And he found himself a woman?"

"He must have," Mydwano confirmed. "And while we're all frantically looking for him!"

After those words they all laughed. Maut, who sensed that the current chase was more an amusement than a real hunt, started barking, but immediately he got the shaft of a spear across his muzzle.

"Quiet, you wolverine," growled Khetanzi – it was he who had hit the dog. "You think Nokho is as dumb as his dad? Now just wait…"

What they were waiting for he did not explain, but from here on all three walked more cautiously and looked carefully wherever the trails of footprints were interrupted by a fallen tree or thick foliage. Eventually the landscape itself aided pursuit: the valley became an ever wider, flat space with only occasional young trees, as if to underscore that nothing could be hidden from Kheno's people. Soon their hopes grew even firmer, for next to a round rock they found traces of blood and a few black feathers with bright green stripes.

"A black grouse," Khetanzi said. "He shot it along the way. Maybe quite recently. If we walk faster, we can catch up with him."

"Yes," Mydwano agreed. "We should move faster."

But none of them budged. Yando took a feather from Khetanzi's hand and examined it, as if he were hoping to discover something else within it. "I wonder," he finally said, "how the old man is going to reward us if we bring him Nokho?"

Mydwano perked up. "Yeah, I wonder about that, too. After all, it would mean that we saved the whole family."

Khetanzi smiled wryly. "He'll give you his wife. I can put in a word if you want."

"That would be just fine."

Mydwano sighed so deeply that Yando and Khetanzi burst out laughing. But Mydwano paid no heed to their laughter, for he had taken Khetanzi's comment seriously. "It would be really nice to get his woman," he said, drawing the words out. "Sunbeam felt really sorry for me that I didn't have a wife."

"That Sunbeam of yours became a widow without ever being married first. She ought to be feeling sorry for herself."

"Yeah, that's true."

Yavlyana, whose name meant "Sunbeam", was Mydwano's cousin on his father's side. Through her mother she was related to Khetanzi and Yando. Her suitor died before he could save up the bride-price. The suitor's name was Lar.

"What reward would you want?" Yando asked.

But Khetanzi did not seem to hear the question. "Let's go," he said. He was the first to rise and start running on, and the others followed him. But they did not run for long: Mitten came flying towards them from far off. The dog moved as fast as its paws would carry it.

Khetanzi's reddish dog could understood human speech, she followed tracks perfectly, found whatever animal, and then handed it over to the hunter, who merely had to shoot it. But the dog also had a keen sense of danger and could warn her master whenever it was necessary to give up chasing an animal or an outsider that might be too much to handle.

Mitten pawed the men's legs as if to prevent them from taking a step further.

"Where is Maut?" Khetanzi muttered. "Why isn't he here?"

That second dog had not returned nor, as everyone realized at once, would it ever.

"They killed Maut," Yando said.

"He killed Maut," Khetanzi said. "He's close. Maut must have attacked him… We're here, have your bows ready."

All three rushed towards where the valley was interrupted by a thin strip of black forest. Yando was in the lead, and he shouted, "Stop! Look!"

He was pointing to somewhere far off to his right, where dark specks had appeared against the white landscape. The specks grew larger, they stretched out into an uneven line and slowly came closer.

"That's not Nokho," Khetanzi said, "it's a pack of wolves. Maut had no fear of wolves. They must have killed him."

Yando mentioned that the three of them had enough arrows to fight the wolves off. Khetanzi, signaling his agreement without a word said, raised his bow.

"Over there! Over there!"

It was Mydwano who shouted. He was standing with his back to his brothers and pointing to the far side of the valley. There, too, some dark specks had appeared and were growing bigger.

The pack

The wolves slowly approached and then stopped at about an arrow's flight away – as if they knew the exact boundary where an arrow would no longer fly with deadly force. Khetanzi counted them: there were four of them for every arrow. The wolves remained where they were.

"What are they waiting for?" Mydwano asked. His voice trembled.

"For you to run away," Khetanzi retorted angrily. After a moment of silence, he went on: "The first move is ours to make. I'll go for the ones on the right, Yando can go for the ones on the left. You, Mydwano, go with him. Keep a distance of at least several paces and don't let the pack get you from the side. Let's go."

Each ran, hunched over like in a real battle, to his assigned place. Khetanzi was the first to stop, drop to his knee, and shoot off an arrow. His brothers' bows sounded in turn. All three were good marksmen, the sort who could make quite a display at big celebrations, but now their luck let them down. The wolves did not require any great agility to avoid death at their hands; each wolf simply walked away from the arrow's trajectory.

The whole pack seemed to act as a single mind, one that could anticipate its opponents' plans.

Khetanzi was the first to realize this, when he saw the leader of the pack separate from the general mass. The leader was a large wolf with a slight hump on its back and a white mark on its side. This wolf ran, in no especial hurry, to the right, stopped, and howled. As soon as his howl died down, new specks began to appear far off – the men had been looking at only a portion of the whole pack – and when the procession of wolves grew denser, the animals all began to run at the same time, aiming to encircle the bowmen.

A chill came over Khetanzi's heart as he suddenly felt less weight on his back – he had already shot more than half of his arrows, and apparently so had his brothers. The wolves began to leisurely construct their noose, waiting for that moment when the men could no longer hold them off at a distance. There was no hope of resisting such a pack with spears, even if the three men had stood back to back.

Khetanzi jumped up and looked around. The same encirclement was being constructed from Yando and Mydwano's side. As if to mock them, the wolves stopped and sniffed at the black-feathered arrows that stuck out of the ground – there were a great many, as many as willows on a riverbank.

"Enough!" Khetanzi shouted with all his might. "Don't shoot. Both of you come here!"

He ran back to the place where they had initially split up in order to launch their defense. Fortunately, Khetanzi's brothers had not shown the same quick thinking as himself; they had not yet become frozen with fear at the wolf pack's united front.

"Did you manage to down at least one?" Yando asked, gasping.

"No."

"I got two. They got away into the forest."

"Don't lie," Mydwano squeaked.

"I'm not lying."

With his two hands Khetanzi grabbed his brothers by their heads and knocked their skulls together. "You silly wolverines. Listen to me: when the wolves get there," he pointed to the path where they had recently walked, "we're done for. We won't be able to fight them off, even if we downed half of them."

The faces of his brothers tensed.

"What should we do, Khetanzi?" Yando whispered.

"We need to run back the way we came, to Fish Lake."

"What about the footprints?" Mydwano asked. His voice shook like he was about to cry. "He's over there somewhere, Nokho is."

"If we can get back to the lake, then everyone can go follow those tracks. That's what Khungal said. Then he won't be able to get away. Stop thinking with your stupid nose and put your trust in your legs instead."

They left the valley, but kept their bows ready. Khetanzi took the rear and often looked back to see what the wolf pack was doing. The wolves moved in the same tightening noose behind the fleeing men and to their left and right.

"They're going to surround us!" Mydwano cried. He was gasping for air.

"No, they won't. Just hold on, things are going to get better soon."

Khetanzi said this with confidence: the valley gradually grew more narrow and eventually it would turn into a gorge where one could pass only in single file. There the pack would have to stretch out and it would be much harder for them to attack the men. Khetanzi was already sure of the pack's uncanny ability to think as one, and he understood that if the wolves were going to attack them as easy pickings, they would do it soon, before the valley narrowed into the gorge.

The pack, however, ran with the same even pace and showed no apparent desire to attack.

"Here, switch with me."

Yando changed places with Khetanzi and ran facing backwards – none could equal his skill at doing that.

They were nearly at the gorge when the pack called off its chase.

"They're leaving!" Yando cried. "The wolves are leaving!"

"Don't stop. Keep moving."

Khetanzi felt a great weight slip off his back, and apparently so did his brothers. They stopped along a river between the wooded hillsides. While they were running, Khetanzi remembered Mitten – she had fled as soon as the wolves appeared. He was not angry at her, for any dog could be expected to yield to the appearance of wolves; the foolhardy Maut had not understood that.

The dog's fate quickly became clear when Khetanzi spotted an even sequence of small pawprints. Mitten had run to Fish Lake in order to summon help for the men while they were surrounded by the wolves.

Khetanzi was so overwhelmed with emotion at the dog's action, he nearly cried.

They went on until darkness came over the gorge.

***

All three men were on their last legs by the time they reached the lake. They spent that night in the branches of an old, chunky pine and they hardly got any sleep. They had been so happy at their good fortune in spotting the footprints, and then getting away from the wolves, that they had forgotten their hunger and fatigue, but the next morning each felt like an elderly or ailing man. The cold had turned fiercer and sapped them of their strength. Some dried meat failed to revive their good spirits, but it at least kept them alert.

The whole force gathered at Fish Lake felt much the same. Forepaw's warriors were regaining their strength, but their thoughts were gloomy – none had found even the slightest trace of Nokho. They had little meat jerky left, but resorting to raw meat demanded courage, and the cold – an enemy against which even the bravest of men are powerless – was becoming ever more oppressive.

Khetanzi's squad were among the last to arrive, but his dog appeared before they did. She danced on her thin legs, ran among the men, whined, and tried to get every man's attention. Some tried to talk to her, but many simply brushed her off. The men understood that a dog returning from the taiga without its master, did not augur anything good. If on this campaign it could have got at least a little warmth and good food, it would have eagerly kept up its pursuit. But now the dog was downcast, and its legs lacked the bounce they once had. Therefore, Forepaw ordered the men to wait, so the last squads would have time to arrive. This was a mere excuse. When everyone else besides those three had arrived, no one moved, no one spoke up, and Forepaw was silent. Everyone was thinking only about himself…

The cave

The news that Khetanzi and his brothers bore, brought the warriors back to life. They gathered around Forepaw and the three brothers, they shouted as if they were now looking forward to an easy war with rich plunder, and even the report of wolves did not dour their spirits.

"What hope would a wolf pack have against forty bows?" they cried.

With such shouts the troop shrugged off any anguish about their own lack of success and the fierce cold, and they set off along the trail. They walked and some even broke into a run. Some snacked as they made their way; ribbons of dried meat hung from their mouths. The path through the gorge into the valley took hardly any time at all. The day promised victory and deliverance. The sun had risen only a third of its way across the sky, and the weather remained clear.

In the valley Khetanzi showed his commander the double series of footprints – even as the brothers were fleeing from the wolves, Khetanzi had ordered them not to tread over them.

"He found himself a wife," he told Forepaw, pointing at the footprints that were half the size of the ones which, he assumed, belonged to Nokho.

Something akin to a smile flashed across Forepaw's pock-marked face. "Big guy."

The other warriors looked in astonishment, but no one doubted that the footprints belonged to the young man who had let Mother Fire's curse lie over them. And they were right.

***

By midday the troop had traversed the valley and arrived among the flat-topped hills. The footprints led towards one of them – a nearly bald one – and then were lost among rocky scree. Forepaw ordered his men to stop. He looked up for a long time and breathed in slowly, as if he hoped to detect in the air the scent of some human abode.

Finally he spoke. "He's hiding on that hill," the commander said quietly and contentedly, as if he could already see Nokho right there in front of him.

Khetanzi was standing at his side.

"Talk to that clever reddish bitch of yours. Maybe she'll show us the way?"

Mitten was keeping her distance from the other dogs, strong hounds of various colors that had grown more subdued after crossing that valley covered in wolves' tracks. Khetanzi put his arm around Mitten's neck and spoke something into her ear, and then the dog went flying up the hill. Her thin, sprightly legs easily found a hold among the rocks. Soon she disappeared from view, and after some time passed a voice came from high up.

"There," Forepaw said, his gaze fixed on the heights.

He turned to Khetanzi and tapped the latter's chest with his fist. "You come with me."

Khetanzi smiled.

Suddenly Yando appeared from behind the commander. "It was the three of us who found the footprints, but Khetanzi gets all the credit?"

"Alright, then, you can come too."

"What about our brother?"

Mydwano, as if aware of what they were talking about, stepped closer so the commander might notice him. Forepaw saw the puffy-cheeked young man look at him imploringly.

"It's too hard. Stay here." After the commander said this, he turned to his warriors and ordered them to surround the hill.

The three of them then began making their way up.

***

They easily found the shelter in the hillside. Forepaw sent an arrow flying into the depths of it – the arrow made a thud that echoed resoundingly – and then he disappeared into the cave himself. Yando and Khetanzi followed.

Light poured into the two fugitives' shelter and it did not take long for their pursuers' eyes to get used to the darkness. Traces of human presence lay all around them: bones, feathers, hare skins. Forepaw made his way down, and as he looked at the damp, occasionally frost-covered walls, he saw that the shelter was not so large and there was no further to go.

"Hey…" Khetanzi was coming down towards where the commander stood. He raised a hand to his face, blew on it, and said in a dull, trembling voice, "It's warm."

"What is?"

"The ash. There was a fireplace up there, I put my hand in the ash. It's still quite warm, like there was still a fire burning there last night."

The commander rushed back up. There he could distinguish, in a slight hollow, the remains of a fire: a few partially burned brands and scattered twigs. He hadn't noticed this fireplace on the way down. Yando was squatting on his haunches, a hand on the middle of the black fire-ring. Forepaw grabbed a fistful of ash – warmth, of the sort he had long forgotten about, came flowing along his fingers.

"How can it be?" Yando asked.

The commander caught his bewildered gaze in the dim light.

"How can it be…"

Forepaw did not know what to say. He was dumbfounded himself.

"This means that he has fire," Khetanzi muttered. "He has fire, but we don't. Why is that, commander?"

No reply came, and the silence lasted a long time.

Forepaw was nearly twice the age of these youths. He had three sons himself, and the eldest of them would soon take over from his father; that eldest had already led men in raids several times, risked death, and seen incredible things. There was only one thing Forepaw knew for sure: to lead men, you need to watch out for the moment when the united will of a troop of warriors might crumble, like a herd from which the alpha male was taken away. Then you have to say something, even if you yourself do not see any way out. Now Forepaw spoke:

"This is not Nokho."

"Then who?" both of the other men immediately asked.

"There are a lot of vagabonds wandering through the taiga."

Khetanzi took something from a pouch hanging from his belt and handed it to his commander. It was a narrow arrowhead with a broken edge. "I found this here. I wanted to keep it for myself. You see the notch? Nokho would mark his own arrows that way. I know him like I know myself. Once, a long time ago, he told me that he and his brother had their own chum that no one else knew about. We're in that chum. This is Nokho, it can't be anyone else."

Their commander rose. He spoke quietly and severely. "If Nokho has fire, and we don't, that means the Mother wanted it that way. Now listen carefully: if you want to return home alive, keep quiet about this ash. Nokho got away. But he's somewhere around here, and we have to find him."

The commander turned and walked briskly towards the exit from the cave.

The first thing that Forepaw saw was the sky showering a never-ending white blanket over the earth.

Kheno

Old Kheno lay in his chum on a bed of spruce branches, oss, and fur that was covered with three skins.

There was only him in the chum and a girl, his granddaughter.

To preserve whatever sparse remains of warmth there were, the smoke-hole had been covered with a fur.

"Take the fur away," the old man bade her.

"Why? Snow will fall on you."

"Take it away and then go somewhere else."

The girl grabbed a ladder and, without saying anything, she removed the fur from the smoke-hole. A shaft of pale blue light appeared inside the chum and clumps of steam floated within it.

The girl set a plate of dried meat in front of the old man. "Here, eat."

"You can have it."

"No, I can't," the girl said and then she began to sob. "I feel sick. Grandpa, do we have to wait long?"

"No, not long. The men are gathering their strength and then they'll go out and search for him again. They'll definitely find him this time – if our distant relatives don't find him first. Just hold on. Don't cry."

The girl stood in the shaft of light and Kheno watched her wipe her wet cheeks with her hands.

"Can everyone really suffer for what one single person did?"

"Yes," the old man quietly said. "The gods don't like jokes."

"But don't they like people?"

"They like good people."

"So we're bad people?"

"Listen, dear," Kheno tried to speak as affectionately as he could. "Soon you'll be warming your hands over the fire and complaining that the soup you slurped right from the pot burned your throat. And shortly thereafter you'll be crying again, but this time from happiness when I find you a prince to marry, the finest man in the taiga. You have so much to look forward to, missy, and that's why you were born such a pretty young lady. Just hold on a little longer… Go now, I want to sleep. Go."

The girl sighed as children do when they have got over their crying. She bent down to kiss the old man and then went out.

***

The warriors had returned the evening before at sundown. The snowfall had not only covered the footprints but also sapped the men's strength; moving without skis became laborious. The news that Tusyada's son was so close at hand but then escaped, left everyone disappointed and grumbling. But there was another side to that news: Nokho was alive, and the blood that the vengeful Mother wanted still flowed in his veins. That angle proved stronger and the people's hopes swelled.

The warriors would lie under furs and seek some warm from their wives' bodies, then they would get up, take skis and sledges, stock up on arrows and that meat jerky (so tiresome now), and set off over the new snow where Nokho would surely leave fresh footprints. Now he would be in more trouble than his erstwhile family, for a whole host of men were now coming after him, while he probably lacked decent skis and warm clothes, unless he had stolen them off someone. He had undoubtedly abducted a woman to cope with the loneliness and, most importantly, stay warm – he would be fearing the cold now, especially considering that the way back to his secret shelter inside the hill was now cut off.

That is what everyone was thinking, and Kheno, too – after the warriors returned, his previous anxiety began to subside. Only Forepaw, who had led the men, seemed to say little and only reluctantly, but he had always been like that…

The old man stared at the fading shaft of light. He thought how the Mother was tormenting every single one of his people, so that they would remember and pass the lesson on to their descendants. He was prepared to endure this to the end. This thought comforted him. The old man fell asleep before he even knew it. It was a deep sleep like in his younger days.

He awoke to someone insistently shaking him by the knee.

"Is that you, granddaughter?" Kheno asked, his eyes still closed.

"It's me."

The old man started and looked up. The shaft of light descending into the chum that had faded, had now appeared again – it was as white as mammoth tusk and as clear as water. In the middle of it Kheno saw a tall, thick-haired man who held a long spear. "Greetings, clan father," Nokho said.

***

The snow had hastened his decision to go and seek revenge.

We realized that now the ground would reveal our footprints to our foes. I tried to hurry Nokho:

"I want to see the people who killed my brother."

"You will," he replied.

A wolf pack appeared not far away – it was the same one that had chased Khetanzi and his brothers. Nokho felt that it was something stronger than hunger that had forced the wolves to leave their previous territory and come this way.

Now we did not descend into the valley by our usual way but headed into the taiga over the top of the hill and along the other side.

Our fear of the wolves had saved us: when we returned from some hunting, we stopped on a height and saw some figures down at the foot of the hill. They were Forepaw's warriors.

Fate itself had given a sign that now there was only one thing to do: head for Kheno's encampment. We trusted that this fate which had brought Nokho and me together would settle everything.

We crept up to the huge encampment without anyone noticing. The people lay in their chums, wrapped up in a myriad of furs, and even an earthquake would not have driven anyone outside.

And now Nokho was standing before the old man.

***

"You came back…"

Kheno hardly heard his own words. The old man was in a state of complete bafflement, he froze like a hunter who had been led by a seemingly familiar trail into some unknown, foreign land.

"Can you sleep when it's so cold?" Nokho stood there motionless.

Kheno looked at him for a long time and could not see in him the sort of person who would make a daring nighttime raid. He saw only the young man he had known. Without even knowing why, the old man said, "I'm glad."

Nokho sat down with his legs crossed and set the spear down in front of him. He smiled. "Me too."

The old man sat up. "Why have you come?"

"I missed my family." The face of Tusyada's son continued to show the same smile.

Kheno suddenly realized that he hardly knew him. Nokho was a strong lad, a good hunter that few equaled. But to Nokho's left, he saw the young man's stupid father and dissolute mother who had brought a curse upon the entire family, and to his right he saw his brother Serkhasawa, who had meekly subjected himself to the knife in order to save his people. Kheno was not sure whose blood was the stronger in him.

"Your family is dying," the old man said dully. "You know that. Look, I'm not your little pet, don't toy with me. You can see yourself that I'm old, and if death has come, then I'll welcome it like a dear guest." After a brief silence, he went on, "There are forty hale men here, another dozen elderly men, and you know that, too. Right now they are sleeping. But even if you killed one or even several, the others…"

"You're afraid, old man."

"Shut up!" The initial confusion had passed. Kheno had now regained control over himself and spoke assertively. "Remember your brother, he is worthy of an epic tale, because he accepted his fate with dignity. We would forget about the cowardice you have shown, we would forgive you for what we have suffered, if you returned here to act as gloriously as your brother did. You can run away from human beings, but only a madman would try to hide from the gods."

Nokho did not answer, he only kept his gaze fixed on the old man.

Kheno went on. "Just be smart," he said wearily. "Don't make things more difficult for yourself. After all, you did come back. What sense does it make if you kill me and then flee into the taiga again? Just to die the same death that's looming over us? But down there," the old man pointed a twisted finger at the ground, "we will meet again. Think about what sins you would have on you, imagine what…"

The old man did not finish his statement, for he sensed the presence of a third individual somewhere behind him. While the old man slept, I had crept into the chum before

Nokho and sat down at the far side in the dark with my bow ready, so that I could launch an arrow if the curtain were flung back.

"Is that your woman?" Kheno laughed. "The one my warriors were talking about? You want to drag her around everywhere with you. Where did you abduct her from?"

"Come here, brother."

Instead of a woman, it was a narrow-faced, slight youth who stood before the old man alongside Nokho.

"This is Wenga," Nokho said. "He was first Yabto's son, then his slave. Yabto you know. Khetanzi, Yando, and Mydwano killed his brother Lar. They hurt him just for laughs, if you haven't forgotten. Wenga came back with me."

"It doesn't make any difference," the old man said after a period of silence. He was feeling slightly embarrassed.

"You're right, it doesn't."

Nokho took a suede sack from his back and drew something from it. It was a bit of birch-bark tinder.

"Watch."

A spark leapt out of Nokho's hands, then another, and soon a small flame danced at his feet. He picked up the burning birch bark and lifted it to his face – his face shone with triumph.

"Want to warm your hands?" Nokho extended the birch bank towards Kheno and said this almost with real affection. He watched the old man start violently and reach out towards the fire. As soon as the old man's hands came near, the fire hissed and went out.

Silence followed. The old man understood completely.

Nokho was the first to speak. "You taught us that people suffer because they lived incorrectly. But you yourself lived properly. And so did we along with you. Is that right?"

"Yes, I have nothing to fault myself for. Except for some minor things."

"You always offered food to the spirits, honored the gods, and you never made an unworthy sacrifice to our lord Nga.

And that is why your family was spared hardships that afflicted or even killed other families. You said, 'Be honest people, don't lie to the spirits, and then nothing bad is going to happen to you.' Is that right?"

"You remember my words well."

The old man looked up, and the look in his eyes was such that Nokho recoiled.

"Why are you even asking?" Kheno said. "What do you want from me?"

"Do you still believe all that? Think about it first. We still have time before dawn."

"You're asking a lot," the old man finally muttered. "To remember what exactly I have done wrong, I'd have to trace back through my entire life, bit by bit like each knot in a fishing net. And it has been a long life. I could hardly manage by morning."

Kheno tried to smile, but instead he only winced as if from a blow. "I only know one thing: it is all your mother and father's fault. Mainly your father's... Any person might act stupidly on occasion, but Tusyada did something that even silly children would never dare. The Mother's wrath is too great."

"If your wisdom, which protected your family and never failed you, could be undone by just one stupid man, than what is your wisdom worth anyway? What are you sacrifices worth?"

"Don't blaspheme. You know what sacrifice the Mother demands."

Nokho threw back his head and laughed, so much that he gasped for air like a drowning man. "Demands? Do you really know that the Mother demands? You saw how fire burns in my hands but goes out the second you get near it. Which of us has she punished? Who is really cursed here, old man?"

Kheno fell silent. Then he suddenly jumped to his feet. "The Mother is protecting you in order to teach the rest of us. To teach us a lesson and then save us. Have you thought about that? If it weren't for Tusyada, you could never find people who honored fire as much as we have. Remember, boy, people who consistently do good might deserve occasional punishment, but never condemnation. Even now our conscience is clear before fire, because we gave it everything that we could. Your mother and father are dead, impaled. And now you're here, you came by your own accord…"

"They're dead?" Nokho asked. He said this as if what he heard had been completely expected. "Well, I wonder what the Mother is still unhappy about."

"Don't blaspheme," Kheno repeated.

"You know, sometimes a woman with child gets a craving for something: fish bladder, fresh moss, magpie eggs. Everyone understands that that's just how pregnant women are. Maybe the Mother just wants you all to die? Just like that, without any lesson to teach. Have you thought about that, old man?"

"Remember, young'un, nothing happens without a reason. Now, the reason might be the gods, spirits, the dead, people, animals, or anything else whatsoever, but not even a grain of sand or a thorn on a stalk will come about just like that. And the Mother's wrath…"

He stopped as he watched Nokho take the spear and set its wide blade by his feet.

"I could stab you right through, in a single motion," Nokho said. "What's the reason that lies behind that?" He said this with no rancor, in fact he nearly laughed.

Kheno immediately burst out laughing himself. "I already told you, you're a fool if you think you can scare an old man with death. You need a reason? Four dozen young men, all sleeping with their weapons… And another dozen old men, and women and children, many of whom are pretty strong. Even the old women draw strength from the hatred they have for you. They might not have any teeth, but they have nails like an owl's claws…"

Nokho motioned with his eyes that I should take up my previous position behind the old man. Kheno did not catch this, he was too overcome with laughter and his eyes were closed.

"Even if you kill me and get away, you and that lad would be found within a day. You know how well Forepaw can lead men in search of the enemy. You think you can get away, silly boy, but all paths intersect, for human beings, for the gods… And you think…"

The words flew forth, Kheno seethed like a pot in which meat broth had reached a furious rolling boil. He had one hand over his face, the other flailed like a raven knocked to the ground as the old man rolled with laughter. But suddenly his laughter stopped.

Kheno froze. His hand fell from his face and his other arm weakly hit the floor. The old man stared at Nokho slack-jawed, eyes bulging, and then he fell sideways like a withered old tree.

Tusyada's son stood there for a moment, dumbfounded. Then he went up to Kheno and put his hand under the old man's nostrils – he felt no warmth coming from there.

"There's your reason," he said to his blood brother and winked.

Two demons

We went out of the chum and got to work. The full moon filled the sky, and the predawn cold bit at our faces. The dwellings of Kheno's great encampment were arranged in circles, like the pattern on a breastplate.

By tacit agreement we set off in different directions. Each of us went up to a chum, threw the flap aside, and launched two or three arrows towards where the men usually slept, then we ran on to the next chum. By the time our quivers were empty, we had managed to cover nearly all the dwellings.

The encampment wailed as one. Men burst out of the chums with arrows in their legs, backs, or shoulders. We finished them off with our spears. Some others ran out with weapons in hand, but they did not even have time to raise them at us.

A ferocious demon had settled into Nokho – he flew along, barely touching the ground, and all courage departed from the warriors.

"Show me the ones who killed Lar!" I cried.

"We'll find them among the dead. Go through the chums and kill them, every single person!"

"I don't need to kill the women."

"Everyone!" Nokho roared. "The whole family, like fat flung from the scraper."

He roared like an icy wind, so great did his hungry heart feast on the killing. Some of the men threw down their weapons and lay face down in the snow in the hope of being shown mercy, but they got only death instead. It was clear that Nokho had no intention of stopping until the only voices remaining in the encampment were those of the victors.

I glanced up at the terrible face of the moon and was overcome with an inexplicable anguish. I ran towards Nokho and shouted as loud as I could, "Stop!"

My shout brought him to a stop. He paused his bloody work and stared at his oath-brother, the way one looks at someone invited to a feast who has decided to head off just as things were getting started. Blood dripped from the blade of his spear.

"Show me the ones who killed my brother. Whether they're alive or dead, just show me."

Nokho roared, and only a few words could be made out: "You… Whose… You… Who…"

"Stop," I repeated. "You have already won."

Nokho did not reply. He turned and rushed into the nearest chum – an instant later, a birch-bark cradle came flying out. Like a bear angry at finding that its prey was not what it expected, he ran towards another chum. I rushed after him, and when I caught up, I hit him on the shoulder with the butt of my spear.

"Stop. I want to speak to them."

Nokho was deaf to all sounds except for the storm that raged within him. Now the fury that had borne him along was turned towards me.

Everyone in the encampment froze and watched these men, who had come to do the will of some higher power, begin fighting with one another instead. They saw how the preternatural power on display now settled on the slighter of the two warriors. This power allowed me to dodge Nokho's blows as he stabbed at the empty air.

The words of Iron Horn had come true, I knew that for sure: the little slave with the heart of a *soning* spoke within me. His heart sufficed to make one single motion that settled everything.

I sprung up and flew through the air, and then in the stillness the people around me heard a brief thud. It was Nokho's head falling onto the densely packed snow. They all screamed like a cliff had collapsed right next to them.

Then silence fell over the encampment.

It was interrupted by another sound that the people there had nearly forgotten: someone striking an iron against a flint.

The mad widow

The only individual that had remained entirely aloof from these events in the encampment was an old crone named Watane.

Even before her husband had passed away she had been unwell, and after losing her husband she turned into a creature so terrible that none of the deceased's brothers wanted to take her into his chum. The widow's dwelling was on the outskirts of the encampment. She was not deprived of anything, but no one felt sorry for her, probably out of fear. The look of darkness and horror that never left Watane's perennially dirty face, her hair that clumped together into locks like dead snakes, and her voice that stabbed at others' ears like iron had made Watane into a convincing likeness of an evil spirit. She lived her own mysterious life which no one could really figure out.

While her relatives were looking at the aftermath of the battle, she had walked up with a bundle of sticks and quietly got to making a fire in a part of the encampment now bereft of any living people.

The widow struck sparks from her flint. The moon shone upon her back. A meandering trail approached the crone – it was blood from Nokho's now headless body. The blood was not absorbed down into the snow, it crept towards the firewood like a snake towards a chick fallen from the nest. More and more sparks came from the old woman's hands, the birch bark took light, and a thin wisp of smoke zigzagged across the face of the moon.

The trail of blood stopped a few inches away from the fire, as if hesitating, and then it rushed forward.

Flames shot up into the sky. The fire devoured the wood with a deafening roar, it rumbled as it were born not from small branches but raged from the underworld dwelling of the great lord Nga.

People came running up to the flames. The young women were first to encircle the fire in a tight ring, followed by children, and then the wounded limped up, leaving a dark trail on the snow behind them. Everyone was holding their arms out at the flames, and they cried out from the sweet pain of regained sensation in their frozen hands. Their initial shouts gave way to weeping. No one tried to hide their tears.

Only the widow Watane was not crying. She had quickly been pushed away from the fire and now she was standing in her usual pose, hands on her cheeks, and staring silently at the throng. Suddenly she shrieked so loudly that everyone froze:

"Over there!" she cried. "Look over there! At him!"

She was pointing at the spot where I stood.

The entire crowd turned as one and then came flowing towards me. They got on their knees some distance away and froze, as if kneeling before a great spirit, and they dared not budge. I could not see their faces, only their backs and the tops of their heads. Gradually they got ahold of themselves and waited to see who would be bold enough to speak first.

Finally an old voice was heard:

"Who are you, warrior?"

I answered. "A year ago, Yabto from the Mosquito People brought Lar to your encampment and called him his son. Lar was promised a wife, but instead he only got a place among the trees. I am Wenga, Lar's brother. I came to see the ones who killed him."

The silence that followed was as long as winter. Then the same old voice said, frightened, "Who's Lar?"

After those words were said, I felt anger rising up from my chest towards my throat. "Someone come up to me now," I said. "My brother and I had different bodies, but we had the same face."

A bowlegged, toothless old man stepped out of the crowd and came towards me. The old man took a long, careful look as if he could not believe his eyes, then blinked in surprise. "People, it was that loser… The same sickly guy that Watane stole food for, that Lar. It's true, they have the same face… Forgive us, warrior, our family is a very big one."

The old man turned back towards his people and cried in a long, drawn-out voice, "Yavlyana, my little ray of sunlight, come here…"

A round young woman came running up to me. She nudged the old man out of the way and fell to her knees. "It was me, warrior. I wanted to marry your brother. But it's not my fault, it was my evil brothers that killed him. He was sick when they brought him, he wanted food constantly, and everyone bullied him. One day he said, 'Alright, let's fight.' I tried to tell them to take it easy on him, but no one listens to a girl. That's how it happened…"

The woman began to wail in lamentation, but then she suddenly jumped up and took my hand. "Don't worry about your brother, you have already got revenge. Come on, I'll show you."

The woman brought me to the place where the battle in the encampment had raged. Bodies were lying in heaps. She bravely rolled one of the dead over to show me his face.

"Look, this was my older brother. Another one of my brothers is lying over there, come on…"

"Damn you!" A tall woman was running up to us. "You wolverine-widow, you disgusting creature. Don't we already have enough sin upon us? Haven't we suffered enough. You want to start something new? Mother Fire got offended at one of our kin, then we deceived her with a false sacrifice and we almost died. Two young lads killed all our strong men, as if they were a whole army. Isn't that enough? You, warrior, don't believe what she says. That's not her brother. Your enemies are still among the living, only one is dead."

Her voice seemed to pierce the throng of spectators, which then roared and flung two men at my feet. They were Yando and Mydwano.

Khetanzi was indeed dead. He and Forepaw, too – the latter had been one of the sleepers whom our arrows killed.

Yando was completely unscathed, but Mydwano could hardly walk and he pressed his hand against a wound in his side. They made up the sole survivors of the whole host of young men.

The women shrieked and fell upon them to force them down onto their knees. I remember the women's eyes, they burned with an eagerness to perform any service.

"What do you want from them? Tell us!" the people cried.

Back in Nokho's secret refuge I had thought about what I would do to these people who killed my brother. But from the great many things I longed to do, only one remained: to ask "Why couldn't you just let Lar live?" and watch them squirm as they tried to come up with an answer.

Yando looked down at the ground. Mydwano was breathing loudly and raggedly. I said nothing. Finally, I decided to act – I put the blade of my spear to Yando's throat.

"Look at me."

Yando looked up. His gaze showed no supplication, no fear, only a mournful acceptance of his fate.

Instead of him, it was Mydwano who spoke. "I didn't lay a finger on your brother. I just stood nearby. Please let me live…"

This young man pleaded in the dull voice of a slave, and that voice swept from me the last remnants of the rage that I had expended on the extermination of the camp's warriors and the fight with Nokho. The heart of the *soning* within me fell silent.

I dropped my weapon, turned, and walked off towards the setting moon.

Yando jumped up and ran after me. "Hey, wait." He spoke softly and nearly breathlessly. "I don't know you, but I knew that you would come. Even back there in your cave I knew that…"

I kept walking. Neither rage nor thoughts of revenge troubled me any longer, and these people had all become alien to me in an instant, just like all other human beings on the earth. I was empty inside now, and I walked without even knowing where.

But Yando watched the reflection of the distant flames dance on my back, and to him I seemed then to be a god walking among men.

"You are one of two warriors who slaughtered an entire host of strong men. Why won't you kill me? You're leaving me alone to survive. Who are you, tell me? Lar's spirit returned from the underworld? What do you plan to do with us? Worse than what we already suffered? Come on, say something!"

He got no reply, but he continued walking after me. Finally, he ran up and barred my way. "I am Yando the Dog. Is that who you want me to be, your dog?"

"No."

"Then why don't you act like a man? What are you hiding from us? Look, if you spare me… After everything that happened, people are going to expect more punishment, this time for unavenged blood. They will go crazy from the anticipation, everyone will become like widow Watane. Me, I'll end up like Tusyada – the same will happen to me like it did to him. Kheno's not around now, who is going to explain everything to him? Listen, let me go with you. You can kill me whenever you want, just don't leave me here alone…"

Yando was running backwards in front of me, just like he had done in the valley when he was escaping from the wolves.

Suddenly he stopped and cried, "Turn around. Look what's behind you!"

I did so. What remained of Kheno's family was coming after me.

"They want to be your dogs, too. Old dogs, females, puppies. Can't you see?"

I looked at the gray figures scattered across the snow-covered field. For the first time in my short, unhappy life I saw people coming to serve me.

The demon at my back, so fickle and unfathomable, descended into my legs and made them step towards the crowd.

Yando ran before me with a mighty cry:

"Our leader! Our leader!"

***

Once the sun was up they buried their dead.

The heaviest body, it turned out, was Nokho's. To carry him, the arms of every man remaining in the camp were needed– and they were mainly old men. They were amazed by the weight of Nokho's invisible sin and they wondered what great guilt could be dragging the dead man down towards the earth.

But the people were even more astonished by the shaman.

He came into the encampment on the same day and said that the spirits had called him to the heavenly smoke, and that very evening he would close his eyes and stop breathing.

The shaman said that he already had a wooden bier prepared, he only asked that someone lift it up into the branches. This frightened everyone and the women cried.

Before the shaman closed his eyes and breathed his last, he said, "Woe to you all…"

The whole family wept and said that they really were a sorry lot, because it was bad for people to be left with no intermediary who could see the spirits and communicate with them.

"Don't you cry about that," the dying man said. "You won't be needing a shaman."

When the people expressed puzzlement and repeated that it was bad to lose such a clairvoyant, the shaman said, "If I am being summoned away from you, it means that there is no longer any need for me on this earth." After a silence, he added, "You yourselves will see the spirits."

No one moved. Some were thinking that perhaps the shaman's secret power would become the possession of all, but he anticipated their thoughts and said:

"Don't get too happy now. It is bad when every person is going to see what should be revealed only to a few, just like there is nothing good about a fish jumping out of the river and flopping around on the grass."

When the shaman had said this, he closed his eyes and stopped breathing.

The face of the tribe

Another day came and I could see the face of the tribe.

It was the face of an abandoned dog that is trying to gauge the depths of its new owner and his strength.

I was given a chum, it was the best one after Kheno's, which I had refused. My chum was covered with new and strong skins, with a wide, soft bed of furs and moss, a big hearth, and a pot in which a whole reindeer leg was boiling.

I was fed like a long-awaited guest – the old men sat around the fire with their arms crossed and watched in silence as I ate. The hot meat put my body to rest, and I fell asleep with an unfinished bone still in my hand. When I woke up, I saw the same faces around me.

Another day passed and the people continued to stare at me without even trying to hide it. From my movements and words they were trying to solve the riddle that tormented them: whence came such strength in such a slight young man, almost a boy? Did it always lie within him, or did it come upon him at some mysterious instant? No one got any clear answer, and each tended towards his own supposition. Those who were completely exhausted after the torments of recent months, believed that this young man was an emissary sent by a higher power. Others – the minority – believed the same, only not as firmly. They wanted to see another demonstration of that strength and then, they felt, their hearts would be at rest.

I did not know what Kheno's people would believe if they knew that the same doubt lived within me, too. But I was saved by my youth, by a young man's tendency to simply take good conditions as a given. Kheno's people, on the other hand, were rescued by a life that did not leave much room for long contemplation.

The family continued to melt away: three wounded men died within a day of the battle, Mydwano among them. The wound on his side was sewn up with hair and the bleeding stopped, but soon yellow pus began to issue from between the stitches. Mydwano had said nothing as the bone needle pierced his skin, but now he cried out from the interminable pain, and this gave way to a moan that recalled a child's sobbing. By morning Mydwano, the man whose name meant "Liver", cried no more.

Of the men capable of fighting, maintaining the herds, or leading caravans, only Yando and Lidyang were left – the old man's brother was much stronger than many of his gray-haired peers. There were also five boys who had already seen their first success at hunting, but were not yet old enough to fully take after their fathers. The rest were hardly capable of feeding themselves. A just and well-fed existence had allowed many people in Kheno's family to live to a great span of years, so among the living there were many elderly men, and especially elderly women, who were revered just like the men. Their feeble legs had saved their lives, for they remained inside their chums and were not struck down by Nokho's iron.

But mainly there were women. Nearly every one of Kheno's forty young warriors had left a widow behind. The widows had children, some of whom lay in their cradles while others – who barely reached up to a grown man's knees – clutched at their mothers' parkas.

Other tribes had feared the Nga people and did not come near their territory without good reason. But suitors from this great people were happily welcomed in the encampments of other tribes. Marrying a blood relative was considered the same as marrying oneself – Kheno honored this commandment like all the other ones. Long ago, the Nga people had been forced to get their brides through warfare. But then everything changed, because the people of that great tribe inevitably proved the victors. Most importantly, rumors spread through the taiga that there were no young ladies in the world happier than those betrothed to the Nga men, for those fearsome people possessed something other peoples did not: unwavering devotion.

The women of the Nga people were at no risk of starvation, even if they were widowed. They were never discarded by their husbands and replaced with another woman. As they say in the taiga, "they eat fat." Very little was demanded of the women except that they remain faithful and not nag their husbands.

Even the disaster of the recent months had not changed the women of Kheno's family. They remained lovely and defenseless homemakers. They were the first to believe that the slight stranger was their leader, sent by the spirits and perhaps even by the great lord Nga himself. The women mourned their husbands, sons, and brothers, but the indelible horror of that night and the miraculous return of fire had led them to view the deaths of their men as nearly justified. Almost none of them suffered from any craving for revenge. They were all faithful and caring wives, honored mothers of warriors, and could not imagine any other lot in life.

It was the men who bore the brunt – this became clear once everyone noticed how the herds had thinned. In good times the reindeer were so many that probably only Kheno knew the true number. The huge corral was guarded by over a dozen shepherds. But when the disaster struck, the patriarch and his people stopped paying attention to the herd. While the young men were off in the taiga looking for Tusyada's son, or bringing the message to the other Nga clans, the three old men assigned guard duty were unable to cope, and wildlife had destroyed the fence in various places. Domesticated reindeer do not mix with wild ones, and those which escaped into the taiga could be brought back, but there was no one to see to that, nor was it worth the bother: the herd had thinned by nearly half, but the old men said that even the remaining reindeer were too many for the number of hale men left in the camp to deal with. Because the family had not migrated to their winter pastures, the reindeer cooped up inside the fence chewed at the earth virtually all the way down to the rock.

***

The month of heavy snowfall was near and the men had to decide how they could survive it. They gathered for that purpose in Kheno's great chum. I was there, too.

I had uttered few words these past days, and the more time passed, the less I saw any need for words. A silence came over me, and I paid little heed to these people as they talked about matters that I did not much understand and which seemed lamentably alien to me. Even these people themselves were alien to me, and I saw them as only another twist in my inexplicable life. I had no intention of taking advantage of the veneration and fear they showed me, I was simply ready for them to vanish just as they had come.

I was not far from the truth in this. Once the people had regained their composure after that night of slaughter, they no longer thought of this outsider as their true leader, albeit an unusual one. Yando, who had volunteered to become my dog, went on living the same life he always had. The old men would bring me the choicest portion of the meat, but if they asked me any questions, it was only for the sake of showing honor.

I remember one of the old men asking me something. Instead of replying I stood up and walked out of the chum.

"Don't mind him," Lidyang told the astonished elders. "I've heard about such people: when time comes to don armor, a demon settles inside them, and in battle each of those men is worth a whole army. But when the war is over, such a man falls into a funk, he lives separately from the others and can't even feed himself. They serve him meat then on a long skewer – they're afraid that he'll attack, like a stray dog."

"And he doesn't attack them?" one bald old man asked.

Lidyang smiled. "I don't think he is as rabid as the ones I've heard about. Plus, we've got so many women…"

The men all laughed at once and flashed their toothless gums.

Lidyang was no longer smiling, however. He went on talking about the women in their encampment, who were too many for such a small number of breadwinners.

"Those women who came here from other tribes and clans can return to their native encampments," Lidyang said. "But we'll talk about that later, after we have survived the winter." After a pause he added, "If any of the women are fated to survive, let it be the daughters of our blood to whom we brought suitors. They are the bones that the flesh of our new family will grow around."

The old men stared unblinking at Lidyang, so amazed were they at his wisdom.

The bride

Late at night I left the chum where the meeting had been held.

It was a sense of melancholy that drove me out. It had pursued me for several days like a persistent foe, and when it caught up with me, I sought refuge in solitude and darkness. The coals in my hearth gleamed here and there. I watched the fire grow colder but did not blow on the coals. Then something nudged me inside – I took my weapons, got on my skis, and set off by moonlight.

I was prevented from getting away, however.

The sky was still dark and crazy Watane, whose little chum stood on the outskirts of the encampment, came running up to my dwelling with a wooden plate. A half-gnawed bone smoked on it. These plates were her longtime obsession, as every member of Kheno's family knew.

The clan had kept Watane fed all these years after her husband's death, but now, when she was soft in the head, she invariably ate only a small portion of what she was offered. She would bring most of the food to the young suitors who had come from other families. The widow was sure that these poor young men would die of starvation before they could ever marry a daughter of Kheno's family. She referred to these young men as her children and proffered food to them twice daily. The young men would laugh and tap their noses, a gesture that indicated that the old woman was not right in the head. The widow would laugh together with them, tap her own nose, and leave the food there at their feet. Once the sun was up, she would come running to those young men again.

Only Lar, whose hunger was never-ending, never refused the widow's morsels. In fact, he asked her to bring more.

Watane would then steal food, because her own food did not suffice, and when there was nowhere to steal it from, she would grab it right out of the boiling pot. For this she was beaten several times, but she shrugged it off and continued to grab piping hot food with her fingers. Boys were given the task of driving the mad old woman away from the poles where meat had been hung to dry. Watane then simply sat down and waited from the boys to wander off, or she hovered around them like a wolverine around a dying elk, muttering curses in a language that she had almost forgotten by now.

She could never feed Lar enough.

When he died, Watane lay under his bier that had been lifted up into the branches. She remained there for several days, until from hunger and a sense of grief beyond anyone's ken she died a sort of death. People brought her back home. Many were convinced that she would die, but she lived on.

When the disaster struck the encampment, people forgot all about her. I was unaware at the time that she had been trying to bring me food with the same zeal as she had served it to Sunbeam's fiancé. Each time, however, the women drove her away from my chum. Watane therefore decided to try to feed me at the crack of dawn, when she thought the encampment would be sleeping.

On this morning, no one stood in her way. She threw back the door of my chum and saw that it was empty. She backed away slightly, set the plate down on the snow, and was prepared simply to wait, when she saw two stripes departing into the taiga. The trail led towards a swaying figure in the distance. In the dim predawn light she could make out the bow and spear on my back, and she therefore supposed that this person had set off on a long journey, perhaps for ever.

Watane got up, grabbed the plate, and ran after my tracks. She plunged into snow up to her knees and cried, "Sonny, stop! Why are you leaving? Who's going to feed you? Sonny!"

The women came pouring out of their dwellings as if they had been waiting for that cry. They gathered into a swarm and rushed towards my chum, and subsequently after my ski tracks. I heard shouting behind me, but I felt so indifferent to them that I did not quicken my pace. As my legs worked in turn, my feelings of melancholy abated and did not torment me so much.

Unlike the men who had treated me with honor and an anxious cautiousness, the women saw in me a higher being, a messenger sent by some unknown entity that could both kill and save.

They were afraid to ignite my wrath, but they were even more afraid of me abandoning them.

The women got on their own skis. As they set off, they knocked widow Watane over and sent her wooden plate flying into the snow. Once they had caught up with me, they surrounded me. They rolled in the snow and grabbed the tips of their skis with their fingers. Were it not for woman's perennial fear of touching a weapon and thereby depriving it of its power, they would have pulled out bows, spears, and arrows and carried me back to the encampment.

I said nothing to them. I could kill these women and regard it as an ordinary thing. It was melancholy that was spurring me to run off, but in fact I was like a cobweb floating through the air that could be stopped by the first branch along its path.

Watane pushed her way through the crowd and then grabbed my bow. The women fell silent and seemed numb. At the widow's feet was the plate with the bone on it, now covered in snow. Without letting go of the weapon, Watane raised the plate up and said:

"Come on. First I'll feed you with my own two hands, and then you can go if you want."

I followed meekly behind her like a reindeer calf.

The women started walking in turn. The widow's comportment had frightened them just as much as their idol's attempt to leave. One of them came up with an idea to console them all: the spirits surely knew that Watane was soft in the head, so they would not get angry that my weapons had been defiled so.

The women did not bother to tell the elderly men about what Watane had done.

I returned to my chum, put my weapons down, took my jumper off, and fell asleep. I did not even touch the plate with the half-gnawed bone which had been left by my bed.

***

On that same day, one wise old woman – it was she who assumed that the spirits would not be angry at Watane's antics – went to Lidyang, her cousin, in order to talk about Wenga's attempt to leave.

"He simply decided to go hunting, and you didn't let him," Lidyang suggested.

"No, that's not it," the old woman muttered. "I saw him, it was like his heart had been removed. He is like an empty body where whoever wants can live there. Except now no one is living there."

Lidyang froze. His sister had repeated almost exactly his remark the day before about the rabid warrior.

"He's feeling down?"

"It's not that," the old woman answered. "He's not feeling anything at all. He has never really lived at all, as if he were captured and enslaved before he was even born."

"Does that really happen?"

"Such things happen as you couldn't even fathom, you old pile of bear scat. But I'll say it again: he's empty inside."

Lidyang and the old woman stared at one another for a long time. Finally Lidyang smiled and said warily, "If he's empty inside, then let someone settle in there."

These words were like a big, juicy piece of fat to this old woman's ears. She smiled and repeated her tease that had annoyed Lidyang back when they were children: "You heap of bear scat…"

***

At twilight that same day, the old woman headed towards my chum.

Not far away, Watane wandered like a lost dog, an empty plate in her hands. Her face was smeared with soot from the hearth, and the locks of her dirty gray hair turned in the wind like slender serpents.

"You there, scram!" the wise old woman said without rancor and stamped her feet.

The widow quickly moved several feet away.

The wise old woman entered into the soul of the empty man as resolutely as she crossed the threshold. She had come to Lidyang with an already formed plan in mind, she only needed it to be said out loud by male lips – then it would be a man's bold decision and not a mere woman's whim.

Over that day she had prepared everything. She got right to the point without any sweeping speeches:

"You are a small person, but great in spirit. It would be hard to find a girl that is a true match for you. But I found one."

The old woman ran to the door, threw back the flap, and shouted out into the twilight:

"Come on!"

An instant later, the forward part of the chum was packed with women. They all stood and waited to be called on. The old woman put some wood onto the fireplace, fed the fire a chunk of meat and, after muttering a brief prayer, she blew the flames hotter.

"Why are you here?" I asked.

Instead of an answer, the crowd of women parted and one woman was pushed towards the fire. She wore an ornate fox-trimmed parka embroidered with pearls. The old woman began to strike one palm against the other in an even rhythm, and the women began to clap after her.

"Well, then?" the old woman shouted.

The girl threw back her hood – the lush fur fell onto her shoulders.

The girl danced.

The women clapped faster and faster, while the old woman blew the fire hotter and screeched like a goose, always keeping an eye on me – she seemed overjoyed.

The one she felt so sorry for, the one who she said was empty inside, was staring with fascination at the girl.

***

She was Kheno's favorite granddaughter.

When the girl reached a suitable age for betrothal, the old man called her parents and said that there was no hurry to choose a fiancé for her, because such an exquisite face – white like mammoth ivory, eyes that could only be compared to sacred pools, a little round mouth – and slender body like the handle of an Ostyak knife meant that she could demand a high bride-price and wait for the very best offer. A family with a girl like that possesses wealth equal to many fine things: such wealth can make for great stability or buy one's way out of trouble.

From that time on, the patriarch's granddaughter had been waiting for a destiny that was unlike that of any other girl in that huge and happy family. Her expectation of future happiness was not dimmed even by the death of her parents – their boat overturned in the middle of a river and the icy waters swept her mother and father away. Springtime Girl fell into orphanhood but was caught, as if she landed on soft, deep moss, by the endless doting of her respected grandfather, and she soon got over her grief.

***

At the old woman's sign, the women stopped clapping and began, all of them except the girl, to file out of the chum. Before the old woman herself left, she bent over and whispered excitedly into my ear:

"There won't be a trace of your doldrums left, warrior. She will bear you many strong children. I am sure of that."

After the old woman said this, she vanished as if she had never been there at all.

"Who are you?" I asked.

"Nara," the girl answered.

***

Many things have faded from my memory, but that day when I first laid eyes on her I remember as clearly as if it were yesterday.

I had nothing, not even a past. After the secret which Man-Effigy had revealed to me, after Lar's death, everything had gone wrong – even the sunny days of early childhood that sometimes came back to me in brief and vague flashes. All that were left were distant memories of Springtime Girl, whose soul was blended with mine and Lar's.

When I heard this girl's name, I started – I felt some inexplicable presentiment within me. That name took on new life…

And then something happened that I could hardly have expected, because I did not even know it existed. She laid down next to me, still in her clothes, and as she turned away from me she said, "I won't let you undo my belt today. Just so you know."

Kinsmen

Several days after fire had come back to the camp, a pack of wolves appeared on the outskirts of the encampment.

The wolves had come at the smell of hardship – they could distinguish it among the myriad other smells, because it got their wolf blood rushing. The smell of hardship heralded salvation for wolves before the terrible month of heavy snowfall, when the taiga is covered in soft drifts and wolves plunge into the snow up to their ears. At that time any small prey whatsoever, be it a partridge or a hare, seems heaven-sent.

The pack descended like a dark cloud and by morning they had surrounded the reindeer paddock.

Lidyang was the first person to spot the wolves.

Snow swirled over the paddock. The herds had begun to run in circles like a ferocious whirlpool. Several wolves came climbing over into the paddock and chased the reindeer, while the others kept a distance an arrow's flight away, like men at war.

Some dark objects lay by the fence. The old man knew, without any need to take a closer look, that these were reindeer carcasses that the wolves had been unable to drag through the paddock's enclosure.

Lidyang ran towards the encampment and cursed his old legs as he went. He beat the chums with his tent and shouted, "Wolves! Bring your weapons!" Without waiting for assistance to arrive, he ran to his own chum, grabbed his own bow and quiver, and rushed back to the paddock. By the time Yando arrived, with three old men behind me, Lidyang had shot nearly all of his arrows, but none had hit their targets. The wolves that had made a bloodbath inside the paddock, vanished. While Lidyang was summoning the others from the encampment, the initial two reindeer carcasses were joined by four more. The wolves had dragged one out of the paddock and tore the fence down as they did. The pack itself had vanished – only when the dim, pale sun rose over the hill could people make out an even column of light gray specks, almost too faint to see. Yando grabbed his bow and an arrow and, without saying anything to the elders, went ahead. A barely noticeable ripple passed through the frozen ranks.

"Where are you going, you wolverine?" Lidyang cried. "You think they're going to wait for you to catch up? Any one of them is twice as smart as you."

Yando spat and turned around. The men said nothing.

"Where did such a huge pack of wolves come from?" one of the old men finally spoke up. "I have never seen such a pack in all my life."

No one replied to that. Yando's voice broke the silence:

"What are we afraid of? We do have a great warrior with us, after all."

"I won't even waste my spit on that remark," Lidyang said with contempt. "Even if Nga himself were among us, those wolves won't leave us alone until we start dropping from exhaustion and can't guard the herd any more. Then they can kill as many reindeer as they want."

Lidyang's remark was so devastatingly simple and true that the old men did not even notice the blasphemy. The wolf pack seemed to possess not only huge numbers but great intelligence, too – every member of it, down to the last cub, knew that Kheno's family was now almost bereft of men capable of running fast and long, and so there was no one to pursue them, surround them, and kill them in the snow.

"They won't leave us alone," Lidyang said.

"What should we do?" the old man with the shiny bald head asked.

"I don't know." After a brief pause, he went on, "They won't leave us alone, so we need to leave from here. At least then we can save what reindeer remain."

"In just a few days the heavy snowfall is going to come, and then the great cold," another old man spoke up. "Who would dare move camp in such weather?"

"Someone who doesn't want to die."

"You are too clever, Lidyang, and you only believe in yourself. Kheno would complain about that…"

Lidyang turned to face the speaker and repeated the late patriarch's favorite retort:

"If you know of something better, say it."

"I do!" the old man raised his voice. "We are members of a great clan. Have you forgotten? Can't we call on our relatives? They would help us!"

"Like they helped us find Nokho?"

The old man fell silent for a moment; he was unsure what to say to that. Finally, he cried, "It was Mother Fire herself who punished Nokho, she settled into the body of that puny lad! Are you blind? Can't you see? If the Mother thought it more convenient to punish him through someone else instead, she would have done so. And everyone respected Kheno…"

"Especially when he had forty young warriors, not even counting the old, and so much wealth that he never skimped on gifts," Lidyang said with the same contempt.

***

The old man shook his head angrily and walked away. But after some time passed, he proved right.

All of the old men, except for those too weak to pull a bowstring all the way to their shoulder, were assigned to guard the paddock.

Lidyang entered the outsider's chum, where a woman was already keeping house, and said, "There are wolves. We need to save the herd. Help us."

I got up without saying a word, took my weapons, and set off after the old man.

A path had been blazed through the encampment: the women brought wood to the paddock on hand-drawn sleds, so that at night a fire would scare the wolves off. The inhabitants of the encampment wanted to hold on until the morning, and then send a messenger to their wider relatives to ask for help. This messenger, as Lidyang decided and the rest of the elders tacitly agreed, would be Yando. He had strong young legs and knew these parts well. He was to leave before dawn, so that he could reach the other encampment by sundown: the family living there was led by a man named Noynoba, which meant "Gauntlet". Even if his family had migrated elsewhere, it would be nearby and Yando could catch up with them. Another day would be needed for him to return with that assistance.

Yando rushed through the encampment like a puppy who needed to get all its excessive friskiness out of its paws. He grabbed at things that he did not really need, and he tried to run after the pack of wolves himself, which annoyed the elders.

Such had been his behavior the night before, when the young lady with the exquisite face had entered my chum.

By midday, there was no longer any need for him to set out: Noynoba's people came to us instead.

Noynoba was a close neighbor to Kheno and about the same age. He had been the first to receive the gifts and hear of the disaster that had struck one of the biggest and most respected families in the entire Nga clan.

It was true what Kheno had sadly concluded: neither Noynoba nor any other relatives whom their messengers reached, began to waste the precious autumn days – so important for stockpiling food – on searching for the rogue whom Mother Fire had cursed. They kept on doing what they were doing, only they did not allow any strangers in their encampments.

Only Noynoba remembered that his neighbors were in peril, and before he led his small family and relatively meager herd to their winter pastures, he sent his people to Kheno's territory. Noynoba comforted himself by saying that the strength and piety of that family would allow them to overcome their hardship. But no news of such salvation arrived, Kheno's people did not come to see Noynoba's, and the old man first felt pangs of guilt, then a burning curiosity.

He sent four fully-equipped warriors. They were led by a giant of a man who bore the Tungus name Yekha, in memory of his father who was a member of that tattoo-faced people. Many years ago that tattoo-faced man had come into their Yurak family for the sake of a lovely young lady, this warrior's mother. The previous autumn Yekha's father was taken by the taiga – he went hunting and never returned.

In order to avoid any need for the warriors to resort to an outright lie, Noynoba ordered that Kheno be told that his people had seen no trace of the cursed lad, but not a word more. The relative that enjoyed such great esteem would assume that Noynoba had not forgotten his request, and had searched for the crazy lad, who had undoubtedly already been killed by some man or animal, or just froze to death to the delight of the crows and wolverines.

When the women saw their neighbors, they burst into tears. The elders bowed to the warriors as if the latter were their seniors.

Kheno had taught his family never to believe in coincidence – the unexpected arrival of Noynoba's men left them convinced once again that, in spite of the harsh lesson, the supernatural powers had not abandoned their devotees.

What Yekha and his companions saw with their own eyes, and heard from the confused account of the elders, freed them from any need to convey Noynoba's message, which they themselves had been loathe to do.

Yando brought the tale of their woe to its conclusion:

"Now we have a great warrior among us!"

He pointed at me. I was standing half an arrow's flight away, but I heard everything.

Yekha the giant squinted towards where Yando had indicated. "Where's the warrior?" he asked.

"Right there in front of you," Yando replied. "There's no one else there, is there?"

The man with the Tungus name stopped squinting and said, puzzled, "That's a mere boy…"

Now Lidyang spoke up, "Yes, that's right." He told the visitors what he already told his own family, about the warrior whose empty soul was inhabited by a ferocious, martial demon.

The kinsmen listened to the old man's words in silence. They had nothing to say in reply to that, just like everything else they had seen and heard on this day. The death of the patriarch and the men of this family, the strongest in the whole clan, hung over their thoughts like a thick fog.

Lidyang could see into these men and he did not allow that fog to settle – he immediately moved on to the pack of wolves that was like nothing they had ever seen before. He spoke loudly and to the point, as if commanding a battle. This lofty speech distracted Yekha, who forgot all about his intention to examine the unassuming warrior more closely.

Yekha looked at the sun and said, "We'll get them by sunset."

***

Now there were seven men in the encampment who were capable of a great hunt – Noynoba's four warriors, Yando, myself, and old Lidyang who assured everyone that he could keep up.

We stood in a semicircle, each two dozen paces from the next, and headed down the gentle slope into the valley where the trail of pawprints led. We ran as fast as we could, in order to reach the wolves before the valley narrowed and was lost in the narrow space between the hills.

Yekha ran next to me and I could see that he covered in a single step a distance that took me four. This amused the giant. He moderated his pace, came nearer to me, and said, "I want to hear how your arrows sing!"

I was expending nearly all my energy on running, and I could only reply angrily, "You will!"

We caught up with the pack just before it would have been able to hide among the forested foot of the hills. Lidyang was the first to stop and shoot off an arrow – the black feather was a blur against the sky and then fell a dozen paces from the trailing wolf in the pack.

Yekha and his men, who were standing at the edges, launched their arrows as they ran. The pack could sense that a strong and dangerous foe was at hand, and it began to spread out across what remained of the open ground. But their foe was experienced, ran swiftly, and shot accurately, and it would not allow the gray blotch to get away. One of the wolves already lay in the snow, while another ran with the feathered shafts of arrows sticking out of it.

"Find the leader of the pack," Lidyang shouted. He was clearly growing fatigued.

The leader, the wolf with a slight hump on its back and a white mark on its side, revealed itself. When its pursuers could see only the tails of the other wolves in the pack as they ran, the leader stopped, turned to face the enemy, and bared its fangs as if threatening revenge.

It ran forward slightly, and then turned around. The other wolves immediately did the same. In an instant, bared fangs replaced the tails we had watched running away. The entire pack might have stopped, and then things would get difficult for a group of humans with empty quivers. Two of Noynoba's men had already hung their bows on their backs and were reaching for their spears.

But something else was in store for the wolves.

The leader appeared right in front of me. I saw its face – it looked almost like that of the young Ostyak slave, only closer and clear – and the same force that compelled me to act before my mind even realized the necessity to do so, made me stop, raise my bow, and shoot.

The arrow pierced the front of the leader's head. It collapsed in the snow and moved no more.

My shot attracted the others' attention. The pursuers all froze. The gray patch took advantage of that momentary confusion: the wolves spread out, then separated into several smaller packs that now reached the foot of the hills.

Only one of the creatures was moving in the opposite direction to this general flight. It was a she-wolf. She ran to where the leader of the pack lay. Arrows jutted from the earth along her path and nearly pierced her paws, but the she-wolf moved with no concern for death.

We now walked leisurely – none of the men had any arrows left. The she-wolf rushed forward to do precisely what she had run towards death to do: she licked the eyes of her slain mate and then, squatting on her hind legs, she gave a thin howl, as if it were a woman wailing.

Once the human beings came close, the she-wolf ran back towards the hills.

"Your arrows sing beautifully," Yekha said to me.

One of Noynoba's men suggested that I take the slain wolf. I pointed with my bow towards the departing she-wolf.

"This is hers."

Again Yekha's mocking voice came, "The great warrior has no need for glory?" The giant with the Tungus name took the dead wolf's body and threw it over his shoulder as if it were a mere fox fur.

We walked the whole way back in silence. Only Yando ran ahead and filled the space around us, on which dusk was now descending, with a joyful cry.

He rejoiced, but not quite at that successful hunt. Together with Yekha, the bright idea had come to him that now the small and unsociable stranger's skills of waging war would inevitably be tested. This presentiment brought a tingling warmth that spread through his body, and the creaking of the snow under his skis barely drowned the beating of his heart.

Yando hated me.

The men arrived back by night. They greedily ate hot meat and listened to the old men's anxious talk about the dark line along the lower edge of the sky, which portended that the month of heavy snowfall was near.

The feast

The giant from Noynoba's family felt no hatred for the little man whom the others had called a great warrior.

He himself was so strong that there was no need for him to hate anyone. But the tale of two furious youths wiping out a whole host of strong men, kindled his curiosity. To satisfy it, Yekha sought some pretext for a quarrel. However, I kept aloof from the others and said nothing, and men of the taiga were not accustomed to challenging someone to a fight just because of an angry look.

Yando spent all morning hovering around Yekha with a look of slavish devotion and admiration. Yando praised his weapons, asked him about his hunting achievements and other exploits, and the son of the tattoo-faced Tungus finally realized that Yando sought the same thing he did. Yekha took his admirer lightly by the hood of his parka, as if handling a suckling puppy, and led him to a distant chum.

At the corners of his eyes, lines appeared that resembled the prints of little birds. He breathed deeply and resembled a boy who had secretly got ahold of his father's bow. None of Kheno's people knew that in Noynoba's family, they all laughed at this son of a Tungus who had grown so huge that draught reindeer collapsed under him, but who, instead of thinking about marriage and amassing possessions, could spent a whole day by an anthill imagining another life.

The laughter died when Yekha had clad himself in iron. "Did that runt really kill half of your men here?" he asked.

"No, Nokho did. He only killed a few and then he killed Nokho. He flew at Nokho with a spear – he hardly touched the ground – and he cut off his head."

"They say there's a spirit dwelling inside him…"

"Yes, the spirit got revenge for his brother, who died in our encampment."

"Died?"

"He was killed."

"By whom?"

"By me and my brothers." Yando stated this truth with evident satisfaction.

Yekha whistled in astonishment. "So how are you still alive?"

"Clearly that spirit was sated by my brothers' deaths. Khetanzi got hit by an arrow, Mydwano died from a wound in his side. I promised that I would become like his dog, just like all of Kheno's people did."

"And did you?"

"Our people, the old men and women, almost worship him like a god. After all, he brought fire back. They gave him their best bride, the one they were saving for some prince. What is he going to do with her?" Yando laughed; it sounded like a hiccup. "But a god should show his strength, and only then will people worship him."

With no fear at all Yando grabbed the giant man by his jumper, pulled him close and whispered, "The old men are saying that we need to leave here, move closer to our kinsmen, so that together we can survive till spring, and then whatever happens, happens. Those are wise words. We will leave soon and take the herd with us. They'll try to convince you and your people to help us, and you'll agree – after all, you've got a good heart. Now, listen to me: tell the elders that they should arrange a big feast before we say goodbye to this place. Here, at our summer encampment, where the umbilical cords of many of Kheno's people were buried. The bones of our ancestors are here, too, and who knows when we'll ever come back. Tell them that. You're a great warrior, they won't refuse you. Let there be a feast. One with pots boiling, games, tournaments…"

Yekha shook off the hand that clutched his chest. "If you are a dog, then you are the smartest of all."

Yando beamed. He sensed that the giant had readily accepted his idea.

"And the mangiest of all," Yekha finished. He walked towards the middle of the encampment, a song on his lips. He liked Yando's idea.

***

The elders liked that idea, too. Yekha did not even have to convince them of it.

"We are an unworthy people," Lidyang said, "and we have forgotten about the lord of our great clan. Death came close but did not swallow us up, and we have not done anything to thank Nga for that. Fortune is kind to people with kind thoughts. There is a black reindeer in the paddock, the wolves didn't get it."

The elders nodded in approval. Only one remained frozen, the one who had quarreled with Lidyang at the paddock on the day when the wolf pack appeared. "Only poor folk slaughter a black reindeer," he said. After a pause he went on, "Kheno would never allow such a disgrace. He would haul you out of here by the beard."

"Perhaps you can suggest a worthier sacrifice?" Lidyang replied, with overt contempt.

The old man turned away and sniffed loudly. He was related to Lidyang not only by blood but also by long years of mutual hostility. In their younger days the hostility had never quite led to a fight, however, and now, as it had grown older, it was capable only of producing some offensive remarks and hateful looks.

Nevertheless, the mention that such a sacrifice might be unworthy raised a hubbub among the elders. Yekha interrupted it:

"Calm down, esteemed elders," he said. "We're going to have a real feast, and that means some real tournaments. Warriors' fun is never harmless, even when we don't have too many warriors now. We are all related in the end, though we come from different families. Perhaps one of us will have the honor of going to the encampment of our great lord and telling him how much we esteem him."

The elders fell silent, amazed by the intelligence of this man with a Tungus name.

All the same, Lidyang went to get the black reindeer. He slaughtered it himself and, as he intoned the required words, he sprinkled the ground at sunset.

***

The next morning was clear, with not a cloud in the sky. The snow in the paddock was pink from reindeer blood. Pots were carried out of the chums. A meaty steam floated over the dwellings. The women – crones, young widows, girls – sang the song of the Loon Bird, who had brought in its beak a pinch of earth that served as the beginning of the firmament. The boys measured their strength against one another and butted heads like young reindeer bulls. Sleds were already lined up and waiting for contestants to jump over them. The men ate and wiped their fingers on their hair.

"It's a good feast," the elders said.

The look in their eyes, however, was a sad one.

Lidyang leapt up and took off his jumper in a single motion. His skin was the color of reindeer hide, and under it his weakened but still formidable muscles flexed. His chest hung like a thin fold over his scrawny belly. When the women saw the old man naked, they turned away and pressed their hands over their mouths to keep the laughter inside; the oldest of them chortled shamelessly. Lidyang was deaf to this. He put his arms out like a bear and jumped around near the fire, wagging the thin tuft of his beard and shouting, "Who is it going to be, then?" The men stayed rooted to their places, they assumed that the old man was joking.

Lidyang grabbed Yando by the arm, lifted him to his feet, and ripped off his clothes like the skin from a burbot. "You whelp, you pile of bear scat, come vie against an old man!"

Yando put out his arms and pretended that he was getting ready for the fight. He smiled, looked around, clapped his hands, and by all accounts looked happy to amuse his relatives.

But anger now rang more clearly in Lidyang's voice. "What are you prancing around in front of me like that for? I'm not some old woman. Why don't you turn your pants inside out and show everyone that they're still dry. Come on!"

His young opponent was slight in build but strong. He realized that this bout was a serious one. He still had the same goofy smile on his face, but now his body tensed and became a mass of smooth muscles. His legs stepped lightly and precisely. He lunged, but his arms grabbed only air. Lidyang effortlessly avoided the attempt, and with a deft motion he came at Yando from the rear and gave his opponent a resounding kick. Yando went down into the snow face-first.

The encampment erupted with hearty laughter.

Yando was momentarily blinded by rage, but he got ahold of himself. He knew what to do: he leapt to his feet, put on the same old smile, and quickly bowed to the people around him.

"Fight for real!" they shouted at him.

Just like the bowstring endows the arrow with its killing force, so he rushed at the old man, but even while he was still flying, an ethereal light flashed in his head and darkness again came over him. Lidyang had, with his long, hard palms, clapped him over the ears.

When Yando regained senses, he heard the same laughter. But now two dark streams flowed from his nose and fell onto his belly.

Lidyang walked up and lifted his head by the chin. "You still alive?"

Yando nodded.

"Then be happy. It's not you who will be going to Nga."

Before the bout there had been no discussion of what the prize for the winner would be, but the old man with the bald pate removed from his belt an embroidered suede bag with his flint inside, placed it into Lidyang's hand, and closed the latter's fingers around it.

The men jumped up and shouted. Yando shouted, too.

Next, two of Noynoba's warriors took their jumpers off. The young widows forgot all about the necessary decorum and shrieked. The boys, too, were antsy with anticipation. But while the two strong men fought, the people's eyes increasingly looked towards the giant with the Tungus name.

Yekha could feel their gazes on him. He already knew the words that he would pronounce when the current fight was over.

The strange young man who had stoked his curiosity for several days now, sat opposite him and chewed on meat with an air of indifference.

The fight came to an end, but by now no one was paying any attention to it. Everyone was waiting for Yekha, and he said:

"Why is the great warrior bored?"

People turned their eyes at me, but the giant continued to speak.

"I know the answer: wrestling is for little kids. That's why the great warrior is bored. Maybe Dog's Ear – that is his name, isn't it? – would like to choose some fun he feels worthy of him?"

I knew that sooner or later Yekha would want to test me. His eyes and his mocking tone of speech had made that clear from the day he arrived at the encampment. But I felt no fear of this massive person, probably because he was too far away from ordinary human beings. I could refuse that trial as easily as I could accept it. I laid my half-gnawed bone down in the snow, wiped my lips with my hand, and said, "If you're looking for fun, then ask the children for one of their toys."

Yekha smiled widely in reply, but I caught a twitch in his face.

Now I know that it was not the boldness of my words that made the man with the Tungus name shudder, rather it was the sound of my voice that offended him. Yekha had grown accustomed to cowardice on the part of his opponents; even those who put on a big act and shouted the usual insults before a bout, were concealing their fear behind this boldness. Yekha could detect that fear among a myriad of other sounds, and he had long since reassured himself that no one was fearless before him. He was generous and never humiliated anyone for refusing to come out against him.

In this voice, however, he did not find what he was used to finding, and the giant shuddered to hear something he had almost forgotten entirely.

Yekha was embarrassed at this brief moment of weakness. Without wiping the smile from his face, he spoke quietly, as if to himself, but nevertheless so that everyone around him could hear:

"Some supernatural force made you like their toothpick: they had feasted on grief and then used you to clean their teeth – and then threw you away. Perhaps on your own you are a mere coward, a hollow block of wood, and you're conning these poor people?"

Silence hung over the crowd. One of the women gasped. Watane, dirty and disheveled, came forward and squatted like a dog in the snow. Her breathing was rapid, her gaze darted about the scene like that of a wounded, dying animal.

Yando stood up opposite Yekha, beat his chest, and said loudly, "Don't take it as an insult, dear kinsman, but that great warrior is showing mercy on you." He then said nothing for a moment and waited for an answer, but before any came he ended with the words he had already prepared in advance. "It's a pity that the brother of the great warrior is not among us. He would have challenged you to show your strength himself. Lar loved the games that strong men play, though he was no strong man himself."

After these words the bald-headed elder gasped. Lidyang froze, and even his thin beard did not stir in the wind.

Yekha himself was breathless for a moment, amazed as he was at Yando's serpent-like cunning. "Thanks for mentioning that, brother," the giant said in a tone as sweet as birch sap. "But my curiosity fell onto the bed of green grass along with me when I came from the womb, and perhaps even earlier. I was so curious to see the fellow who slew half of the warriors in Kheno's big family, I couldn't sleep or eat, I couldn't do anything. I'm ready to give up the iron I'm wearing – and it's the finest Ostyak iron – and my weapons. Maybe that prize will help the great warrior quit showing such unnecessary mercy?"

"Wenga!"

It was Lidyang who shouted – and now it was I who shuddered, for I heard my own name spoken for the first time in all these days. Kheno's people referred to me as "the great warrior" and nothing else, as if they were afraid to disturb my name that might prove apt.

"What are you going to wager?" The old man spoke loud and clear. His words hung in the air like a resounding slap in the face.

Before I could come up with a reply, something incredible happened that neither Kheno's people, nor I myself could have predicted: this affair of men was now interrupted by a woman, it was Nara.

She stepped forth out of the crowd of her relatives, sat down in the middle of the circle, and said, "Besides me, he owns no other property."

She uttered not a single word more, and the people, astonished, each quietly thought their own thoughts.

Lidyang was the first to break this silence. "Would she suit you as a prize?" he asked Yekha.

"Certainly," the giant replied. He jumped to his feet and stood at his full height.

The fact that if he were to win, he, a relative, albeit a distant one and moreover half Tungus, might wed his own flesh, was not something Yekha was thinking of at that moment. No one was.

While everyone was silent, I stared at that woman who had been given to me to lift my spirits, and I expected her to look at me, too. But Nara's gaze was directed somewhere above everyone's heads, and though I saw only part of her face, I sensed that all her strength at that moment was directed to holding back her tears. Suddenly something welled up within me: my will to live had returned.

"My weapons are in the chum," I said.

"I'll wait," the giant replied amiably. He always had his own bow and quiver with him.

But before I had managed to take several steps, my weapons were already in my hands – Yando had brought them and handed them to me, beaming a smile. "I did promise to be your dog," he said.

***

The two opponents walked out of the encampment, to an open space where the men of Kheno's family used to amuse themselves by "catching arrows".

Those men who really knew how to catch arrows in flight, lived so long ago that they were now mere legend. Only the name of this pastime remained, though it was now something harmless and simple for the people of the taiga. Two opponents would stand opposite one another at a distance just over half a arrow's flight. Each would then shoot in turn at the other a blunt-tipped *tomar*, the sort used for taking down ermines, martens, and squirrels.

But among the Nga people, such a pastime was considered something silly. In many families adolescent males were made to stand under real arrows, so that they would gain the same experience as their fathers and lose their fear of death.

The Nga people took even their games seriously. Surprisingly, however, so rarely did anyone die in these trials that few could remember such cases. However, they did remember something else: the showdowns that were sparked by an insult or some hard and irresolvable dispute never ended just like that. Among the Nga people, such a fight was measured not by the number of arrows launched – as lesser peoples do – but by the death of the guilty party, for the blame always went to the loser.

This time, wise Lidyang had found a middle ground: he announced a total of ten shots and ensured that each of us had only three iron-tipped arrows. Yekha dared not complain, after all, he was a guest there.

"Even more fun," he said as he accepted the *tomar* arrows from the old man. To even things out for his opponent, the giant took off his jumper, then pulled his chain mail, its plates sparkling, over his head and hung it on the trunk of a bent, dead birch tree.

Lidyang clicked his tongue as he looked at the armor. "One could happily pay fifty reindeer for something like that."

"My father got it somewhere," Yekha said as he put his jumper back on. "I don't know where and how."

Lidyang came up to me. "Don't be shy, now," the old man whispered with a slight smile. "Yekha's big, it'll be easy to hit him. You are thin and much shorter." Then he fell silent. I could see that Lidyang was gathering his strength to say something important. "Tell me, is it in you now, that spirit?"

"What spirit?"

"The one that killed Nokho."

"I don't know…"

"Maybe you can call it to you?"

"Spirits choose their own battles to fight. If it wants, it will come."

Lidyang's smile vanished. He asked no more questions but only said, "Nara is a woman of our blood. She can be only your wife. Try to win."

"That was your gift, not anything I chose," I replied, without even looking at the old man.

***

Nara was not among the people who had come to the site of our showdown. She stood alone in the encampment, where a gentle wind turned her wet cheeks to ice. The patriarch had promised her a prince, the most magnificent man under the sun, but the "prince" turned out to be someone as slight as a child. Nara understood that the disaster that had fallen on the family was to blame – it had taken her grandfather away before his time.

But Springtime Girl was wracked with resentment against her relatives who had given her to the odd stranger, as if she were a mere slave and not Kheno's favorite granddaughter. That hit her especially on the day when a wise old woman came into her chum and imperiously announced the girl's fate: she saw here the others' revenge for all the doting that she alone had received from the patriarch of the family. Nara followed after the old woman submissively and silently, and did as she was told. Somewhere deep inside she hoped that her humiliating dance in front of the slight and unsociable stranger would win her some pity, if not from that old crone then at least from the other women. Those women, however, did not see her sorrow and were quite content, she could see it on their faces. Nara did not worship the stranger as a god who had brought salvation from death, along with the slaughter of their men, but in everything that had happened she knew one thing: the great fortune that had been promised to her would never come.

When she lay next to me, she hoped for my eventual death. Several days later, that longing for my death led her to do something unspeakably brazen: to make herself the prize for the winner, who would undoubtedly be the giant from Noynoba's family.

But during these same days, something else happened: Nara felt an ineffable presentiment that a great change would come. This presentiment arose from a look the stranger gave her, one that she would never forget. The stranger seemed to be looking into her eyes and not just admiring her beauty, but detecting there something higher than beauty. No man had ever looked at her like that before. Though she continued to harbor ill will towards her bridegroom, that look remained in her mind – on the contrary, it began to reside there alongside her resentment and was so persistent that there was soon no room left for resentment. Nara tried to shrug it off, she shook her head and even cried out whenever that look rose again before her in her mind, but the memory of that look was tenacious. Springtime Girl made an effort to revive her resentment, which she regarded as the reasonable emotion to feel. Yet the look would not leave her.

On the day of the showdown these opposing forces squared off inside her just like the men who were about to shoot arrows at one another. Resentment shot the first arrow and awaited the reply.

Nara's sunken eyes saw nothing but vague spots: white, brown, blue. She could not understand what was going on inside her, she did not even want to. She felt like she herself was merely an arena for a duel.

Now came the reply of resentment's foe.

Suddenly the tribe she had considered her own appeared before her and laughed with mouths open wide – mouths toothy and toothless, children's mouths – and Nara shuddered. That laughter surrounded her on all sides, she was overcome by horror. Just as a beast, once surrounded, rushes about trying to find the slightest gap in the hunters' ranks, so that it might break free and live, so her soul did the same, and she saw that there was only one escape: the look in the stranger's eyes. It alone was not laughing, it alone had no desire for revenge. Run to that look, and then you would be saved, she thought. When Nara saw it with remarkable clarity, a new feeling of horror came over her: the person who would be her sole salvation, she herself had sent to certain death, and perhaps while she was standing there in the deserted encampment that death was imminent...

Nara's legs bore her swiftly towards the site of the showdown.

***

With her eyes so dulled, she could not see the sole man who stared at her from afar, who stared the whole time that the two opponents were setting up on the field. That man's soul, too, was riven by a presentiment such that his clenched lips turned white and he could barely hold back a cry.

It was Yando.

As he stared then at the girl with a body as slender as the handle of an Ostyak knife, he hated the whole world, and even more he hated old Kheno, who had made him and Nara blood kin. This hatred came in waves like a toothache.

But unlike many other people, Yando kept his wits about him even in shame and despair, and the faithful dog ran slightly ahead of his master.

The whistling of the first arrow soothed him.

***

That brief singing of the arrow was cut short by a dull, barely audible thump – as if a shaman, beginning his dialogue with his drum before going to visit the spirits, lightly struck the stretched skin with a finger.

Thus the *tomar* which I had shot hit the son of the Tungus man in the chest and then fell into the snow. Yekha had not even thought to dodge it.

"You lost, you big hunk of meat!" the bald-headed elder shouted.

Nobody spoke up to support the old man. Yekha drew his bow and now the eyes of the people gathered turned to his unassuming opponent.

I had just managed to set my weapon down and stand back up when an invisible whip burned across my shoulder and knocked me off my feet. Even after its flight had been weakened by the obstacle that I was, the *tomar* continued flying on behind me for a distance nearly equal to that separating me from the giant of Noynoba's family.

Yekha was satisfied, for that had been his very intention, to knock his opponent down without wounding him. A second thought came after the arrow was already on its way: with his next shot he would shatter his opponent's knee, and with the next – just to be sure – he would ravage his opponent's chest and leave him unable to breathe. Then his curiosity would be more than satisfied. He was confident of what he had guessed at: no raging spirit had settled into this youth, he was as empty as a hollow trunk. The people of Kheno's family would be convinced of that, too, and they would praise Yekha as the one who had opened their eyes.

The son of the Tungus man recalled also the prize that lay in store for him...

An instant later he nearly paid dearly for this daydreaming. A *tomar* roared past his right ear – his opponent had aimed for his head.

The giant felt a surge of righteous, martial anger and began aiming his next arrow. He held the tip of his arrow over the little fellow for a long time, as if he wanted to fix his target firmly. He aimed at a tiny point, one almost too small to see: his opponent's knee.

Clearly, however, the heart of the little *soning* had not fallen completely silent within me – I felt no fear, the heat of danger flooded over my body and let it sense every slight movement of the air.

I dodged the *tomar* with the only sure motion. Just as he had done, I aimed my next shot at Yekha's knee – and I hit him. The giant collapsed into the snow, and though I stood far away, I could see that his face was filled with true rage as he stood back up. I could see that rage whisper to him that he needed to draw an iron-tipped arrow from his quiver and put an end to these silly games.

This feeling then gave way to shame, however, and it was another *tomar* that Yekha took out.

As he made his sixth shot, he limped slightly in his left leg. His opponent remained unharmed, though Yekha was not at all amused by the fact that the little fellow dived down into the snow like a partridge.

One of the old men, excited by the spectacle, shouted, "Bring out the iron-tipped ones!"

The giant's hand reached for his quiver, though it was not even his turn to shoot.

I drew first a heavy arrow from my quiver, its tip resembled a swallow's tail. When it hit its target, it would remain inside the opponent's body and stubbornly drain the life out of it. But now my strength was fading, and my arm that held the bow trembled, so the shot ultimately flew far to Yekha's side.

The Tungus man's son prepared now to end the silly games, but without great hurry.

He was sure that the life of the person opposite him now lay in the fingers of his right hand as they gripped the plumed end of the arrow's shaft. Clearly, however, Yekha was in no rush to take this life.

He thought of how his opponent was a strong lad, albeit an unsociable and perhaps ornery one, but there was surely no raging warlike spirit inside him, it had visited him only once on some mission beyond anyone's ken.

At that moment, the giant's curiosity felt satisfied and ceased to nag him.

***

Yekha never made his shot. Fate came down on top of him like a rockfall.

As the iron-tipped arrow rested against his bowstring, a gray apparition flew forth out of the crowd of women and into the giant's face. The Tungus man's son roared like a bear and collapsed into the snow.

This apparition was Watane. With a fury that made even the knees of Noynoba's warriors tremble, the widow slashed at the giant with her talons. The air echoed with her cries.

During the showdown, no one had paid any mind to the mad old woman, but she had stood there among the crowd and followed every action of the two opponents with wide eyes, hands on her cheeks, and muttering something. Before the Tungus man's son had managed to launch his arrow, the raging demon settled into the widow's body.

The men present managed to separate the two, but it was like splitting the parts of a tightly glued bow. They flung the widow a dozen feet to the side, she fell into the snow and wailed like it was her own flesh which had been ravaged, and not the man with the Tungus name.

Yekha bored his head into the snow and crawled on his hands and knees around the spot where, a moment before, he had been standing and aiming at his opponent. He no longer cried out, only a terrible, visceral moan rumbled from him. When two of his comrades were finally able to set him upright again, everyone could see his eyelids sunken into his skull where his eyes had once been.

The heavenly caravan

The fact that Watane had been mad for many years saved her from instant death.

One of Noynoba's men was already pointing his spear at her, but Lidyang stopped him from striking.

"We'll take care of it ourselves," the old man pleaded.

The warrior let his weapon drop. Before he left, he said, "Your guilt here is immeasurable, and the old woman shares but little of it."

Lidyang shuddered. He had been wracked with worry in recent days, and now a black pit of despair was pulling him in.

The old woman was no longer crying out. She lay on her side, eyes closed and with a hand placed on her head. Lidyang stared at her dully and finally noticed the barely perceptible swaying of her slender back under her parka – Watane was breathing as a sleeping person does after making a great and righteous effort. Something closed around Lidyang's heart like a tiny, vicious dog.

He jerked the widow face up and slapped her violently across the cheek. It was as if several more dogs clung to him when he realized that Watane really had been sleeping – the slap woke her like the first light of day falling through a chum's smoke-hole. His anger was like a ringing pain in his chest. Lidyang could not find any words. "You snake…" was all he managed to get out.

Watane did not seem to hear him. She wiped her face with a fistful of snow and smiled. "Is that sonny of mine still alive?"

Her voice was as clear as if it had never known sleep. When Lidyang heard it, he froze. But then he recalled the wooden plate, the bone with bits of meat still on it, and the mockery of his female relatives' husbands. The angry dogs within him quieted down.

"He's alive."

The old man then spat down by his feet and walked away. A mighty cry stopped him, however:

"Lidyang!"

He turned and saw Watane standing up straight and seeming totally composed. All that remained of her former insanity were her dirty clothes and the gray locks of dirty hair entwined like serpents.

Lidyang could hardly believe his eyes. It took some time for him to get ahold of himself. "Even if you are not crazy and fooled us all these years," he said, "you still won't live to see sundown."

"I know."

"I'll cut your throat myself."

Watane chuckled quietly, in the way that those who know something hidden from others do.

"And not just yours," the old man continued. "Noynoba's people said, 'The worthless life of that old bitch is too small a compensation for the blinding of the great warrior.' They are being generous here, because that shame might have cost all of us our lives. Look at what you have done..." He fell silent for a moment. "We need to give them the head and the skin of that runt that you fed scraps to. Now he's an ordinary human being like anyone else."

"It's too late," Watane said. "The great caravan is already on the move." She tilted her head slightly to the side. "And you talk like you know what fate has in store."

"I know that I'll cut your throat. That's enough."

"The great caravan is already on the way," Watane repeated. "It will be here before you could even bring your hand to your face. And you will follow after it, while some will ride on it. Kheno's land is no longer your land. Other people will dwell on it."

The woman was still mad, Lidyang concluded, and he walked away.

After he had taken a few steps, he thought that he ought to tie the widow up, because there was no guarantee that some other spirit – an insidious one that would bring death to all of them – would not settle into her heart. But as soon as the thought came to him, he heard from behind him:

"Look down into the valley."

Lidyang turned – he raised his hands but, before they reached his face, they froze as if in prayer. The shouting of the people inside the encampment suddenly quieted.

***

From that direction where the hill sloped smoothly down to the lightly forested riverbank and became a plain, a white wall was coming towards the camp. It took up the entire space between the ground and the sky.

The people had been awaiting the imminent arrival of the month of heavy snowfall, which announced its coming through dark lines in the great distance. But as they looked at the white wall, no one was thinking about that impending change in the weather, and one of the old men spoke in a whisper that then spread through the encampment:

"The Seven Heavenly Snows…"

The snow was coming not from some heavy cloud but from the very depths of the sky – from each of the seven heavens, even from the very utmost, so infinitely far away that it had forgotten about the earth, but now remembered it and shed down a white stream.

Probably everyone in the taiga knew that there had once been a flood due to the Seven Snows. The great river Yenisei had swelled and the entire earth was depopulated.

But this snow was bringing different tidings.

Through the flurries, the outlines of human beings appeared – first only vaguely, dimly, and then so clearly that one could make out sledges, reindeer, and people both mounted and on foot. The widow walked towards this wall and the people of Kheno's family watched her. Astonished by this spectacle, they forgot all about Yekha and about how shortly before, they had been afraid to even approach Watane – everyone except Lidyang.

"What is this?" he asked.

"A big caravan."

After this reply, a silence hung in the air that the old man found unbearable. "Who are those people? Where are they going?!" he cried.

"The dead. They are departing," Watane's voice remained just as steady.

"Before the living leave some land forever, the inhabitants of its graves leave it. Didn't you know that?"

"Forever… Why?" Lidyang asked, bewildered. Her initial remark about how the land had already been given to others, he had taken as mere ravings and immediately forgot.

"Because that is how it was ordained."

"By whom?"

"By the one who sent this snow."

The old man's bafflement turned into anger. He took a great and determined step towards where blind Yekha was seated on a fur and swaying like marsh grass. He tore the spear out of the hands of one of Noynoba's warriors standing next to his chief – the warrior readily yielded his weapon to him. Lidyang headed towards the wall, first walking and then running – and then he stopped.

He saw two shadows now coming towards him, a large one and a smaller one. They appeared from out of the snow, walked past Lidyang as if he were not even there, and approached the widow.

Now their faces were clearly visible. When Kheno's people recognized them, they screamed and recoiled as if a tree were falling right next to them.

It was Tusyada and Mayana.

The foolish man and his unfaithful wife knelt down in front of Watane and brought their faces to her feet that were clad in torn boots – this was how one showed thanks for a kindness to which there is no adequate answer, for any expression of gratitude would seem too meager.

They rose back up, and the widow bowed to them in reply.

Tusyada and Mayana turned towards the crowd of people and, staring with empty and immobile eyes, they began to remove their parkas – everyone watched as they caressed the widow's feet. On the left side of each of the two's bodies were small, identical gashes, from which a black trail of blood snaked across the gray skin.

It was Watane who had crept into the sanctuary by night and ended their suffering by means of a knife attached to a stick, which Kheno's people had mistaken for a spear.

Mayana and Tusyada put their parkas back on. They did not bow to the people gathered. They turned towards Watane and gently took her hands in order to lead her away with them.

"It's not time yet," she said. "Go, my dears. Go."

The foolish man and his unfaithful wife let go of her hands, stepped into the white stream, and became indistinguishable from the rest of the caravan.

"Don't be afraid," Watane addressed the dumbstruck crowd. "Maybe someone else will want to come out and express their thanks to someone among you."

But no others among the dead wished to show themselves to the living.

They headed towards the Yenisei, so that they could then float along its current to the north of the world. The great caravan had gathered, from all of the clan cemeteries in those lands, those souls whose fates – so obscure and mysterious to the living – had been decided.

The dead peered at the living, but many could not find any familiar faces there, and those who did recognize someone did not recall such kindness worth falling at their feet for. Only for an instant did an elderly face appear through the white sheet that some recognized as Kheno's.

The people there watched the caravan march on, and no one felt the passage of time – it all seemed to happen in a single moment. As soon as the man and woman disappeared, a lanky man stepped out of the snows. Watane ran up to him, hugged his gray body, and said with a heavy sigh:

"Finally I can see both of you. Like before."

She turned, raised her eyes towards where I stood – apart from everyone else, as always – and uttered the most crucial words of my life:

"Come to me, Ilget."

I did so.

MAN OF THE EARTH
(THE SECOND NAME)

Mother

The woman squeezed Lar's hand and tears streamed down her cheeks. She beamed, and I could find no trace on her face of that dirty old crone with snake-like hair who had run after me with the wooden plate.

The woman hugged me and from here I felt only a sense of warmth and purity. The woman stroked Lar's chest and said to me, "This is your brother Balna, which in our language means 'Bird-Cherry Staff'. You're Ilget, 'Man of the Earth'. The dead do not speak. Say to your brother, 'Greetings, *ket*'. That is how your people greet one another, for you are an Ostyak."

I looked at my dead brother, and my mind had already concluded who this woman was, but my heart was still overcome with astonishment and unable to accept the word. I wanted her to show pity on me and I asked, "Who are you?"

She told me, all the while smiling and shedding tears:

"I left you not long ago… It was the place we would hunt in the summer, our family's place. Your father, his father, and many generations before them would travel down our native river to the Yenisei and catch fat fish there. We would erect a chum and live there together, me, my husband, and our dogs – the Ostyaks don't keep reindeer like the people here. It happened that the four of us were migrating to our winter camp. You were born on a bright day when the riverbanks were covered in flowers from the late sun. I buried your umbilical cord there on the shore. Then we went there again in early spring and left when you were a year old. When we took the chum down and gathered our things on our big boat, your father saw large taimen splashing in the water and he rushed to catch them in the loaded boat. He was an ardent man and would chase a catch like that even if it killed him. I shouted to him, but he was so keen on the fish that he didn't hear me. I only watched the boat sail away and eventually disappear, as if the fish had taken it with them. We were left all alone on the empty bank. We shouted for him all day, and then I gave you my breast and laid you down in the moss – our women always did that when we had no one to leave the child with – and went off to find my kinsmen on the other river, our native one. We arrived back together at sunset and I hoped to hear from far off you two crying out from hunger. But it was quiet, even our dogs had left you and gone downstream – they missed their master."

My mother heaved a heavy sigh and wiped her tears.

"My kinsmen never forgave me for that. They abandoned me there on the riverbank and said that I was a terrible mother, though they themselves would leave their children in the moss. I was left alone there, but then the Yuraks came, and one of Kheno's men took me as his wife; I was still beautiful then. A new life began for me. My husband died, but I didn't miss him, because missing you had drained all the life out of me like marrow from bones. But the gods were merciful: they saved me from perishing by taking my wits away. In every little boy I saw you two, or one of you. It seemed to me like you were needing something to eat. Then my son Balna came… Though he eventually died, I would at least have him. And now you arrived. My life has come full circle, and soon I will depart. Your life has only just begun. You are an Ostyak from the Great Perch clan, and you have a native river and a native land. Go there."

When I asked where exactly my river was located, my mother smiled and said that it was a left tributary of the Yenisei, but there are an infinite number of such rivers, and it was hard to say which of them was my own.

"But when you get there, erect a chum and dwell there. Ostyaks will come from the neighboring rivers, tell them that you're Ilget, son of Belegin."

"I don't know the Ostyak language..."

"Don't you worry about that. Everyone knew Belegin, and your face is his face. Just like Balna's face. There are not so many people on this earth that one could mistake you for someone else. Just say the name: Belegin."

"Who can show me the way?" I asked.

"Only the person who took you away from there," she replied. "You are the last of the family."

"That person is my enemy and he wants me dead."

"That doesn't matter," she said. "You must go there all the same. The spirits have cleared the way for you, they have sent demons who have subjected you to trials or rescued you in order to bring you here, to this place where you found almost everything you were looking for. You found me, your brother, your name, your people. Now you must get your own land back, and it would be foolish to do anything else. Don't you know that the Yenisei is the Tree on which the world stands?"

"That's what they say."

"So know, too, that every person has his nest somewhere on the Tree. No one is born a wanderer or slave. A person comes into the world with land and sustenance – otherwise, why should he be born? Only afterwards do many people lose what they came into the world with. Do you understand me?"

"I do."

"Go find what you have lost, Ilget."

My dead brother took her by the hand in order to lead her away with him, but my mother freed her hand and hugged me.

"What is your name?" I asked, and then burst into tears.

"Among our people, a woman loses her name after she has given birth to a child. I am the mother of Balna and Ilget."

I continued to cry and did not want to let her go. I was ready to act like a fool, to ask about the wooden plate and say that I was hungry, as long as she would stay there with me. But instead, I said, "I once was able to hear birds from half a day's flight away…"

"If you have such a talent, it will remain with you. It is time for me to go… I beg you, don't abandon the blind fellow, he lost his sight for your sake. And don't abandon that girl with the exquisite face. Don't abandon all these poor people."

Tears welled in my eyes, and I did not even notice that my mother had removed her arms from around me. Nor did I see my brother lead her away into the Seven Heavenly Snows.

The white wall disappeared.

***

At the moment I heard her say those words, my enemy was close by, perhaps a mere half a day's journey away.

In the morning the remnant of Kheno's family departed. They took as many reindeer as would make a caravan of two dozen sledges and they set off for the summer pastures of their kinsmen. Two of Noynoba's warriors went ahead to catch up with the patriarch of their family and, if he had already begun to lead the clan off on its migration, to tell him to wait.

We found the warriors on the second day. Under some trees, on snow trodden and stained, they sat like children who had been scolded, with heads low. Nearby, women, children, and men lay in a tangle, they had been shot in the neck with arrows. All of the warriors had torn jumpers – the enemy had stripped them of their armor without caring about their clothing or other possible booty. Noynoba himself was still alive and said that they had been ambushed, out of the blue. The attackers had been only a few men, around a dozen, but skilled and fearsome. Once they had killed everyone, they loaded a single woman's sledge with iron, arrows, and dried meat and vanished as mysteriously as they had appeared.

"Two of ours left with them," the old man said.

The men who had attacked him spoke Yurak, but he did not know who they were. They had been led by a man with a remarkably stout body and virtually no neck.

"Which way did they go?" I shouted into the old man's face.

"That way…" Noynoba's arm made a motion that seemed to encompass half the world.

Yabto

On that day in early autumn when Nokho saved me, Yabto carried the body of his elder son on his back.

When he saw the bare pine and the body with an arrow in its back, he realized that the battle was over for him, so he did not go looking for the one who had called him an enemy and killed his son.

Yabto made his way along the riverbank. He slipped and fell on the mossy rocks, but he was oblivious to the pain, he only noticed the thud that Yabtonga's head made when it struck the stones. He lifted the heavy body back onto his shoulders and walked on.

The stout man was already exhausted when he reached the bend where the river had cast Yawire's body up onto the rocky shallows. Just like his brother before, he lay face-down with an arrow in his back.

Yabto dropped Yabtonga in a dry place, then went for Yawire. He turned the latter over on his back, dragged him by the hood of his parka to the shore, and laid him next to his elder son.

After Yabto caught his breath, he removed his bow and quiver, took his ax from his belt, and went to a nearby grove to make a stretcher from young fir trees and the bits of the rope which, without thinking, he had picked up and tucked away.

His thoughts were occupied with finding suitable trees. He found a fir, a thin and springy one with a gay tuft at the top. He chopped at it once, but then dropped the ax – a thought had suddenly come to him.

He forgot all about the ax and rope. Instead, he went back to his sons and sat down next to them.

He looked at their faces, which were now white and washed clean by the river. He was struck by how little sense there was to what he was doing – and not just the business of constructing the stretcher but everything that he and other people had ever done before.

He might have told his sons, "Get up," and they would recognize their father's voice, jump to their feet, and rub their eyes, so fresh did the two of them look.

But this was not to be, for they were dead, and a dead man is no different than someone not yet born. And even if Yabtonga and Yawire's souls hovered somewhere nearby and saw their pure faces, saw their father sitting there on the stone, they would do nothing to help the stout man who now had to get to his boat, cross the river, return to his encampment, and somehow live his life.

That crushing idea of the rest of his life fell on Yabto's heart and caused unbearable pain.

But the pain awakened his mind and told him that it was silly to make such a big effort for the dead. Better to lie down next to them and never get up. Mourning the dead is something that only carefree people do. When people mourn the dead, they merely feel sorry for themselves, their insignificance, and find therein consolation and even satisfaction.

Yabto looked at the fir-grove where he had left his ax and suddenly had a vision of himself as the last man left on earth, dragging two dead bodies through the endless taiga. He would ask that lone man, "What are you doing that for?" Was it so that other people would not castigate you for not seeing your sons off to the lower world as is proper, for not raising their bodies up into the branches of the Mosquito clan's sanctuary? But there were no longer any Mosquito People around, nor any other human beings. They did not exist any more, just as the souls of slaves do not exist. There is only you, Yabto, your body that is still filled with strength, your mind that can come up with ideas to save you, and your heart endowed with great strength of will. That strength of will stood against the disorder into which his life had been submerged.

Yabto recalled how a similar vision had come to him several years before, when he made the lash and intended to gather his family together like shepherds whip their herds into shape. At that time – he now realized this – only part of the truth had been revealed to him. But the truth lay in the fact that he would end up alone. In this there was clarity and freedom – the sole and most reliable blessing. If there was some design by the supernatural world therein, it lay precisely in this and in nothing else.

Yabto thought also of how half a day's journey from this bend, the mountains would divide and lead everything to the same Bountiful River. It had been by this way, a longer one than he and his sons had traveled, that his puny enemy had walked. He had surely hidden the iron he stole somewhere along the way.

The iron, and not his sons, would serve as the continuation of his will – it was the iron that was worth thinking about now.

Yabto stood up and returned to the fir-grove. After he had chosen a small area of soft earth among the stones, he set about digging a grave for Yabtonga and Yawire with his ax.

***

His expectation did not deceive him: in a thicket, almost at the very bank of the river, he spotted a dry stick that been placed as a marker, and so ineptly that even a stranger would have guessed that it denoted a hiding place. Yabto clad himself in the gleaming Ostyak armor, cut a shaft for the incredibly wide spear-blade, and then walked along the riverbank in search of his boat.

When the moon had become only a thin, curved strip of light, and the wind was sweeping off the last remaining warmth of autumn, Yabto arrived back home. Early one overcast morning he pulled his empty boat ashore and strolled into his encampment like a conqueror. Uma stood up and bowed to her husband. She saw the mail shirt with its shining plates at the chest that Yabto had put on over his parka, as well as the broad-bladed spear, and she understood thereby that her husband had achieved what he had set out to do.

Kiss Woman's heart sank. All these days she had been thinking about the runt, recalling how he alone of all the children had never bit her breast, and she wept at his fate.

Now that Yabto was back, she made a fire in the summer hearth under an empty pot. A large container of water stood nearby, The stout man was hungry and realized that it would take a while to get any hot food. He walked off towards his chum. A sound of ringing iron came from inside there – he had taken off his armor, and he laid his restored honor there in the sacred part of the chum.

He then walked out, sat down on a large stone, and stared at his wife for a long time. This stare made Kiss Woman nervous, her flint slipped from her hands and fell into the hearth, destroying the little chum of wood chips and birch bark she had made there.

"Are you waiting for our sons? Don't. I buried them on yonder riverbank."

Uma froze, a guilty and stupid look came over her face. She had long since grown used to her husband's affability and was ready to hear any remark, only not words like that. Uma knew that Yabtonga and Yawire would come along any moment now, when they had done what their father had ordered them to do: take care of the boat, or their catch... They would bring Wenga, who was probably tied up. She wept for the runt, but she was unable to fathom his death either.

Uma rose and ran to the shore, her round, ample body shaking. When she returned, Yabto was still sitting on the stone, in the same pose with his hands on his knees and his elbows jutting upwards, as if he were just about to get up.

"Where are my children?" Kiss Woman said dully. "Where are Yabtonga and Yawire?"

She had seen the empty boat, which had been hauled far up onto the shore, right into the willows, and she was unable to believe her husband's words.

"Someone killed them. I don't know who, but I'll find him. He killed them when I went into the forest to catch a bird for dinner. That person also took away Dog's Ear – I had caught him and tied him to a tree naked. That's everything for you to know, don't ask anything more."

Uma collapsed to the grass. The stout man slowly got up, took the container of water, and splashed some of the water onto her face. When she opened her eyes, Yabto was speaking quietly, as if he were merely asking a favor and not ordering her:

"If you want to make a big fuss about this, better go into the forest. I'm tired."

He went to his chum and laid down on the furs. Inside he had first raged at the lack of a hot meal, but now he wished only for some peace. He closed his eyes and suddenly felt an unbearable regret at what had happened to his children. He regretted that he would never again hear their voices, never see them as fully grown men, never speak with them about raiding, big hunting, or abducting a bride. But as Yabto thought about his sons, he also felt regret at his own life, which might have turned out completely differently if, when his sons were little, he had not listened to his wife and gone to the Yenisei to catch fat fish. He recalled that devastated encampment at the mouth of the unknown river; time had not blunted his memories, on the contrary, it seemed to make every tree and stone more vivid.

However, Yabto's anguish soon passed – it was replaced by the concerns of his weary body. As he fell asleep, he thought about how if Uma was wallowing in grief or went away into the forest to cry, she would not be cooking any meat, and he would have to resort to some jerky when he woke up. But he had no desire to get up now and order his wife around. The stout man recalled the vision, that the old times were never coming back, and now he would have to get used to the lonely life that had been ordained for him.

Yabto awoke at dusk and found next to his bed a plate of warm meat. He eagerly got down to eating it. When his hunger was sated, he was amazed at his wife, for after all, it was Uma who had set the plate there.

Kiss Woman was sitting by the now-extinguished fire and absentmindedly stirring the coals with a stick. Ashes had been thickly smeared on her face, hair, and hands, as people do when they have lost a loved one. The sight of his wife reassured him and at the same time astonished him – he had expected a very different kind of mourning from a woman who came from the People of the Scream.

As if aiming to reconcile Uma to the life they would now live, Yabto said, "You won't get your sons back." The stout man fell silent and then wanted to tell Uma that it would be better if she washed her face off, but he changed his mind and left his wife alone.

***

He stepped into the small chum that belonged to Man-Effigy, in order to carry out what he had promised to both that man and himself.

Over the last month the man who would never die had grown utterly frail and could no longer leave his chum, even to use the toilet. Uma had cared for him like for a baby. She stuffed his pants with dry moss and removed them once a day in order to carry them down to the river. Before she dressed the old man again, she washed his legs, now little more than purple sticks, with warm water. At this time, however, Kiss Woman had not seen to her uncle since the day before, and Man-Effigy reeked like the pit just outside their encampment.

Yabto had no desire to stick around and chat. He only told the old man that the next day, he would do what he promised: he would carry him off and leave him in a place he had long had in mind, where Nga would finally remember about the existence of this dry old husk.

The old man slightly tilted his head without even opening his eyes – he had heard what Yabto had said. The stout man then left.

His wife was no longer by the summer hearth. Uma was sitting in her sons' chum, stroking the furs that Yabtonga and Yawire had once slept under. Her entire body was shaking and to Yabto suddenly seemed decrepit, like an old woman's.

He watched her for some time and then said, "We don't have any supplies. Before the river rises, let's go to the Yenisei and catch some fat fish." After a pause, he added, "You do like fat fish, after all."

Uma did not reply.

"We'll set off tomorrow," Yabto said.

That night he slept alone. He knew that his wife's grief would be like the pain of a stubbed toe: sharp, but brief.

Not even a year passes before widows seem to grow young again and start looking for a new husband. Women who have lost children bear new ones. And Uma could still have more children, though that would be the greatest foolishness. True grief comes to a woman only when others begin to disdain her. But such grief had not come to Kiss Woman, for she had a husband.

So Yabto thought.

***

In the morning he carried the old man in his arms.

"Why are you wasting your strength?" Man-Effigy whispered. "If you want me dead, you could kill me just like that."

"I can't," Yabto said. "I'll do you this small honor."

He set the old man down in the middle of the boat, amid the nets and the supplies for their journey, and he whispered into the old man's ear as one does when sharing a great secret with someone:

"It's a problem that you're still alive. Everyone dies after they have lived their span of years, except you. Even you don't remember when you were born, no one does."

"You're right."

"I've got to remind the gods of their mistake, and if they realize it, then I will believe in them and respect them. You see, old man, the whole world is like an encampment with a negligent owner: things are just lying around randomly, the fishing nets are all tangled, the dogs are mangy, the weapons haven't been cleaned. And someone who ought to die, won't die. Why is that, old man?"

"You tell me, if you're so wise…"

"I'm no sage, but I know a thing or two. I know one place high up that you could never get down from, and no one else will take you down, either. It's very visible from the river. As I'm heading back home, I'll see you – maybe I'll already see your bones – and my heart will be at ease. It'll mean that the gods are not as messy and untidy as I thought."

The old man slowly opened his toothless mouth and spat from it the last bit of laughter that had soundlessly quaked inside him. "You mean to starve me, like you wanted to do to Lar, and you'll think that it was Nga's doing?"

"Yes, that's exactly what I am going to think," Yabto replied calmly but angrily. "It's a good place, the very best. Nga should see you there and feel ashamed of himself."

"You want to shame a god?"

"He should have been flogged long ago. Just like all the others…"

The old man sat up, revealed the dirty whites of his faded eyes, and for the first time in his life he looked at Yabto with contempt. "Listen, I will die all the same. How are you going to see that Nga is shamed?"

"There will be more order in life. Those who ought to die, will die, not like now."

"And if that doesn't happen? How are you going to flog a god?"

"Don't pretend that you're like an innocent babe that doesn't know such simple things. I'll hack his idol apart and whip it with my lash."

After Yabto said this, he lost any interest in talking to the old man.

The stout man put him into the boat and then called to Uma so she would come down to the river.

***

Yabto sailed to the place he had noticed long before. It was a tall rock that lunged like a wrestler into the body of the river – part of the rock that joined it to the riverbank had fallen into the water. In bad water the base of the cliff foamed with turbulent water, while the top with its willows and sparse, stunted trees looked like a head from which most of the hair had been torn out.

Every time Yabto sailed past this point, he would look at the promontory and try to find a path up it among the rocky folds. He thought it would be fun to climb up sometime to that balding head and get a view of the area from those heights. His former curiosity had not been in vain.

The stout man's boat sailed thrice around the rock. Yabto deftly paddled against the current and peered carefully to find the path up that he had noticed before. Once he found it, he made several mighty strokes with the oar, brought the boat right up to the rock, and moored it to the roots of a dead tree that had been crushed by rockfall.

The weather was calm. The current kept the boat pointed straight and it was fixed in its course as if it had been laid on the firmament. Uma said nothing and only looked down at her feet.

Man-Effigy, too, was silent. His head was raised, and though his eyes were closed, he seemed to be able to see through the lids and watch Yabto prepare his journey to his final resting place. "'Every possible thing in this world has already happened to me,'" Yabto recalled as he looked at the old man. Yabto got down to business and prepared the shoulder harness that he had made the previous evening, before he went to sleep. The harness consisted of two straps attached to a flat piece of wood, and a length of rope. After ensuring that the attachments were strong, Yabto set the harness down at the front of the boat, then stepped over to the old man and picked him up.

"You don't weigh more than a couple of capercaillies," he said, pleased at his own inventiveness.

He carefully set the old man down on the wooden seat and bound the rope around his chest – this was the same rope with which he had tied Wenga naked to the pine. He then turned around and put his arms through the straps, and an instant later the old man's legs were already up in the air. Man-Effigy now faced Kiss Woman.

"Say something to your niece!" Yabto said. "Something nice."

"You will find happiness," Man-Effigy said clearly.

Uma did not reply.

"There you go," the stout man said and boldly stepped out into the water.

He leisurely made his way up, carefully judging every stone before he set his foot on it or grabbed at it. Yabto got halfway up the promontory with the confidence of a big, many-legged spider. But at that midpoint the stout man realized that the bulk of the weight was represented by himself, and not the old man that he carried on his back – even the ax at Yabto's belt seemed heavier. Moreover, the wind had picked up and sent Man-Effigy's legs fluttering, so knocking Yabto off balance that twice he nearly fell. He felt a yawning pit in his stomach, he froze and gripped the rocks until his heart began to beat more slowly. Some time passed and then he looked up as far as his neck would allow: the cliff that had seemed small from the river now towered far up into the sky. Yabto looked down – his large boat had dwindled to the size of a titmouse and he could barely make out there the gray ball that was his wife.

Yet his heart continued to beat frantically, his knees ached, and shameful thoughts darted into his mind like gray lizards. The first of these – "Go back down!" – was pushed out by another thought that was just as shameful: trying to go back down with that burden still on his back would be even more dangerous and difficult. As for his wife, the stout man was not even thinking about her. The third thought – the most despicable of all – whispered that Man-Effigy could surely sense his weakness and would say so, choosing words that could kill him more surely than iron-tipped arrows. This fear proved stronger than the others and Yabto, like he had done in childhood when his father's palm struck his face, winced with eyes closed tight. He stood there in darkness for some time.

The wind eventually grew calmer, however, and the old man continued to be silent. Yabto's ability to think clearly now marched on; it had not abandoned him for long. That host of cheery thoughts was brought by the demon that dwelt between his shoulder blades. There was no need to head back down, said the first rank of this army.

Things are going to get impossible, said the second rank. Yabto could simply shrug off the straps, and as his burden plunged down towards the base of the cliff he could say whatever mean words he wanted to – they wouldn't even reach Yabto.

The third, strongest rank of this army of thoughts waved its weapons and shouted that only half of the journey upward remained, or even less, and Yabto needed merely to make a little effort that wasn't even as great as his weakness claimed. He needed to be resolute in doing this, so that he would not pine for the rest of his days from the disorder in the world and his own insignificance. The supernatural world would laugh at you, Yabto, and that would be worse than death. To avoid it, he needed to make a small effort.

This last thought got his blood flowing, his heart grew more ardent, and the stout man went upwards and traversed the remaining distance before he even knew it.

***

There, at the top of the cliff, Yabto experienced the happiness that had been augured for Kiss Woman. He saw his native river that looped around his encampment, he saw forested hills and their bald tops, he saw the world as soft, pliable, so much so that he might have straightened the serpentine river with his own hands, or pulled on it as he might pull the string of his horned bow.

The stout man spotted a large, flat stone. He set Man-Effigy down on it and freed his shoulders from the harness.

"Here you go," the stout man said with a heavy but content sigh. Man-Effigy could hear how pleased Yabto was and opened his eyes. Yabto and the old man stared at one another for a long time.

"What about me?" the stout man broke the silence. "What do you have to foretell for me?"

"I can see your wish," the old one said.

"What wish?"

"You seek to tame everything around you. Whatever lives freely, lives on its own, sparks fear in you. You tame dogs, reindeer, children both your own and adopted, my niece, the demon behind your shoulders. You brought me here to tame me and not have to be afraid any more. Not everything worked out for you, but now that doesn't matter, because you thought of something really great, though you aren't really aware of it yourself."

"What is it that I've thought of?"

"Taming fate itself."

Yabto had been listening to the old man with one knee on the ground. After those words he slowly got up. "Oh," he said, still catching his breath after the effort. "What a simple thing, and I really wasn't even aware."

"You see, Man-Effigy is good for something."

"Tell me, who are you?"

"You don't know already? Your wife's uncle, the brother of her father, from the People of the Scream. You took me in after my encampment was struck by plague, you fed me for long years and did not require me to do any work. Thanks for that…" The old man gave a respectful bow, something he had never done before.

This only annoyed Yabto, however. "Again you're lying to me. You always lie. My wife's father was decades younger than you. How could you be his brother?"

"Think whatever you want, Yabto, if you refuse to believe me." The old man was silent for a moment. "Why don't you ask me about something else, about what really matters?"

"What's that?"

"You must be keen to know where fate lives and what it looks like."

"Does it live somewhere?"

"It does. Inside you. In your will. All people are good at times and bad at times. They are fickle, and that is why fate drives them along like a herd of reindeer. Choose something and stick with it, and then you'll run along on your own, without any shepherd over you. You already took such a step when you made that lashed stick. And you killed the Tungus out of the simple fear that he was doing the same. And out of stupidity, too. Iron Horn was a brigand, but he was also a weak man, he took a liking to the runt…"

As Yabto listened to the old man's words, he recognized something that he had never quite seen before.

"Flogging idols is silly, it's only for old people who have lost their minds. The supernatural powers merely laugh at it, and then get their revenge." Man-Effigy fell silent, inhaled the pure wind up there, and closed his eyes. "But to tame fate itself," he went on, "it's not enough just to put your own life in order. If the world stands on the Tree of the Yenisei, you would need to shake the whole tree – anything less would not bring you the peace you seek. You are strong, try it. Just don't give up, otherwise you'll regret it. Now go. You left your sons, now leave me, too. I'm tired."

Yabto took the old man under the arms and carefully put him down on the ground. He leaned with his back against a rock and, after removing the ax from his belt, he headed for the way back down. He found it easy to descend, and he swept the rocky handholds away after him, so that no one else would be able to use them to get up.

Uma

Yabto erected a chum at the mouth of his native river.

His own river was a noisy one, but the Yenisei seemed in no mood to talk and only blew a damp cold over their camp.

The stout man prepared his fishing tackle for the next day. Uma was making a fire from birch bark in order to cook a meal from their meager supplies. Contrary to his habit, the stout man simply set the net down in the boat without untangling it. The autumn light was quickly fading, and Yabto was unable to distinguish one section of the net from another. In the end, he simply crumpled the net up, threw it into the boat, and went to the fire.

The fire came to life, embraced the pot above it, and danced along with it.

"You could have brought that net up to the light," Uma said.

These were the first words she had uttered after several days of silence, and the stout man was astonished by how calmly and boldly they were spoken. After all, Uma was talking about something that was men's business. He had forbidden his wife from bothering him with loud weeping over their sons, but he still expected some crying from her. Yet his wife had been silent, and the stout man was overcome with astonishment and anxiety.

"Tomorrow," he said.

Uma stirred the broth with a stick and as she did so, she spoke without looking at her husband:

"How are you going to untangle that net when it gets light out late in autumn, and you got it so tangled up that you'll miss the good morning fishing, and we'll again end up without any fish, just like before..."

"Be quiet"

It was as if Uma did not hear him, she continued to stir the pot and talk. "…without fish, without meat. How could you have wasted this fat autumn, Yabto, when the elk and reindeer are fat to bursting, when even the mosquitoes have forgotten about the cold and decided not to die off after all? You went looking for your stolen iron, Yabto, and you found it – you turned my sons into iron, you have become an iron husband, and now my sons are gleaming in the sun and protecting your chest, your back, your shoulders, your head…"

"Be quiet."

"… so no arrow, spear, or ax will get you, because unlike other women, I careful cleaned my teats, washed them in running water, when I fed each of them, even that rebellious Lar, even that runt Wenga. They've been turned into iron…"

Yabto realized that this marked the start of her mourning, and it was different than he had expected.

Her mother's grief was now breaking through the blocked exit from its lair, to emerge as a fearless beast of blind rage. He grabbed his wife by her parka and shook her as hard as he could. The boiling pot tipped and spilled noisily into the fire. But when Yabto let go of her, Uma picked up the dropped stick.

"…they would protect you, because it was not for them that I washed my teats but for you, Yabto."

The stout man made an effort to suppress his anger. "I told you that I would find the men who killed them. Calm down." He said nothing for a moment, but then added dully, "Go ahead, cry."

Kiss Woman stopped stirring the pot and stared at her husband.

In the flickering light of the flames, Yabto saw her round, haggard face and realized that never would tears appear on it – a beast had emerged, in whose flaming innards all tears had been burned away, and all that remained was the conviction that he, Yabto, had killed their sons Yabtonga and

Yawire. This woman who once wished to be a fish, so that children would issue from her like roe, now lived only on hatred for her husband.

The stout man understand this look, though he found no words for it. He saw the beast. He realized that the beast in his wife's guise would never leave him be, never die on its own – it would live as long as the stout man lived. The beast would hide its eyes, look down at the ground, but in all things in the world it would see only Yabto.

"Get up," he told his wife. "Let's go."

***

Uma got up and walked ahead of her husband.

She did not ask where they were going and why, she did not show any fear or say terrible words – on the contrary, Kiss Woman bore her heavy, round body along smoothly, she stepped deftly and never stumbled in the darkness, as if she had an owl's eyes. It was only due to her hatred for her husband that she was stronger than him, and that hatred gave her a light step – the same step with which she had once, laughing, lured the young Yabto into the taiga, some distance from the camp, so that they could enjoy some lovemaking, and Yabto would run after her with a heavy, headlong run, breathing heavily and wiping slaver from his month…

The only light that guided them was a piece of the sky, sprinkled with stars, through a break in the hills. Yabto's eyes were growing used to the darkness and Kiss Woman's light step filled him with fear. The stout man did not give in to this fear, but it leapt around somewhere nearby and mocked him, and several times this annoyance led Yabto to stumble, swear in a dull voice, and nearly lose the ax at his waist. It seemed like this journey was the prelude to a duel, and the further he walked, the clearer he saw in Uma a strong foe and prepared to confront that strong foe.

Yabto realized that the moment had come to strike a blow.

When the moon appeared through the crack in the hills, he saw an open space covered with rocks. A stream was burbling somewhere nearby. The stout man ordered his wife to stop. Uma stopped. Without turning to her husband, she looked up and took in the place, as if she was settling in there.

Yabto's brazen, mocking fear told him it was no use wasting time on words. He took the ax from his belt. Uma, who still stood with her back to her husband, said:

"Over there, a bit behind you, is a fallen tree. A big one."

Yabto turned and saw the wide trunk a few steps away. He went up to it.

Uma came up, too.

"Other women were jealous of me. You've got a good husband, they said. He inherited a little wealth from his father, and he keeps everything in order, and the storehouse is always full. And now you have filled that storehouse to the very brink, only a little bit remains to be placed there, so that you won't have to worry for the rest of your days."

Kiss Woman dropped to her knees, laid her hand on the wide trunk, and ended by saying, "Just know, my iron husband, I will not leave you."

Anger flared up inside Yabto. He raised the ax, but an instant before striking the blow, his reason told him that a sharp ax would be unable to defeat the beast in Uma's guise. That beast would be killed only by some long, hard, and inescapable suffering that was equal to the hatred for Yabto that the beast bore within itself.

The stout man turned the ax around and used the butt of it to break his wife's arms and legs, then he walked off into the darkness. He walked with wide steps, without paying any attention to his route and not remembering the way back to their little camp. But after some time, Yabto stopped, stood still, and stopped breathing – he listened carefully and tried to catch any far-off moaning. There was nothing.

"It doesn't matter," the stout man grinned and began to carefully search in the darkness for the lost path to the riverbank, where his boat and small chum were.

The birth of an army

He found the way back and arrived at the camp before dawn, and then he got into the tent and fell asleep.

In the morning he ate the food that his wife had left, gathered his fishing nets, and took down the tent, and then he sailed down the Yenisei for about half a day. In a flat, open space free from foliage, the stout man founded a new encampment. He had decided never to return to the earlier one, so that he would not have to remember the past and meet people who knew where he lived.

The stout man worked with no concern for sleep or rest. In the morning he set his nets out – sturgeon and redfin taimen swam right into them, as if the fish were aware that Yabto was lacking supplies here at the threshold of winter. By night he speared burbot and pike in the shallows. Soon the hole that he dug into the permafrost and lined with fresh spruce branches, was full of big fish. Whitefish, peled, and other small catch he dried on ropes, but now the heat and sun were gone, so Yabto dug another cold store.

His attention was completely consumed by this happy daily battle with big fish that had to be beaten hard before they could be loaded into the boat. He felt no regret or yearning for anything. He saw himself now on the true path of his life, and he considered his plentiful catch a sign of this.

The stout man stopped fishing once the severe pre-winter winds came and the great river began to thicken into ice. He insulated his chum with some panels made from birch bark and began to live without caring about supplies or whose land he was living on. The place undoubtedly belonged to someone, but the lands along the Yenisei were so vast that no single clan or tribe could protect all their territory from squatters.

When the first snow fell, Yabto went off into the taiga to hunt. When he had left his native territory, he never considered that he might never return, but out of his usual habit of being prudent and packing whatever might be necessary, he had taken his skis lined with beaver skins. The stout man caught some birds. Merely for his own amusement he shot two squirrels – their bodies now sizzled on a skewer, while Yabto simply threw away the fur, which had not yet reached its winter beauty. He was surprised at himself; he would never had done such a thing in the past.

One day followed another and the stout man began to turn wild in his solitary encampment. He was increasingly worried that he would not manage to catch enough meat. He walked ever farther into the taiga and sometimes overnighted there, but the larger game turned out to not be so ready to submit to him as sturgeon and taimen were, and the hares and fowl only left the stout man in a foul mood.

One day, however, as he was off on one of these expeditions, he saw a fresh ski track, and he rushed after it as if it had been the prints of an elk.

He reached the person who had left the track as the sun was already setting. From the shabby fox fur with which the old coat was trimmed, he recognized that the man was a Nenets. The hunter was tall, with huge hands like bear paws, but a tiny head like a baby's. He had a bow and quiver on his back, an ax at his belt, and a spear in his hands. Upon hearing the footsteps of another man, this unknown hunter turned to face Yabto. His mouth surrounded by black bristles slowly stretched into a smile, and he raised his weapon.

Without exchanging a word, they set their bows down on the snow and then rushed at one another – without any arguing, without any of the insults customarily spoken before a fight – they rushed at one another like loved ones after a long separation. The taiga now rang with wheezing and hoarse cries. The unknown hunter was a good fighter, but

Yabto was even better. With a deft movement the stout man knocked the spear from his opponent's hands, and the latter man did not have time to draw his ax from his belt before he ended up on his back in the snow. Inside of doing his opponent in with the iron blade of his spear, Yabto jumped on top of him, put the wood of the spear across his throat, and slowly pushed down. The hunter struggled with his bear-like hands to keep Yabto off him, but as the weight of the spear grew heavier on his throat, his strength was fading and, defeated, he began to speak.

He said that there was no need for one of them to kill the other, and if Yabto needed game, he knew just where to get it. There was vastly more game there than Yabto could have stolen now from him, and together the two could go raiding, so that their only worry until the end of the great cold would be just keeping the fire going in the hearth.

Yabto stopped pushing down so hard. He liked how this tiny-headed Nenets did not beg for mercy but spoke reasonably, and almost calmly, as if he knew that reason was the stout man's good demon. Yabto took his spear off his opponent's throat and helped him sit up.

The man came from a big family that was part of the Willow clan. He was a vagabond with no hearth of his own, just as Iron Horn had been and Yabto had now become. There was no hope for him of returning to his own people. As he sat there on the snow, he began to tell Yabto of how, a month before, he had slain his younger brother, because their father had given that brother nearly all of their herd. The old man expected to die soon and kept the younger son there in his encampment, so that that son could close his eyes and lift him up into the branches, and then wait for their mother and elderly aunt to die so that he could see them off, too, into the lower world. The stranger said that he did not even ask his father how he, the elder son, would survive with a meager dozen reindeer – the injustice of the situation had left him so appalled that he was unable to speak. The younger brother died from an arrow to his temple the next morning, just after he had taken possession of his inheritance.

"I hammered his head to the bed," the warrior said with a smile. Then he turned sad and added, "My father never loved me. It was like that since I was little. Well, his problem. Now let him fear me."

Willow – that is what Yabto started calling him – led the stout man right from the place of their fight along the route that he had made.

***

From far off they saw a caravan.

People – evidently they were Ostyaks, since they had no reindeer – were migrating to their winter pastures. Their four sledges were pulled by dogs. They were assisted by four men, and three women walked behind the caravan.

They ambushed the two tallest Ostyak men and killed them. The women screamed and hid behind the heavily laden sledges. One of the surviving men drew his bow, while the other unleashed the dogs.

Yabto's new buddy wounded the man with the bow in the shoulder, while the stout man saw to something even more important: he killed the dogs without a single missed arrow.

The wounded man collapsed to the snow. The other man stood with his hands down and watched, frozen, as the attackers slowly walked towards his caravan. He was a young man with wide Ostyak eyes, a straight face, and skin the color of iron. He recognized the Yuraks, the old enemies of his tribe, by the fur on their shoulders, and he remembered the few Yurak words he knew, so when his foes approached he began to speak an odd mixed language. He begged them to spare his life. He waited for their reply, but none came – his foes, with heads tilted slightly to the side, scrutinized him.

Then the young man said how things seemed to him: the men who defeated him were free men, and he might prove useful to them.

"You're a coward, and cowards are no companions of ours!" Willow cried.

Yabto pointed to the wounded man. "Who is he? How is he related to you?"

"He's no one."

"Then why are you migrating with him?"

The Ostyak began to mutter and from the hodgepodge of words Yabto understood that one of the women hiding behind the sledges was the wounded man's sister.

"For two years he wouldn't give her to me. He says I don't bring enough birds back from hunting."

"Say it in Ostyak, I understand," the stout man said, smiling. He drew his short knife from its sheath and held it out to the young man. The latter understood without any need for words: he took the knife, ran up to the wounded man, and finished him off right there and then. The women, who were no longer trying to hide, were struck dumb with horror.

"Which girl there is the one you wanted?" Yabto asked.

The Ostyak indicated a young lady with a pockmarked face who stood there in the middle.

"That's a lousy woman," the stout man said. "Don't take her. You can come with us then."

The Ostyak nodded eagerly. Willow drove the women away – they ran off into the forest, wailing loudly as they did.

The caravan was laden with dried beaver meat, beaver skins, fish, scrapers, and the sort of arrows that only this people who called each other *ket* made. Yabto could see that their plunder was not as ample as Willow had promised. But what he really gained from it was that he now had two men who felt awe and dread at him, like dogs.

The three of them carried out two more raids, on a tribe which Yabto did not know and did not care to know. They got a second mail shirt made from shiny iron plates – Yabto was wearing the first under his jumper – and yet another man. Like the first two men, he had been nursing a grudge.

Again Yabto's wits, which had so often saved him, whispered: wherever more than one person is living, there will always be someone angry at his lot in life and desiring revenge, which ordinary human cowardice and propriety prevents him from carrying out. Such men were his men, warriors of the army of outcasts and vagabonds. His mind told him: during raids grab plunder, but also leave at least one of the men alive, the weakest one but with strong legs, so that he can spread word of you. Then the glory of your army will fly ahead of your arrows.

Yabto readily heeded his good demon, and soon he had around him a motley array of warriors, among whom were, besides Willow and the Ostyak, a Selkup in a fox-fur hat and a Tungus with a tattooed face.

By the time the stout man crossed the ice and entered the land of the Nga people where he attacked Noynoba's family, he had already gathered ten warriors.

Noynoba's family gave him another two men. Whatever grudge they nursed, Yabto did not know – these young hunters had heard somewhere of the army that was growing like a storm front, and they themselves asked the stout man to take them with him.

During the month of great cold, when life in the taiga seemed to die out and people did not leave their encampments and only tended their fires, Yabto's glory swelled – when people sat idle, they started to recall all their old grievances, and their thoughts naturally turned to the army of men who were outsiders everywhere.

The army became like an incorporeal spirit that drifted through the chums.

Yabto took his men to the encampment where he had left his boat. His things were all untouched. A hillock of snow had formed around his tent, the top stuck out of it. The warriors were carrying plunder with them. They erected their own dwellings and covered them with the finest skins and birch bark. In the month of great ice, when elk huddle in herds of ten or more, the army managed to save itself from hunger with a single successful hunt. Each of the warriors, even the slightest, felt that he was now capable of doing anything.

Before spring came, Yabto carried out a raid without launching a single arrow. His army surrounded the encampment and, when the people began to emerge from the chums, the stout man called out, "Anyone feeling angry? Come with me." Five men did so. Yabto spared the rest of the people and only ordered them to go away into the taiga and wait until the next morning, when he would have already seized whatever plunder there was.

When the rivers began to shake off their ice, the stout man ordered the army to come to his native encampment. The army paddled against the current in a long line of boats. Yabto had once dreamed of four warriors young and loyal, but now he had a dozen more, and nearly all of them clad in iron.

Yabto went to his old site even though there was no need to. The encampment surrounded by the river was convenient for fishing, but risky for war. The stout man knew that his victories – though they were still rather small ones – would not go unanswered. There, at that encampment, his army could be assailed from all sides, and therefore he would have to set patrols along the entire loop of the river. But the stout man did not go back in order to permanently dwell there. He went there only for his own consolation, to see where his old, stupid, and wrong life had been lived, in order to see it now through different eyes and cast it away from his memory, like fat flung from the scraper.

He was looking forward to encountering the spirits of the place, who would probably be frightened at the new appearance of the man who had been resident here. Only one cloud hung over the joy of that journey: atop the rock Yabto caught no sight of Man-Effigy, neither his bones nor his clothing.

His annoyance did not last long, however. "The crows might have carried everything off," the stout man decided and ordered his men to paddle harder.

After he and the army had spent some time on the Bountiful River, they returned to his new encampment on the banks of the Yenisei. He would have previously considered such an excursion a mere whim, but now he saw himself not as a householder but as a leader of men, and his thoughts now centered around a special sense of authority.

The quiet wedding

Noynoba had not managed to move far, and we returned to his summer encampment. The journey took no more than half a day. But this journey had initially seemed like it would never end – my heart, stupid and impatient, was roaring to chase after my enemy. Now I was linked to the stout man even more than I had been before, when my life was in his hands and freed only by the whim of some unknown demon. I felt no sympathy for Noynoba, nor any memory of the people my mother had told me about. I turned to follow the barely visible track, what remained of it after the snowfall.

Lidyang brought me back to my senses. "Where are you going?" he asked, squinting at me. "You want to die just like Noynoba? What were you thinking, young man?"

I boldly told the old man that I was not afraid of death, because it could no longer come – I had been appointed to take up a place that had been assigned to me before I was even born, and dwell there.

"Has the miracle really not taught you anything?" Lidyang lowered his gaze and spoke simply and straightforwardly, without any contempt for my youth. "Perhaps that is how things shall be. But after the great snow comes great cold, we have few supplies, and less providers than ever. You want to survive, so do we. If you can help us in hunting, you can save some people. Your mother told you not to abandon these people – the women, the blind man, your bride. If you don't want to lose what was assigned to you, then don't break that covenant, Ilget."

So I remained – not out of any pity for those people, but out of fear of disobeying the supernatural forces that had sent the miracle.

We erected chums, made our first fire in the new encampment, and started to live there.

***

That night Nara undid her clothing herself.

Nara revealed to me a life that I had not known before, and any thought of departing alone went away.

Only later did I realize that she had been aware of everything, though she did not possess any gift of foresight. The presentiment that warred within her against her resentment at her fate, ultimately won out, and obviously against her will. She realized that this is how life was, that life had to go on, regardless of anyone's wishes, regardless of what she would have chosen. Nara was an image of that power that is stronger than wisdom, stronger than reason – and that power fell upon me. The first thing she said was, "Poor, poor Ilget."

She undid her clothes, and I was dazzled.

I stared at that small, white, nearly translucent body, which revealed what makes up life, and I returned to that world, warm like summer moss, from which I had fallen upon being born.

We spent several days thusly. At dawn I would go off with the men into the taiga, then return at sundown and have my fill of her, and once sated I would lay my head between the little, sharp-pointed hillocks and listen to the quiet murmur of the living streams of her body. I would listen, while the wind roared over the chum, and the mad snowflakes that flew through the smoke-hole died halfway to the fireplace.

During these nights we recounted our lives to one another, and once she asked me, "When you look into my eyes, it's someone else you're seeing. Who?"

I told her about Yabto's daughter, who was part of a single soul divided into three. I told her about my secret stash of arrows and bird bones.

"Was she your sister?"

"No."

Nara stared at me for a long time, then turned away and fell asleep.

The following night she asked me again. "Are you thinking about her?"

"Yes."

Nara asked nothing further until the night after that. "Are you always going to be thinking of her?"

I told her that Yabto's daughter had been married off to a Tungus clan and was now far away.

Nara said nothing for a long time but stared at me fixedly. Then she said, "Go on, think about her, then. It doesn't scare me. But know this: I am her. We have the same name and the same fate. You have received your due, my prince. Think on that and never leave me."

***

During these days, the other women gave me a strange look that I could not understand.

Then a wise old woman came with a drum and performed a rite. She fed the fire and summoned good spirits to our bed. When her ritual was over, she sat by the fire with her legs stretched out and said, "Our lives have gone all downhill like a hat rolling off your head. A wedding, but no feast. People don't have much meat. Things are going to get hungry."

She rose. "I'm going to feed the blind man. So the food doesn't go right past his mouth."

Yekha lived in a chum with a kinsman of his, the only warrior from the entire tribe who had survived unscathed – I do not remember his name. The son of the Tungus man kept silent, just as people are silent when they do not yet understand the changes that have taken place within them. He maintained the same silence as he accepted food from others.

Nara caught up with the wise old woman. "I'll feed him, you go to bed."

"What about your husband?" The old woman asked archly.

Nara smiled and said nothing in reply – she just dropped a bone with some meat left on it into the old woman's container and walked away.

"You fell right into the trap, young man," the old woman said.

Ants

One morning there was one provider less: Yando had left.

His ski tracks went east and then disappeared from sight down in the valley. A frozen sky the color of bloody milk hung over the taiga. When the women learned that Yando – a quick-footed man, a good shot, and a handsome lad – had gone off, they were at first bewildered, and then they raised an uproar. The women knew that Yando had not been able to stand my good fortune. I was the sole person who was oblivious to this.

Yekha emerged from his chum, leaning on his kinsman's shoulder. For the first time in all these days, he spoke:

"What are you crying about, good people?"

The women fell silent, amazed. Yekha had spoken as if he were one of them, in a peaceful, straightforward manner.

All of them had witnessed the giant's blinding at the hands of the feeble old woman, and everyone knew that this was the doing of supernatural forces. But probably no one could believe that this man who had turned, in an instant, from a great warrior into a helpless cripple, harbored no anger against the people responsible for his bitter fate.

Everyone had felt there was something bad about Yekha's silence. They cared for him like for a baby, but it was difficult to say what motivated them more: compassion or fear. Now suddenly he was talking as if nothing had ever happened. None of the people knew – nor did I – that his blinding was only the start of another miracle, one hidden from the eyes of others.

A day came when Yekha told me about this miracle.

His name made no sense, inasmuch as it meant "Battle Cry". From birth he had been larger than others of the same age, and as he grew up, he grew enormous. No one expected any other path in life for him than that of a great warrior. Yekha lived up to their expectations, he alone was worth two dozen men. But the unusual strength of his body softened his spirit. Men went to war, inflamed by hatred for the enemy, summoning a fierce spirit into their hearts. Yekha used his physical mass to fight the enemy, but the fierceness that he displayed, and which struck terror into so many, was something that he put on like a shaman wears the face of another.

He realized this quality, he felt ashamed of it, therefore he forced himself to go looking for opponents, to go and fight men who had done nothing at all wrong to his family. He respected his people, and so he could never entrust them with his deepest, darkest secret: to never fight again. The more this shameful dream tormented Yekha, the angrier he became.

His relatives laughed at how he loved to sit for days by an anthill, but it was a gentle mockery at the harmless pastime of a great warrior who was so useful to his family, and moreover a young man who still did not know woman.

In the lives of ants, he saw the best life that any living creature could have. Every one of those tiny, intelligent creatures hurried along on its own way, and the Tungus man's son was amazed that whenever they ran into one another, they parted peacefully and simply hastened to see to their mysterious but surely important business, as if each ant had not even noticed the other.

He was amazed at how ants were all more or less the same, there were neither big nor puny among them.

But one day he saw an ant war.

A small squad of black ants attacked a hive of red ones, and at the head of the black ants was one noticeably larger than its comrades. This was their leader, and what few foes lay along his path, he crushed in a single blow. Yekha said that the life in the anthill had not stopped, each ant continued to bear its burden, but from somewhere deep inside appeared red ants that had clearly never carried anything on their backs. They came scurrying, one after another, down towards the foot of the anthill and the first to descend immediately met their death, for the black ants were noticeably bigger.

Yekha was enthralled by this spectacle and had already grabbed a twig in order to intervene in this dispute between others, but he held back. The forces of the red ants were arriving en masse, they swamped the enemy, and the battle became a moving blur in which red was becoming the dominant color. Then the defenders retreated, and the Tungus man's son saw the red ants haul, through their defeated foes, the body of the big black ant: it had been torn to pieces.

Yekha was deeply shaken by this sight and began to cry.

From that day on, his shameful wish became ever stronger.

"When I sought a pretext to fight you, I remembered that black ant," the Tungus man's son explained to me.

But then Noynoba ordered him to take four of his comrades and go help Kheno's family. And when my mother, driven by some higher power, took his eyesight away, Yekha was plunged into darkness and felt nothing besides pain. Then the pain went away and only the darkness remained. But then came a day when, it seemed to the Tungus man's son, that darkness ceased being darkness.

He was fed by his kinsman, then he received his food from the warm hands of the old woman, and then Nara fed him – and Yekha realized that war would no longer be part of his life, even if his life depended solely on the mercy of these people who felt guilt towards him. No longer was anyone expecting him to put on a raging face. He had become like a useless old dog, kept fed only out of appreciation for past services and for letting children play with him.

Now another thought came to the Tungus man's son, not a shameful thought but a strange one: he was happy to be blind. This was such an awkward thought that he could not quite make sense of it, and Yekha – like he had formerly in-flamed his rage – sought sadness within himself.

There was only one thing to be sad about: he would never again be able to watch the lives of ants. But this sadness could not completely overwhelm him, because in exchange for the loss of his sight, the Tungus man's son now heard sounds that he had never been aware of before. What he wanted most was for some sighted person to always stay alongside him and explain where these sounds were coming from. In this way, the concerns of the people living there became more familiar to him, and when he heard the women's uproar, he asked his kinsman to lead him outside and he spoke – calmly, like one of them, and to everyone's amazement – the words:

"What are you crying about, good people?"

They told him.

Yekha asked his kinsman to bring him to me.

"I thought that Yando would cut your throat," he said to me. "While you slept."

"What for?"

"When you lived at Kheno's, you only looked down at your feet. But I saw his face and heard his words."

Yekha told me that Yando's face had been distorted by a wicked grin as he spoke of the gift that a runt like me wouldn't even know what to do with.

I was shocked. "Nara is his own blood. Are there really no other women out there for him?"

"No," Yekha said. "So now you don't have to worry. More-over, I got Nara – she feeds me like a good wife, puts dry moss on my face. I won our duel, it turns out."

The giant laughed and so did I.

Lidyang came up and scolded us as old men do. "Do you even know where he ran off to?"

"To live on his own," I said, though I sounded unsure.

"You silly wolverine. Alone without shelter or supplies. A man won't survive like that at this time of year."

"Don't you worry, old man," Yekha said, laughter still ringing in his voice. "Anything might happen to that lad, but I'm sure he won't die."

"That is exactly what I'm worried about," Lidyang said gloomily and then went to join the other elders.

***

Three of us went hunting. The lords of this forest were merciful on us and gave us a musk-deer. The people's hunger was sated and they forgot for a time about Yando's disappearance. But that musk-deer marked the end of any mercy from the lords of the forest. Animals got away from us, our traps lay empty, and in the middle of the month of great cold we had to resort to eating the draught reindeer.

We would wander through the taiga, but return to camp and drop like frozen birds, too exhausted to even put an arm over the threshold. In the chums, the people recalled the tale of the abandoned wife who had to catch mice under the snow and was barely still alive when a kind and strong man found her in the taiga.

That winter no one disturbed us.

That winter hunger decided who would live and who would not. Three old men and the same number of old women soon died – the old men thought it unfair that they should live when there were children to consider, five boys that were as tall as a grown man's elbow, and they gave those children most of their food. But three of those children – the littlest – did not survive either.

Mothers buried their children and lacked the strength to even cry, but they were secretly happy that their children had found peace.

The wise old woman held on like a strong pine-cone, but she, too, complained sometime before spring that she was tired, and then she immediately laid down, closed her eyes, and never opened them again.

Lidyang refused to consider himself an old man – he would go out into the taiga with me and Noynoba's warrior, and he was given that share of food allotted to the men. They refused to let Yekha the giant perish, though he was as useless as any baby – Nara, without even asking me first, would take some of my food and bring it over to the blind man. His sole surviving kinsman gave him a little of his own food. Yekha remained unaware of how little the others were eating.

None of the people grumbled about how the food was divided, for the age-old law of every tribe was that the lesser portion of food should be given to the weakest.

The widows' rebellion

As the difficult month of ice passed, the taiga sent us an elk, a scrawny one as they are in spring. It had broken away from the other elk with which it spent the cold season, and it then grew weaker. Its hooves left tracks in the hard crust of ice that topped the snow. The animal seemed to be downright happy to see us and it simply stood there waiting for its arrow.

This big catch allowed us to survive until the spring meltwater began to run down from the hills into the valley. By now we were reduced to four men, my Nara, and another dozen women – the young widows of Kheno's family.

In spring the women staggered forth from the chums, looked at one another, and began crying. Many of them had been young and fresh, but this winter had turned them into old leather. Only now – and not during the cold season itself – did they finally understand the great change that had taken place in their lives. Their well-fed lives in Kheno's stately family had taught them to look at themselves more often than married women of other, weaker clans. The women wanted their old lives back, and this desire grew stronger by the day and drowned out the only reasonable thought: that the past could never be restored. They did their usual work, gathered the first herbs, walked around in the vicinity of the encampment in search of food – at least those mice that the unhappy abandoned wife of legend had subsisted on. The widows would, however, sometimes gather together and spend a long time quietly discussing something. Anyone who saw them assumed that they had gathered to mourn together their misfortune and find some consolation therein.

The only person who could hear them when the hunters went into the taiga, was Yekha. He would come out of his chum on his hands and knees and perform the only work he was capable of: breaking the branches that the young widows had brought from the forest.

Time passed, and the women's discussions grew louder. They stopped gathering all at once, then would come together in groups of only two or three – and finally a day came when one of them pulled another woman's hair.

The women had turned into men.

They had been bonded by their bitter fate for only a short time. Now the infighting began, though they realized that there would be more people hurt by it than contented. Each of the women wanted their own man to provide for them, for they considered that something any woman should have, especially a beautiful one. They refused to think about anything but what they considered theirs by right. They turned into she-bears as they are in early spring, and now they feared nothing.

The widows' enmities against one another, however, proved short-lived. It was Forepaw's widow who put a stop to them. She was no longer young, but she was strong, tall, and as taciturn and sharp-sighted as a lynx.

Lidyang could hunt game, but he was not a man who could satisfy. Yekha was probably good in bed, but he needed care like a baby. The most attractive catch was the young, stately warrior from Noynoba's tribe, the kinsman of the giant. While her relatives were screaming and pulling each other's hair, Forepaw's widow saw the warrior walk down towards the river. She surreptitiously followed him, and in a place where they could no longer be seen by others, she pulled him down into the dry grass and sucked the will to resist out of him like sweet marrow from a bone. The warrior was tall and broad-shouldered, but quite young and all he thought about was women. When Forepaw's widow pounced on him, and proved inexhaustible and insatiable in lovemaking, he stopped thinking about any other women and he stuck to her shamelessly, like a reindeer calf following its mother.

When the other women saw this, they knew that they were defeated, but it was too late: the widow roared terribly in order to discourage any of them from coming near and challenging her over the man she had caught. She knew the same secret of authority that her slain husband had known.

The attempts to capture Lidyang and Yekha ended in failure.

One of the women – I don't remember her name, nor the names of many other women there – was a mother to two boys that had become so emaciated over the winter that they were translucent like leaves. She went up to Lidyang and said, with no attempt to dissemble, "You're a widower, Lidyang. I'm a widow. You're a strong guy, and you've got a lot of time left. Be my husband. Feed my sons."

The old man knew how desperate the women were becoming then, and he asked with a wry smile, "What are you going to give me in return?"

Without blinking, the woman replied, "Everything that I've got. I am half the age of your late wife. Let's go, just get a look at me and you'll be young again yourself."

She held out her hand to the old man and repeated, "Just feed my sons. They will respect you like their father."

Lidyang shrugged her hand away. "I have been feeding them…"

"No." The woman took a step towards the old man. "Feed them like any father feeds only his own family and enjoys only his own wives."

Now Lidyang's ire was awakened. "And just let the others die?"

"Just let them," the woman said, and then she burst into tears, as she realized that her attempt had been unsuccessful.

"You wolverine's daughter," Lidyang said. "Don't you come around here again, otherwise I'll give you a lashing. Like a real husband would."

Yavlyana was the first to learn that the old man had rejected the mother of two boys, and so she was the first to rush after the remaining catch. While Yekha's kinsman was utterly occupied by Forepaw's widow, Yavlyana visited the giant alone and said that he could lean on her shoulder if he wanted to walk around – and thus she lured the Tungus man's son off into the taiga. She returned to the encampment around evening and asked the men – at the moment we were coming back from hunting – to bring Yekha home.

"Let him have a she-bear for a wife!" cried the girl once betrothed to Lar through her tears.

Everyone laughed at her, and the widows most cruelly of all.

***

But several days passed, and the jealousy of all of them found an outlet.

It was now directed at Nara, Kheno's favorite granddaughter, the only woman of the big family who had gained a husband when other women lost theirs. Granted, it was a man of unimpressive build, but strong and favored by the spirits. They feared me, these women, but the triumph of Forepaw's widow, who had tamed Noynoba's warrior in no time, proved stronger than their fear.

One day when the three of us were returning from a brief hunting expedition, I walked into my chum and saw Nara, her face scratched and bruised.

"Who did this?" I asked.

She refused to answer and only clenched her jaw.

I called Lidyang in. The old man stared at her for a long time and rather indifferently, and then he said, "Got to kill one of them. To strike fear into the others."

But the women now were completely fearless.

After a silence, Nara spoke. "When they get themselves husbands, their madness will pass. You don't need to kill anyone."

With an angry, intent step, Lidyang went off to his chum. When he emerged from it, he was holding in his hand a few large, ring-shaped leather straps. This was what remained of the harness of the last deer of Kheno's once-great herd.

"Who hit her?" the old man shouted.

The women backed away from Lidyang. Only Forepaw's widow remained where she stood.

"Enough." She spoke calmly, without fear.

"All in good time," the widow said and with a barely visible smile she glanced at Noynoba's warrior. The latter was standing several paces away and we saw him wince.

Silence dragged on and the widow's face filled with triumph.

I was with Nara then. I wanted to stroke her face, but she slapped my hand. It was not that Nara feared my touch would hurt, rather she knew something I did not: to caress and feel sorry for one's wife, especially in public, was to act shamelessly.

She looked at me, and her glance was like Yabto's lash.

I jumped to my feet and walked up to Forepaw's widow.

"What's going to happen next?" I asked.

The widow laughed and said nothing in reply. Noynoba's warrior took a step towards us. His fingers lay on his belt, where he carried a long knife.

I addressed the women. "You are so stupid that you don't understand the problem you all face."

"Everyone has their own problems," the widow replied slowly, so that everyone could admire her. After she said that, she went up and stood next to her tamed calf.

Then I told that woman who had inherited not only the clan name but also the spirit of her slain husband, "That's right. Therefore, listen to me. In order that your common problem doesn't become my problem, all of you should just be killed, like sick reindeer cows. Then I won't have to worry about my home and my wife any more."

The women quaked at my words, but the widow burst out laughing, a deep-chested laugh like a man's. She went on laughing, and I saw Lidyang's severe look, but I continued talking.

"You hassle us and demand food. You're right to laugh, woman – everyone indeed has their own problems. There's another way to get rid of an intolerable burden like beautiful widows. We'll do like everyone does: every provider focuses on feeding himself. Now I'm a man with my own household, I've got a wife and also my own native river, I should go there. Each of the men can do the same: choose for themselves a wife and a place to live. Anyone else can go make whatever life for themselves that they can. After all, isn't that what you wanted when you started to divide the men up between you?"

The mother of the small boys was first to start crying, and it was like a strong wind passed over the women's heads and sent their heavy locks of hair fluttering. The women wept, each over her own problems, and in that crying I could hear a plea to kill them if I must, but never abandon them. Stronger than their crying, however, was Lidyang's look – I saw how hostility welled inside him, and Noynoba's warrior was already gripping the handle of his knife.

This confrontation was interrupted by the sound of cracking, so deafeningly loud it was like thunder in the sky.

Yekha had been sitting in his chum and listening with his heightened sense of hearing to our words. He resolved to step outside without waiting for anyone to come and help him. As he emerged, he stumbled and fell onto the pile of dry branches that had been brought from the forest.

The women rushed to him, but the son of the Tungus man got up on his own, took two women by the shoulder at once, and ordered them to bring him to where the people were gathered. Yekha addressed me, but he spoke for everyone to hear:

"When you were still known as Dog's Ear, one young man promised to become your dog. But he ran away, and now there's a calamity. We don't have any dogs at all. It would be good to have at least one dog, even a blind one, as long as he could bare his teeth. I will be your dog, Ilget. Before you go into the taiga, tie me to your wife's leg with a long leash and just go hunt animals without worrying about anything."

The only response to this was silence.

With those words, Yekha put an end to the infighting. There was probably no need for his services, no one was thinking of getting revenge on my wife, though she stood apart from the other women, but those women who had no hope of winning one of the men, found in the Tungus man's son their savior. After he had spoken, the women realized the boundless stupidity of their plan. Even Forepaw's widow fell silent.

Yando

Driven by desperation and a canine instinct, Yando found Yabto's new encampment. On the day he had set off, a blizzard swiftly wiped out the footprints left by the army of the disgruntled.

As Yando walked, he trusted that there would be vengeance for the injustice he suffered. His faith was strong, it never flagged as he spent nights on the snow under a blanket of spruce branches, it never fell prey to any beast. Over the ten days of his journey he ate no more than two partridges hastily roasted over a fire. He made it through, however, and he got his reward: he found the traces of a camp of a large number of people. This success left him feeling renewed, and for another five days – snow-free and clear ones – he walked after the trails that a multitude of skis had left, as if following a beaten path.

His strength was dwindling as he reached the flat road that was the frozen Yenisei, but when he saw even columns of white smoke rising in the distance, he began to crawl the rest of the way without resting, as resting might turn into sleep, and that would mean death.

He had crawled only a short distance when a warrior who was cutting a hole in the ice with his spear-point, caught sight of him.

Yando entered a chum where a warm fire blazed. A stout man was seated in front of him on a high bed of skins and held out a spoon made from bone.

"Eat," the man said and pushed a bowl of steaming meat broth towards him.

The newcomer began to speak once his insides had been warmed. "Are you Yabto of the Nenyang people?"

"Where do you know of me from?"

"The whole taiga knows Yabto of the Nenyang."

"Not all of them, not yet. Why have you come here?"

"I brought you a present. For your warriors and for you."

"What kind of present for me?"

"Do you know Wenga?"

"Is he still alive?"

"For the time being."

"That's good. Where are you hiding my present?"

Yando set the spoon down, rose, and showed Yabto his ten fingers. "It's that many days from here. He alone among many mouths is dying of hunger."

Yabto thought for a moment. "Wenga isn't going to die just like that," the stout man finally said.

"I think so, too. The spirits favor that runt."

"How do you know that?"

"I saw it. He alone killed half of the men in Kheno's family. A raging demon settled in him. But now the demon is gone. Only an empty shell is left."

When Yabto heard this, he froze and closed his eyes. "And Kheno himself?" he asked after a silence.

"The old man is dead."

"And who are you, then?"

"My name is Yando. I am of the Nga people. I remember you, big man, from when you visited our father and brought Lar."

Yabto smiled and leaned back on the furs – he was satisfied and continued listening.

"If you want to get your present…" Yando began.

"I do. You have made me pleased."

"…let me eat for a few days, and then I'll show you the way. Your warriors will get a present there, too. Not all of them, but many. I know you want to found a great encampment of men who have suffered injustices…"

"I do."

"There are over a dozen women with Wenga. They will be wives for your men, the first mothers of your future tribe. A great tribe!"

"You speak like a wise man," Yabto repeated Man-Effigy's words. "What do you want for yourself, after you have been so generous to me?"

"Almost nothing, just one of those women. The smallest."

The stout man burst out laughing. "Obviously you are randy like an elk in springtime, if you almost died in the taiga for her sake."

"Not for her sake."

"How's that?"

"Not for her sake. Understand, big man, a time has already come when one can do things that were considered impossible. It is right at hand, for you and for me. Just a ten-day journey… And for an army like this, fleet-footed and without any fear of great cold, let alone other men, what is a journey like that?"

"You speak like a wise man," Yabto repeated. He was no longer laughing. With every word he liked this fellow more and more because he was a man after Yabto's own heart – perhaps not as sure and confident, but he had a sharp mind.

"Give me time to regain my strength, and we'll go," the newcomer repeated.

Yabto nodded, but then thought for a moment and replied, "No."

***

The stout man had some four dozen warriors of various tribes at his back, all clad in the finest iron. Yet Yabto felt that this force was small.

During this winter, once the great cold ended, he had resolved to lead his army north, in order to gather all men unhappy with their lot in life, from the mouth of the Upper

Katanga – which the Ostyaks call the Mouth River – to the Middle Katanga. The death of Dog's Ear would have pleased the stout man, but he did not want to expend men and time on it when he could be gathering a truly large army instead.

Yabto confided these thoughts to this man whom he had seen for the first time in his life. "Soon I will be able to do anything I want, and getting ahold of the runt will be like touching my own nose."

"A lot can change while you are moving about."

"You're right."

"What should I do, then?"

"Eat your fill here. You're coming with me." Yabto rose and prepared to leave.

"Listen, big man," Yando said. "If you don't want to go there with your army, then give me supplies and one of your men. I'll make it so that the runt comes running to you instead."

"I'm not going to do that," Yabto said. He stepped over the threshold and then turned around. "How would you manage that? Tell me."

"Those women were happy in Kheno's family. Now they are widows. They're all dreaming of new husbands. I'll tell one of them – just one – that there is a place, and you'll determine it, where they can all find husbands. And not just husbands but heroic men in shining iron. Some time will pass, and they themselves will harness the runt and the other men like reindeer and drive them forth. The women of Kheno's family are capable of such things. Tear my hair out if that doesn't happen."

The stout man was so amazed he was speechless. Then he told Yando, "When we travel on the Yenisei, you'll be at my right hand."

The campaign

That winter Yabto traveled over the ice of the great river, sowing chaos and gathering men.

He knew languages and dialects, and the army made up by his men of different faces and tribes embodied, as it were, the whole habitable world along the Tree of the Yenisei. The army marched without a flag of war – the name of its commander was its flag.

That name spread along all the rivers, it reached even those places where the rumor of this unprecedented army was considered the product of a sick mind.

He encountered the first people already on the second day of the journey: three men with big-eyed Ostyak faces were chopping at the ice with their axes. Their sledges laden with fishing gear were nearby. While the men worked, their dogs – strong and self-contented – were sleeping on the snow and noticed the strangers only when the latter had already approached.

The dogs' barking interrupted the men's work: they saw the armed caravan and realized that it was too late to run away, nor was there any point in trying to defend themselves.

The army and the fishermen stared at one another for some time. Then a man separated from the crowd of strangers and came towards them – it was Yabto. He greeted the fishermen in perfect Ostyak.

"What do you want from us?" one of the men asked.

"From you? Nothing."

The Ostyaks were wary. They said that they belonged to the great Burbot clan, the mouth of their home river was nearby, and if this stranger wished to raise the flag of war, then he ought to think carefully about it first. The Burbot people were many, they were brave, and their iron was strong.

From the fox-fur fringe on Yabto's coat they saw that he was a Yurak, a man with black soles, and a foe of the Ostyaks – a people with white soles – and therefore they did not even ask what the reason for war might be.

The stout man replied that he would wage war only on those who wanted it – he had no need for the Burbot people's territory.

"Then why are you leading so many armed men?" the same Ostyak asked.

"So that people know that Yabto of the Nenyang is marching, the founder of a new tribe where no man goes without his fair share and respect. Tell your people only this: 'Yabto of the Nenyang is marching.'"

The Ostyaks froze – they had undoubtedly heard this name before.

The stout man smiled. "I'm sorry that you didn't manage to catch any fish."

After he said this, he turned and walked back towards his own people. The army stood waiting for the fishermen to harness their dogs to their sleds and flee towards the mouth of their own river.

Yabto traveled on, and as the sun set they pitched their field tents. The warriors were not afraid to make their fires right there on the ice, for at that time of the year it was exceptionally strong.

They never saw those Ostyaks again, but what the stout man expected to happen, happened – his name had penetrated deep along the banks of that river, from one mouth to another, and spread throughout the encampments. Soon the army began to swell with new recruits.

The first to arrive were people with no hearths of their own. They were vagabonds like Iron Horn, who had grown tired of a peaceful life among his kinsmen and craved danger.

There were also truly unlucky men. For some, poverty had taken their homes and families away, while others had lost them through their own carelessness, and a third set had never had them to begin with and lived like a cobweb swept by the air. They wandered through the encampments of relatives, survived on the latter's grudging charity, and were frail and weaponless. Such people were of little use, but Yabto received them cordially, though he never remembered what tribes they came from, let alone what their own names were.

Then brigands arrived who were tired of having to lay low and reach for their weapons at every rustle of a branch, men who were pining from loneliness and their inability to rejoin human society. There were a few of these.

What Yabto was especially looking forward to, however, were the angry and strong men, men like Willow who had slain his brother.

As the army was passing through a region with a large number of islands, where the Yenisei roared loudly from each spring until the arrival of the first ice, the stout man's hopes were fulfilled.

***

A small group of Somatu people, who dwelt on frozen swamps and envied those who lived on solid ground, came down to the big river in order to fish and plunder. They spoke nearly the same language as many Yuraks, but the two did not consider themselves related. The Somatu knew nothing of Yabto's army.

When their leader – his name was Soymu – saw the army that greatly exceeded his own group of men, he did not think to run. He ordered his men to shoot their arrows at once, and then immediately ready their spears and axes – those would come in handy when the large army dispersed and began to encircle them. His men readily obeyed him and said nothing.

These Somatu lived a hard life, they did not fear death, and even the Sleeping God who created heaven and earth they considered a poor orphan who had no one. They had little regard for their own lives and considered cowardice to be foolishness.

Soymu shot off two arrows, but the arrows failed to scatter their foes: the enemy hid behind their shields and remained where they were. He started to reach for a third arrow, but stopped.

Yabto did now what he usually did: he went out alone to meet the enemy, unarmed. The leader of the Somatu, who felt dejected at the bravery of his foes, followed his example.

"I am Yabto of the Nenyang," his enemy said.

"I am Soymu."

"I know things are tough for you, Soymu. It's unfortunate to live in swamps when other people are living on solid ground and drinking water from clean rivers."

"I don't need your pity."

"It's not pity, it's a fact. If the Somatu were as numerous as the Yuraks, they would trade territories."

The leader was taken aback by Yabto's straightforwardness. He hesitated for a moment, then said "You're right."

The stout man allowed him no respite but went on. "You ought then to go and lay claim to the solid ground that's waiting for you."

"And where is that?"

"Wherever you want. I am gathering men who are looking for their fair share. When such men come together in a large number, no one can stop them – not other people, not the spirits, not the gods. Do you understand what I'm talking about?"

It was the great demon at Yabto's back who said those words. The Somatu were a proud people and preferred to live in the swamps rather than recognize any one else's authority over them, but the great demon had crushed, as if with a bear's paw, Soymu's will to resist. The leader sat down on the snow and stared at Yabto for a long time. He forgot all about the plundering and fishing he had come to do.

The group of Somatu filed into the ranks of the stout man's army. That same evening, elated at having some hot meat, Soymu accidentally stabbed one of the vagabonds who had just arrived. Fortunately, the dead man was so insignificant that his death did not cause any strife among them.

***

Soon Yabto had gathered around a hundred men, but he was still dissatisfied, for he considered this too small an army to shake the Tree of the Yenisei. But his demon told the stout man that his work this winter was done, that he now had to head south and reach some encampment before the ice started to weaken. The army needed to be fed and prepare for its great task.

In their encampment, the new people would be able to defend themselves against any foe.

He would build a fence of logs and reinforce it with earth and stones from the river, as the Selkups do, assign the warriors their tasks, and gather strength.

His plunder so far consisted of only weapons, and that was not enough to live on. They needed pots, fine clothes, strong chums, and meat, a lot of meat so that every man of the new tribe and those who wanted to join, could see that their lives had changed, that they could look forward to a better life, one worth facing adversity and the horrors of war. The stout man's cares did not wear him down, he could see that the time had come when everything he expected in his youth would work out, and that undoubtedly was his destiny in life.

He ordered his army now to go hunting and fishing, so that they would not lack for food on the journey back. His men spread out along the riverbank, cut holes in the ice, and fished without any fear of the owners of that territory – the owners themselves were afraid.

The battle of the islands

The name of this remarkable commander reached the land of the Nga people.

It posed no threat to this great clan, for there were no resentful men among them. But the rumor of the growing army got the men stirred up, and finally one of them, probably some old man whom people trusted unthinkingly, said that it was surely these people who were guilty of wiping out two respected families – Kheno's and Noynoba's – and the Nga clan's agitation was joined by a thirst for revenge.

The Nga people decided to stop Yabto of the Nenyang.

They did not know the exact number of his warriors, but they believed in their own prowess, the greatness of their clan, and the patronage of their dread god of the underworld. A troop of their fifty best warriors was assembled, each of whom was capable of catching an arrow in mid-flight. The Nga people had no flag of war, because they did not march forth to measure their strength against others or argue over territory.

The days grew brighter and snow no longer fell. The army went onto the ice of the Yenisei and immediately came upon the enemy's trail. The caravan moved quickly, the warriors' heavy weapons had been loaded onto sledges while they themselves walked alongside; they wore goggles to shield their eyes from the blinding light off the ice.

The sun betrayed the Nga people to the enemy.

In the morning the sun rose right over the course of the river, blinding those traveling north and making things clearer for those headed south. Yando was the first to spot the hostile force, though he himself remained unseen.

He had taken a few people to hunt an elk whose tracks he had found the day before. They walked far and caught sight of a caravan in movement. Yando dropped down to the snow and ordered his companions to do the same. They then crawled, dragging their skis behind them, to a forested island, where they got up and rushed to find Yabto. The enemy had not even noticed them.

The stout man quickly realized what he needed to do. Fortunately, the greater part of his men were there alongside him.

He sent the Somatu and several other men ahead.

The Nga people took that band for the whole army and took their weapons from their sledges without any particular haste. They then advanced and, once they were near the enemy, they shot their arrows all at once.

Soymu had been instructed to feign cowardice and conceal any desire to fight. The Somatu leader did this perfectly. His men shook their weapons, shouted insults against the opposing force, and when a flock of arrows came whistling towards them, they backed off, abandoning several of their own in front of them – these were some worthless men who lacked shields and did not know how to dodge arrows. Soymu had taken them along in order to make the enemy drunk on a false sense of easy victory.

When the Nga warriors saw their first victims, they began to move faster, while the Somatu retreated to an island on which low, sparse trees grew, and there was nowhere there to hide. In spring this island – only one of many along this point of the Yenisei – would be flooded under the ceaseless roar of the rapids. In winter the river here grew calmer, and at the place where foamy water roared, cliffs rose from icy boulders covered with thick snow.

If the Nga people had been a little more careful, they would have guessed at what the opposing force was planning, but their bravery and their contempt for the lesser peoples of the taiga drove them onward.

Finally, the Somatu stopped retreating and stood their ground with their shields up.

The enemy decided not to waste its arrows in vain, and so they lay their quivers down on the snow and reached for their axes and spears. They closed their ranks and rushed forward – the Nga people wanted to end this in a single blow, load the enemy's scalps onto their sledges, and head home quickly.

***

That Yabto proved able to hide over fifty men in an open space on the edge of the island, many considered the work of a demon and not a man. Just as the Nga people came up to the Somatu, death came at them in a thick flurry from both left and right. They realized that they had fallen into a trap, halted for a moment, but they did not lose heart. The band knew what to do: vanquish the men standing against them with a single blow and, once on open ground, retreat as far as they could, wait for the enemy to expend their arrows, and draw them into a fight with axes and spears – in such a battle, no one could win against the warriors of the Nga people.

They gave a fearsome roar and rushed forward. Those who were at the edges covered with their shields the ones running in the middle. But just as the wooden shields of the Somatu were right in front of them, it was as if a brisk wind blew in, and the Somatu vanished: Soymu's men had darted to the side or dropped down into the snow, so they would not be hit by the arrows from their own side.

The Nga warriors found themselves in front of the open space for which they had rushed forward – and this was their undoing.

The edge of the island descended into a valley of snow-covered boulders, and the first ranks tumbled right into it without noticing the danger in time and stopping. They were easily picked off like reindeer crossing a river. The fates of those who remained were decided just as quickly, as if they were mere youths and not the finest warriors of a great clan. The bows of countless foes twanged just a few yards away, and the Nga men's skills at catching arrows proved useless.

The Somatu consoled themselves after their feigned cowardice by tearing one man away from the doomed Nga band and raising him up on their spears. One after another the Nga men collapsed into snow stained red, and when the last of them had fallen, Yabto ordered an end to the battle.

***

The day was short, but enough of it was left for the new tribe to enjoy their plunder. Every one of them, even the lowliest, could don armor and trade their ragged coats for new ones. Then they took the strength that had been contained in the hearts and livers of those brave men – the laughing mouths of the new tribe were stained with blood. Along with the weapons and clothing, the victors also got the Nga caravan, which consisted of many reindeer and sledges laden with supplies.

Yabto spoke with a prisoner, a tall young man with long hair who was slightly older than his own sons had been. The prisoner glared at Yabto and answered him impertinently.

"What is your name?" Yabto asked.

"Soroga. Was it you who killed Noynoba and his family?"

"It was me."

The stout man stared intently at the prisoner and tried to detect any change on the latter's face. The prisoner's expression remained the same.

"You're a fine warrior, Soroga. Will you join me? I've already got one of yours. See that young guy?" Yabto pointed to Yando who stood several paces away. "He is from the Nga people."

The warrior did not even look at where Yabto had pointed. "He's not one of ours," he said. "Ours are laying dead here."

"I could let you go, give you supplies and a sled."

After he said this, Soroga laughed soundlessly and said that Yabto was the one who should be begging for mercy. "Before the ice even weakens, an army will come, one so much greater than your rabble that you would be like a squirrel fighting a bear. It will not be as careless as we were. We are expected back in a few days, but we will not return – and soon everyone will know about our disaster. Everyone! And not only our clan, other tribes will hate you, Yabto of the Nenyang. So why do you taunt me by falsely promising to let me live? You're a dead man yourself." The prisoner laughed even more bitterly, then fell silent. He was tired. "If you want to do something good for me," he said dully, "then just hurry up and kill me."

Yabto drew his knife from his belt.

***

The short day ended. The yellow light of campfires dotted the darkness that had fallen over the island. The new tribe celebrated and hailed their leader.

Yabto sat motionless as a stone and despised his people and their shouting, for it only hindered him from being able to hear the demon at his back. That demon remained silent, however.

Yando came up. Yabto took him by the arm and led him to his own chum.

"Did you hear everything?"

"I did."

"What do you have to say about it?"

"That lad was right. The Nga people overlooked it when Kheno died. Their attempt at revenge for Noynoba didn't work out. They can't allow things to go wrong a third time."

"Will they manage to gather an army while the ice still holds?"

"If not this winter, then definitely next. We won't be able to escape the Nga. But remember, big man, you became the first to ever win against the warriors of that great clan. You can gather an even larger army than they can. While there is still time, go along the rivers, and don't just wait for clans and families to throw you their refuse."

Yabto smiled and said that such a wise advisor would get from him whatever he wanted.

Yando smiled in reply. "I don't want much, only the girl I already told you about."

"What is her name?"

"Nara."

Now the demon at the stout man's back spoke up.

***

Yabto had forgotten about her.

The daughter he had married off two years before to the Tungus clan of the Kondogir had faded from his memory after the deaths of his sons and Uma. He had severed all his former bonds of kinship and was now founding a new people, who might rid the world of its annoying disorder. He had already grown accustomed to thinking of himself as a lone man, the last man on earth, and he shuddered to hear that name spoken, for it reminded him it was not so.

His glory would soar even higher when those dwelling along the tributaries of the Yenisei learned who had first beaten the hitherto unbeatable clan. But this glory, his demon said, would engender fear together with respect, and the inhabitants of the region would strive to avoid any encounter with Yabto, so recruiting for his army would take a long time. The Kondogir, however, a clan to whom Yabto was related, were strong and numerous. Through that family connection they would be his allies.

He returned to his men's feasting and asked Soymu, a frequent visitor to those parts, whether the mouth of the Middle Katanga was far away.

The Somatu commander held up his five fingers. "A five-day journey. But now we've got a lot of reindeer, so less."

By sunrise Yabto knew what to do. He called Willow, Yando, and Soymu and told them that a big war was coming where they would need allies, and he already knew just who. He said that no alliance could be concluded without offering some gifts, so his men should not take the finest iron. Instead, that should be loaded onto sledges, and his men should take only the lesser stuff for themselves. He indicated to Willow and Yando that they should prepare for a journey.

"But you, Soymu, my brother, will stay with me," the stout man said. "Don't you leave here, and please, don't get anyone killed."

The Somatu commander puffed out his chest and instantly forgot his resentment at having to part with the finest plunder.

That same day, a caravan of ten reindeer set off towards the north.

Only one thought troubled the stout man's heart: it concerned meeting his daughter again. He did not feel any personal guilt at his son's deaths, and even when he broke his wife's bones, he was not killing Uma but the raging beast inside her. One could fairly claim that it was fate which had decided all that. But the very thought that he would see Nara and his new relatives not as a head of a family and a householder, but rather as a man who had lost everything, buzzed around him like a gadfly and prevented him from enjoying the fruition of his hopes. He sought some pretext to drive this gadfly away and finally he found one. He remembered Man-Effigy's words: "All people are good at times and bad at times. They are fickle, and that is why fate drives them along like a herd of reindeer. Choose something and stick with it, and then you'll run along on your own, without any shepherd over you."

The vexatious thought vanished, and the stout man smiled to himself.

Molkon

The lands of the Tungus clan of the Kondogir stretched from the mouth of the Middle Katanga nearly to its headwaters. Scattered families lived along the rivers that flowed into it. The Kondogir hunted, kept boundless herds, and were a content and friendly people. Any news which one of them heard quickly spread to all.

They knew of the fearsome army founded by Molkon's relative by marriage. One day Molkon, who was patriarch of the strongest family in the clan, called his son Altaney and said that he should get ready and go greet some visitors properly, while the latter were still on their way to the encampment. Altaney gathered some three dozen men and set off for the mouth of the river. The old man remained at home. He proved prophetic, for on the very same day Altaney met his father-in-law. Molkon was only wrong in that he had expected the whole army, but instead only three men had come.

Altaney bowed to his father-in-law and led him to his own father. Along the way he asked no questions and uttered not a single word beyond what politeness required. He was a taciturn sort – Yabto saw that at once and said nothing himself.

This stately man, a head taller than Yabto, was Molkon's treasure. Of the patriarch's many children, only six had survived: five daughters and that lone son.

The old man met them at the edge of the encampment.

"Are you aiming to find offended and resentful men among my own people?" he asked instead of a greeting.

The stout man replied at once, "There are no such men among those who dwell with you, Molkon."

"There are," the old man smiled archly. "All Kondogir are resentful, and myself most of all. Why did it take you so long to come and visit?"

They embraced.

"You see from how many fires smoke is rising?" Molkon went on. "The kettles are boiling and full of meat, and you're expected."

"How did you know that I would come? Are you a shaman?"

"For someone who is old, the world is small. If you hear a man's name, it means he's somewhere nearby. Come, now I'll show you something great, something you would never imagine…"

***

Nara had got pregnant while still on the journey from her native encampment.

She came out to meet her father in a new parka embroidered with shining fur and beads. The woman who came out bore no resemblance to the tender young woman who had left the banks of the Bountiful River, and Yabto was dumbfounded at the sight of his daughter.

Nara bowed to her father. Tears flowed down her cheeks.

"Show him," the old man ordered her.

Nara opened the flap over the chum and an old woman, the eldest of Molkon's wives, brought out two boys.

"Your grandsons, Yabto."

From the clothing that had been made exclusively to their measure, the stout men understood that these children of the Kondogir clan were cherished above all others in the encampment who, like every infant in the taiga, wore hand-me-down clothes from their forebears' childhoods, often their grandfathers'. But Yabto was even more astonished that there were two of them – and at first he was not sure whether that was something to be happy about. They took after their father and had eyes like short stitches sewn with a black thread. They were two years old, but even in that heavy clothing, they could keep upright.

The stout man picked his grandsons up, asked their names, and immediately forgot them.

Nara stood nearby and occasionally wiped her wet cheeks with her palm. "Are my brothers alright?" she asked. "Is mother alright?"

Yabto bent down and deposited the boys onto the snow – they immediately went running to their mother.

The patriarch prevented any answer to her question, he only barked at his daughter-in-law, "Later." Custom held that one should not ask a guest questions until after he had been fed.

Springtime Girl looked down and led the children back into the chum. She lived in constant, reverent fear of her husband's father.

Many guests gathered in Molkon's chum. Besides Yabto and his two companions, the patriarch's brothers and his best men were there.

When the pot and container of fish meal were empty, the old man said that the ample food had made him sleepy, and all the Kondogir men besides Altaney rose and began to file out.

"Are these good fellows your army?" the old man motioned with his eyes towards Willow and Yando. They had not said a word while in Molkon's encampment, they only glanced pathetically aside at the smoke rising from the wealthy clan's myriad fires.

"Having over a hundred guests at once would be no fun at all. Even for such a rich man as you."

The old man smacked his lips to show surprise, but Yabto could see that he was not particularly surprised.

"I knew your father, a fine man, and when I first saw you, I knew you would outdo him in everything. Where are your men?"

"Three days' journey from here."

"No one would leave his native land, let alone a river called the Bountiful, but you did… Well then, are your sons well, dear Yabto? Your wife?"

The stout man looked the patriarch right in the eye and told him calmly and bluntly that his sons, Yabtonga and Yawire, died at the hands of an escaped slave that he had wished to bring up as his son, and now regretted. The death of his sons had awakened a raging demon inside his wife, and to kill it, Yabto was forced to kill his wife.

The stout man looked at the patriarch and waited to hear what he had to say. He expected sympathy, but Molkon's eyes narrowed like those of a snake and he said this instead:

"You walked around the taiga, gathered men, and by promising them honor and satiety you raised a mighty army, you went along the Yenisei and filled every living thing with fear – and all for the sake of catching a single slave? Is he some kind of giant?"

"No. He's a runt, but the spirits favor him. Are you making fun of my grief? You shouldn't."

"Forgive me." After he said this, he continued to stare at Yabto with the same look. "If, as you say, he is favored by the spirits, then perhaps your grief was their will?"

Yabto began to speak. He said that the Nga people had sent forth against his army a band of warriors, each of whom could catch an arrow in flight. "Every last one of them is lying dead not far from here, among the boulders on the islands. No one had ever defeated the Nga people before. Whose will was that?"

"I don't know," the old man said. "But now I know why you are going around the taiga from river to river and gathering men. You want to shake the tree of the Yenisei so hard that every nest comes tumbling out of the branches, and in those fallen nests you want to find the runt who made your life so horrible. You may well succeed. But, dear fellow, once you have shaken the tree, do you really need that escaped slave? Do you need anyone at all, when all the nests are lying there at your feet?" Molkon fell silent for a moment. "I understand your grief. You were a man like everyone else, but you know who you are now?"

"Who?"

"Listen. Stay here at my home. I will die soon, you can share authority with my son."

"I am a Yurak."

"If I bequeath authority, my people would consider even an Arin or a Somatu one of theirs, or any other person, even a fish or a crow. You saw your grandsons. Now this place is your blood, too, dear fellow. Where else should you be? What do you have to say about that? Do you miss your army?"

"Now you listen to me. Every word you said is true. But the Nga people will make another attempt, and they'll come for me with a much bigger force – it's as certain as the sun coming up in the morning. My men are brave, and there are many of them, but they would be weak against Nga people who are riled up after their previous failure… If I took your wise advice, they would come for me here even if I didn't have any army. You know that, Molkon."

"I do."

"You've got a lot of strong men. A whole lot."

"Is that what you came here for?"

"Yes. Help me, Molkon. After all, we're family."

The patriarch's face grew pale.

"I brought you the finest iron," Yabto said. "What the Nga warriors had on."

"You brought war," the old man said dully. "I am a cunning fellow, but you are even more cunning. I was but a hollow bone before you."

The stout man saw victory in sight and took a step closer towards it. "If you are worried that the Nga people will come for me while I am in your territory, I'll leave tomorrow."

"No, don't. Was it a really a bad thing for me to welcome you? Sleep here in my chum, dear guest. And lodgings have already been prepared for your men. Stay here in my encampment."

Altaney rose. "My wife will be asking me," he said. "What shall I tell her?"

"Tell her what you heard," Yabto said, and was embarrassed at how feeble his own voice sounded.

***

The stout man did not leave from there, in fact, he was not even thinking about it.

He made his grandsons little bows, with real larch-wood arrows with bone tips. He was a kindly grandfather.

Only Nara, when she bowed to her father in the mornings, would not say a single word to him. For his part, the stout man did not try to strike up conversation with his daughter. Altaney had saved Yabto from any need to tell her what had happened, and every time the stout man saw his daughter, he felt grateful to his son-in-law. But time passed, and he began to realize that Nara had something to say to him. He waited for her to say it. There was more curiosity than anxiety in this waiting, but with time, his anxiety grew stronger.

He would go hunting for partridges with Molkon and they feasted every evening, but the old man no longer spoke with him about war or armies. Yabto trusted that his relative felt trapped and so he, too, said nothing. Instead they had happy, friendly conversations about simple, pleasant matters. But time went by, and they both wearied of these conversations. Each of them knew what they were keeping silent about: once the ice weakened, and the rivers swelled and overflowed, they could forget about waging any big war until next winter.

Finally, the stout man's patience was at an end. One evening, as he nibbled at a bone and tried not to revealed how concerned he was, he asked Molkon what his answer was.

"Things here are alright for you, but while the ice is still strong, I need to lead my men."

"Go ahead and do that," the old man replied.

Yabto repeated his question.

"To gather a big army, they would need time," Molkon said. "They will hardly manage now. Go now and don't worry until next winter."

Yabto was disappointed and his heart sank. He did not reveal this, however, and after he had thanked the old man for his food, he went to lie down.

****

The next day he stood by a loaded sledge – his son-in-law had generously gifted one – and said goodbye. Nara brought out the children.

Yabto squatted and patted each of them on the nose. "Grow up strong, the both of you. And give me something to remember you by."

The children said nothing. Nara took from her neck a thin string from which little birds, sculpted from bone, dangled and she spoke for the first time in many days:

"This would be a good memento of two little boys. Take it. Let it always be with you."

"Where is this from?"

"It was a gift from Wenga, when we were children ourselves. Farewell, father. Give my greetings to my mother. And my brothers. Try to find them good brides." After she said this, she bowed and led the children away.

Yabto was astonished by his daughter's words. He looked around for Altaney. Molkon's son himself came up and said gloomily that it was time to go, for the day was short. The stout man looked once more at the birds sculpted from bone – they were still warm, imbued with the warmth of a human body – and he placed the little birds into the bag on his belt where he kept his flint.

Molkon embraced his relative and quietly said, "Leave the Tree alone…"

***

They reached the river mouth at midday.

Altaney saw the guest off. At the point where they would go their separate ways, he called Yabto aside, took his knife from his belt, and cut his hand open.

"Do the same," he told the stout man.

Yabto shed some of his own blood. They clasped hands and waited for their palms to stick together like the parts of a bow.

"There is not much left of the winter," Altaney said, "and the Nga people will not raise an army. But even later, father will not war against them. I will. I swear that I will give you warriors and come myself, once the ice thickens again."

While they were traveling together, Yabto was tormented by a desire to ask Altaney whether he had told Nara what he had been instructed to. Now those nagging thoughts vanished and were forgotten. He asked instead about something else.

"Why will you join me?"

"You wanted to shake the tree of the Yenisei. I like that. No one has ever done that."

"Will you go against your father?"

"Yes."

"What's so bad about Molkon?"

"He lives too long."

After mighty Altaney said this, he drew his hand away from Yabto's and walked off.

∗∗∗

Yabto arrived back at the place he had departed from: the site a ten-day journey from Noynoba's summer encampment.

There, where the old man's family had once lived, he was protected by surging lowland rivers, and moreover impassable swamps that were covered in perennial clouds of biting insects.

There was a place there for fishing, and now the army set their weapons aside and wielded fishing gear instead.

Yabto remained aloof from these common tasks – he lay on furs and turned the bird bones over in his fingers. One day he called Yando and said:

"You promised a present: for the warriors women, and for me the runt. Take what you need and go."

Yabto looked into those keen eyes and felt assured that little time would pass before the one who made these birds would be here, tied to a tree.

My faith

Yando set off to do what he had promised the stout man, and even more so, had promised himself.

During the lonely winter months, people had grown un-used to hearing strangers' voices, so Yavlyana almost died from fright when she heard her name out of a clump of willows. The voice was not unknown to her, only somewhat forgotten.

They embraced, rubbed noses like brother and sister, and that same evening in the encampment Yavlyana spoke in Yando's words:

"Ask the men, and most of all Ilget. Tell them, all of you. Tell them all as one: we want the fat fish, the fish full of caviar that our men used to catch for us, in that wonderful place at the mouth of the river where fish gather. You need to go out to the Yenisei and then a bit down it. There, my sisters, handsome men in shining iron are waiting for us, and each woman will have her own hearth and her own husband, and the life we lost will be restored to us."

From that day on, the women began to wear us down with quiet, insistent nagging.

The first whom they convinced was Lidyang. He knew the place, for Yando's words about the banks of a bay where fish gather had been true.

The old man hesitated, however. He was still Kheno's brother, and though sometimes he detested the widows, ties of blood bound him to them. He had wanted to bring them to their kinsmen's lands, but for himself he just wanted to live his own life, which he had already planned out from beginning to end.

The memory of the wonder that had occurred – the inhabitants of the graves departing into the Seven Heavenly

Snows – weighed on him for a long time. Lidyang nevertheless planned to return to the site of the great encampment
and live out the rest of his days there, where his umbilical
cord had been buried. He decided to carry out that plan, even
if no one wanted to go with him and he had to live all on his
own. The prophetic words that Kheno's land would be handed over to others for ever, now only sparked anger within
him and an infantile, contrarian desire.

"They're right," Lidyang said about the women when the
three of us were sitting at the fire and roasting small birds
over it. "They need to gather strength so that they can go
on living." The old man looked up and asked me as if I were
some bystander, "Will you come with us, Ilget?"

"Yes, I will."

"And then? Then where will you go?"

I replied that now I was a man with a name, a tribe, and
a native river. Now I was a man like all others, and my path
was set. "My nest on the tree of the Yenisei is empty and it's
waiting for me," I said.

The old man chuckled. "Your nest… How are you going
to find it? Do you know the way?"

"No."

"Maybe you know someone who can show you the way?"

"Yes, I know someone. And I know that he blames me for
his misfortunes and wants me dead."

"There, you see? Who is going to help you? Finding your
particular river along the Yenisei is like finding one marked
needle on a whole pine tree."

I found it hard that the old man – like probably everyone
else – did not share my sense of faith. I gathered my courage
and said, "Destiny will show the way."

"Destiny? What do you know about it? You're just a kid…"

"You heard it yourself," I said coolly, "that no one is born
without his own land and sustenance, otherwise why should
he be born at all?"

"Have you ever seen slaves, captives?"

"I have. I have been a slave myself."

"Then remember them, remember your own self, and realize how silly your words sound, how silly you are."

"And that wonder that we all saw?"

"Oh, you son of a wolverine. Do you think seeing the dead is a wonder? When our shaman was alive, he would chase them away from the encampment like stray dogs. They all kept trying to come back, they missed their good life in Kheno's family so. The dead, if you really want to know, are the same sons of wolverines and fish crap as the living – they don't want to live their present lives, either, and so they go looking for a better one. If you live to become a dry old bunch of bones like me, you'll understand that. We have seen that you can do remarkable things, but you can't do them solely through your own volition, whenever you need to. No one can. So, be happy just to be alive. You're a small guy, but strong. Be happy that you have a wife, a beautiful one that others could only envy. Look, our brother here," the old man nodded towards Noynoba's warrior, "found some unfresh meat, but he's happy."

The warrior rose, spat at Lidyang's feet, and walked out. He was fed up with Lidyang's hurtful jokes about his submissiveness to Forepaw's widow. Lidyang however went on, without even noticing the warrior's spitting:

"Even a blind man is simply happy to be alive. That, my boy, is wisdom that you lack."

I did not know what to say in response to this. I felt nothing within me besides anger at the old man. I was angry because the truth of his words attacked my own trust in my destiny.

Nara knew a certain truth, too.

None of the women bothered her, though they continued to stay aloof from her. But the women were unable to conceal from her their secret, that it was Yando's message that

Yavlyana had repeated to them. Yavlyana's shrill whisper came flying up out of the smoke-hole of the unclean women's chum and landed at her feet.

That night Nara told me, "We don't need to set off there with everyone else."

"You don't want those fish?"

"We would only find death there. Yando came. He wants to offer your life as a present to the man you know. The women will try to coax you into going, but don't go, Ilget."

Anger flared within me again, and I told my wife that now my destiny was clear, and if it had assigned me this path, then I had to walk it fearlessly.

Nara hugged me and her tears ran down my face and body. "Don't be an enemy to yourself and to me," she kept repeating.

That only sparked even greater determination within me. "My enemy is anyone who does not believe in my destiny."

"Those are just words," Springtime Girl cried. "But words aren't worth risking your life for, even if they are prophetic."

I still remember how her words left me blind with rage. I leapt up, grabbed Nara by her hair, twice slapped her, and flung her into the unclean half of the chum. I then got dressed, stepped out of the chum into the deep night, and laid down on the ground. I looked up at the stars and listened to the river roaring in the distance with the dirty waters of spring. I thought of nothing, felt nothing, besides the fact that I had done something special and done it on my own.

I went back inside. The fire in the hearth had gone out. Nara was lying there where I had thrown her. I repeated, in order to drive away that which had quenched my faith and sparked fear:

"Whoever does not believe in my destiny is an enemy. Don't be my enemy, wife. Get up."

***

I sensed that Nara had been telling the truth, but how I should act based on that truth, I did not know. All that I possessed within was faith in my destiny, and it told me: if your fortune lies in the hands of a single man, then you must go to him, even if he is your enemy. Faith, however, is not reason. Faith can kill if it does not have anything to defend itself from the enemy with. All people were my enemy, because they did not share my faith, and my wife was probably among them.

In the morning, when we set off on the journey, she walked alongside me but said nothing. I saw neither anger nor resentment in her. She walked obediently, with her head down, and she looked distractedly to the side. She seemed to not even feel Yekha's massive hands that rested on her shoulders – she was serving as the giant's guide.

We had no boats. We walked along the banks of rivers that each grew from one another, to eventually disappear into the single great river.

After one overnight stop, I was overcome by despair. I said that on this day, I would not go anywhere, and the women who had been staring at me insistently the whole journey, did not start to argue – they were tired.

I took my bow, said that I was going hunting for birds, and walked off into the forest. Noynoba's warrior was inspired to come along, and the motivation had been none other than nagging from his well-worn wife. Lidyang however told the warrior, "Just let him go. Leave him alone."

I walked along without looking up or looking for game. I was still thinking of the one enemy who was stronger than any people and had assailed my faith. Who had arranged it so that my share, my place on the tree, my life was in the hands of a single man who sought my death? It was that thought which was my enemy.

As I sought some weapon to use against it, I recalled the wondrous things that had happened in my presence, but this weapon proved weak, because faith is not something that is understood, it is something that is felt – it gives off a warmth in the chest. That warmth is faith. I realized that Nara had said the truth, I could see that these widows of Kheno's family were leading me along in order to trade me for their happiness, but I went along nonetheless, hoping that through my stubbornness I could lure out that warm feeling of faith and it would aid me.

But instead of warmth I felt a black pit yawning inside me, and it was filled with the turbulent waters of fear and shame.

From the bottom of this pit I heard something, I heard a voice like the creaking of a dead tree. The voice called out to me, "Hey, hunter! Hey, hunter!"

I turned and saw someone sitting on the stump of a tree.

It was Man-Effigy.

The pike's spine

"I guess you want to ask how I ended up here?" he asked.

I was speechless.

"Yabto left me up on a rock so that Nga would remember that I existed and take me. Yabto was so sure that the god would listen to him, that he didn't even stay to watch me die. He got in his boat and sailed off. Granted, he almost fell off that cliff as he was hauling me up… I waited for a crow to come by, I grabbed it by its legs, and together we flew down to the riverbank. The crow fed me, too. You don't believe me?"

Memory of the voice awakened inside me. "Who are you?" I asked.

"Your stepmother's uncle." He laughed his familiar laugh that sounded like merely the creaking of a dead tree.

"Who are you?"

Man-Effigy was silent for a moment, but then he spoke. "Back in the days when a person wouldn't think about death, I had a name – I forget it now – strength, and joy in my heart. Back then I was crossing from one bank of the Yenisei to the other. Spring was already in full force. The sky was bright-blue. I was in good spirits, because I went to abduct a bride who knew I was coming to abduct her, and she was so impatient she couldn't sleep. When I thought about her, I laughed from joy, and in that very instant, the hard ground under my feet started drifting: it was ice giving way under me. I had strong skis lined with beaver, and I sped up in order to get through this dangerous place faster, but the ice was cracking louder and louder, and it seemed like I was going downhill. The ice floe under me turned over and I went into the water. The water grabbed my skis and dragged me down.

I managed to quickly free myself from the skis and I grabbed onto the edge of the ice with both hands. I held on with all my might, fear had made me desperate. My hands slipped, but I was afraid to release one of them so that I could get rid of my quiver and my ax from my belt – the water was grabbing at them, too, and I grew even more afraid. If someone had come along and put out a stick, I would have been saved, but I was all alone on the big river.

"But then came a moment when everything froze, as if just before a heavy rain, and I thought, is my life going to end just like that? After all, I was on my way to abduct a bride, one who was looking forward to the abduction. Who had I angered? Who needed my death? How was I any worse than other people who were now happily living their lives, while my strength was quickly running out? That thought took hold of me, I felt an inexpressible sense of longing. I looked up at the bright sky and remembered the highest god, the one who is asleep. Why was he sleeping while the current pulled me under the ice? Why didn't he wake up and save me?"

The old man fell silent, smiled, and looked at me. "He did wake up and save me… Even though I hadn't made the slightest prayer, I hadn't promised him anything as people usually do when they ask the supernatural world for something. He sent a man, a Yurak from his appearance and speech. That man took off his skis, laid down on the snow, crawled toward me, and held out the shaft of his spear. He pulled me out.

"Then he helped me up onto the riverbank, where he had an earthen hut, and he made a fire there in the fireplace. He laughed and asked me, 'Well, did you get a good look at Death?' I replied, 'Yes, I did.' But then I said something else, I don't know why: 'I'd like to never see it again. I'd like to never die.' The man chuckled. 'If you don't die, you'll eventually get tired of life. Ask old people what their lives are like.' 'No,' I said, 'I wouldn't get tired of it.' 'What do you need to live forever for?' I answered with the first thing that came into my mind: 'To see what other people wouldn't see, because life is too short – everyone regrets that.' 'Well, if so, then go ahead, never die,' the man said, and he jokingly but powerfully slapped me on the shoulder. I fell backwards and we both laughed. Then, I remember, I asked him his name, and he said he was from the Cape People and called Rich-in-Reindeer-Bulls. 'Only I don't have a single bull. I got rid of all of them.' 'Why?' I asked. 'Long story,' he replied, and then fell silent, but it would have been rude of me to ask more. I told him, 'Be my elder brother. You saved me, after all.' 'I will,' he replied. 'Come visit sometimes, it's boring here all alone.' The next morning he gave me his skis and some jerky, and I set off the way I had been going, to abduct that bride."

"And did you?"

"Yes, I did," Man-Effigy replied, then he cried, "Is that really so important, you marrowless bone?!"

After a pause, he went on:

"It isn't so important. What's important is that I didn't die. I outlived my children, grandchildren, great-grandchildren, then my great-grandchildren's great-grandchildren, and then I lost count."

"Is Uma a relative of yours?"

"No. When my grandson died – and he was an ancient old man when he did – people started to shun me. To avoid bothering them, I went off into the taiga and never returned. If a man finds it strange to live so long, other people find it downright scary. They thought as they could be expected to think, and felt better. I sat down on a fallen log, and I stayed there all day, evening, and night hoping that I would die of hunger, but I was taken in by someone already the next morning – since then I have lived from people's charity. I lived with them, then outlived them, and left… Sometimes I was taken in by the People of the Scream. Uma's father felt so sorry for me, an old man whose evil kin could not dissuade him from going into the taiga to die, that he called me his brother. Then plague struck his encampment, which naturally left me unscathed. Then there was Yabto… By then I firmly knew that it was my gift to never die. Just like it's your gift to hear birds from half a day's flight away. But I didn't start wondering about that right away.

"I remember how in my youth I went to visit my rescuer, Rich-in-Reindeer-Bulls. I loaded a boat with gifts for him – the best that I had – and yet I could not find even a trace of his earthen hut. Granted, I figured that a man living along in an earthen dwelling and not a chum, was hiding from someone and covering his tracks… Before I reached even ordinary old age I was already thinking different: he had no reason to hide, because he was not one of us, not a human being."

"Who was he, then?"

"If only I knew. He saved me, then slapped me jokingly on the shoulder, and death no longer came to me: not from floods, or famines, or war, or disease. I witnessed all those things and yet remained alive, though I wasn't trying to hide from death."

Then I asked the old man, "In our encampment you were no longer even able to walk, so how did you end up here?"

"You, like many people, consider the slightest wonder to be something grand. Believe me, for a man like me, walking was the most insignificant of all the wonders that happened to me. You'll realize later that this is true. It'll be something wonderful when I learn why the spirits played a prank on a lad who said 'I'd like to never die.' After all, every gift is given for a reason, but what was mine for? So that living would bring me satisfaction? But life is no satisfaction, believe me. To free me from any fear of death? That might seem the real answer… But I wasn't afraid of it. So, what was the reason?"

"What was the reason?" I repeated after the old man.

"Perhaps it was for what I asked for: to see the things that other people would not live long enough to see."

"And did you see them?"

"Yes. Life and people are all the same. Nothing changes, no one changes. That is all I have managed to see, and it would have been better not to see that."

After Man-Effigy said this, he fell silent, and I seemed to catch the glimmer of tears in his faded eyes. To prevent the silence from dragging on, I asked:

"Where were you going?"

"To find you." The old man's answer was straightforward. "You'll feed me. Like before. And where were you going?"

"To find Yabto."

"Why?"

"My nest on the tree of the Yenisei is empty. Only Yabto knows where it lies."

"I have been there, too. Why don't you ask me?"

"You have forgotten…"

"Yes, I have. The eyes of an old man only see big stones, and the small stones are something only the young see. Memory is the same. But I can bring the memory back. If you help me."

"I'll give you the best piece."

"I'm not talking about any piece. Help me, do what I ask you."

"I'll do it."

"Don't say that right away. Think it over."

"I'll do it. What do you want, old man?"

"Take my gift from me. Never die."

"Tell me how to do that."

"Take my heart out – you've already seen how that is done. Burn it and then rub yourself with the ashes."

I stood and backed away from him.

"You can't do it?" The old man hung his head. "A weak young'un, a mere boy. But I'll die someday all the same."

"You're not immortal."

"Only spirits are immortal, and probably not all of them. I didn't tell you the main thing: with that man I ate a pike, a big one – its head filled half of the pot. After we ate it, he laughed – and we were always laughing and treating everything as a big joke – and he gestured at the fish: count how many bones there are here, he said. I said that I couldn't count them. He said that it didn't matter, that I would live for as many generations as this pike had bones. 'Then we'll meet and you'll tell me whether you have had enough already or not.' 'What about the tail?' I asked. 'Suck on the tail and spit it out.' 'And if I want to die?' 'Take out your heart, burn it, and smear someone with the ashes.' And we collapsed onto the furs laughing. It seemed so funny to us. Maybe I have already reached the tail. Or maybe I've got a ways yet. How can I bear it?"

"Can't I kill you like any man?"

"My appointed fate, foolish boy, lies in the fact that I'll never have anyone alongside me who will cut my head off and then throw it from a distant mountain, so that it can't crawl back to my body and reattach. Yabto couldn't do it. You couldn't do it either."

***

I heard people's voices. They were looking for me.

Noynoba's warriors and several women, among whom was Forepaw's widow, had been running through the forest. There were many paths, but they just happened to choose the one that they found me by.

"Who is that?" the widow asked.

"An old man. Can't you see?"

"How did he get here?"

"He landed on a tree stump."

"Who are you?" the warrior shouted. "Tell us!"

Man-Effigy did not reply. He only closed his eyes and became as I had been used to seeing him.

"He was abandoned by his family. He's a Yurak. He'll be coming with us." After I said this, I stood up, took the old man by the arm, and lifted him up onto his feet.

"I can walk on my own," again came the voice like the creaking of a dead tree. "Just support me."

"What do we need those old bones for?" the widow cried.

"Yeah, why?" Noynoba's warrior shouted.

I said nothing in reply, I only led Man-Effigy to the camp on the riverbank.

The women and the warrior followed after me.

"Don't we already have enough cripples?" The widow refused to leave me alone. "Get rid of him!"

I told her that if she did not cease, I would get rid of her, and everyone else, too. Behind my back I heard the women – there were four of them – discussing something, and anger and dismay could be heard in their voices.

Finally, a shout came from the widow, it flew like spit into the face of her young suitor. "What are you just standing there for? He's right there. Tie him up! Come on!"

I took my hand from Man-Effigy's shoulder – the old man did not fall. I quickly moved several steps away and grabbed my bow.

The point of my arrow fell over the face of Noynoba's warrior. His arrow was looking at mine.

"How great it would be, brother, if each of us killed the other," I said.

"I will kill you," Noynoba's warrior hissed.

The widow said nothing, she was waiting for the outcome, but the three other women who heard our words made a sound. I saw my opponent glance at the woman who had him hook, line, and sinker – he was unsure what to do. The widow remained stone-faced. Without looking at anyone or uttering a word, she started from the place and ran down the slope. The warrior lowered his weapon and rushed after her. Then the women left, too.

***

When I brought Man-Effigy to the riverbank, the women were standing in a tight rank, like warriors ready to meet the enemy. Lidyang, my wife, and Yekha stood apart from them.

Forepaw's widow stood in front of the others. I did not know what she had said to the people there, but I could see that everyone was hostile to me. She was the first to speak:

"We're going on foot when others go in boats. We're making our feet bloody on all these stones just so we don't die of hunger, and this guy is collecting carrion in the taiga!"

"Now we have another mouth to feed!" one of the women cried.

"What kind of provider could he ever be?"

The arrival of Man-Effigy had stunned Lidyang. He walked up to the old man.

"Who are you?"

Man-Effigy said nothing, nor did he even open his eyes. Instead it was I who answered. "A Yurak abandoned by his kin. I'm talking him along."

"Can you handle him on your own?"

"Yes I can."

"You're being foolish," Lidyang said. "We're barely making progress, because we've got a blind man who keeps stumbling over stones. Now you want to haul these dry bones with you? If you do, the fish are going to get away. This old man probably came out here himself to die. Why get involved?"

I pointed to Noynoba's warrior. "He's a strong guy, he'll help me."

Suddenly the alarm on the women's faces subsided, and I caught several words quietly said by one of them along the lines of how only evil people would bring the elderly out to die on a tree stump, plus the old man was so weak that he would soon die on our journey and then there would be no delay or reason to quarrel.

This was shattered by the angry voice of the widow:

"He's not helping to carry anything!" She grabbed her suitor by his sleeve, "Don't you dare get involved with that dead meat, you hear me? If you won't listen to what I'm telling you, don't you dare come to me again."

"The man is mere carrion indeed," the warrior said submissively.

Suddenly a woman cried out – it was one of those who had gone through the forest to find me. She was pretty and ardently detested Nara. "He threatened to abandon us if we didn't let him take the old man. Well, let him, then! Just a few more days, and we'll be eating fat fish. Just leave us if you want. Take that bitch that was given to you and the blind man! Stay here and try to catch fish with your bare hands!"

Lidyang ran towards the silly woman to chastise her, but Noynoba's warrior flung him aside with a single blow.

Now Yavlyana got involved and revealed everything she had been hiding. "Sisters, have you forgotten? We would never be able to manage without Ilget. Without him, Yabto of the Nenyang won't accept us in his tribe – he said so himself. If he doesn't want to go, then we'll bring him there by force instead of that old man. Tie him up! Like a reindeer!"

She screamed those last words, her eyes on Noynoba's warrior. What had happened earlier in the forest now repeated: we each grabbed our bows, I backed away some distance and leaned against a warm wall – Nara had brought Yekha, and he bear-hugged me and shielded me with his back.

"I'll cut off the head of anyone who touches him," the son of the Tungus man quietly said.

Everyone fell silent.

Lidyang rose and walked towards the women, wiping blood from his mouth as he did. "What husbands are you talking about? What Nenyang? We're going to get fat fish…"

"Go yourself," Yavlyana cried in reply. "As for us, we're going to get ourselves husbands, Yabto of the Nenyang's warriors! All of them in shining iron… New chums, new pots! We'll have our old lives back! Shoot the blind man!"

Everyone watched as Noynoba's warrior lowered his weapon, and then let it fall from his hands. He revered the giant like an elder brother and feared him even though the man was now sightless.

Lidyang dropped onto a stone.

For a time everyone was silent. Lidyang was aghast at the lie. The women – even Forepaw's widow – were overcome with despair. It was clear to all now that no one could separate me from the blind man.

But then a woman, the mother of the boys, cried, "Maybe he needs Ilget, fine, but Yabto's warriors need wives! They are pining away without women. They'll see how strong and beautiful we are, and Yabto won't stand in their way."

With that, the women's despair blew away. And with those words, we went our separate ways.

***

Several days later the widows arrived at the great encampment of the new nation, at the river mouth that was teeming with fat fish full of roe.

Their arrival nearly cost them their lives.

The Somatu, who stood guard, were the first to spot them. They dropped whatever they held in their hands as if it were a mere trifle, pushed Noynoba's warrior aside, and began to strip the women's parkas off. The Somatu had no idea where this great fortune had come from, they growled and pawed at the bodies they had been missing all these months of living alone and dangerously. These swamp-dwellers then suddenly let go of their catch, grabbed their weapons, and prepared to defend what they saw as theirs and no one else's. Soymu ordered them to desist, however, as he saw that Yabto of Nenyang was approaching.

The stout man had watched these events. The widows of the great family took advantage of this pause to crawl away to the sidelines. They said nothing, and even the two boys, who had remained unscathed, did not make a sound.

From among the bunch, someone quietly asked, "Who are these women and where did they come from?"

Instead of answering, the stout man just called Yando and said that he could not see the present that had been promised to him.

Yando rushed up to Yavlyana. "Where is the runt?"

Yavlyana was scared half to death. "He didn't want to come," she stuttered. "We had a fight about some pathetic old man who came out into the taiga all by himself to die, I guess. But Ilget refused to let us leave him behind."

"Who is this Ilget?" the stout man asked.

"The person you're looking for," Yando said. "He's an Ostyak from the Great Perch clan. Now he has his name and his people back."

"What old man?" Yabto asked dully, almost ambivalently.

"A Nenets," the woman replied.

Yabto turned to Noynoba's warrior. "Why didn't you tie him up? You've got a weapon."

The warrior hesitated to reply and tried to meet the widow's gaze, but she stood far off with bruised and bloodied face. "Yekha defended him," he finally said.

"The big, blind guy," Yavlyana explained.

Yabto repeated his question.

The warrior gathered his strength and replied, "He's my brother."

"Weren't you told that the runt is the gift you have to bring in order to join my tribe?"

"Yes, I was."

"So how dare you, the only armed man, arrive here without the gift that was promised?"

"How could I attack my own brother…"

"He's obsessed with that woman of his, like a puppy dog!" one of the women cried.

Yabto laughed and briefly glanced at Forepaw's widow as she wiped her bloody mouth with her hand. The whole time that the stout man had been talking, no one had seen his hands – behind his back, his fingers gripped the wood of his spear, the wide blade of it lay on the ground…

Before the people there could even draw breath, the iron whirred and the head of Noynoba's warrior went rolling down towards the river.

"These women are my gift to you," Yabto said among the silence.

He ordered Yando to line them all up and wash their faces, so that everyone could examine them – it was not such a bad gift after all.

"We are a new people, and there is no people without its women. Let these be the first."

He waited for someone to ask whether this gift was too small for an army that could lay claim to everything, but no question came.

The warriors saw the women no more on that day. Yabto ordered them to be hidden away in a distant chum and kept under guard, otherwise the guards' heads would roll just like that of Noynoba's warrior, whose name he didn't even know.

Before the battle

It was not that he had again let his scrawny and mysterious foe slip away, nor was it the news of that old man, which occupied his thoughts, though it slightly rankled. Rather, the demon at his back whispered about something else, something more important.

Yabto gathered his warriors and told them, "What if an army was being prepared that was ten times stronger than ours? Who can I go to meet it with? With dogs that couldn't remain with their owners and gathered into a pack of strays?"

"You called us a new people, and now we're just a pack of strays?"

The commander raised his voice. "What is a new people?" he asked. "Huh? Who will tell me?"

No answer came from his army. Finally, someone shouted that a new people lives by fairness, that in it no man is without his fair share, and Yabto himself had talked about that many times.

"By fairness? Can you fairly divide up, and with no man left out, those women that are quivering with fear that you'll tear them apart?"

The army was again silent.

"If you don't have anything to say, then I'll do the talking. You just listen closely to every word I say. It is not you who found me. It was me who gathered you, according to the will of gods and spirits whose names we will know soon."

He spoke quietly, addressing each man in turn. "You there, Willow, your father took away your inheritance, made you poor, and you want revenge. You, Tendo, slaved away working for a kinsman, and he did not even give you a bride."

He rose and walked among the rows of seated men, nudging each of them in the chest. "You were driven out of home, because instead of a skull you've only got a stone there. You took offense at how a caught bird was divided up. Isn't that right?"

"You know our stories, Yabto."

"You can kill the man who got a herd and didn't deserve it. Willow already did that. Take all the daughters from a man who was unwilling to provide even one. Destroy the home of this numbskull's family…"

Now a hubbub arose that was unanimous: yes, that is exactly what should have been done and shall be done!

"Look how foolish you are, like a hunter who is chasing a hare when an elk is running right alongside him."

"Tell us what you want!" the men cried.

"I gathered you by the will of the gods, I gave you shining iron instead of threadbare clothing, I gave you victory over the best warriors in the taiga. And for what? To run from one encampment to another and get revenge on those who insulted you but did nothing wrong to me personally? No. I'm hunting after something different."

"What?"

"The good demon behind my shoulders calls it Peace. My quarry is peace over the entire tree of the Yenisei. Under that peace, the best will not die instead of the worst, and there will be no dishonesty in dividing up territory, hunting catch, or brides. Let there be peace, like the encampment of a good householder, where everything is in its right place, and he could migrate from one end of the earth to the other and find his things untouched. Wouldn't you all like a world like that?"

The Somatu commander spoke up. "In that world will we end up with the same frozen swamps?"

"Soymu, brother, boggy land will go only to those who deserve it. I can see that it won't be you and your kinsmen."

　　　　　　　　　　　　

Soymu beamed. "Then I like your world. You speak like a wise man, Yabto."

"Everyone does what he ought to, and gets what he deserves – that is what the demon between my shoulder blades constantly says. The same holds for each of you – otherwise, why would you have come to me?"

Then the men, enchanted by Yabto's words, asked how such a world could be achieved.

"We are many, but we are still nearly insignificant," the stout man replied.

He looked at his men and saw that they did not follow. He went on:

"Once I was walking along the top of a cliff. The path was narrow and the cliff was high. The wind was beating me from every direction, it wanted to push me off. But I had to walk this cliff, there was no other way for me to go on. Down below I could see certain death, if not from the height than from the weapons of others. So, I'm walking along and I think, my entire life depends on not making a single motion to the side. At times the way became so narrow that even a glance to the side risked getting me killed. I realized that I would make it through, I would survive, only if I kept looking ahead, even if all the demons in the heavens started dancing around me."

"But what if someone came towards you?" Yando asked.

"I would have flung him aside, even if he were my brother. Or he would have thrown me off. A path like that could only be walked by a single man, who maintained a singularity of purpose and never looked to the sides or down. That was as sure as your cleverness at asking questions… The great hunt that I am inviting you on demands the same strength of will that led me along that cliff." He fell silent for a moment and then asked quietly, though loud enough for every man to hear, "Tell me, who am I to you?"

"Our leader," several voices piped up.

Yando now jumped to his feet – he had been sitting to Yabto's side, but his mind, keen as a lynx's, could sense Yabto's commanding look.

"You," Yando poked the Somatu commander in the chest with his spear, "You called him a wise man! Where have you ever seen a man as wise as this? In your swamp?"

Soymu reached for his knife, but Yando shouted even louder:

"If Yabto of the Nenyang is a leader who gathered all who are hungry to get even with the people who offended them, then we are no people, not even an army, but a pack of dogs! Yes, a pack who don't have their own hearths, who are doomed to wander the taiga, raid encampments, and ultimately die of hunger, cold, or a trunk cleaned bare. If Yabto were just a leader of men, then soon the skin from our flayed faces will be swinging from a tree at a confluence, in order to warn other packs against raiding."

He shouted then with all his might. "Yabto of the Nenyang is our very strength of will! The will that will get us past the cliff's edge. We have no other will. Whoever wants this, stand up!"

Everyone besides the stout man rose.

The sparks from the bonfire, mixed with steam from a hundred mouths, floated over the taiga on this night when not a sound could be heard.

Yando fell to his knees and looked into the face of the man he had called their will. "Tell us, how do we get started?"

Yabto did not move. He spoke, with unchanging expression:

"Just like a pine tree that soars into the sky, begins from a tiny seed, our work, too, begins from a single short word: 'death'. Death to anyone who strays from what we desire in even the slightest way – who takes another man's possessions without asking, who strikes a comrade, hides food, or takes more from the pot than he ought to. That is what I can suggest as a start. For waging war there will be other rules, but they will be similar to what I just told you."

"Yabto!" the new people cried.

From that moment they ceased being a hundred armed men, they were divided into squads of ten men each. No one was allowed to remain dwelling where he had before – each ten-man squad was assigned three chums and a commander who was provided, in addition to his rank, a woman. The women mended the clothes of their husbands' subordinates, cooked food, and knew their honor was kept safe by that same single short word that protected everything else.

Thus the dream of the young widows of Kheno's great family came true – they were all satisfied. The stout man took Forepaw's widow for himself, in spite of expectations that he would choose a woman of fresher age – and there were such women. The actual name of that widow also remains unknown to me.

***

The Nga people and Yabto of the Nenyang were presently on the same side of the Yenisei, the left bank. Although the stout man had left his native river, he nevertheless remained on the same bank. Spring gave way to summer and swamps swelled as they were fed by small rivers, shielding the two enemies from one another. With the warm season also came a lot of nice work to do, and of the bad work there was only pillaging and some minor revenge. The enemies did not seek either of those. They waited for autumn, when the month of heavy snowfall would make the ice on the Yenisei so strong that it could bear myriads of men, reindeer, and iron, and would not melt at the abundance of blood that would be shed.

Without neglecting their herds, the Nga people careful-ly considered what lay ahead of them. Their scouts main-tained constant surveillance over Yabto's encampment and, when they returned home, they told of incredible things: how women had arrived at the encampment, looked after the men, and apparently were undoing their belts for all one hundred of the warriors, while the men, as if their minds had been damaged, assembled into shapes resembling a block of wood for slicing meat and performed strange dances with their weapons. The stout man himself sat like an idol on an elevated place and occasionally raised one arm or the other.

What was being discussed in the enemy's camp, however, the scouts were unable to report. The elders demanded to know whether Yabto had many reindeer and sledges, though they realized it was a foolish question – he had few reindeer, for the riverbank and thick taiga could not offer room for a large herd. But the elders knew that Yabto possessed a keen mind, and therefore they were not ashamed to ask something that might seem silly.

They also asked the scouts whether the army's ranks were being expanded by other men unhappy with their lives. The scouts swore that they had kept painstaking watch, and not a single new man had arrived, moreover there was not a single new fire blazing in the encampment.

The elders of the Nga family castigated themselves for the loss of that band of their best warriors, but time passed, the pain lessened, and a grudging appreciation of the enemy's cunning fanned a calm and confident desire to cut out this rot that had appeared in the world that stood on the Yenisei. The anger they felt was a composed and righteous anger.

Everything changed one day when a man returning from his scouting mission, said that axes were ceaselessly ringing at the enemy's encampment, and tall trees came tumbling down one after another. Several days later, the elders learned that the riverbank was covered with rafts, and there were fewer chums standing. "They are leaving for the other bank," one of the elders said. Why Yabto of the Nenyang would abandon that convenient camp together with all his warriors, women, chums, weapons, sledges, and plunder, and moreover risk losing some of the reindeer in the move – this was a riddle, and it shook the Nga elders out of their complacency.

One of them said that it was no mystery, that Yabto was simply afraid to go to war and wanted to get far away. "He's a smart man, he finally understood how things are."

Some were pleased by these words. But now another elder spoke up. "Gray hair on an empty skull! Is he really sailing far away? To the islands, where the roaring currents will smash his rafts to smithereens?"

In that silence which an incontrovertible truth leaves behind it like a wake, one word was spoken:

"Molkon."

That word shattered their composure.

"Molkon, the leader of the Kondogir, is Yabto of the Nenyang's relative by marriage," the same voice went on. "That kinship obliges him to provide help. The ice forms at the mouth of the Middle Katanga earlier than it does here. In the forested islands, the roaring waters calm down by then. That's where they're going to meet us, just like those men of ours who all knew how to catch an arrow in mid-flight. The Kondogir have many reindeer, and also many men. Besides their fellow Tungus, they can call on Somatu and Tau – they always agree to join in a big war."

Dozens of wrinkled hands slapped gray heads, and the long, flowing beards shook as if in weeping. How could so many wise men overlook a thing like that?

***

The sun had not yet set when four of the Nga people's best scouts ran through the taiga. Their light dugout canoe slid over the grass. By nightfall they had reached the Yenisei, and when they saw the fires of a temporary camp on the other bank, they ran on. In the thick willows they hopped into their boat and rowed as hard as they could. Each knew that one of them might never return home, if not all four of them. They had to reach the great encampment of the Tungus man Molkon and learn his thoughts about the coming war.

The taiga was covered in golden rays when the scouts finally returned. Their report sparked celebration. Molkon, they said, would not fight on Yabto's side. Moreover, he did not want anyone else to join in this foul business that Yabto had started. He was not obliged to do anything for Yabto of the Nenyang, and if it weren't for the two fine grandsons that the daughter of the man from the Bountiful River had born, then he wouldn't want to maintain any further ties with the man, not even a passing acquaintance. If the man did not refrain from his mad plans, then he, Molkon, would be happy to see the Nga people put a stop to him once and for all. That was the reply given by the most esteemed member of the Kondogir clan. Moreover, the scouts added, they were welcomed not as ordinary warriors but as emissaries of a great clan, though there was little time for ceremony.

They also learned that Yabto of the Nenyang was creating a new encampment not far from where the rapids began. No one knew why the leader of the new people was doing this. Some said that the Arin and Assan people living on the Upper Katanga, who other peoples called the Angara-Muren, were prepared to join with his forces, but they hardly gave any credence to that.

A place for mustering had already been set: downstream along the Yenisei, several days' journey from the mouth of what had once been Yabto's own river. Men clad in shining iron came streaming towards that spot. More smoke rose from the encampment on the riverbank by the day. Once the first blizzard subsided, during the month of heavy snowfall, was when the war would be launched.

We, too, arrived at that location.

***

Man-Effigy, who knew everything that went on in the world without ever leaving his spot, showed me the way. He said, "If you want to be closer to your enemy, then better you go there with a big army instead of all by yourself." He then chuckled, knowing that it was impossible for me to respond to such wisdom unkindly.

Lidyang was the brother of the late Kheno, Nara was his favorite granddaughter, and Yekha, though half-Tungus, belonged to the family of Noynoba, also late and lamented. They were all of the Nga people, members of the same tribe.

We were received by a man who bore, by a whim of fate, the same name as Nokho's brother, the one whose blood was shed in spite of his innocence: Serkhasawa, "White-Headed One".

But if the other Serkhasawa had white hair from birth, this one received it in old age, and it was clear that it was the last name he would ever go by.

The old man wept at the sight of his relatives. He held Nara's wet cheeks between his palms for a long time, reached out with trembling fingers towards the giant's face, hugged Lidyang for a long time, and looked ambivalently at Man-Effigy who sat in the snow. He listened to Lidyang's brief explanation that the old man was a Nenets of uncertain background, and apparently his evil relatives had abandoned him.

When it was my turn in line, Serkhasawa's tears stopped. "Who is this?" he asked.

Nara was standing next to me and said, "My husband."

"For a beauty like you, who was being saved for a queen, they couldn't find any nicer-looking man?" There was no trace of humor in the old man's voice.

"He is open to the will of the spirits," Lidyang said. "And a good archer."

"Every man is open to the will of the spirits. So, who are you?"

"I am Ilget, son of Belegin, brother of Balna, an Ostyak from the Great Perch clan," I said and looked the old man in the eye. Then I added just as firmly, "I was once a slave to Yabto, whom you intend to fight against."

"Oh…" the old man drew out, and before I grasped what was in that sound, he said, "May you live to ripe old age, *ket.* Isn't that what your people say?"

"They do."

***

We arrived without draught reindeer, like poor people, and one chum was provided for all of us. There, at the far end in the sleeping area, Nara got out of her parka after burying me under a heap of old, ragged furs, and as she pressed her entire body against mine, she tried to undo her tightly fastened belt. Her nails became claws, so great was her haste. She started to cry, "Well, come on, undo it." She brushed my hand away from her belly and spoke into my ear with moist lips, "I've already got someone inside of me. I need more, I want there to be a lot more."

"That's not how it works."

"What about you and your brother? What if you don't come back and all that I got from you is a single child?"

"I'll come back."

"Stop listening to my body, be a man like other men… You might not come back."

"I will."

"I want more, I want sons like you… You might not come back."

Man-Effigy coughed unceasingly, Lidyang tossed, turned, and groaned, and Yekha slept soundlessly, but it seemed like all three heard every word and sound coming from under the furs.

The son of the Tungus man must have found them especially hard – the following day, he asked to move to a different chum. But even without Yekha there, everything repeated three nights in a row. Nara wanted many kids and for certain.

There was no fourth night.

The battle

"Your wife misses you even though you're still alive," Man-Effigy told me. "No need for that."

"Will she find another man?"

"You'll make it back alive."

"Are you still dreaming about someone setting your heart alight?"

"Nah," the network of lines on his lips suggested a smile. "Not any more. I want to see how everything turns out. How they will bring him here."

I said nothing in reply, I just went out onto the ice, where a seemingly endless line of men in iron stretched. Lidyang had stepped out before me: to his spear and bow he had added armor, obtained from who knows where, made of leather soaked in glue, a Selkup wicker shield, and an iron hat with a high peak. He knew I walked alongside him, but he was in no mood to talk. He had firmly resolved – if he survived – to return to Kheno's territory and dwell there, even if he were all alone. Really, he was just like me, because he lived with the same desire to occupy an empty nest on the tree.

The men who led this army refused to give me a shield. "You're already too hard to hit," they said, laughing.

As for my own weapons, I had my bow and my spear.

***

Humankind had fought on the ice a countless number of times before, but there probably had never been a battle so strange, brief, and terrible.

The night before we went out onto the ice, the elders of the best families in the Nga clan came together in the big chum. As commanders of their forces they chose three men, who assumed for the battle the names Khe "Thunder", Khekhsar "Storm", and Khekhtu "Lightning". For three nights before that, the shamans had performed their rite in dark chums, descended to the underworld, sought to learn the will of its dread ruler, and ask his favor. They returned exhausted, and from their confused speech we could learn only that his will was unclear.

What secretly and jointly tormented the wise men was what should be sacrificed for a clan that knew that worthless gifts only insulted the supernatural world. Even were the blood of thousands of black reindeer to be shed at sunset, that would be hardly anything at all, and moreover every reindeer was needed for our campaign. The number of slaves, too, was insignificant. Then one of the elders said:

"Yabto of the Nenyang is not just a villain who has gathered and armed a rabble that do not have their own hearths, and what he says is and does are not just words. Rather, it is a plague sweeping through the world. Even if the Kondogir refuse to fight for him, I am certain that new men will join him, for disrespect for one's parents, elders, and other people's lands might sound like fun and make a scoundrel out of a good person. This war is about more than revenge for Kheno and Noynoba's families, and the death of our warriors for which we, frankly, are to blame. If we leave things as they are, if we kill as many as we can and scatter the rest across the taiga, nothing would change. The plague would rise back up again and come for us. Therefore, our sacrifice should be everything under Yabto of the Nenyang's banners: his warriors, his women, children, reindeer, dogs, and even the mice that burrow in the snow next to his chums. It would be good for Yabto himself to remain alive, for we know a fate for him that would not only restore our honor, and make up for the loss of our kinsmen, but also please our great patron god: it shall be a death that would terrify death itself."

The elders nodded and stroked their beards.

But now another respected elder spoke up:

"You're so confident in our victory. All of us are. But you know, luck is fickle…"

"You're right. Then it is we who would become the sacrifice, every last one of us. Yabto has probably reinforced his encampment with walls, like the Selkup do. We will not do that. Our families – women, children, the infirm – will stay in our present encampment on the riverbank. If Nga turns his back to us, then Yabto will come and do to them what we would do to him should we prove victorious. Is that not a real sacrifice?"

The elders again stroked their beards.

***

The journey was long. Several times the howling winds forced men to hide under furs and buried the iron caravan in snow. The wolves followed after us with a reasonable hope for easy prey. We passed the mouth of the Upper Katanga and reached the islands: they rose as snowy, sparsely forested hillocks.

As we traveled, we expected that some encampment might appear on the riverbank, but the riverbank was deserted, there was little forest, and we did not have to fear ambush.

The army made camp on the snow. Night fell. The commanders ordered that large fires be lit. A yellow glow dispelled the darkness. We expected to see the same lights close by, but the sky over the islands remained black. We sent scouts out – they did not return.

Thunder – the most senior of all – refused his comrades' reasonable suggestion to let the army get at least a wink of sleep. But the men sitting at the fires slept.

***

In the morning, the army of the Nga people assembled into ranks across the entire width of the river and waited for the enemy. The distance to the islands was more than several arrows' flights and remained deserted.

The first man appeared before sunrise. He bore no banner. He came close and stopped just out of arrow range, whereupon he took from his reindeer's back a bag, whirled it with all his might, and then hurled it towards us. Then he turned around and left.

The bag contained the heads of the scouts.

Some time passed, and then a mounted man appeared with the red flag of war. One of our commanders – it was Lightning – went to meet him carrying the same flag. However great the enmity between two foes, custom demanded that one discuss the rules of war, even if the aim were a trifling one like abducting some powerfully-chested women without paying any bride-price or seeking forgiveness. But instead, Yabto's emissary said only the following:

"You, Nga people, will win if that god awakens who is asleep in the utmost heaven and knows nothing of the existence of humankind, or even the world on the Yenisei."

"Where is Yabto of the Nenyang?" Lightning asked.

"You will see soon. You'll see everything soon."

After the rider said this, he headed back to his own people.

***

Yabto appeared far off, and only those who stood in the first ranks could recognize that this was the leader. For Yabto that was enough, for the commanders Thunder, Storm, and Lightning stood at the head of our side. The stout man sat down on a dais that had been carried behind him.

The Nga people's enemy came into sight. In two thin, equal streams they came running from two sides separating the islands from the riverbank (where Yabto had hidden his army on such a cold night, remained a mystery to the commanders). They did not scatter across the open space but remained in distinct formations that were equal, identical, as if a skilled craftsman had hewn them with his ax. Each of these formations were framed by an array of shields, made from glued leather and wood, that were just as identical and expertly wrought. Over these formations, polished iron shone.

Instead of an unnecessary discussion of the rules of the war, instead of the mutual threats and insults that serve to get warriors fired up before the battle, Yabto had decided to dazzle the enemy with something else, with this wonder that he had created out of the rabble of the taiga.

Yabto raised his spear – and the even formations scattered like beads spilled from an overturned container. An instant later they stood in four lines, and the line of shields had been smoothly rearranged and remained unbroken throughout. With another wave of Yabto's spear, the lines turned into round, equal-sized stones as one can find among the middle of a shallow river. These stones bristled with spears.

Our army stood dumbfounded. The Nga people knew war well, but this was the first time they had ever seen such a thing.

Thunder broke the silence. He spoke loudly enough for many to hear:

"Enough of their dancing. They are a hundred men, just as they were before. Yabto is dancing in front of us because he knows that we will withstand their blow. Moreover, we have enough men to go around the islands and surround him. Even if he hid an ambush there, it would be a small one. I can see he has no reindeer, only men on foot."

"No more waiting. Launch the arrow!"

A black-feathered arrow, whistling more like a flute than an arrowhead, came flying from deep within the ranks, and its song had not yet ended before the Nga warriors rushed forward. The ranks in the rear ran blindly, snow dust having been kicked up by those before them.

Before the opposing sides met, Yabto gave a third signal, and the river stones disintegrated to form a single massive spear point. Its tip plunged deep into the enemy army. This was unexpected, and it was such a powerful blow that the commander named Thunder, who had been standing right in the middle, barely escaped death. He was knocked from the back of a black-headed reindeer bull; the bull wheezed under men's feet and tried to get up, but soon died.

The commander, however, survived. He struck to the left and the right and shouted to his warriors to form tighter ranks. The voices of the other commanders carried over the battle, and every Nga man knew that their army was alive. Soon the strike of that unprecedented iron wedge would begin to weaken and vanish. The Nga warriors would then be fighting the battle of strength against strength that they were used to.

I was there somewhere, too. Where was I? I slashed with my spear, and whether I killed many, I don't know. The heart of the *soning* that had come to me in the form of the puny slave and performed wondrous things in Kheno's encampment, had not yet spoken inside me – I was a man like any other. Yet while men were dying around me, I remained alive.

One of the senior warriors grabbed me by my sleeve and ordered me to run to the edge of the forest, where bowmen were massing.

"It doesn't make sense for you to be here," he said in a merry tone. "Strike the enemy when he begins to retreat. Strike our own people if they try to run away. Understand?"

I rushed towards the place that he had indicated: the shaft of my spear broke, and all that was left was the wide blade, but my bow was still intact and my quiver full.

The bowmen formed a chain along the riverbank. To one side I saw the Nga army, with great bloodshed and torment, absorb the iron ball that Yabto had come up with. I heard the voices of Storm and Lightning – the voice of the most senior of the three could no longer be heard. The bowmen were talking about how the army's rear was standing around idly and soon the commanders would order them to surround the islands.

That is probably what would have happened. I saw movement begin deep inside the army. The mounted men dismounted – fighting from a reindeer's back on rocky terrain is certain death – and came together. The commanders shouted something, and it looked by all accounts like they would soon start moving…

But something else happened instead, something that caused the battle to freeze.

****

Dark specks appeared in the landscape between the islands and the riverbank: they were people.

A voice cried over the bloody field of battle, "The Kondogirs!"

Everyone, from the most senior and strongest down to the youths and the wounded who watched from the baggage train, knew that the Tungus would not support the war, that Yabto's relative by marriage found him repugnant. But the Kondogirs – men in bright, embroidered breastplates with the same intricate patterns tattooed on their faces – had arrived nevertheless. This news came as a harder blow to the Nga army than that human wedge at the beginning of the battle. Already someone was cursing Molkon's name.

In that moment when the battle had stopped, Yabto ordered his warriors to enter into formation. He stood up in his elevated place and shouted under a sun that reflected blindingly off the ice, "It was already said to you, Nga people, 'when the god in the utmost heaven awakes, he who is unaware that humankind or even the earth exists…'" The stout man now turned and opened his arms wide, ready to greet someone.

The man he was waiting for, was Altaney. He alone of all the Kondogirs was mounted, his bull moved at a leisurely pace and deftly found its way among the icy stones. Molkon's son got down from his reindeer and hugged Yabto, his blood brother. Then, without even looking aside, he reached his arm out towards his army, and a banner was placed into his hand. The red cloth was similar to all the other banners of war, it was the red flag that everyone goes to war with. But Altaney's banner was of the sort that one could not have imagined even in the cruelest times.

The pole from which the banner flew was crowned with a gray head: it was Molkon's.

The battle had begun before daybreak. Now the sun shone in a clear sky and everyone, from those who stood in the first ranks to the warriors with the baggage train, could see that this man had made his father's head his banner.

Altaney planted his pole in the snow and once more hugged the stout man.

****

Among the talents that every human being is endowed with, Molkon's eldest son had received – besides his remarkable good looks and stature – a keen mind. Though he had not heard what Yabto of the Nenyang told his own soldiers about the strength of will that led him along the cliff's edge, he could sense these thoughts merely looking at the stout man. When the two had clasped their bloody hands until they stuck together, Altaney already knew that he would go even further than Yabto himself. The trusty demon between his shoulder blades was silent about only one thing: it had probably already forgotten how to see such things.

The taiga lived by killing. It sometimes happened that people raised their weapons against their parents or their own children. But to make one's father's head a banner of war, such a thought had never come to even the most rebellious imaginations. Altaney was the first to do this – he did not do it out of malice, but because his father had barred his way along the cliff's edge. He kept his word and brought his own forces.

The Nga people, on the other hand, every last one of them, had never heard the talk of the cliff's edge and the pact between the two lofty minds. They knew what had been told to them: that Yabto's army was not a band of brigands, not patricides, but a plague that had to be eradicated, just as an abscess is cut out with a red-hot arrowhead. Otherwise, that plague would spread through the whole taiga, through the whole world that stood on the sacred Tree of the Yenisei. It was with this conviction that they went to war.

Now, when the Nga army saw the head raised on the banner, they did not experience the fear that arises even in strong men when they face death. They saw that from which death is born, something like the sticky egg of a reptile dwelling deep in a swamp, something that even the foulest spirit would find foul. Their fear suddenly gave way to anger, as if the heart of the *soning* had settled into the entire Nga army.

There was no need to issue commands or form ranks – from hundreds of throats such a roar issued that caused even the reindeer to falter, and the warriors seemed to run with their legs not even touching the ground. The anger of the Nga people swept over the islands and devoured in an instant everything that stood on them.

I, too, flew along as part of that furious mass, and I made it out alive.

***

   ALEXANDER GRIGORENKO

As evening fell, specks again appeared far off beyond the islands: men on reindeer. They held their bows ready to shoot.

These were Kondogirs from more distant herding grounds. They had learned of Molkon's death and set off to get revenge. They did not arrive until the end of the bloodbath, but it had not quenched their anger. In the dim moonlight they walked among the bodies, seeking out any with an embroidered breastplate or tattooed faces, and they struck with their iron at both the dead and those still alive.

The remnants of the Nga army did the same. Fatigue weighed on them, but they would not yet give in to sleep – only the dead slept.

The next morning it became clear that less than half the men of the great clan were left. Among them was Lidyang, and that brought joy to my heart. His face was pale, his eyes sunken into their dark sockets, but there was a trace of a smile on his lips. We embraced, and it seemed like the old man's chest heaved. He told me something about what he had seen, but I remember nothing of it.

Thunder had died at the beginning of the battle, but Storm and Lightning remained among the living. By midday they stood on a height and shouted to the survivors to assemble.

Of the Kondogirs who had come under Altaney's banner, most were slain on the islands, while the remainder fled over the frozen Yenisei to distant lands, knowing that retribution awaited them in their native encampments.

They made a painstaking search, both among the living and the dead, for the man who had killed his father, but they did not find him.

Yando, the man so famous for reindeer-racing, had disappeared without a trace.

Yabto of the Nenyang's new nation had ceased to exist. By nightfall they even got to those who had managed to survive by hiding under the heaps of bodies.

Only the fate of the women left in the reinforced encampment beyond the islands, remained uncertain. It was said that the Nga warriors broke into the encampment the next morning and found empty chums and abandoned items. Whether the widows of Kheno's family had fled into the taiga, as they had no hope that the victors would be merciful to them, or whether they left with the Kondogirs as those men returned home – no one could say. Drifting snow had covered the tracks leading away from the encampment, but the warriors had no intention of following them and returned to the site of the battle.

The Nga people, so overcome by their experience of victory, were not thinking – nor could they even know – that blood had been shed beyond measure. Their victory in the battle among the islands had cost the lives of so many strong men, that after it the great clan would cease to exist, it would fragment into families and smaller clans, each of which would go by a new name. Rather, the army was presently concerned about something else.

Yabto of the Nenyang had survived.

In the last moments of the battle he had stood fearsome, like a boulder dropped from the sky. Bodies were heaped around him like the solar motif of a breastplate, so many men had the stout man's spear cut down. Eventually, however, his strength was obviously flagging, and an arrow that fell between the armor over his knee and his greave robbed him of the last of it…

They overcame Yabto and tied him to an old pine that had was bare at the roots.

Everyone who could ran towards the tree. The most senior warriors had to expend their last remaining strength on fending the crowd off, so that the celebratory sacrifice to their patron god could go on interrupted. But then the commanders of the army arrived and said that such a celebratory sacrifice should not be rushed.

"Let the anxious waiting serve as the first of his torments!" Storm cried.

Those words changed everything: the shouting died down, and in an instant the army, exhausted, was overcome by sleep.

***

Four young warriors volunteered to guard the stout man, as they were strong and had no need for sleep. The commanders readily agreed and left for their own tent. At first the warriors held firm, but when everything quieted down, they immediately began to doze off, and clearly the shafts of their spears were keeping them upright as much as their own legs.

Fires blazed, but no one sat up next to them – the living were now as supine as the dead. Only three figures among the stillness knew no sleep: Lidyang, Yabto and myself.

I stood together with the old man a dozen paces from the pine and watched the guards struggle to stay awake, while the stout man only stared with a cold gaze at the fire.

"Let's go," Lidyang whispered to me, and when we came up to the tree, he told the warriors, "Go get some sleep, boys. We'll relieve you."

Without saying a world, the warriors walked a mere few steps away and immediately collapsed.

The old man glanced at me. "As long as I have known you, you wanted to see this man again. Go on, talk with him if you want."

Yabto, however, was the first to speak:

"Pity there are no mosquitoes, like back then. You remember?"

"Tell me where you found me. Me and my brother."

"So many rivers flow into the Yenisei. How could I name the exact one?"

"Would you be able to recognize it?"

"How could I not recognize that place where my life went to hell? I've looked back on it all these years. Sometimes I feel like I can even smell the stones on that riverbank."

"Guide me there."

He laughed. "Tomorrow they are going to treat me so harshly, it would scare even death itself. How could I guide you?" His laughter then subsided. "Look, aren't there enough rivers out there? Any of them would be fit for you."

"My umbilical cord was buried in that place. My own and that of my brother, who you sold away and caused to die. That is my nest on the tree of the Yenisei – you tore me from my nest. What do I need all those other rivers for?"

The stout man seemed like he wanted to say something, but then he only sighed deeply and fell silent. He looked at me as if entreatingly. I could see that only talking with me was keeping him above the waters of anguish that his whole stout body had already been plunged into, with its head on a nonexistent neck, with its shattered dreams of a world in which everything was run according to rules, with the demon between his shoulder blades – with everything that was in him and on him.

Lidyang was standing with his back to us and listening to what we said. The old man abruptly turned and brought his face close to Yabto's. "You're already a dead man, I can see that from your empty eyes." Then he addressed me sharply, "Let's go. You can help."

We made our way through the darkness, unafraid of waking any of that army that had been totally overcome by sleep. Lidyang chose one from among the dead, and together we hauled the body up to the pine tree. The old man used his knife to cut the rope that bound Yabto – the stout man looked at his freed hands with astonishment.

"He won't run away," Lidyang said and grinned.

The three of us tied the dead man to the pine – it was someone from among Yabto of the Nenyang's new nation.

"Help him find his river," he told Yabto. "Don't try to trick him."

"I won't."

"What about you?" I asked Lidyang.

"I'll come with you."

I smiled.

"Just do what I tell you," the old man glared.

We hastened to the outskirts of the army, where the baggage train was. There Lidyang kicked the sleeping guards – they were youths who had been brought to a battle for the first time – and in an authoritative voice he demanded a long sledge with supplies, two of the best reindeer, and a black banner. They asked him what it was all for.

"We're headed for home, so that word of our victory can arrive there by sunrise. These two are coming with him. Khekhsar's orders."

The red flag was a symbol of war, the black flag a sign of victory.

Yabto collapsed onto the sledge and I joined him. Lidyang stood in front and whipped the reindeer so hard they roared…

***

We knew that our deceit would be discovered as soon as the sun rose, or perhaps even earlier. But this was not to be, for the army's sleep was so sound that many men, who had not taken care to cover themselves with blankets, froze to death in their sleep.

When they woke up and saw the dead man tied to the pine instead of Yabto, the sun was already shining.

They initially thought that the warriors assigned to guard the prisoner, had been murdered. But then they saw that the snow under them had melted, and under their armor they were clearly breathing. These men were hauled up, beaten, and thrown onto a sledge. The same was done to the boys who had guarded the baggage train.

By the time the warriors finally got to grips with what had happened, the day was already over.

We drove the reindeer on through the darkness and by morning reached the encampment.

The women, children, and infirm came pouring out onto the ice once our black flag came into view. They wept and flung their arms around Lidyang's knees, while Lidyang shouted to them that all nearby communities should learn of the victory by sundown – that was what the commanders had ordered.

Before our pursuers could catch up and our deception be made clear to all, we managed to get another pair of reindeer with a sledge for Nara, Yekha, and Man-Effigy. Regarding me, it was said that this fellow from a nearby Yurak clan was in a rush to get back to his native territory, as his wife would soon give birth. The women wept and kissed me and Nara…

Amid the rejoicing, no one even asked about a big bundle that was tightly wrapped in furs – this was Yabto.

***

How many harnessed sledges were chasing after us, I do not know. Probably many. But luck turned out to be on our side, it let us get far away, and more than once it sent snow that covered our tracks. It also dimmed the wits of our pursuers, who searched in the mouth of every small river thinking that we might be hiding there, and so they wasted their time and effort.

But eventually one of our four reindeer fell, and the old man asked Yabto whether it was still far to the place.

"Still a ways away," Yabto said.

We were again rescued by another snowfall.

Lidyang asked us to give him half of our arrows. "Harness one reindeer to the sledge and let it haul the weak. Walk alongside as long as the wind blows like this. When they come, I'll meet them."

I said that I would not leave him behind, but the old man yelled at me angrily – he was capable of yelling so harshly that a tree would be reduced to smithereens – that I was a hollow bone, fish shit, that I had got so many people killed and would get more people killed, and never even make it to my nest on the Tree, cursed be it.

"You yourself wanted to go away to your own land and dwell there," I shouted. "Why don't you? Why help me?"

"You?" the old man's bony fist grabbed the collar of my coat. "Her." Lidyang's hand released my coat and pointed to where Nara stood. "She was my brother Kheno's favorite granddaughter, the jewel of the family, my old blood. How could I live on my own land knowing that I didn't keep her safe? It's not you I'm helping but her. We're the last members of our family: she's a woman, I..."

He stared at me for a long time, so long that I remember that look to this day. I have never met a man who felt as sorry for me as Lidyang, only he was ashamed to feel that pity and concealed it under anger.

"They'll be here soon," he said dully. "Go. Don't worry about anything." After a silence, he added, "I'll catch up with you."

***

Lidyang's action managed to give us a day of tranquil travel, but the journey itself became unbearable for my wife.

"How much longer?" Nara moaned. "How much is left, my tormenter..."

"Soon," Yabto spoke up.

Suddenly I thought of how I had not feared the stout man the whole time we were pursued, even though his arms were unbound. He could have broken my neck, grabbed my weapons, and fled into the taiga – no one was going to stand in his way. But Yabto was quiet, he eagerly helped gather firewood for our brief overnight stops, he wrapped Nara in furs, and did everything that a man with strong arms could do – he acted as if my journey was his own. But I did not detect in him any fear, let alone obsequiousness as might arise from feelings of guilt. The stout man probably did not give any thought at all to what awaited him. Yabto was hollow inside, just like I myself had once been.

Only once did he act strangely.

Before sunset, our pursuers appeared far off. They moved on two harnessed sledges, but it was difficult to tell how many men sat on them. I grabbed my bow and the stout man did the same. Our reindeer, though tired, were running along remarkably smoothly. The Nga people's reindeer, on the other hand, were clearly worse for wear – their harnesses seemed to drop into the snow, and the distance between us grew no shorter. We looked at them with nervousness, ready to fight, even when darkness came over the frozen river. But now Nara said, "Look, wolves!" From a low bank far off, dark specks were weaving their way onto the flat white expanse. I felt like this was the same pack that had pursued the men of the glorious clan when disaster had struck their family. "Wolves," Nara repeated and burst into tears.

So far the stout man had keep his eyes fixed calmly on our pursuers, his hands tightly clenched his weapon, but at the mention of the wolves he suddenly went limp, shuddered, dropped his bow on the sled, and hid under the hood of his overcoat.

I thumped him on the back and shouted, "Get up!" but Yabto was like a dead man. He, my enemy, had never been a coward, he had never feared any man, let alone a beast – I was astonished at his faintheartedness, and moreover the fact that he did not even try to hide it.

Clearly, however, luck was still with us. The pack understood, as if a single mind, that it was not alone in this hunt and its prey would have to be divided up with the men borne along on the two harnessed sledges. Having decided that, the pack chose the more difficult but more abundant prey. Moreover, the pursuers' reindeer were weaker than ours, and in the semidarkness the wolves could easily avoid the men's arrows.

The wolves cut across the frozen river and began to encircle the Nga people's sledges. I watched the pursuit come to a halt. We could hear our pursuers shout, and their bows plaintively twanged far off.

The exhausted reindeer were frantic with horror, and the chase that had lasted so many days, from the islands at the mouth of the Middle Katanga to the first hills of the Sayan region, ended.

We went on, while our pursuers fled into the darkness and quickly vanished from sight. When night fell, I halted our reindeer. A blissful warmth spread through my chest, and I did not even think that Nga's people might be able to fight the wolves off and then resume their pursuit.

I thumped Yabto again on the back and said loudly, "Get up. There's no one after us any more."

The stout man emerged, stood up, scooped up a handful of snow, and spend a long time wiping his face.

"Are you so afraid of wolves?" I asked disdainfully.

He did not reply. I wanted to see his face, but the darkness was already so thick that I could barely see my own hands.

Without saying a word, the stout man took the ax from the sledge and went off to the nearby riverbank to chop firewood.

***

The sun had already made half of its brief course across the sky when Yabto sat up in the sleigh and said that we needed to stop. "We're close now. Go slower."

We got off the sleigh. Yekha walked holding onto Nara's shoulders – he barely touched them, aware that he had heavy hands and was not the only burden that my wife now carried.

At first I could not see anything – Yabto stopped and raised his arm:

"Two tall rocks that look like arrowheads. An uninterrupted stretch of river, three boulders – one twice as big as the other two. The river then immediately turns to the right. It's small, your river. We're here."

Homecoming

Three utterly exhausted reindeer, two sledges, a little dried meat, a few threadbare skins that might be suitable for covering the tiniest chum, a spear, skis, two bows and a few arrows, a wife with round belly, the blind giant, a feeble old man, and my enemy – that is what I had with me as I arrived home to my nest.

The winter had now reached the month of severe cold, but I initially was not thinking about that at all. I wanted to think about how what had happened to me, had happened for real. My heart was quiet, it trusted in that truth of things, but I wanted to look upon the truth as I might look at my own two hands.

I got on my skis and moved along the riverbank that was littered with large stones and fallen trees, as one finds along many rivers that flow among tall rocks. Yabto walked after me, up to his waist in snow, and he looked around as he did.

Soon he grew tired and went back to the others. I could hear his ax ring – the stout man was preparing a place for us to settle into.

The whole river was now under ice. I could see that in some places this river was wide and would be navigable in a small boat.

Finally I caught sight of something. Not far away a thin column of steam rose. It was a hole in the ice, not one made by man but rather due to warm water that came flowing from somewhere into my river. I walked up and saw a fish in the unfrozen water.

The fish seemed to be waiting for me. It was a perch. It swam against the current and slowly wiggled its big, dark-green body, and then it brought its eyes up to the very surface and stared fixedly at me. Occasionally the current would pull it back under the ice, but the perch always swam back up. I stared at it just as intently. This went on for a long time, and the fish seemed like it might say something any moment now, so wonderful and blissful did my heart find this sight. The perch said nothing, however – an icy wind swept over that patch of ice-free water and then I saw the fish no more.

***

What my mother had told me on the day the Seven Heavenly Snows bore her and the other dead of Kheno's land away, had now come to pass. A man in baggy clothing came by, he was short, bow-legged, and had a cheerful, pockmarked face. He looked at me for a long time just as the fish had done, waiting for the necessary words to be spoken. I said them:

"I am Ilget, son of Belegin."

"I see," the man said in Yurak. "Belegin passed away a long time ago, he drowned." After a brief silence, he said with an old man's severity, "You are an Ostyak, you ought to speak Ostyak. Where is your brother Balna – don't you share the same face?"

"He's dead."

"He died just like that?"

"No."

"Did you get revenge?"

"Yes."

"And is the mother of Ilget and Balna still alive?"

"She was taken away to marry a Yurak. She died, too."

"Ah," the man drawled. "We kinsmen of hers cursed her for being a bad mother, she hid you under moss and ran away."

"She wanted…"

"I know. We shouldn't have done that. But clearly, such was her fate. I am Tyney, your kinsman from the neighboring river. But here you are, Ilget, you alone of all those people came… Well, may you live to ripe old age, *ket!*"

ALEXANDER GRIGORENKO

We embraced.

"What hearth have you been living at all this time, Ilget?"

"Good people fed me."

"Yes… There are a lot of good people in this world."

Tyney asked about the people who had come with me. I pointed to Nara.

"Wow, you've got a lovely wife," he said. "You're really lucky."

I said that Yabto was Nara's uncle, Man-Effigy her grandfather, and Yekha my sworn brother. The whole time we talked, the smile never disappeared from the giant's lips.

"What is he smiling for?" Tyney asked me. "Did his whole brain go out his nose?"

"Ever since he went blind, he is simply happy that he doesn't have to fight any more," I replied.

"Tell me, old man, are there a lot of anthills in these parts?" Yekha asked, and Tyney nearly fainted, for Yekha had said it in Ostyak.

Once Tyney regained his composure, he said, "Yep, you really have lost your mind. What do you need anthills for, blind man?"

Yekha laughed.

Tyney told me that my river was not the most abundant, but no one had ever starved, because the *kaygus* here were kind, and I had to make friends with my *kaygus*, which might appear as a sable, or a stranger, or most frequently of all a large perch. Moreover, we were near the Yenisei, and people around here did not usually fight over the fat fish – there were enough for everybody. Mother Fire harbored no anger against the people living here, only my wife had to learn how to respect her and use the right words.

I asked what my river was called.

Tyney looked at me with astonishment. "That's what your river is called, the Ilget. Besides you, there's no one else here, you see. Truth be told, we also come around here sometimes, so that the river isn't totally deserted. For a long time, so long ago even our great-grandfathers can't remember when, hunters known as Biryusa lived here, so sometimes people call it the Biryusa River, but now it's yours. It's a great thing when a wandering man returns to where he belongs."

The next day, people came over from Tyney's own river: his wife and three young men who were close relatives. On sleds that white, wide-chested dogs barely managed to pull, they brought everything that we needed to survive that winter: coverings for chums, arrows, two pots, tackle for fishing under the ice, and furs for bedding, as well as three puppies that had just been weaned, for the Ostyaks keep no reindeer. In a single day, a whole new encampment rose up. It consisted of two chums, insulated at the bottoms with birch bark and snow.

"How can I repay you?" I asked Tyney.

"All that's mine here are the puppies. Belegin left the rest for you, think of it that way. He himself sank to the bottom, but his boat washed up on an island, not far from here. He was on a loaded boat chasing after taimen, the mad fool. We recovered what we could."

Then he put his hand under his coat and pulled out a small leather bag used to store one's flint, and he carefully placed it into my hand. Inside the bag was a tiny wooden doll – time had covered it with a sparking patina.

"Your *alel*. The waters cast it up. It came back as if it knew that you would be arriving. Well, now you're home at last."

***

We slaughtered the reindeer and our neighbors gave us fish – thus we survived the great cold. Tyney visited often – he always brought something with him, but mainly he came so that, through our chats, he could teach Nara and me the Ostyak language. Yekha, who knew some of my people's

   ALEXANDER GRIGORENKO

language, continued the old man's work after the latter left. Though Yabto apparently knew every language and dialect on the Tree of the Yenisei, he did not participate in this – he lived in the other chum together with Man-Effigy, who said nothing, while Yabto only spoke when he was forced to, mainly when someone asked him something. This did not, however, get in the way of our hunting or ice-fishing together. The big perch did not appear to me again, but clearly the *kaygus* of my river was generous, and we did not perish from hunger.

One day the stout man called me. Amidst a flat hollow, the snow had been trampled down until it was hard as stone, and there Yabto was sitting on a stump – at his feet was a long block of wood made from a dry, debarked larch.

"Only little boys make arrows from osier. I'll show you how to make real ones. Watch and learn."

With an adze, he separated a finger-thick piece of wood from the block, checked whether it was even, and then he drew a short-bladed knife from his belt and began to sharpen the body of the arrow.

"Here," he pointed to the middle of the arrow-shaft, "make it a bit thicker than at the tips. The arrow will be rather heavy, but when it flies from the bowstring, it won't wiggle in its flight – your shot will be precise and powerful. The Selkups do it this way, and I found it very clever."

The stout man had everything there with him: a thin piece of sinew for attaching the arrowhead, and an owl feather, which I understood had been carefully selected.

"This block of wood, if you work smartly, will be enough for three dozen good arrows. You can learn to fashion the arrowheads yourself, after all, you're an Ostyak."

He got up and walked away.

***

In the spring, when the hard, frozen crust atop the snow began to soften, Nara gave birth to a daughter. Tyney's wife and widowed daughter-in-law came to help with the labor. Nara managed easily, only she was upset that there was only a single child. Some time passed and then other kinsmen came by. We sat in the chum and accepted their gifts. Yabto was the last to enter the chum. He took a small bag from his belt and drew from it a strip of old suede on which little bird figurines, made from now-yellowed bone, had been strung.

Nara accepted the gift, then stared at it for a long time and smiled. "Where did this come from?" she asked.

"It was given to me as a keepsake of two little boys. Now you will have it. I have nothing else to give."

The sight of those birds made from bone touched my heart.

From that day on, I longed to speak with Yabto.

I felt no fear towards him – that had been left behind in the encampment on the Bountiful River. Nor did I feel any hatred towards him – that had been quenched by the happiness that fortune had brought me, a happiness concealed in the wise world that stood on the Yenisei. It was something else that burned me – I wanted to know what my anguished life had all been for. Why had my path been so long and painful? I was not sure whether I should seek some answer from Yabto – by all accounts it did not seem worthwhile. But everything important that had happened in my life was bound with this man of stout body and almost no neck. He had been my father and master, I had been his son and slave.

Finally, I asked him, "Tell me, do you still think me your enemy?"

He laughed, nearly too quietly to hear. "No."

"Because I saved you from death?"

"I saved you from death, too."

"To make me a slave."

"Since I couldn't get a son out of you..."

"Who am I to you now?"

"Someone who kindly provides me some shelter on his land."

"Why do you humble yourself like that?"

"How else can a dead man act?"

"But you're alive. You can hunt, fight. Can you go off and live a normal life?"

He thought for a moment. "You come into this world from who knows where, like a snowflake falling into the smoke-hole, and you disappear to who knows where. Everything else is just tricks that the spirits play, like the fact that I still walk across an earth on which I no longer even exist. The fact that they won't let that poor old man die, though he is so old now that his own name is lost – that's also a trick they have played."

"Do you envy Man-Effigy?"

"You fool, he ought to envy me. All your Tree of the Yenisei is good for is spitting on its roots."

Then I stood up and took him by the hand. "Come on, you promised to show me the place where you found me and my brother."

"It wasn't me, it was my black-snouted bitch. She was a good dog, especially for squirrel-hunting… The place would be covered by snow now."

"You'll find it. You promised. If you no longer want anything for yourself, then do it for me. If you aren't even here any more, then what difference does it make?"

He stared at me for a long time – my words had clearly struck him – and then abruptly got to his feet.

We walked down into a hollow where, under heavy snow, there was moss that seemed bottomless.

"It was somewhere here," Yabto said. "I remember this tree, now it is twice as thick. And you can see the riverbank from here, too."

The bank really was close by.

"Tell me," I said to him, "like the master of these places."

"Tell you about what?"

"Tell me why you made other people so unhappy. Me, my brother, your wife…"

"I made them happy, and the very life around them, too. I can see that you understand nothing of what you have seen, let alone what you couldn't have known. Sit down."

Then he told me everything, starting from that day when he lay in a chum that had already been robbed of its weapons. He began to go over all that he had lived through like a tangled fishing-net, in order to find that one day when his life had gone wrong.

As he stood up, Yabto said that he felt no guilt at the fact that he had not succeeded. If anything cut through the darkness over his soul, it was only the thought that he had aimed for something no one else had ever imagined, and perhaps a time would come when such a man would be born who would succeed in everything.

"Now I'm alone," Yabto said. "The only such man in the whole world."

There on my own territory I saw no threat in him, neither to me nor to Nara, even though the stout man could have easily picked up a weapon.

But after he had spoken those words, I found that he weighed on me unbearably, like a stone tied around my neck. I knew everything now, and we spoke to him no more.

The she-wolf wife

At the very beginning of spring, Yabto went off to hunt birds and did not return.

I found him the next day. He lay not far from the river-bank with a gaping hole in his throat. It was apparent that the stout man had died without putting up any resistance.

I looked around. On the other bank, where some large, flat stones made it easy to cross the river, a she-wolf lay several paces from the water. She seemed to have been waiting for someone to come along and see what she had done. Her eyes stared at me intently, as if this were no mere animal.

Finally, the she-wolf got up and leisurely ran off towards a nearby mountain.

We buried Yabto just like anyone ought to be buried: Yekha, myself, and two of Tyney's young relatives could barely lift the body up a man's height into the tree.

But the night after the burial, the she-wolf returned. It came in a dream and led me to the site of Yabto's death and even farther, beyond the mountain, into a valley with three streams, where her pack awaited.

The wolf pack followed after the she-wolf like they would follow a leader – calmly, with their muzzles low and not seeking their own path. Alongside her ran five wolves with broad skulls and light-colored chests – the she-wolf's sons.

At night the pack halted. The she-wolf stood in the middle of their circle. She lifted her head towards the sky and howled…

Once she had howled, the wolves pressed their whole bodies against the ground and hid their muzzles in the snow, or moss, or dead leaves. This was no ordinary howl to gather the pack or to warn of prey or danger nearby.

It was a life unknown to wolves that howled thus…

The howling repeated with gaps, but each time the she-wolf howled to exhaustion. Once she felt silent, she lowered her muzzle onto her forepaws and pressed it against them with all her might, until her back ached, so that she could feel the last traces of warmth in them – she still remembered when these paws had been hands. At first they had been white, soft hands, with plump, slightly pointy fingers, then they had been swollen with green streaks at the wrists, burned, rough, but nevertheless warm.

For the last time these hands, powdered with the shining scales of whitefish, had held a small stick and poked at something in the cooking pot, while that man who had been killed half a day before was trying to untangle a fishing net.

The last color of her hands was the color of deer liver, her fingers were swollen from the blood bursting everywhere in her body…

She heard the footsteps of her husband as he walked off, she heard them for a long time, she heard the sound that every stalk made as it broke under his feet. He fell, got back up again, walked on… Then the footsteps disappeared, a frozen silence hung, and pain began to flow into her numb arms and legs that seemed hardly to exist at all. The pain spread over her body in a slow trickle, it crawled along her spine, reached her neck and the back of her arms, and plunged her into oblivion. This lasted for a short time and then Uma came to – and the pain, too, returned, only it was of a different kind that pierced her whole body. Oddly, she still had her wits about her, and she wanted to scream, so that she could at least get some meager part of what tormented her out, but her voice was stuck somewhere in her innards – she opened and closed her mouth like a fish, but only a few weak, sibilant sounds emerged. She again fell into oblivion, woke back up, and once more wallowed in a mute darkness where there was only pain…

Uma opened her eyes when it was daybreak. She felt now thirst, and that thirst proved stronger than the pain. The freezing autumn forest had little moisture to offer – Uma greedily licked at the frosty grass, and at everything else that was in reach, but it only made her desperation for something to drink stronger. The pain remained, but on this night she had already learned to speak with it. A dead tree lying right in front of her face got in her way. Uma gathered all her strength, sat up as much as her little body would allow, craned her neck serpent-like, and saw that beyond the tree was a little pool of water, about the diameter of a small pot. The pool was so clear that she could make out the jagged edges of fallen leaves at its bottom. She twisted her body and tried to crawl over the trunk, but this tree that had lived a full life and now prepared to serve as a huge home for myriad insects, was too thick for a person with broken arms and legs. Kiss Woman attempted several times to get over the trunk, by gripping the branches with her teeth and rolling over to the other side, but the trunk was too slippery under her, there were no usable branches, and she rolled back down – each of these attempts to save her life was punished by fresh pain.

For the first time she burst into tears, bitter, miserable, and angry ones. This crying clearly served as a balm, though its effect was but fleeting. She wiped her face with the collar of her parka, which was now huddled around her neck and left her belly exposed, and she decided that she would crawl along the fallen tree as long as her strength would last. After sinking her teeth into roots and wiggling her body, she had crawled only a short distance and then lay exhausted. The tree boasted not only a trunk of respectable thickness but also great height, and the path along it – whether in one direction or the other – suddenly seemed insurmountable, as long as the whole Yenisei itself. She again burst out crying, but her tears no longer brought consolation – fear had now come upon her, the horror of death. She realized that she would die, but for some reason she was mostly afraid of dying of thirst. Like before, she licked the grass, but it was now late in the day, and the frost and even the moisture resulting therefrom had drained into the earth, in order to return the next day along with the morning chill. Uma addressed her pain and begged it for a little sleep, so that she could survive until the frost reappeared...

That night she awoke and heard movement among the rustling of the wind. She opened her eyes, sat up, and saw green pinpoints wandering close by.

Instead of the horror that might come over a defenseless person surrounded by a pack of wolves, Uma felt joy. If she could, she would have crawled out of her parka so that the wolves would find her even easier prey. She waited, but the wolves did not approach... In the darkness she heard the subtle sounds that their paws made as they stepped.

Only one wolf approached her. The sky had cleared enough for Kiss Woman to already make out the wolf's outlines: it had a broad chest, long legs, and a barely noticeable hump at its mane. The wolf came right up to her and began sniffing her from head to toe, as if it thought that some part of her body might belong not to a human being but to some other creature. After it had smelled her, it sat next to her and howled – a brief, hoarse sound.

Only later did Uma recognize what this howl meant – it was to forbid the others from coming near. The remaining wolves sat far off, some lay, and others expressed unease...

She lay on her side and looked at the yellow, red-streaked eyes that remained motionless opposite her. The wolf once more glanced towards the pack and then slowly laid down next to Uma. It lay with its back to her and snuggled up against her, and with its head on its paws. Its warmth was transferred to her body, and she buried her face into the fur on its neck and said, "Water" – and again she plunged into oblivion, this time deeply. The pain that she felt even while unconscious, subsided somewhat.

She came to, and not where she had been lying but far from the dead tree. The wolf had dragged her by the collar of her parka. Along the way it was forced to chastise another wolf who dared violate its prohibition on coming closer. The humiliated wolf went off into a ravine in order to lick its wounds. After this, the leader – and this was undoubtedly the leader of the pack – came back to her, dug its teeth into her parka again, and did not stop dragging her until Kiss Woman's face fell into an ice-cold stream. She almost choked as she drank and drank, caught her breath, and then drank some more… The wolf stood alongside her.

From that day she ceased to consider it a wolf, but she did not know what it was. She only saw that this hunchbacked beast had been her salvation, it had preserved her life that was still needed for something or someone. From then on the wolf was almost always at her side, it would only leave for a brief time in order to bring her food. She would take the raw meat from its maws, chew it, drink water from the stream, and then fall asleep. The pain was no longer a harbinger of death but mere pain, and Uma would not even stoop to speaking with it. The pain did sometimes draw attention to itself – it beat harshly on her legs, and the wolf would pull her boots off her, first one, then the other. At night the wolf would lie next to her, pressed against her like a spouse, and begin to lick her legs where her bones had been broken. This went on for many days and nights, and eventually there was no longer any pain in her legs.

Then, when the first snow had fallen, the wolf began to tear at her clothing – it ripped open her parka in order to get at her deadened arms, and eventually it tore everything off her. Snow fell, but she was left completely without clothing and was now completely in the wolf's power – the wolf seemed to stick to her, to this white, fragile, and naked creature. It licked her broken arms and wrapped itself around her – and the same miracle happened to her arms, too: the pain went away. The wolf no longer went to fetch food, rather its loyal kin brought it. The wolf seemed downright inseparable from her, and Uma began to talk to it.

"Are you a god? Tell me, and I'll start to pray to you. Just tell me…"

The wolf not only apparently did not understand her, it was not even listening to what she said.

"Darling creature. You must have had a wife you loved, and you lost her…"

Kiss Woman muttered these words as she pressed her face so deeply into its fur that she gasped for air – already that inexpressible feeling known as coming back to life had taken her breath away. She said the words that she longed to say when she had been the old Uma, from the People of the Scream, but life had brought her such suffering that these words had remained pent up inside her, just like her dream of becoming a fish that children would issue from like roe. She no longer felt pain, nor cold, and the smell of the wolf's fur, the wolf's tongue became her smell. Those suppressed unspoken words came forth, but suddenly everything stopped.

The first blizzard came. The wolf lay atop her, covered her from head to toe, and Uma could hear a sound inside its body like the crying of an infant, and she herself began to cry. After the torrent of words came a stream of tears. She cried at not being capable of a sacrifice that could balance out what this hunchbacked beast had done for her. It was not due to her pain that she wept, as the pain was now gone, but rather due to her inability to show the same love that she had received. All that remained in her were those words.

But then night fell, cold and snowy, and by the middle of the next day the blizzard had abated. Kiss Woman suddenly realized that she was unable to say anything, and this was not due to the cold but a problem with her larynx: it had lost the very capacity for speech. The wolf was sleeping. She looked at her hands and saw fur along their sides. Several days later, her fingers had grown shorter, then turned into claws, and fur grew along her entire body. The wolf stayed by her, but it already permitted itself to leave for brief periods.

At the beginning of the month of great cold, the pack was joined by a new she-wolf, and probably the happiest and most devoted of all. She led the pack to paddocks and slaughtered the reindeer inside, as if she had no memory left of being human, and she was more feared than even some males. However, her happiness lay in something else – now she could thank her husband.

With a heavy belly she was finishing off the great herd that had belonged to Kheno's family – she would eventually bear five sons and they would be proud, pure, and fearless. Their wolf father never got a chance to see them, however. On the same great hunt an arrow went through his skull. Uma saw who shot this arrow: it was the adopted whelp that she had fed with her own breast, back when she was human.

Then in her grief she realized that there was a meaning to her life as a wolf. The reason for Kiss Woman's existence had been her children, husband, and cooking pots. The she-wolf's purpose was to ensure the death of both of them: the man who lacked a neck, and the adopted whelp. Yabto was to die first. With what remained of her human thinking, the she-wolf understood that he was the root from which all her woes sprung.

In her brief happiness, she had not forgotten her all-con-suming hatred for the man who had taken all her human joys away from her, and traded for some iron her own children Yabtonga and Yawire, for whom she had carefully washed her teats unlike other women. Yabto broke her arms and legs, but he did not slay the beast. Her words as a human, "My iron husband, I will not leave you," turned into a persistent, never-ending howl.

Once the now-widowed she-wolf gave birth to her sons, she never let any wolf near her. She led the pack from one victory over prey to another, and the wolves never grumbled at being led by a female. They followed her, and she followed the trail of the stout man – she could sense his proximity like a growing pain in her breast, and that pain finally led her to the Ilget River, to my river. There the she-wolf spotted her enemy standing on the riverbank, armed with a bow and arrows, and she made her way towards him over the large stones that jutted out of the water. When the man saw the animal, he froze, dropped his weapon, and meekly gave himself up to death – he lifted his head, so that the wolf's teeth could more easily reach what little neck he had. As he died, the she-wolf felt that he did not push her away but rather pressed himself against her.

After killing Yabto, she remained by the river, knowing that people would come along sooner or later, and among them would probably be the man who murdered her husband. That murderer came, he was alone. But the she-wolf had waited for him for so long that her ardor had cooled, being fully sated by the vengeance she had already obtained. Her heart was so at peace now that the she-wolf no longer bore any anger.

The gates of paradise

They searched for the wolf, but the pack left for some other region and was soon forgotten. Our neighbors were concerned that we had lost a provider. My soul let out a slight sigh.

I had something else to worry about: Man-Effigy was going mad. He had clearly reached the last vertebrae in that spine of his remarkable lifespan, and now a disgust for life afflicted him like an illness.

Tyney visited me regularly and we would listen to his stories. He often recounted the same one:

"The heroic Albe wanted to vanquish Khosedam, she who is death itself. He cut through massive rocks with his sword as he chased her, and the Yenisei came flowing through these cut rocks. One day he would have caught her, had Khosedam not turned into a sterlet and fled into the water. Albe turned into a taimen and would have inevitably caught up, but Albe's brother was sitting atop a rock and playing the flute. The hero started listening to the flute-playing, and Khosedam got away. Then, when the melody was over, Albe got angry and shot an arrow at his brother – the rocks by the islands are red from his blood. He deeply grieved for having killed his brother, so much so that he left for the heavens. If you look up, you'll see Kay – that's the path of his reindeer-drawn sled. Khosedam, however, got away and now in the far north, among the eternal ice, she waits for the dead to come to her, and when she shakes her filthy mane, snowstorms sweep across the earth. That's how it was, kids."

The dead tree creaked, "If it hadn't been for that idiot with the flute, human beings would have become immortal, wouldn't they?"

"Probably yes," replied Tyney, somewhat taken aback – he was used to people crying after this story.

"Idiots with flutes are worse than evil. If you killed them in time, no one would think as they looked down at a cradle, 'You'll die, too.' But everyone dies. Even you will, kids." He pointed to my daughter, whom Nara held in her arms, and to Tyney's grandchildren. "You'll all suffer, then croak. And whoever croaks in old age, when everything hurts, and not from plague, hunger, or the weapons of others, people consider that person fortunate. All because of some fish shit who got in the way of something important. Forgive grandpa for carving you whistles from willow."

Tyney led his grandchildren out – he did not appear again for many days. Man-Effigy, for his part, crawled away to his own chum, still shaking with laughter.

Man-Effigy became more unbearable by the day. People stopped visiting us. Nara hid our daughter from him and, as she prepared to bear another child, hid herself. She begged me to save her from the old man who gave off such a hatred for life. She feared that the old man would creep into our chum and spit curses into the cradle. She asked me to move Man-Effigy farther away from the encampment, and I did. I continued to bring him food, but the old man would not sit there in silence as he once did – he wore me down with the same request he had made long ago: to burn his heart and accept the gift that had become for him a torment.

He said, "You arrived at your own river, you ended up back in your nest. Your dream came true – why don't you want to take this gift from me? You're afraid?" He went on to mock me. "You're weak. What kind of a warrior are you if you can't do just a little thing like that? How are you going to protect your wife and children?"

I listened without replying, and finally I asked, "Is it so hard for you to witness my good fortune?"

"Yes," the old man readily answered.

Then I asked another question, "Tell me, was it so hard for you to outlive the people you loved?"

"If you're talking about love, I have forgotten what that is. I know that there is such a word, and such an affliction that makes people do silly, ridiculous things. I know that it sometimes drives people mad."

"So how could I outlive the people that I love?"

"That will pass… With time it will pass. People dying will become as ordinary a thing as the snow falling, and perhaps my gift will give you something that it didn't give me. Remember, this was a god's way of playing a joke on me, and I don't know which god. But listen, young man, immortality is a weapon, it is useless, dangerous even, in the hands of someone who doesn't know how to wield it. But you learn how to do that, young man, you learn. I'm sure you'll succeed, I can see it. You'll live as many generations as a pike's bones, and you won't suffer like I have, when you get to the end. My experience taught me to predict things that haven't even happened yet, to sense what anyone is saying or thinking – and it will be the same for you. Do what I asked you, young man. I helped you, after all."

"And I helped you."

The old man chortled. "Someday, perhaps very soon, you'll do what I ask. You'll have no other choice."

He creaked with repugnant laughter as I left him.

The days passed, however, and I began to realize that Man-Effigy was right.

Yabto – a taciturn member of our encampment and a beaten, empty man – was the first burden that remained from my former life. Wise and just fate had freed me of him. The old man was the other weight that I ought to free myself from and thereby do a good thing for everyone: for myself, Nara, the children, neighbors, kinsmen, and the old man himself.

Only I had no intention of burning his heart – and it was not from fear. I wanted to be a man like any other, I looked forward to a quiet old age, of the sort that one could not imagine a happy life without, and I wanted to have a happy life.

When the ice grew thick, I cut a hole in it, and the next morning I went to the old man, picked him up, and carried him to the river. While I was chopping at the layer of ice that had formed overnight, Man-Effigy sat shivering on a stump.

"What about the fire?" he asked anxiously. "Where are you going to burn my heart?"

Instead of a reply, I went up to him, drew a knife with a long, narrow blade, and planted it in his left chest.

"Enough."

"You liar… you fish shit," the old man said angrily and closed his eyes. Perhaps that angry remark was the ultimate wisdom that he had arrived at.

I dropped his legs into the hole, and my river quickly and obediently pulled the body under the ice. My work done, I set off back home and, as I walked past that warm spring that existed along part of the river's flow, I saw the large perch, it stared at me with astonishment.

"Forgive me," I said to the perch.

It continued to stare.

When I arrived home, I told my wife that death had finally remembered that man whose true name was unknown to everyone, probably even to him.

Nara rocked the cradle. "May his bones rest in peace. May his soul rest," she said with visible relief.

People began visiting us again. Good Tyney asked about the old man's grave.

"The river is his grave…"

"Ah," Tyney made his own realization. "The poor man, he suffered so. That's why he was so angry."

Yekha did not ask about the old man at all. He had learned to chop wood blind, and to carry water, and these chores occupied him more than anything else in life.

   ALEXANDER GRIGORENKO

Springtime Woman

After Man-Effigy's departure, wise fate did not stop there. It worked far off, many, many days' journey from my own river, at the mouth of the Middle Katanga, where those Kondogir men faithful to Molkon dragged the body of the patricide Altaney by leather straps.

The men who had come to aid Yabto were left on the islands where they lay. In the spring the rapids roared and the water swept all the bodies north, to the Icy Crone.

It was purely out of rage that the Kondogirs dragged the corpse – it was no longer possible to get revenge on him, and among those who survived in the great encampment there were no worthy avengers. The traitors' widows went their separate ways among the families of the vast clan. The large encampment lay empty.

There was one widow, however, on whom all the Kondogirs' fury was poured.

Nara was their enemy's daughter. The same blood, mixed with the cursed blood of the patricide, flowed in the veins of her sons, who were barely four years old. They did not kill her, instead they merely threw Altaney's body into the chum where she had once lived with her husband and children. They ordered her to remain there with the corpse. The children, too. Her former relatives forbid her from leaving the chum under pain of death.

Nara and her children spent the rest of the winter with the corpse. Only once did the widow come near it, in order to drag it to a place along the wall where a cold draft blew through an old tent-covering. Only a few solitary people remained in the encampment that had once been great – these were old widowers who did not want to leave for other families. Initially they were reluctant to speak to her or even throw her children a bit of meat. Sometimes they looked in to see whether the widow's face had been sufficiently smeared with ashes. Springtime Woman set traps for hares and partridges, but animals rarely fell in. Her boys first cried from hunger, then grew quiet. Their hearth barely smoldered.

In the month of winds, the handful of residents that remained in the great encampment grew tired of being angry at the widow. They began to toss her some pieces of dry meat, and piping-hot bones from their pots.

When spring came, Nara washed her face with snow and staggered into one of the chums, in order to declare that she had no intention of praying to the spirits and gods any more, that they might forgive her for fate having made her Altaney's wife. Moreover, the corpse already stank so badly that they had better kill her, if they considered her guilty. The next day, men came from a neighboring encampment, carried the body out without saying a word, and hauled it into the forest – in the opposite direction from the clan's sanctuary.

By this time, the fury of many Kondogirs had subsided, they allowed Nara to live as she had before. But she no longer had any man to provide for her, and no man would marry her and be willing to adopt her sons, however fine they were. Nara was well aware of that.

When the next winter came around, she went herself to one of the senior Kondogirs and said that she would no longer feed her children with mice and carrion, like the last winter. Let them decide her fate now, for such a glorious clan could not endlessly take their anger out on a single woman, even if she were the widow of such an unparalleled villain.

In Springtime Woman's words was a foolhardiness born from despair, but the Tungus showed her mercy. The most senior of them said that she did not deserve death, but since the clan had rejected her, it would be best that she return to her own river, where she had been taken as a bride. Nara said that there was no longer anyone of her family living along that river, but the elder noted:

"Perhaps someone will take you. After all, no river remains completely deserted for long."

She was given two reindeer, a large woman's sledge with supplies and furs for shelter, and an ax, and they set her on the strong ice. The reindeer ran south and after several days reached the islands and the red rocks – the site of the last battle, where Springtime Woman's husband and father had sought to shake the Tree of the Yenisei.

By now, my mother's prophecy that appeared in the Seven Heavenly Snows, began to be fulfilled: other people had come to dwell on the lands that once belonged to Kheno's glorious family, to the once-great and now scattered Nga clan. This region was now settled by Assan and Kot people, who had not yet divided up the lands for hunting and fishing. The Abundant River, for its part, had been settled by Selkups come from the west, who intended to share it with the Nenets, Yabto's kinsmen.

As Nara reached the river mouth, she was unaware of all of this. But when she saw the familiar rocks, she cried and told her sons that she had been born and grew up here, but returning to this land in a dead time and dwelling there, would be too much for her.

***

What Altaney had kept hidden from her – that her brothers had been killed, and her mother was no more – Molkon told her later. Once Yabto left, he was overcome by an unbearable feeling of pity for his daughter-in-law and grandsons. He came, stroked her hair, and cried together with her. He himself lost his head several days later – in the middle of the day, before the eyes of many young dogs with tattooed faces who bowed before Altaney. There were no human beings around her any more, only madness in human form.

She did not speak with her husband after this, for he went off to fight. All that was left behind following his departure was a pain in her breast. Initially it was a quiet pain, but it would not go away. Nara lived with it for the whole period from one winter to the next, and she lived with it now. The pain it turned into something that she could touch with her hands. It was her grief.

"Better we go south, wherever fortune brings us," she told her sons.

And so they went. Several days on, a blizzard swept across the frozen river and one reindeer fell. The animals that pulled her sledge were tired now. Springtime Woman wrapped her and the children in furs and tried to wait the bad weather out, but it persisted, and now death loomed.

During these same days, my own wife was doing well. Her stomach grew round and she began to demand that we set off for some fat fish. Tyney, my constant and attentive visitor, said that every change in life starts with a demand for fat fish, especially for a pregnant woman, and now we were in a time of year when it would be easier to reach out and catch a star than catch those fat fish.

"There must be a reason for it," he said as he left.

But Nara remained anxious, and finally she told the truth. "You didn't get to your native hearth on your own – fortune brought you here. And now you don't need any-one."

"What about you talking about?"

"You look into my eyes, but you're really seeing some-thing else there. The first time that happened, I was sur-prised. But now those other eyes are overflowing with tears, and they freeze as they fall…"

She grabbed the string of birds sculpted from now-yel-lowed bones and threw it in my face. "Those eyes. Go find them now. Take the dogs, Ilget, and go! If you sit here in this warm chum, it's a sin. And I need to give birth. Go!"

They were two different women, but with the same name and a single heart.

I called Tyney and told him that I had received news: my sister was coming to find me but facing freezing conditions along the way. The old man did not ask where I got the news from, he only pointed upwards and said:

"That's your fat fish."

***

That same evening we set off with two harnessed sleighs. After several days' journey along the frozen river we came upon a snow-covered mound with the outlines of a sleigh; it was topped by reindeer antlers. Steam rose in a white, barely visible column from the mound, as if from a bear's den. We scraped the snow off and the people under it – mother and children – were still alive, but numb with cold. I took my glove off and slapped the woman across the cheek. She started, looked around, and stared at me with baffled eyes.

"Nara! Nara!"

I took her face in my hands – I could see the thin, white trace on her right cheek, the scar from my bone-tipped arrow. She was different now – Nara had turned from a lanky girl with a round face into an ample-bodied woman.

"Who are you?" Springtime Girl asked.

"I'm Wenga, the runt."

"Oh…" she said and closed her eyes.

Together with Tyney I carried Nara and the children into our own sleighs, rubbed their faces with fat, and covered them with furs.

"We need fire," the old man said. "Otherwise we won't be able to warm them up."

We pitched our tent and made a fire inside. There Nara asked, "Why does that old man call you Ilget and speak Ostyak to you?"

I said that now I had my own river, I was an Ostyak, and Ilget was my real name.

"No," Springtime Girl smiled. "You're Wenga, Lar's brother."

I took the yellowed birds on a string out and said, "Let it be that way."

Nara took the birds. "It's all over, runt."

"No," I said. "Everything is just beginning."

"Do you still love me?"

I looked down. "You're my sister… I have a wife with the same name as yours. She bore me a daughter and soon she'll bear another child, probably a son."

"I loved Lar. All that I have left is his face – you have the same face."

"I know. Lar is dead."

"So, only the face is left…" She looked at me in silence for a long time, with a weary smile, then she suddenly asked with no change of expression, "You won't abandon my children?"

"I won't."

"And you'll take me as your second wife?"

"Ostyaks only take a single wife. Don't think about that. You're alive and you're going to live on."

All this time Tyney had been watching us, and finally he said, "Enough talking Yurak. Let's get some sleep."

✳✳✳

We set off back home – and there I saw, after I had gone ashore for firewood, a ragged Yurak shirt laying at the base of a young pine trunk with a sharpened tip. The shirt was on the trunk because formerly it had been on a human being, and the human being on the stake. He had died long ago, then his body rotted away and animals hauled his bones off, but the shirt remained. It had been Lidyang's.

I rolled the shirt up as tightly as I could, so that the others on the sleighs would not see what I carried, and I hid it under my coat. Thus no one else ever saw Lidyang's shirt.

***

Nara accepted Nara like her own family, as if she had known her for a long time. There was no jealousy in her, no fear, in the way that a person filled with peace and contentedness cannot be jealous or afraid.

In the evenings we – myself and the two Naras – would talk about what we had gone through, and each of us could see how fate had woven our lives together. Things were good for us now.

We wanted to marry the stout man's daughter off to Yekha. Though blind, he had got the hang of almost any task, except that he could not shoot. Yekha said, however, that first one usually looks at a bride, and then feels her. The former he was not capable of, and therefore he was embarrassed to do the latter, and all in all my idea was silly.

"Better that she help me or walk with me, so that I don't fall into some hole in the ice," he said with embarrassment, and everyone laughed.

Then Tyney promised he would find her a suitor from one of the nearby rivers. Thus Nara, Yabto's daughter, lived with us. It was her hands that cut the umbilical cord of my second daughter. Originally I had seen Springtime Girl like the northern lights: something I could admire but never possess. Now she saw me that way.

A year later, her and her sons already spoke Ostyak well. One day the stout man's daughter asked, "If you were ever left alone with my children, you wouldn't be like Yabto, would you?"

Her question surprised me. "Why are you saying that?"

Fate desired that everyone bring you gifts, like to a prince for his storehouse. For some it was their lives, for others their ideas, or a piece of their heart, or their eyes. I brought you sons – you won't have your own, I can see that from your wife's face. Don't ask why I'm saying that, and don't be embarrassed to accept my gift. There ought to be one happy man in this world, so let it be you, who people called the runt. Just don't be like Yabto."

I said nothing in reply, I was so stunned by the clarity of her words, for she was really saying farewell to me.

The pain which had clotted in the middle of her chest, had grown larger while my Springtime Girl subsisted on mice, her face smeared with ashes, while she froze on her sledge on the Yenisei ice, and when she came to life after arriving at my river.

She now told me of the pain in her breast that she felt.

"Why didn't you say anything?"

"It only hurt a little. But now it's hard to breathe."

I remember how I cursed then and ran off to find Tyney, so that he could find the shaman.

"The shaman lives at the mouth of the Mana, on an island there, and the ice is already bad. It's a long way if you're on skis."

"We'll take the dogs."

We went on a light dogsled over the river ice. A day later the shaman was already at my encampment. He looked Nara in the eye for a long time and said something to her – she did not understand – and then he began to perform his rite. After his drum fell silent, he went up to the ill woman and ordered her to take her parka off. He then put his hand on her breast, tore off a bloody chunk, and flung it next to the hearth.

"That's the disease right there. Just don't feed it to the fire – the fire would be offended."

Then he went to lie down and did not even accept food, he was so tired.

Only a brown spot remained on Nara's breast. My wife helped her dress, wrapped her in a blanket made of squirrel fur, and a big reindeer hide. We blew the fire hot.

By morning Yabto's daughter had stopped breathing.

People gathered – Yekha, Tyney, and his wife. To make sure, the old man took the traditional step of putting a fox fur up to Nara's face – the fur did not flutter. We sat there in silence for a long time, only occasionally a sound similar to laughing erupted from the giant's mouth – he had no way to cry.

A long time passed before the shaman finally woke up and asked for food. We told him that his efforts the night before had been in vain. He quickly jumped up from under the furs, walked up to the deceased, and asked what clan she was from. I replied that she came from the Nenyang, the Mosquito People.

"Why didn't you tell me she was a Yurak? Instead of hers, I took hold of some other person's disease – I healed some Ostyak. Take me back to my island."

Tyney walked out of the chum without saying anything. The dogs started barking…

Nara's sons were six years old then. They already knew a little about death, but they did not understand the change that had taken place in their lives. They did not cry.

That is how I accepted Springtime Girl's gift.

✷✷✷

Three more years passed. Now I had four children: two daughters and two sons. When the boys were nearly nine years old, I gave them Ostyak names: Togot and Balna. When I looked at them, I could see a distant resemblance to Yabtonga and Yawire, but that meant nothing to me. Though their umbilical cords might have been buried in other parts, they would live just as other people live in their own nests on the great Tree, enjoying the gifts that wise fate gave them, and desiring nothing more.

Together with me they would hunt for bears, track elks, set fish-traps, catch birds in autumn, and go for fat, roe-filled fish in spring. I would teach them how to make arrows from larch wood, to boil thick fish glue and use it to glue a bow together and then string that bow, to fashion sledges and recognize the leader of a sled-pulling pack already as a puppy. In time, I would send them off to find brides.

I would teach them the greatest wisdom that my own fate had given me: to be content with what one had and covet nothing more, and to pray to all the higher powers, lest some insidious spirit blow that poisonous and deadly thought up your nose. Then, with the first breath you took, that thought would poison you and everyone around you.

I would teach them so, because I had already seen for myself how life is ordained for a person from the very beginning. Who had ordained it this way? I do not know... But I think that it was the one they call the Sleeping God, who dwells in the utmost heaven. He created this beautiful world and then, feeling assured, he went to sleep. It had probably happened exactly that way, I thought... Men said that he no longer remembers that the earth and human beings exist. But as I looked at the workings of fate, I realized that his wisdom had remained behind on the earth and spread across the great Tree of the Yenisei on which the world stood, inhabited by people in their different tribes and by trees, animals, and spirits.

Together with my sons I went up to the tops of the forested cliffs on a sunny day. I pointed to the serpentine body of the great water and said to them, "Look how beautiful it is!"

I knew whom to thank for everything that had happened: the Yenisei became my god. I would go up there alone to see its majesty, and I prayed to it with the words that my heart suggested.

That went on for many years until one day in late autumn when I went up to the heights to pray, and blood flowed from my ear.

My talent that I had almost forgotten – hearing birds from half a day's flight away – awoke, but the tidings took my hearing away completely.

My head rang unbearably and I crawled back to the encampment like a reptile. Nara, the children, Yekha all came running up to me, and they shouted something when they saw the blood…

Tyney boiled a big chunk of birch bark in a pot. Then he rolled it up into a trumpet – narrow at one end and wide at the other – and showed me that I had to put it up to my ear. I did what he asked. He shouted something into the trumpet, then he looked me in the face and I understood from the movement of his lips that he was asking "Can you hear me?"

Only a distant ringing reached me, and it left a resounding pain at the back of my head. "I can't hear anything," I said.

The old man stood up, shook his head sadly, and walked out.

A day later the shaman arrived – Tyney had brought him. The shaman spent a long time performing his rite, and then he dropped his drum and stick and fell, exhausted, onto the furs. The old man and my wife went up to him, obviously to ask if he had reached some agreement with the spirit that had sent me this sudden affliction. The shaman did not answer, however, he only walked past them and spoke to me – slowly, so that I did not even need hearing to make out his words:

"The spirits are gone. The world is empty."

What exactly had I heard up there on the cliff? What tidings? I did not know then. I know now.

I heard the Sayan Mountains riven asunder.

DEAF-AND-BLIND
(THE THIRD NAME)

This house alone of those which had stood opposite the gate called Namazgokh, was destined to survive.

They say that a man had once lived in it, he earned a living by making bricks from clay and straw. He dug the clay here, close by. They also say that not far away, a small, muddy river flowed that was no more than a brook. It no longer exists, nor does the man himself, nor those who lived with him.

The house has survived, however. Craftsmen needed it to store the strong wooden beams they made while they were still hot, and therefore its walls remained untouched by sledgehammer or spade. The other houses were demolished, so that their rubble could be carried into the ditch. Granted, one could not call this house whole, for half of its roof was missing; I do not know why it collapsed. The surviving part is enough for me to escape the wind and the winter rains, and in summer the midday heat.

I spend every morning by the wall. A long shadow extends west from it. I sit and look out towards the flat-topped hill on which the city once stood. People swarm about the ruins, but less of them by the year, and the hill itself is covered with sand.

That morning shade is short-lived. When the shadow begins to creep up my knees, I go deeper into the house and lie my head on a beam that the craftsmen left behind. It is the root of a mulberry tree, worked with an ax and soaked in saltwater until it became as hard as iron. The salt does not vanish with the years, rather the wood grows harder…

I am alone, but I know that they will come for me soon – I only have to lie my head on the beam and close my eyes. They will come, they will stare at me unblinkingly, as if asking how I will pay for their lives. They nag me like hawkers, but I lack the courage to send them away.

"What are you staring at me for? Can't you see how wretched I am?"

Their eyes remained fixed on me, however, and they say nothing. In the silence I hear, "You're still alive, but we are not."

I tell them:

"Am I really to blame for that?"

They answer without speaking a word:

"Are *we* really to blame for anything?"

And who is to blame for the fact that the world turned out to be different from what we thought, that it is ruled by a power that we were not even aware of?

Bloody Sky

Perhaps fate was merciful that I was completely deaf when those days came upon us.

What did I see then? I saw an open mouth that gaped, a black, bottomless pit of fear. The mouth was shouting something, and our people were shocked by what they heard, they could not believe what had been said. I, on the other hand, saw only the blackness…

People from tribes that I knew nothing of then came pouring into our lands. At first they fled along the riverbank, on foot or on the backs of horses – I was seeing those animals for the first time, too – and when the ice over the Yenisei grew thick, whole crowds of them came. No one drove them away or tried to stop them, neither us nor those who controlled the neighboring rivers. People teemed along the mountains and froze to death in crevices there.

Tyney had lived a whole lifetime now in these parts, which lay close to the Mountains of Paradise. He talked with the arrivals about something, then walked off and sat down on a stone, deep in thought.

I went up to him and asked "What are they saying?" – I knew that I would not be able to hear the answer.

Tyney quietly spoke, then shouted a word – a word that I did not know and was uttered with a single motion of his lips.

Bloody Sky, the warlord, my people called by the concise name Des, and that is the name that the old man shouted. It was Bloody Sky who had put to flight the peoples of the steppes, the tribes of the mountains from which the great river springs, and he himself was coming for us, too.

The people whom he caused to flee bore along with their terror a secret that left me stunned.

To comprehend it, I did not need to be able to hear.

There, beyond the Sayan Mountains, where I – and many others – believed that paradise lay at the crown of the Tree, the abode of the luminous spirits, many of whom were destined to be born and come into the world – ordinary human beings lived, and these people were fierce and bore the name Mongols.

They were led by a single man who lived in a huge white yurt on wheels, which a herd of harnessed bulls pulled over the earth. This man held the fate of the whole world in his hands, and he had called on Bloody Sky.

****

Then much was revealed by what my eyes had not seen, and my ears had not heard.

Ten years earlier, when destiny had just led me to my own river, the Mongols had already arrived on the upper Yenisei, where the steppe ruled by the Kyrgyz people extends.

The Mongols' existence, as well as their strength, was no secret to the Kyrgyz. As the Mongols moved towards the Kyrgyz lands, they easily subjected every tribe along the way, and the Kyrgyz, too, thought it best to show submission and thereby escape death. Four of their princes who joined forces and summoned the commanders of neighboring tribes, themselves went to their prince, knelt before him, and offered gifts: white horses, white gyrfalcons, and white sables. The Mongols' prince – his name was Juchi – was satisfied by what he saw and received. He was kind to the commanders of the Kyrgyz and the forest tribes, and as he was not greedy for senseless bloodshed, he returned to his own steppe after ordering them to obey every order the Mongols gave.

The power of Bloody Sky had then only partly awakened, as if only one of his eyes.

But a year passed, or perhaps a slightly longer time, and one of the Mongol lords set out with a small retinue of warriors to the Tumat people, to take their thirty loveliest girls and give them to his khan; only Bloody Sky was higher than he. The Tumat leader, just like the Kyrgyz and others, knelt in submission and offered gifts, but the demand for such a payment offended his pride. He imprisoned the Mongol lord and slaughtered his retinue. The Tumats lived deep in the mountains and hoped that those mountains would protect them. The khan sent out one band of warriors after another, but they met the same fate as the first. Then he ordered the Kyrgyz to show loyalty and raise an army, in order to chastise the Tumats. The steppe commanders, however, recalled their wounded pride, and they decided that the power of their overlords was not infinite. They therefore donned iron, got on their horses, and set off against the Mongols themselves.

Now Bloody Sky opened his other eye and began to rise to his full stature.

They went down into a valley where two of the Yenisei's headwaters came together. It was like a battle of wolves versus dogs.

In a single blow, the first Mongol detachment beat the Kyrgyz back into the steppe. After that first detachment came the numberless mounted warriors of Prince Juchi over the thick ice.

Juchi spared no one. He traveled for a month down the river, and for every living man who managed to reach my encampment, there were thousands of dead bodies and hundreds of captives collared and tied to long poles.

I would eventually see both with my own eyes.

***

When I crawled down, with bloody ears, from the height where I had prayed, Nara wept, tore her hair, and screamed loudly, as if she wanted to break right through my deafness. Everyone who visited me lamented. After several days, however, even Nara was no longer thinking about her deafened provider.

Within the terror that the howling, black mouths brought was a single word: "Run."

We did not immediately flee after these people. For a taiga man, abandoning his own river would be like a bird throwing her fledglings from the nest. It was hard to take such a step.

But now Tyney drove up with two harnessed sledges. On them were his elderly wife, his widowed daughter-in-law and his grandsons. He shouted in my face and gestured with his arms that I needed to harness my own sleds, and then he rushed over to speak to Nara. She immediately disappeared into our chum in order to gather our possessions and our daughters. Our sons were running through the encampment and calling the dogs, but the latter were reluctant to heed their young masters.

We were ready for the journey, unaware that our sluggishness had already doomed us.

My dogs were already standing with harnesses around their necks when I got up, went to the riverbank, and saw a snake come creeping far off – its scales were glittering iron.

When the other people, both my own and the outsiders, saw the snake, they ran like mice, and some fell on the ice and remained lying there. Tyney jumped onto his sled and drove up to me. Nara ran up waving her arms, I could not see the children…

I watched the snake.

Tyney grabbed me by the arm and pulled me to the edge of the encampment, but now what people called madness came over me. I shook my arm free, clutched at the roots of a pine that grew on the rock, and shouted so loud that my very bones rang: "No!" Tyney's expression turned angry and he walked off, obviously convinced that I was intent on dying on my native river and would do my wife and children the same honor. It was not they whom I was thinking of, though.

It is a hard thing when one man betrays another, but I was betrayed by my god. I saw it and I could not believe it. I saw the gray, iron-covered snake crawling along the glimmering Tree of the Yenisei to which I had prayed...

A powerful jerk tore me from the pine roots: Yekha had run up to me, grabbed me by the collar, pulled me to the ground, and then used his lariat to tie me to him – he did this with a series of flawless motions, as if he could still see. Along with the rope, he had brought the birch-bark trumpet, and now he stuck the narrow end into my ear. A human voice, the first I had heard in all those days, came to me as if from far away:

"If you try to free yourself, I'll kill you."

From that moment, Yekha became my hearer, and I became his sight. Together we were a single entity. The two of us were even referred to by a single name: Sewsi-Khasi, which in Yurak means "Deaf-and-Blind". The Tungus man's son came up with it himself. But that all happened later.

He dragged me, like a puppy, over to the sled where Nara sat and threw the reins in my face. The children were on the other sled, which Balna steered.

By this time, however, it was no longer possible to escape. The snake was already close, and when it caught sight of us and the other people, the sky was blackened by arrows. One of the men on the ice fell.

The snake arrived and swallowed us whole.

***

 ALEXANDER GRIGORENKO

By the time it reached my river, the snake had already had enough dead, it wanted living human beings.

An army such as the taiga had not seen for an eternity approached us. The riders dispersed into a multitude of equal-sized threads similar to the weaving of a net: people were caught with lariats, and those who lay on the ground were swept up like some dropped object.

Thus we, too, were taken and forced into a large crowd that was surrounded by men on horseback. A number of Mongols dismounted and ran into the forest, axes in their hands.

I examined the snake up close. Its scales were men in fur caps tipped with iron, and armor made from iron and leather soaked in glue – the same as we made it. I felt that they bore no enmity towards us and did not even consider us the enemy – they were simply hunters collecting their catch and pleased that there was a lot of it.

We waited. Steam rose from the crowd. Many people's faces were distorted with weeping. We were still all together, Nara stood frozen and pressed our daughters' heads against her chest; our daughters' shoulders heaved with crying. Our sons Balna and Togot stood next to us as well, with a bewildered look on their faces.

"They won't kill us," I shouted to them. "They won't!"

Nara said something to me, having forgotten that I was deaf. Then she buried her face in her hands and kept it there for what seemed like an eternity.

The throng pressed more tightly together and we stood at its very center. Due to my slight build, I did not see the return of those Mongols sent into the forest for wood. Yekha, however, towered above everyone, and he was the first person to be dragged forth out of the crowd – I was hauled off in his wake and they were amazed when they saw a man tied to the giant who barely reached up to the latter's elbow. One of the Mongols now came up with a knife to cut the rope that bound us together, but the Tungus man's son, sensing this disaster, held me close to him and yelled something, while pointing to his eye-sockets and then at my ears and the birch-bark trumpet.

The Mongols did not understand his language, but they understood what he was trying to communicate and they laughed.

Then they began to divide up their catch: they separated out the men, women, and children, and tied them in a chain like fish hung to dry. Several old men from among the Kyrgyz and peoples of the taiga from unfamiliar rivers, they simply drove out of the circle – they were letting those go.

Yekha, due to his great stature, was the last to be tied to a long pole along with the tallest men, but my neck remained unbound to the pole – I walked like a reindeer calf following its mother. One of the Mongols who had laughed at us squat-ted down, smiled at me, muttered something, and drew his finger across his throat. I nodded.

Soon the frozen river was covered by groups of people bound together, and the horsemen rode around them. Everyone had now been mixed up; I saw many people from the taiga, but I recognized no faces among them. I forgot all about my deafness and shouted my wife's name and my children's. I assume that others were doing the same.

Whips flashed over our heads...

***

We marched on until the Kyrgyz steppe where, among stones erected in memory of someone or something, the bodies of people and horses lay, and black birds that had flown here from every direction prevented the snow from covering the bodies. Then we turned towards the sunset. We walked along the valleys of frozen rivers and among hills similar to ours, and then we left them behind. The landscape around us increasingly opened up, and I saw only a sea of people, an endless sea of bobbing heads, and somewhere deep within it were my wife and my children.

Sometimes, as we walked, Yekha would ask me, "What do you see?"

"Snow, a valley, people."

"Many people?"

"More people than you have seen in your entire life."

When we stopped to rest, we were not untied from the poles. Food was brought to the Mongols by nearby tribes who had submitted to them just like the rest of the world had. Once a day, or sometimes less often, we were thrown some piping-hot offal from their pots. When we rose to continue walking, they would leave behind a few people who were practically dead from exhaustion. How long this journey took, I do not know. I only remember that by winter's end we arrived at a place where the mountains had given way to wide valleys and then disappeared entirely.

The main camp of the Mongols was here, the greatest of all camps that a nomad could erect.

People were divided up here, too, the women first. Yekha heard among the myriad voices Nara's, grabbed my trumpet, and shouted, "She's alive! She's here, alive!"

"What about the children?" I shouted.

The Tungus man's son did not reply, however. The women were taken away to somewhere deep inside the camp, behind a solid barrier of wagons and yurts. We never saw them again.

Then the fate of those who remained was decided. The first people whom the Mongols allowed to live where those who had mastered some craft, though when they had set off on that campaign among mere forest-dwellers, they realized that they were unlikely to find many such men.

But then came an order from their leader: every warrior was to bring ten strong captives back from their campaign, even if those captives did not know how to do anything useful. The warriors, knowing that they would lose half along the way, took as many people as they had poles for, so that they would not be punished later for failing to meet the quota. They quarreled among themselves as they counted the captives, but no one dared reach for his sword. The Mongols went on shouting like this all day as they untied people from the poles, felt their arms, and poked them in their chests to see whether they could stand up well on their feet. Those who fell down seemed exhausted to the point that their eyes expressed total indifference, and the Mongols took them outside the camp and then came back wiping their swords. When it was my turn in line and Yekha's, I realized that we would also be led outside the wall of wagons. The Mongols would hardly waste food on cripples, and that is what we were.

Apparently, however, they had all already met their respective quotas, and they ceased arguing with each other.

When it got dark, countless campfires were lit. The Mongols saw that their work was now done, they relaxed after their hard campaign, the grim expressions melted from their faces, and they turned merry. By the firelight they saw that the empty pen for the captives still held a giant and a very short man tied together, and they laughed heartily at that. They gathered together, drank from their skins, and one Mongol pointed at us and said something to his peers. I understood what amusement they were now looking forward to: tiny eyes and huge ears walking together, one tied to the other.

The man who had pointed at us rushed up to me – I recognized the Mongol who had allowed me to remain unbound to the pole – grabbed my birch-bark trumpet, and twice shouted into it "Boorchu!" Then, laughing, he slapped himself in the chest. He was telling me his name. Then he stepped back a few feet and began to clap rhythmically, and his fellows did the same after him.

     ALEXANDER GRIGORENKO

Yekha, who so far had stood as immobile as an idol, shouted into my trumpet, "What do they want?!"

"For us to dance."

"Dance, then," he replied at once.

"I won't."

The Tungus man's son pulled at the rope and yelled so loudly that I could hear him without the trumpet:

"Dance, you wolverine! Dance, fish shit, if you want to live."

"I don't want to live!"

"Well, I do! Understand?"

He raised his arms and, beginning the dance of the angry bear, moved around in circles – I was still resisting, but Yekha dragged me along with him. He jerked at the rope again and tried to give me a kick, but his foot struck only empty air. I saw the men in furs and iron fall to the ground laughing, as if they had been shot in the stomach.

I, too, began to dance, albeit mirroring Yekha's movements. When he made a leap, I fell down. I lost my birch-bark trumpet, and the Mongols rolled on the trodden snow. I shouted at Yekha to make him stop, so that I could pick up my birch-bark ear which was now being tramped under the giant's feet. He stopped, and I crawled on all fours towards the trumpet. Yekha obediently followed where the rope pulled him, while to me, in spite of my deafness, it seemed like the very sky was laughing at us. Out of the corner of my eye I saw several men in shining helmets step out in front of the crowd – these were Noyons – and their initially stern expressions melted like snow in a pot.

The dance went on for a long time, until seemingly everyone living in the great camp had gathered to watch. That dance saved us from death, and it also allowed several other unfortunate people remaining in the pen to survive this night, as no one remembered about them until the next morning.

That morning, we were led off, stiff with cold. The Mongols drove Yekha on, as they got pleasure from watching my inability to keep up with him and falling face-first into the snow.

We were led to the center of this great city. There, in a vast open space decorated with a multitude of tall, multicolored flags, and filled with ranks of men in shining armor and ranks of other men in ragged clothing, I saw several large yurts mounted on wheels.

It was in one of these, which resembled a snow-covered mountain, that the man who now owned the world lived.

At this time he was content that his son, bright Juchi, had laid the peoples of the forest at his feet, without even a drop of precious Mongol blood shed. When the Mongols learned that he was satisfied, they wanted to amuse him with the curiosity they had brought back from the taiga.

I saw him from far off when he stepped out of the yurt, and I shuddered as I did, for he bore such a resemblance to the stout man.

They brought him a high seat and he sat down. People in bright clothing ran up to him one by one and laid bundles of black furs at his feet. Then they brought up the people in ragged clothing who had been taken to fill his quota and therefore remained alive. Then two Mongols grabbed Yekha by his sleeve and quickly dragged him towards the mountain of felt that seemed snow-covered, but before they had managed to bring us there, the man rose and went back into his yurt.

We were returned to the pen – by now it was empty – and when the daylight gave way to campfires, they again dragged us towards the great dwelling on wheels. Inside the Mongols

          ALEXANDER GRIGORENKO

were eating meat and the man presided over the feast. We were ordered to dance, everyone had a good laugh, and the man smiled slightly and said something.

The feasting men laughed at his words, but this time their laughter was more restrained. Now I could see the man up close, and he no longer seemed so similar to Yabto.

He said something again and looked askance at us – he probably wanted us to hear his words. A short-statured man ran up to us and said something to Yekha. The man seated on the throne threw us a chunk of meat, which I immediately hid under my jumper. We were led out.

In the pen I put my birch-bark trumpet up to Yekha's mouth and asked, "What did they tell you?"

"'Look how pitiful a man who wants to live is. Whoever clings to his life will lose it in shame.' Now give me some meat."

The hunt

Several days passed and then we saw something remarkable. The secret behind this spectacle was revealed to me only several years later, but I will tell it to you now.

The man was waiting for his tumens to arrive from other countries.

During any break from fighting, the Mongols were to spend that lull maintaining their equipment and hunting – that was the man's command. And as he was feasting there, the hunt had already begun.

The forces assigned to it had already set out a month ago, maybe more. The detachments spread out so that they were many days' journey from one another, and they followed one rule: they were not to kill their game but drive it onward, and not allow a single animal – even were it a hare or a ground squirrel – to escape in the opposite direction. The hunters formed ranks as they drove the animals onward, and while they had stood an arrow's flight apart at the beginning of the hunt, now their ranks had to draw together and serve as an insurmountable wall for the game. Behind these ranks stood specially assigned men who watched out and were harshly punished for any animal that slipped away. When they came across the occasional stretch of forest, the horsemen would gather together and pass between the trees like an iron comb, in order to drive the creatures back out into the open terrain, and then they would disperse again.

The hunters got no rest, day or night. The sun set, they would light campfires, and while some slept, others wielded torches and with incessant shouting terrified the animals. Each animal would run ahead, assuming that it would find salvation somewhere.

This roundup of game shattered the ordinary boundaries by which predators lived: wolves in packs that had long since divided up the earth between them, now met and fought, and so did foxes, jackals, and wildcats. This fray was short-lived, however, because there was now a lot more prey around: antelopes, wild asses, deer and myriad small game ran ahead of them. The predators hunted these and ate their fill, forgetting all about their competition, but their happiness did not last long, because others arrived and now those predators themselves were hunted.

This formation that the Mongols called a *nerge* grew ever denser. The animals continued to be driven forward out of fear. At night the bonfires were not just some far-off smell, the animals could see the fire. They had already forgotten about their former territories, and they had to think less and less about their prey, which now barely tried to hide or fled in order to save its life.

Suddenly the princes of the local animal kingdom appeared: tigers and long-legged, spotted cats that were like apparitions; the other animals had seen these no more than most people had ever seen a ghost. Then great howling arose, and some animals, crazed with fear, ran as far as they could towards the human smell of their enemies and were inevitably struck down with arrows.

Those princes no longer felt any temptation at the sight of such dense herds of wild reindeer, goats, and asses up close. Their stomachs were already full, and they laid down under the scattered trees or rocky outcrops and watched the general confusion, perplexed by this change that had come over the world. When the horsemen appeared from far off, they got back up and bared their fangs, but the fear that had filled the whole landscape forced these princes, too, to run on just like the other animals. The princes also assumed that somewhere ahead everything would be resolved, that the earth is vast and their lives would return to the usual routine.

A day came, however, when the same formation appeared up ahead, the same fires and shouting.

Then animals both great and small were overcome with despair. The herds rushed at one another, their backs and horns swirled together in great maelstroms, wolves perished under their hooves, foxes darted about in search of shelter and crammed themselves into burrows where rodents and hares were already hiding, the jackals merged with the packs of wolves, and the animals could no longer distinguish their own from outsiders.

The *nerge* moved slowly, between sunrise and sunset it covered not even a small part of a rider's usual distance, so there were days when the animals thought that the chase had ended. Some decided that if they could not seek salvation ahead, then it might lie to the right, where distant mountains could be made out, or to the left, in the low, barren hills that stretched on endlessly. It was in the latter direction that the wolves ran, as they were no lovers of mountains, and the herds rushed after them, but even before darkness fell both groups of animals had been brought back.

Ultimately, there came a moment when every animal, great and small, had become convinced that there was no salvation in store. Neither ahead nor back the other way, neither in the mountains nor in the hills. Though the horsemen and fires were still far off, they were everywhere. In the course of this mad flight, which had been full of changes that no animal's mind was able to comprehend, a month passed, perhaps longer, but everything led to one simple understanding: there was nowhere to run, they would not be able to save themselves. Herds froze from this fear, burrows and dens were filled by every animal without distinction, and the packs of wolves seethed like boiling water.

Then the princes of these parts rose, and every other animal watched them.

It was the princes who were the first to decide to break through the *nerge*, realizing that only they possessed the strength for such a desperate move. Yet if any of them were able to succeed in this plan, it could only be the spotted cats, for that was the only beast in this world that can run as fast as a flying arrow. The men were aware of this quality and had already made preparations – a warrior who let a hare, jackal, or wild ass slip through might get off with only a beating, but anyone responsible for losing a spotted cat or a tiger would have his neck broken.

The men continually looked about to spot any fleet-footed beast, so that they could catch it at that sole moment when it could still be stopped by a rain of stones and arrows. Usually the first animal killed would put an end to everything, as its death would deprive the others of any remaining hope. The tigers, who were far superior to the spotted cats in physical strength, lacked their fleetness of foot, and when they saw one of their peers killed, they would growl angrily and try to frighten the men with their savageness, but the men of that world did not know fear.

The princes returned to the herds and wolf packs, and to the shelters in the earth and under rocks, where they huddled together drearily. Sometimes, in their impotent rage, they might kill some other animal along the way, but if the humans saw this, they would shout with joy, and the other animals were indifferent to it all.

∗∗∗

Even this dense mass into which they had been forced, however, was freedom compared to what would soon come. The *nerge* not only drove the animals onward, the bands of men standing around were guiding them towards one particular direction, towards the great camp and the yurt like a snow-covered mountain at its center. When there was less than one day's journey left, those bands began to come together. They made their way shouting, banging iron, and brandishing fire, and then they stopped at a signal from the leader of this chase, when he saw that all the warriors sent out in sundry directions a month before now formed a single visible circle.

To this circle throngs of slaves were ordered, carrying bundles of stakes on their backs, and so were camels and oxen laden with old skins, felt mats, ropes, and wooden mallets. The throng surrounded the *nerge* as the latter closed together, and soon a never-ending sound of stone rubble arose – it was mallets pounding hundreds and hundreds of stakes into the earth. Ropes were then stretched between these, and the old skins and felt pieces with patches of red fabric were hung over the ropes, so that the circle would become a wall.

I was among this crowd that built the wall. Yekha hauled a cart that was piled high, while I led him by a rope in order to show him the way, to the great merriment of the Mongols. Though this joint entity known as Sewsi-Khasi offered them daily amusement, it nevertheless did what the other slaves did. The Tungus man's son could haul the same weight as a good horse, he pulled the wagon on its tall wheels, while I helped him load it and then guided him where we had been ordered to go.

On this day the hunters were in high spirits, because the hard work was already behind them. Now only a single horseman could stand in for a dozen men from the *nerge*, but most importantly, tomorrow or the day after there would be the celebration of the mighty khan's great hunt, and each of the hunters – with the exception of those that had got a beating – would receive a reward.

***

                                    ALEXANDER GRIGORENKO

The sun set as the wall was now complete. The slaves were ordered to remain along the entire ring, in order to make the wall truly impenetrable, and so we spent the night there.

Yekha sat on the ground and leaned against the tall-wheeled cart. The moon rose, and I looked upon its frozen face. My brother seemed to be sleeping. As the wall was being built, they had beaten us with whips in order to make us work faster, and so my sweat-drenched eyes only once glanced the inside of the great ring, and my fatigued mind was incapable of feeling amazement at the vast amount of animals of all different kinds. Night came, and so did hunger (we had not been given a morsel since morning), so I wanted to wake Yekha and suggest that we eat the leather strap that bound us together. But the giant, who must have been even more tormented by hunger and fatigue than me, said nothing and chose to sleep – that was the only nice thing available to us then. When I realized that, I felt embarrassment at what I had been thinking to ask.

Like many people in the taiga do when hunting, when they want to know whether any large prey like elk or wild boars are around, I found a small stone half buried in the earth and, my stomach pressed to the ground, I gripped it with my teeth and lay still. A sound like a quiet splash of water passed through my bones. I then got up, groped for my rumpled birch-bark ear, and then pointed it towards the circle, but from there I heard only the same splash-like sound, and it told me nothing.

Then I felt a jerk at the strap attached to my belt – Yekha was not sleeping.

Without any change in his expression, he had tugged on the strap. "What do you see?"

"Animals. A great many. No human being has ever seen so many before. What can you hear? Tell me."

He grabbed the trumpet and shouted angrily, "Don't lie. There are no animals there, it's people weeping! They captured more people, you marrowless bone! You can't tell people from animals, silly wolverine!"

In a single motion Yekha broke the birch-bark ear and hurled the fragments away into the darkness. He shook and clenched his jaw tightly shut lest he erupt with weeping.

Then I was truly deaf – and I shall never cease to be grateful to that man who took my hearing away from me.

***

The next day, the slaves were led away with the carts and oxen to a neighboring hill.

From there we saw a plain, and it was framed not by the outlines of distant mountains but equal-sized formations of men on horseback: under multicolored banners the tumens stood waiting for their lord. Those fluttering banners and the iridescent fur on the horsemen's caps were the only things that moved in the vast ranks. Just as motionless stood the warriors who were posted at equal distances along the wall of wood and skins.

A steam rose from inside the ring, and under it a motley array of creatures shimmered, like thick fish glue boiling in a pot. These animals driven into the circle without distinction, lived now as a single body and were doomed to a common fate. I forced my eyes to make out the hoofed animals, which huddled in dense throngs head to head, and the wolves, foxes, jackals, that ran ceaselessly and dejected among the bodies of the others. I made out islands of empty space around where the bright backs of the princes of these parts could be seen. The smaller animals teemed like insects and it was barely possible to distinguish one from another.

Yekha tugged at the strap that bound us, he was shouting something and pointing towards the circle. I could not make out a single word of what he said, and there were many. I only shouted back, "There are animals there, lots of different animals. I'm not kidding!" The giant sniffed the air and tried to make sense of what he was smelling, but the scent was unfamiliar. He said something, at length, speaking quickly, but I could not make any sense of the movement of his lips, and I turned away from him.

At midday people turned their gazes to the west, where a distant glow could be seen. Something approached that re-called the snake that had crawled along the body of the Yeni-sei, only that snake had been the color of dark iron, while this one sparkled in the sun and had a head: it was a white yurt that resembled a snow-covered peak. The man was moving inside the yurt and accompanied by his beloved army. He had clad this army in the finest armor on earth, considered it his own flesh and blood, and he prayed to it as one would pray to the gods on whom life and death depend.

The snake came up towards the ring until it was about an arrow's flight away, then it stopped. A horse was brought for the man, he left the white yurt, and the whole formation surged forward. Banners and clouds of steam rose over the tumens.

The shining horsemen crowded at the wall and their backs prevented me from getting any glimpse of the man. He re-appeared only later, when he rode, together with several of his men, into the circle. There the many-colored mass of animals backed away, leaving an empty space in front of him. I could not see any weapon in his hands – he simply stood and looked at the animals, and this went on for a long time. Then a horseman in a yellow helm rode up and handed him a bow.

He shot his arrows one after another, and so tirelessly that the men who stood behind him handed him a succession of full quivers, like containers of food at a big feast. After the first arrow the living mass inside the ring trembled with one united motion, steam rose in clumps from hundreds and hundreds of animal throats. Yet the man kept on shooting and shooting... How long this lasted, I do not know – I only remember that he turned and watched as Yekha and all the others in ragged clothing on the hill covered their ears, to escape the horrific sound that came from inside the ring.

When movement across a third or perhaps half of the ring had ceased under his rain of arrows, he lowered his bow, turned his horse around, and leisurely headed back to his white yurt. His position was then taken by others, riders in yellow helms, and then these were joined by men in armor of shining iron, followed by men in leather jerkins and big fur hats – there were eventually many people there, they rode around in circles, as easily as over empty ground, in order to seek out and kill whatever game remained.

***

By evening there was no longer any movement inside the ring.

After those horsemen came others, a lot of people in gray felt clothing. Some picked up the arrows, others looked for the carcasses that they required. I watched as several princely, striped animals and one spotted beast were hauled to the other side of the wall, and the men dragging them out were met by a sea of extended hands.

Little else was taken out of the ring, however, only the wild asses and deer. The Mongols had no need for the other animals.

The tumens under their banners now marched forth from their positions. When they arrived, they forced us slaves to get up and begin disassembling the ring, and also to collect whatever game remained.

Yekha took up our cart. The Mongol who commanded our group of ten men – they divided all their slaves, just like themselves, into equal regiments and set a boss over each – gestured that we were to haul not the stakes, felt mats, or mallets, but rather the dead foxes. The boss picked a fox by the tail from right under him, pointed to it, barked some command, and threw it onto the cart. By sunset the cart had been heaped high, though we had not covered even half of the ring. There were so many animals that we hardly found a patch of empty ground to tread. Some of the slaves hid under their clothes hares and large ground squirrels such as we had never seen in the taiga.

That was the hunt of the great khan and his people.

The *khashar*

Boorchu – then the only Mongol that I knew by name – made me a present.

He loved the dances performed by the single entity more than anyone else. After the great hunt, he came by night to the slave pen, found the entity sleeping, and kicked me in my side. He shouted something, and the sound woke Yekha and made him jump to his feet.

When the Mongol saw that I did not have my birch-bark trumpet, he fell silent and walked off.

Several days later, again by night, something hard was jabbed into my ear. The pain was followed by a distant sound:

"Hey, Sewsi-Khasi, hey!"

Boorchu had brought a hollow horn from some massive ox – probably of the sort that pulled the white yurt – and it would serve as a replacement for the birch-bark trumpet. The Mongol had ordered a craftsman to file away the sharp tip of the horn, and also to attach a strap so that I could carry it around without losing it.

Without further ado, he grabbed me by the collar and led us towards the campfires of the army. His men were gathered around one fire, where they ate meat and drank, pouring a rich-smelling, intoxicating beverage out of skins and into their cups. When our dance was finished, we were given both things. First we ate until we were sated, but the drink led us to immediately vomit everything up. The Mongols laughed, and I was choked with bitterness.

That was the last time that we were brought to serve as entertainment. Soon the Mongols' merry faces gave way to stern ones.

Spring came, the great camp set off from that place and proceeded far along the plain that had now burst into flower.

We walked over grass and stone, across unknown rivers that we did not know and which looked nothing alike – their banks were rocky, like my own river, or sandy like Yabto's – and made our way around a chain of snow-covered mountains. On this journey we spent a whole year, only a little of which has remained in my memory, yet that bit I remember to this day.

***

What I remember most from that year is the amazement I felt when I saw a town for the first time.

In the middle of the flat landscape, a gray cliff towered up unlike any I had ever seen, and it lacked the usual top. We came closer, and I could now see that the top of the cliff was as if embroidered with beads – these were human beings. Soon I learned what these cliff-like structures served for, but at the time I could feel only utter astonishment. On that day I walked only because I was being led on, and I lived only because I did not die, and if I had been able to consciously reflect on what I saw, then I probably would have understood that those walls were the only way to hide in this flat region that offered no shelter to anyone.

I do not know what that town was called. It was much smaller than the ones that I would see later. Yet those no longer produced any amazement, though others who had been born in those regions would look, tears in their eyes, at the walls that grew ever taller from one city to another, at the clusters of varicolored dwellings, and their lips would move in something like a prayer. For me, towns remained something from which I kept a distance, like from something alien and almost repugnant.

When we stopped, Yekha would always shout into my horn the same words: "What do you see?" That is what he asked this time, too. "I don't know," I answered. The Tungus man's son shouted again – he wanted the eyes that walked ahead of him to serve him as faithfully as his ears served me.

I told him that I saw a huge anthill, only instead of earth, twigs, and pine needles, it was made out of stone, and instead of ants there were human beings.

Yekha froze, as if he had heard something in my words that he had expected. He let go of the cart and stepped forward, as if he wanted to look at something, and then he asked, "Are they red?"

"Who?"

"The people in the anthill."

I answered that I could not make out what color they were. Yekha stood there for a time, facing the city, then he turned around and I led him back to where his hands could take up the cart again.

The Tungus man's son was lost in thought after that.

I rarely had to ask him what he heard – the flat earth hid nothing.

The landscape was filled with people. By the morning of the next day these people had surrounded the town almost entirely, and they were not warriors. What I saw now is what I had seen a year before during the great hunt, and that had not served to feed the rulers of this world, but rather it taught them how to treat other peoples.

When the Mongols approached any town or city, their commanders would dispatch bands of warriors on all sides. These bands would work like a *nerge* and drive forward anyone who lived in these parts as nomads or settled populations, only during this hunt they did not enclose their prey in a wall of stakes, ropes, and skins. Instead, the hunt would end with a *khashar*.

The word meant "joint effort" in one of the local languages, and it was simple and easy to understand. It was both a quarry for the hunters and a means to pursue other game in the future. During the *khashar*, the Mongols would drive the people out of the towns, and each person in the *khashar* was called a *khasharchi*.

Long lines of people filed along, accompanied by a few men on horseback, and each of these people carried whatever had been picked up along the way: baskets filled with stones, bundles of firewood, or entire tree trunks. We ourselves had done the same earlier; Yekha's cart was full.

Gathering and hauling stones and wood was a *khashar*'s first and simplest task, and for this everyone was divided up – just like the army – into groups of ten men led by a Mongol overseer. Our overseer was a lanky man with a pitted face. The entity known as Sewsi-Khasi did not concern him in the least, it even angered him – whenever I dropped a stone, he would strike me with his whip and bare his long teeth. Fortunately, this Mongol was killed by the very first arrow as we approached the walls, though such a death was unusual for those who directed the bands of *khasharchi*.

The *khashar* would then use these stones and wood to fill in the moats around towns, so that then huge machines for demolishing walls and launching stones – both ordinary ones and burning ones – could approach. A few bands of ten men would make their way under a wooden canopy as arrows, stones, scalding water, and boiling pitch rained down on them. But if there were not enough such canopies, then they would haul the siege machines without them. The Mongol overseer always walked behind them, for his job was to drive the slaves on as fast as possible and deliver the machines to the places they were needed. If a whole group of ten slaves perished under the arrows and stones, then that Mongol would be appointed to another group of ten. The only men whom the Mongols made an effort to protect were the engineers, who would hide behind their machines.

Approaching the walls was the second task of the *khashar*.

The third and last was referred to as "breaking stone with one's head". Under a torrent of hot pitch and iron, the *khasharchi* stood by the battering rams, made excavations, and when the need arose, they would be the first to climb over the walls, but not in order to take the city. Rather, it was to make the enemy expend the greater part of its strength, arrows, and stones on that unarmed crowd which fear and despair had driven towards them. It was hard to call the *khasharchi* slaves, for their only job was to carry rocks and wood, climb over the walls, and die. The *khashar* served as mere fodder for war. The local regions abounded in such fodder, and the Mongols used as much of it as the land produced. Thus, sooner or later every town and city would submit to them, and the *khashar* could only pray that any of their relatives standing on the walls would not try to stubbornly resist.

The towns differed among each other, however. Some surrendered quickly – like that first town and several subsequent ones did – and so the crowd of people survived to be driven onward, its ranks filled with new human beings along the way.

There were towns that seemed hungry for victims, and Otrar was an example. After that town, only a handful of people remained from the *khashar*.

But there were cities that were downright insatiable, and our journey was leading us towards one.

The moat

When I talk about Samarkand, I talk about all the towns that I saw from afar while our cart was laden with stones, or that I saw through the cracks of the wooden canopy that sheltered me as I made my way towards the walls. It was at Samarkand that our destiny found its fulfillment – we were mere grains of sand in a sandstorm.

Samarkand had been preceded by another great city: Bukhara.

We approached it at the beginning of a wet and muddy spring.

Bukhara saved many of us by its unwillingness to resist.

The farther south we went, the more fodder for war there was. Ever more frequently we encountered dwellings with the same flat roofs. Men with beards on their narrow, swarthy faces streamed, hauling wood and stones, in a ceaseless flow of human beings.

This flow constantly changed, and so I do not remember a single face, even those of the men who had walked alongside me.

The army assembled at a distance from Bukhara's walls, and the *khashar* started to fill the moat. The overseers used their whips to make their men work faster, but their ire soon abated, for hardly any disturbance came from the walls.

The army waited there two days (apparently without launching a single arrow or stone), but on the third day the gates opened and people began to file out. The Mongols met them and led them off in order to begin a process they were well used to: dividing the people into groups of ten, into the needed and the useless, into those who would live and those who would die. Some gates let forth people, others swallowed men on horseback, and soon hardly any of the army was left around the moat.

After the Mongols had surged into Bukhara, we spent several more days by its walls. From a high point I could see a tower inside the city. Clumps of smoke rose atop that tower, and human beings rushed around in that smoke. These were the few residents of that city who were unwilling to lay down their weapons and leave with everyone else through the gates, in order to be divided up. They had instead locked themselves in the tower, and that tower was now ready to devour the *khashar* that had met no resistance at the walls. I, and probably many of the *khasharchi*, expected that we would soon be driven through the gates into the city. Yet this did not happen – instead of the captives they had taken earlier, it was those Bukhara residents who had surrendered whom the Mongols sent against the tower. So clever were the rulers of this world, as they knew that a *khashar* always prayed that a city would be unwilling to resist, and it was good indeed if the *khashar* prayed in the same language as the warriors standing up there on the walls.

Smoke still hung over the tower when we were ordered to move onward. The army proceeded along both banks of a river that burbled gaily in springtime. The early warmth of the year extended across the earth covered with flowers and the first greenery, and dotted with an endless series of settlements. I remember telling Yekha about the incredible things I saw, about how encampments here were so numerous and so close together, that a person in one could shout to the people in another; that people here scraped at the earth with sticks and made it look like a scarred face; that the trees here were all alike, squat, and grew in even rows, as if they had grown not from seeds that dropped from branches but by some other power; that there were no forests here, and it was unclear where any animals might live, as well as his beloved ants.

"There is another kind of ants here," Yekha said dourly.

The *khashar* walked ahead of the army. So it had been ordained: the captives were to absorb the first blow of any enemy that decided to attack the Mongols on open ground. By this time, however, all people so foolhardy had been wiped out, and so it was with no fear of imminent death that we walked towards the hill on which this city stood.

***

The boss of our ten men gave Yekha a long stick with some black fabric – it resembled a banner. The Tungus man's son stood at the head of a formation of new captives, the tallest of which barely reached up to his shoulder. I was hidden behind Yekha's back. Our overseer occasionally peered ahead and barked something.

Samarkand rose before us.

As we came up to it, I was looking ahead at the flowering landscape, and so I could not see how the army behind me, like an Ostyak scraper wrought from strong iron, was picking from the earth everything that existed thereon. This was probably the biggest siege force that the lords of the world had ever gathered.

People bore on their own backs or on carts the rubble of their dwellings. As they approached the city, they were ordered to drop their load, lie down on the ground, and wait for darkness to fall. At night the entire *khashar* was made to stand in even ranks at a considerable distance from one another, so that at dawn the men who stood watch at the walls would see an army beyond measure and be overcome with fear.

There in the formation, behind Yekha's back, I went almost unnoticed by the overseer. I turned and saw the vast host that now filled the valley. In it were islands of siege engines, yurts carried on wheels, camels, and oxen. On one side of this massive flow of people, logs, stones, and the rubble of dwellings waited immobile, while on the other side the tumens stood in a dense mass like towering cliffs. It seemed as if the entire world that had once lived so peacefully had now been driven here.

Fascinated by what I saw, I missed the signal – I only saw how some men, struck with whips, began to pick up the logs and stones, while the ranks of slaves that feigned an army parted to let the warriors through. I barely escaped being trampled.

***

Only from far off did this accumulation of human beings resemble a flowing river. In reality the people in it had been neatly divided up, just like we were, who were pretending to be part of the army. Banners and wooden shelters appeared from somewhere. The *khashar* behind us went up to the walls not as an unruly mob but as groups of ten men, each headed by a Mongol, but instead of weapons they carried what was needed to fill in the moat. Though we had stood in front of everyone else, we were the last to start moving. Yekha carried a log in each arm, while I hauled a large stone.

From far off the moat looked like a quiet little river, the sun reflected in it. It looked even smaller against the massive wall, the top of which was completely covered by soldiers. We would soon discover the force of their arrows.

The moat was still far away when the first dark clouds came flying. The entire *khashar* froze. Whips flashed above the crowd.

When we began to move forward again, we could see how only a few of the first ranks managed to reach the wall, and then they turned around and ran to pick up new things to haul. Those who followed had to make their way around the bodies, logs, and stones that now lay on the ground, but soon there were so many that the Mongol overseers saw that most of the slaves were hauling their loads up in vain. They began to call back those slaves that the arrows had spared, and ordered them to pick up whatever had been dropped. The large shields now protected only the commanders – our previous formation was forgotten. At the edge of the moat was a frantic mass of human beings that became easy pickings for the archers on the walls.

The archers shot while what survived of the *khashar* retreated from the moat and ran towards the tumens, which still waited far off. The Mongols did not use their sabers to stop their retreat; on the contrary, they deliberately drove the fleeing men farther from the killing rain of arrows.

The Mongols sped this retreat not out of any mercy towards us, but merely from their conviction that the death of anyone – be it a noyon or a slave – had to be justified and beneficial.

Fate ordained that not only were we among the survivors, but we also did not experience the blind panic that caused many to perish by the overseers' swords at the very beginning. Perhaps we were chosen ones, because the faces that ran alongside us were constantly replaced by others; yet in the end we made it out alive.

A man who is thus chosen is momentarily endowed with a lack of thinking that saves him. I was also saved by Yekha, as he protected me from the horror that might have sucked us in. Whether he was hauling a cart or carrying logs, the Tungus man's son always resembled a god walking over the earth, one who kept his gaze directed somewhere above everything that was happening, and who was indifferent to the flying arrows, spears, and fiery stones. Even if he still had his sight, I know that he would have been the same. The Mongols could see his strength and fearlessness, and that is probably why we were struck by their whips less often than the others. If I were killed, Yekha would undoubtedly have been assigned another man to guide him. Without him, my life was worth nothing.

The *khashar* was left alone until sunset – only a few men were made to drag trebuchets closer to the walls.

At each new city, foreign craftsmen – these were real slaves, that is, valuable men that had been taken captive long ago – would build new siege engines from whatever could be found in the vicinity. All they carried with them were the ropes and some specialized parts from iron.

As night fell, the *khashar* was again forced to go to the moat in order to drag away the dead and whatever they had failed to carry all the way to the water. In the darkness Samarkand's soldiers shot practically at random, and the fires that blazed atop the walls helped us more than them. Yekha was again ordered to take up his cart – several men joined me in loading it. By the time the dark sky began to brighten, the moat had swallowed everything that had lain on the earth. Already half-dead from fatigue and hunger, we were led to where heaps of stones and logs lay, and there the Tungus man's son leaned against a cartwheel and shouted into my horn:

"Is it day or night?!"

I answered that it was near dawn.

"The sun's rising will be the death of us," he said and immediately fell asleep.

***

That city, I now know, had four gates, but at that time I saw only one, which was kept closed with a massive drawbridge.

The sun rose, and already the overseers roamed and struck the sleeping slaves with their whips – and now I saw a wondrous thing.

The city was opening its maws: the drawbridge was slowly lowered across the moat, and the shining red-metal gates opened to discharge a torrent of iron-clad men on horseback. They rushed past the siege engines, past the slaves in the *khashar* who pressed themselves against the ground, past the heaps of logs and stones, and past the rubble of the dwellings that had once huddled against the city. The horsemen flew towards the tumens, who had stood waiting that whole first day while the *khashar* kept moving.

Everyone – both the Mongols and their fodder for war – turned to look as the warhorses came flying. Something strange was happening. All we could see was a dark maelstrom that slowly moved away from us.

How long we stood there, I cannot say, but soon something else happened that no one had ever seen before, or could even imagine.

The horsemen rode back towards the city. They were no longer the same tight, surging stream, and there were far fewer of them. As they came near, the *khashar* could see what prevented many of Samarkand's warriors from driving their horses so quickly onward: many of them dragged on ropes men clad in long clothing and with partly shaven heads. These were Mongols.

The riders who dragged those spoils swept past us and shouted something to the city. Those who had not yet seized such cruel booty lingered in order to kill the slaves who maintained the siege engines – they were so horrified by what they saw that they began to scatter when swords flashed above their heads. The city was already preparing to close its maws, however, and the soldiers were in a hurry, so both the slaves and their masters survived.

"They're beating them!" I shouted to Yekha. He stood motionless, facing the far-off battle, as if he could see it himself, and he said nothing in reply.

When the last horseman had departed across the moat, the city raised the drawbridge and we were left standing in front of the water.

We were not immediately forced to go up towards the walls, for the rulers of the world were somewhat taken aback after what had just happened. They never gave up, however, and by sunset a portion of the *khashar* was again hauling their loads to the walls, while others were sent to demolish those dwellings that the city, to its own misfortune, had hosted on its outskirts. The Mongols had probably assumed earlier that what was carried to the moat was enough, and so those houses had remained standing.

The very sight of the moat sowed despondency. I do not know how many stones were dropped into it, how many trees, pieces of rubble, and human bodies – it seemed as if it had swallowed everything that had existed upon the earth between Bukhara and Samarkand, whether living or non-living. I saw corpses bobbing on the moat's surface, like leaves on a stagnant pond. The moat seemed bottomless, it delayed the city's death and brought our own closer.

Yet that night, death passed us by. Yekha was given a sledgehammer to knock down the walls of houses – just as long ago, in another life, he had chopped larch trunks blind. I led him up to walls and said, "Now hit here," then we loaded the rubble onto our cart and made our way under a rain of arrows shot blindly.

***

Dawn of the third day saw a repeat of the previous one: the city lowered the drawbridge, opened the gates, and sent forth men on horseback. They swept past the *khashar*, siege engines, and heaps of rubble just as they had done before, but this time none of them came back.

That man, the one who dwelt in the yurt that recalled a snow-covered mountaintop, now declared his wish: the moat was to disappear by the time the sun set. He pronounced these words, and whips immediately flashed across the whole mass of the besieging slave force.

The decimated *khashar* was renewed by a fresh crowd driven here from somewhere in that vast, heavily populated land. The whip served as the Mongols' main weapon, followed by the sword, and no one dared slow from a run to a more moderate pace.

I found it inexplicable that the Tungus man's son did not simply drop to the ground; I don't know what fueled his massive bulk. I, however, became like one asleep. I no longer felt my body at all, and I had long since forgotten my hunger, fear, and the prospect of death itself.

How many times we ran up to the moat, I cannot say. I only remember how that night the water surged up out of it and flooded the land bordering it. The water mixed with soil, blood, and stones there to form a slime. We constantly slipped and fell in it, and when campfires were lit (by people oblivious to the fact that this could aid the archers on the walls), I saw how all the people bustling at the moat's edge were now the same color as the earth, the same color as the faceless, eyeless spirits of a bog.

***

On the fourth day it became clear that the man's orders had not been carried out perfectly. The moat had now overflowed and its waters spread across the low ground around it, but there was still a gaping expanse to cross.

The city no longer opened its gate, and it no longer rained arrows and stones down from the walls as abundantly as in the preceding days. The city was tired now, though the enemy had not yet gone into its main battle. The *khashar* had been renewed and all that troubled it was the strange, annoying waiting.

The day went by in a gloom, and that evening the Mongol overseers saw that the *khashar* would soon have nothing more to resort to: the surroundings were now bare, only a few dwellings remained that served to protect equipment for the siege weapons and the flaming projectiles. The moat still did not allow the heavy machinery and men with ladders to reach the walls.

Perhaps, I thought, fate would grant us some rest, until new stones could be gathered from the earth, but what happened next was something different.

At sunset, a cloud of dust rose from somewhere behind us – a herd was being driven to this place. Just like the stones, wood, and human beings, it had been gathered and then kept some distance away for the army's needs. The herd was to be used to fill in the moat and thereby execute that man's orders. Here the Mongols showed some inventiveness, they attached bundles of branches and baskets of rubble to the animals. The *khashar* was ordered to grab sticks, stand in a row, and push the animals on towards the moat. Overseers and ordinary Mongol soldiers moved behind the *khashar*. When they reached the moat, they struck the mooing and bleating animals with their spears, and pushed them down into the moat together with many slaves. The carcasses fell, as if onto soft, deep moss, and lay in a wild heap on top of what had been throw in earlier – yet this first herd forced into the moat raised its bottom by only a hand's breadth.

Another mooing and bleating series of animals followed. Again we stood behind the animals, and then we ran to force a third set in… Another night fell. The trebuchets were brought right up to the moat – streaks of lightning flew over our heads and burst against the walls with blinding flashes of white flame…

It was then, as I ran behind the herds, that Yekha collapsed.

He fell face-first and pressed his hands over his ears. He had heard all the sounds of war and remained a marching god, but now the sound of dying animals was too much for him, I had already seen that on the great hunt. I kicked him and shouted, "Get up, you'll be killed!"

He got up not because I had kicked him and shouted, but because he chose to do so himself. He sat there on the ground and I saw in the white flashes of light how my brother brushed the dirt from his face, his expression stone-faced, and then reached out and wiggled his fingers as if feeling for something. It was my horn that Yekha sought.

"I can see now," he said.

"What?"

"I can see the red ants carrying the parts of a black ant that had been torn to pieces. There are a lot of red ants, they are coming in waves…"

He had talked often about ants, but now I sensed that his wits had left him entirely. Figures in large, sharp-pointed hats were approaching us. "Get up!" I repeated, and the Tungus man's son docilely rose to his feet.

In fact, his mind was still sharp, and he could see better than my own eyes.

Again a herd was driven forth, then the *khashar* brought stones from somewhere, and then another herd, but it had still not been enough to fill the moat – there was still a little bit remaining before the battering rams could be passed over it and men with ladders could run across.

Then the Mongols took one final step.

A tumen approached, dismounted, and assembled into a *nerge,* a formation that was vast and impenetrable. With shields joined together they walked towards what remained of the human beings and livestock.

We stood there as the *nerge* approached. Some ran away from this advancing wall and towards the moat. The members of the *khashar* were forced with the dull ends of spears to move on – the blow caused Yekha to run forward several feet.

He jerked me closer as he always did when he was angry. I watched his hands – they were like bear paws – break the leather strap that connected the joint being that was Deaf-and-Blind. Then his massive hand came down on my head, and everything went black.

Then my brother was used to fill in Samarkand's moat.

Everyone who the *nerge* had pressed forward died. But Yekha alone was worth a whole *khashar*, so massive was his body, so great was his soul.

***

I came to as everything was rushing towards the walls: horses, men with ladders, battering rams, trebuchets… I had apparently been taken for a dead man, or probably not noticed at all. How could one notice a tiny individual at night, and moreover one who was now the same color as the filthy earth? The whole army swept past me and yet I was not trampled, but at the time I was not even capable of feeling astonishment at this.

I looked up and saw that I was the last of the accumulation of people who rushed towards the walls. I was now behind them, and in front of me there was only darkness. I got up and ran into that darkness, ran until I felt grass under my feet. I turned and saw a pale, distant glow.

I collapsed and hit my face against a stone as I did so. I clenched my teeth around the stone and through my bones the death rattles of the world passed, and with each one resonated "Who are you who gave everything and took it away? Who are you who gave everything and took it away? Who are you who gave everything and took it away? Who are you…" Then I shouted those same words, meaningless words that had come upon me out of the blue. I shouted so loud that blood gushed from my nose.

Then I was tired – I laid down and slept, and so soundly that I remember the silence in that sleep to this day.

When I awoke, it was day, a warm, nearly sweltering one. I walked on, after I had gone some distance, I saw a settlement. A dog like a big rat came bounding from somewhere and, after it saw me, ran away. Of many homes only their skeletons remained, but there were some structures that were still whole. In one, a meek bird sat on a heap of dry grass in the corner. It did not know how to fly and, like the dog had done, it scampered away from me. The bird had laid a few eggs. After I ate them, I laid down on the bird's roost and again fell asleep.

****

In the middle of the night, an inexplicable fear came over me and drove me towards the city. That fear, as inescapable as the Mongols' *nerge*, drove me from my peaceful spot to where men had disappeared into the moat, whole hosts of men, and it drove me as if death had lurked in peace but there I would find salvation.

When I arrived there, all that remained outside the walls were the trebuchets with their engineers and an occasional few men on horseback. Heaps of bodies lay under the walls.

I stood next to the wheel of a siege engine. A ragged, mud-covered man from the *khashar* approached. He held a stick and intended to drive me away, but I grabbed a rock and shouted in Ostyak that I would break his skull. He dropped his ridiculous weapon and, with an air of indifference, he sat down by the wheel and next to me. A Mongol rode past and turned to look at us. His white teeth flashed as he smiled and, after he had lightly spurred his horse on, he headed for another siege engine.

The mud-covered man suddenly shook my shoulder, gave me an intent look and began quickly moving his lips: he wanted to tell me something, unaware that I was deaf. He waved his arms to indicate something huge, he drew his twig-like finger across his throat, tapped me in the chest with his fist, and lifted his arms, then he suddenly fell silent and stared into space. Then I watched him cry and rock back and forth, opening and closing his mouth like a fish.

It was only then that I noticed that I no longer had my horn trumpet.

***

Now I know what the man was trying to tell me.

On the fifth day, when the filled moat allowed the battering rams to pass, and the *khashar* fell from the walls in bunches, the city again opened its maw, but instead of horsemen it let out three old men in long robes and round white hats. A noyon in a yellow helmet rode forth to meet them. They briefly conversed.

That gate was named Namazgokh or the Prayer Gate. The old men undoubtedly called it so. In accordance with the custom of these parts that one should not directly ask for anything, they merely said that while some men were putting up resistance along the walls, others were praying that the great khan would show mercy when Samarkand fell.

The old men were led to where the yurts stood, and the first tumen surged through the Prayer Gate. Then the other three gates were opened, and the city accepted the entire army that had stood outside the walls.

What they had prayed for was not granted.

The city continued to put up resistance even as it was overrun by the enemy. Like in Bukhara, there remained inside it some who preferred to die rather than be divided up into gangs of ten slaves. They locked themselves in a fortress deep within the city. The fortress was high and those who stood at its walls could see movement far off and the smoke of battle. The men who had prayed for mercy while others fought, now climbed the walls so that they could die of their own accord.

On the next day people came streaming from the gates. This was a new *khashar*, it filled the whole plain in front of

the wall and again I was swept up by it. We were surrounded
and forced to head for somewhere behind the hills. Along
the way, horsemen would separate out bits of the crowd,
and those people would remain behind while the rest were
driven onward. When the whole *khashar* had been divided
up, they began to arrange the people in a chain that stretched
across the hills all the way to the city. Then carts loaded with
something went past us...

What our overlords had in mind became clear when
movement passed along the human chain – something was
being passed from one slave to another – and soon the man
who stood alongside me handed me a leather pail filled with
a shining black liquid...

It was rock oil. Behind one of the nearby hills it seeped
out from under the earth. Until night fell, filled buckets were
passed by the slaves from that source all the way to the city.
It was the first time I had ever seen that black, shining water
and I could not understand what our overlords needed it for.
By the time our work was finished, it was already dark. The
horsemen gathered the chain into a large crowd again and
drove it back towards the city.

A glow rose over Samarkand – the fortress had been
doused with the rock oil and now it was burning.

Flames soared into the sky all night long. The next morning battering rams went to work, and men driven up onto
the walls began demolishing them and the gate towers with
sledgehammers. Soon all that remained were heaps of stone –
only the Prayer Gate was left for going into and out of the city.

Fate did not let me enter the city on this occasion either.
The weather turned hot and the Mongols ordered that the
bodies be buried and the moat covered with earth, as they
feared that plague could follow on the army's heels. At the
other towns the *khashar* had not been tasked with such a
thing; there everyone and everything, human beings and animals, were left wherever death had come to them. However,

Samarkand had taken a greater quantity of human beings than all other cities…

I was among those assigned to dig graves not far from the moat, which was now completely full. Others gathered the bodies along the wall, loaded them onto carts, and brought them over to us. I was so tired that I hardly knew what I was doing; to me the dead were no different from any other trash on the ground, while the overseers did not permit us any rest and soon, it seemed, I might even fall into the grave that I myself had just dug. Someone standing behind me pushed me and I fell down into the mud. When I got back up, I saw a Mongol horseman. He looked at me for a long time and smiled, as if he was waiting for something.

"Sewsi-Khasi?" I read from his lips.

It was Boorchu – the only Mongol who knew me by name. He had probably recognized me by my clothes, by my wild Yurak jumper – I was probably the only person wearing such clothing to make it all the way to this land.

Boorchu kept speaking and gestured, his hands imitating a trumpet pressed to his ear. He wanted to know what had happened to the present he made me. I stood there and said nothing.

He looked at me for a brief moment longer, then rode up, grabbed me by my collar so hard that I nearly suffocated, pulled me up onto the croup of his horse, and then bore me off somewhere.

The Mongol brought me over a hill, then pushed me down to the ground and pointed with his whip to a ditch that had been dug for some reason and then abandoned. I crawled down into it and looked at the horseman, waiting to see what would come next and not feeling any fear at all – fatigue and hunger had long since driven it out of me. He rode up closer, put his whip against my head, and pushed – I understood it as an order to lie down in the ditch.

I lay face down and waited, without thinking about anything, but no arrow pierced my back, no sword blow came.

When I raised my head and looked around, the Mongol was
no longer around.

I spent all night in that ditch, and the next morning I crept
up to the flat top of the nearby hill and looked out: on the
plain that Boorchu had borne me away from, the Mongols
were forcing people along in order to divide them up and
apportion life, slavery, and death.

I was not among those people.

The spectacle that was taking place on the plain in front of
the ruined city was something I had seen many times before.
The landscape filled with human beings did not surprise me,
nor did it scare me. Another desire within me was stronger. I
crept down from the hill and began to collect some dry grass.
After I had gathered a whole armful, I placed it at the bottom
of the ditch, then laid down and slept.

On the beam

One normally measures a peaceful life out by the changes that take place in it. A person goes from childhood to young adulthood, from young adulthood to maturity, then he looks ahead to old age and death. Along the way his appearance changes, children are born whom he teaches to shoot a bow or set traps, then he looks for brides for them or starts thinking about the bride-price – that is what marks the particular age of his life. I did the same...

Here, however, I had no appearance, nor age, nor children. After that war I measured my life out by my thoughts. They came one after the other, and each lingered for its set period – from spring to autumn, for a year, or for several years. They were different, and nearly always painful, but for the most part I remember only them. Everything else that happened to me seemed unvarying, and little of it was worth remembering...

Once, a *tau* told me something: even the *bonka* people, who wear clothing made from wolf skins and have lost any human appearance, know that no man dies before his time. A person lives as long as his task is not done. People are unwilling to understand this only out of their foolishness or their resentment at how short is life.

Here, on the mound known as Afrasiyab, my life, too, should have ended. After the death of the entity Sewsi-Khasi, there was no longer any need for me. That is what I was thinking as the Mongols departed.

Yekha had selflessly traded his life for mine, but why Boorchu saved me, I did not know. He apparently did it out of random kindness, such as is found even among the rulers of the world. If fate played a role in his action, then for what was I fated to remain alive? This mystery was like a nagging wound with the arrow still stuck in it and – hard as it is to believe – after the Mongols left I initially missed the *kha-shar*; the eerie emptiness and stillness of the landscape left me feeling afraid.

I settled into a lonely house with a big hole in the roof – this flaw did not bother me, on the contrary, it helped, because the lack of a cool breeze would have been stifling. I used a stick to dig a little ditch to drain the rain that came in, though rain seldom fell in these parts.

The wooden beam that had been heated and soaked in saltwater, lay there, too. Initially I paid no attention to it, but once, when I was weary after searching for food, I fell asleep on it and saw a person.

It was Nokho. He looked at me without saying anything, and since dreams follow their own logic, I was unable to ask him anything. But one day I laid down, closed my eyes, and recalled that dream – and everything happened again. Just as a person emerges from the darkness in the night time and sits down by the fire, so Nokho appeared. He looked at me, and past me – I could not make sense of his gaze. There were no wounds on him, no blood.

"Say something to me," I begged.

Instead of an answer, he rose and disappeared back into the darkness.

From that day on, I realized that I could summon people, I could call them of my own will and not just the logic of dreams. I would lay down, close my eye, and bring to mind the life that I had left behind on the Tree of the Yenisei. After Nokho, Iron Horn visited me. He was riding his black-headed reindeer bull and smiled at me, and the reindeer tattooed on his cheeks stretched as if leaping upward. Behind the Tungus sat a little man in a filthy jumper whom I did not immediately recognize, but when I did, I shuddered – it was the *soning*, Togot the smith's slave, who had given me his heart. "Stop!"

I cried aloud. Both Iron Horn and the little man vanished at the sound.

After these first encounters, I could not figure out where my visions came from – were these spirits visiting me, or simply my memory speaking? Later I was almost certain that they were spirits, because only dead people visited me, individuals whose death there was no doubt about. After I realized that, I made every effort with my heart and mind to summon Nara and the children to me, but they did not appear at my call, and I supposed that meant they were still among the living. That thought brought me joy, though it did not last long. The people that I longed to speak with – Yabto's daughter, Man-Effigy, Lidyang, Yekha, did not appear no matter how much I called them. Moreover, I was unable to speak. Then I understood that these were not spirits, but merely the past settling in my memory. Even the first time I heard speech did not dissuade me from this conclusion. A woman came, it was Forepaw's widow, and she said without even opening her mouth:

"You're still alive, but I am not."

"Is that really my fault?"

"Whose fault is it, then?" she asked and then disappeared.

After I heard that, I decided to throw the saltwater-treated beam away. I rolled it out of the house and dropped it into a depression that a stream had once run through. I spent several days without it, but then I hauled it back up and into the house, a task which left me exhausted. In those days I almost died from the loneliness, it was unbearable, and I decided to let those people stay with me and go on tormenting me, even if they were spirits and not my memory – what difference did it make?

Worst of all, my conscience would awaken even without them. It spoke much more harshly than Forepaw's widow had.

Every other life seemed clear to me, sung to the last word, and especially those lives which had been given up for me when I was going to my nest on the Tree. Everyone brought their treasures to me like they might to a prince for his store-house – in that, Yabto's daughter, my adopted sister, had been right.

Nokho led me to it, though he lived for revenge. Nara, Yabto's daughter, accepted suffering so that she could give me sons. The stout man himself, when he decided to shake the Tree, was actually bringing me to my own river, while Lidy-ang paid with his death, on a tree stripped of its branches, for me to stand on my own river's bank again. Man-Effigy who longed to die revealed his secret to me, and as a reward he received what he had long been waiting for. Iron Horn made me understand that I was a human being, too, while Togot's little slave gave me his daring heart, and my mother departed with the caravan of the dead, feeling assured that I now knew my path and I was not alone. Even people less intimate, like Noynoba, Kheno, his warriors and widows, contributed what they could for my sake, though each of them assumed that they were simply tending to their own business.

My mind pieced together my life like the shards of a clay vessel, and this brought an unbearable thought: these gifts had ultimately resulted in me living in a foreign land under a dead sky, near a city surrounded by a horrific moat.

I recalled the look of astonishment on the shaman's face as he pronounced the words "The spirits are gone. The world is empty." He discovered earlier than any of us that over there, beyond the Sayan Mountains, lay not paradise but the Void. There were no wondrous talents there that people might be endowed with, no whims of the supernatural powers, no Seven Heavenly Snows, nothing.

Suddenly, however, the thought came to me that the Tree was no lie, that my god who glimmered in the sunlight was not the sort who would betray me. He had simply proven weaker than the Void, the latter had split the Mountains of Paradise apart and vanquished him. Such things happen among both men and gods, someone proves to be the weaker…

Yet I did not know what I should ask the Void, how I might speak with it.

***

A stench oozed up from under the earth, and people were drawn to the ruins. Whenever the wind picked up and brought the stench along, they would walk up the hill that had become dotted with jagged stones, and they searched for something among the rubble. Such was their lives, and this aroused in me neither curiosity nor compassion. The city remained for me, even once it had been defeated and laid waste, something of a monster, and if it were not for that house where I was left unmolested, I probably would have moved farther from the hill so that I would no longer even see the city.

My lonely house stood two or three arrows' flights from the Prayer Gate. People dwelt in what remained of the houses to the sides of other gates. I lived alone and spoke to no one, and I escaped dying from hunger only because nearby, in a lowland, several scrawny trees grew that had survived only thanks to their small size, and they bore big, yellow fruit. Not far off was a grassy field where a yellow plant grew in tufts, and from the tops of these I could pick soft grains and eat them, as I had seen many in the *khashar* do.

In the same nearby place I found a deep pit with water at the bottom – it was what remained of a well after the stone that ringed it atop had, undoubtedly, gone to fill in the moat. Among the things that remained after the battle, I came across a leather pouch with a drawstring, and now I placed therein a flat stone, tied to the pouch the rope that remained from the being Sewsi-Khasi, and used it to draw water up. I drank as much as I could and then poured the rest over myself. The inside fur of my clothing that had once saved me from the cold, had now become rough and a torment to wear, so I escaped the torture by pouring water over myself.

Once a day, or less, I would satisfy my hunger, then return to my dwelling and not think about the future, about what would happen after I picked the trees clean and drank all the water in the well. My death was probably only a matter of time.

Instead something completely unexpected happened: my hearing returned.

Sounds

It happened after the hot season arrived. I was dozing in the morning shade, leaning against an outer wall. The wind picked up and, along with the stuffy heat, it brought to me something that made me tremble: bits of far-off sounds. Initially I assumed that the sounds had simply arisen within me, and perhaps someone was calling me to the salt-treated beam, hard as stone, to talk, but the wind continued to blow and the sounds did not go away. I got up and saw through the thick haze of the heat a string of people making their way to what remained of the Prayer Gate.

Now I ran towards those sounds.

The Void revealed its first miracle, but at the time I was not even thinking about it, just as a man who was famished to the point of fainting does not even think about what food he is eating.

Since the Mongols had departed, all that comforted me was the thought that no one would force me towards the terrible moat – now I went running towards it myself, and as I did I barely even noticed it. Figures with veiled faces were walking over the bridge, under the surviving arch of the gate. They raised their hands to heaven and sang something that sounded like mourning and wailing. I listened to the singing, still not completely certain that this was no trick.

*****

They told me that more people had lived within those walls than the entire Mongol army along with the *khashar*, and now so few remained that one could count every individual.

I, too, was noticed.

All that had survived was a settlement along the road, already familiar to me, that led from Bukhara. A wide, dusty path ran from there up to the walls. People walked along that path towards the city, and I now went towards those people. I heard the roaring of the wind, distant singing, and each of the people on foot turned their eyes at me, though they showed no surprise.

Then I learned that on this day, in accordance with their faith, they were commemorating the dead. That is why they were singing and lifting their hands up. They would go over to the ruins, however, whenever the wind picked up. They were looking for any items or food, and though both had been poisoned by the stench, they apparently had no other choice.

The first people I saw were old men and women. The Mongols had left almost no adult males behind, and that is probably why the first old man I came upon beckoned to me and said:

"*Injo biyo… Injo…*"

Those were the first words I heard and, most importantly, I understood what they meant.

When vision is lost, a person's hearing grows stronger, and the other way around. One might even say that I had begun to understand foreign speech – and there were a lot of foreign languages there – with my eyes. My eyes had become finely attuned, they now caught on any correspondence between sounds and the movement of people's lips, and my hearing was greedy for any sound at all – during those first days I would listen, with inexplicable relish, to the buzzing of the biting insect of these parts, a fly that would gather in huge clouds to torment people.

***

The old man found my clothing strange, but not my face. While the city of Samarkand had lived, it greeted caravans and no one here was ever surprised to see foreigners. The old man asked me something and as I shouted the answer in Ostyak – "I don't understand what you're saying, old man" – I was happy to be able to hear my own voice. He could not make sense of a single word I spoke, he only looked at me for a long time, then got up and went into a house where one wall had been replaced by hay stacked high. He brought me some bread, a piece about the size of my hand that was covered in ashes. I ate it, while other old men and women gathered around and stared at me in silence.

With that piece of bread the old man had lured me like a dog. I did not abandon my solitary dwelling, but I began to walk into the settlement every day.

A few days later, he gave me a ringing blow with a stick when, after satisfying my thirst, I poured what remained in the leather bucket over myself – I still did not realize that water in this region was the most precious thing of all. He swapped my Yurak jumper for the kind of clothing that men here wore. It was a long, soft garment with a sickly smell. I put it on and blended in with the local people.

Again I hauled stones and wood, this time not to fill in the moat but for dwellings and fireplaces. I was fed, but I went every day to those people because I needed the conversation more than the bread. I greedily took in every sound, and I waited for the Void to speak, or what I considered the Void.

A year on, I had already begun to understand the old man and his fellows, and several years later I began to understand the speech of the people who arrived here, as well that of the Mongols, who occasionally came by.

Initially, however, the two of us would converse, like children who have barely learned how to walk, and this level of speech was still not capable of answering what filled my thoughts.

My former life was now clear to me, but my current life was still obscure. Where was it leading me?

I took the return of my sense of hearing as the continuation of a life that had been interrupted, but life brought thoughts that were telling me something different than what I had expected.

***

Once I learned to speak and understand, I pointed to the city and asked the old man who was to blame for its destruction.

"Tyngis," the old man replied. "Didn't you see him yourself?"

"Who's that?"

"The Mongol," he looked at me with surprise, but then suddenly realized what I had been asking about.

"Tyngis is the flame of Allah's wrath."

"Who is Allah?"

"The lord of the world, the compassionate, the merciful, praise be to him."

"The sleeping god?"

"Only the hearts of the unworthy sleep. Allah is awake always."

Then I asked how that city, and many others, had angered this Compassionate, Merciful One.

The old man jumped up. "When a flame sweeps through, the straw remains silent," he hissed. "Remember that, infidel."

From that time I began to wrestle with a riddle that occupied me for some years.

I suddenly realized that the old man had got angry because he knew the truth and feared it more than anything else in the world. Neither Allah nor any other supernatural force had a hand in creating what I called the Void… Therefore, it was impossible to castigate fire here, because it is not a being but only the burning of wood, and it was impossible to anger the spirits by abandoning one's chase of an animal that had already been wounded. Here they do mollify the *kaygus* but only take what is necessary to live. Blood feud did not exist in this land, because the blood here possessed no memory. The population of this land was not divided up into tribes and clans but into those people who were needed and those people who were useless. The latter, without being subjected to any further torments, were simply beheaded or their necks broken. The former group were divided up into gangs of ten men, into hundreds and thousands, and made to live as a single body. All this, because this world had been created not by gods and spirits, but by living men who bore the name Mongols. They were the cleverest people of all, they had honed their wits to the point that they were incapable of making any missteps, and therefore everything submitted to them.

They did not have their own Nga or Sleeping God, because their god was a living man, and one need not be a shaman to look upon him. He was so great that he himself came to serve as the symbol of the lives of a countless host of peoples, and of my life, too.

***

After I spoke with the old man, I laid my head on the salt-treated beam and I began to call to me not the people from my former life, but rather that man whose name I did not know, and if I had known it, I would have been afraid to disturb it.

He came to me several years later, when word had spread of his death.

Then I managed to ask him only one thing:

"Are you the flame of wrath?"

"Yes, I am the flame..."

He disappeared for a long time thereafter. I was stubborn enough to keep calling him to me, and patient enough to wait.

But while I waited, many things changed. I learned something that I had not expected to hear. Horsemen clad in iron and felt stopped in the settlement to spend the night, and they openly talked of how men of precious Mongol blood were presently tearing each other apart with infighting.

Nevertheless, I still wanted to know something from him, and my patience was rewarded. One day we continued our conversation.

"I was at your feast. A short, deaf man and a blind giant, tied together, danced in front of you. Do you remember?"

"Everyone has danced in front of me..."

"You said then, look how pitiful is a man who clings to his life."

"Yes, pitiful."

"Why did you kill?"

He was silent for a moment, then asked a question himself:

"Have you ever seen how I hunt?"

"Yes, I have. And I will never forget it."

"You have understood nothing, then, if you saw it and continue to ask that."

"What should I have understood from your hunt? Why kill so many animals if it isn't to eat their meat, to make clothing out of their hides? Among our people, the spirits would respond with punishment so harsh, that it would be better if that hunter had never been born."

"I am not a hunter at all, and you are a fool, or you were standing too far away... There is the ordinary course of things, where the strong kills the weak, where prey is stolen from the one who dawdles, where birds begin to peck at a sick animal while it is still alive... The same happens among human beings, too. But have you ever seen a tiger coexisting with a baby goat, a wolf pack mixing with hares, a fox and a marmot in a single burrow? No. No one ever has. That exists only in the ring I made. There it does not happen that some kill others, and others use cunning to save themselves."

"But all the same, you killed them all."

"Of course, for it could have been no other way. If I let them all go, they would go their separate ways and then live according to their natures, like they always did. But there is a great moment, a very short moment, when they become completely different, starting that very instant when the ring is enclosed, and until the very moment when I launch the first arrow. The same change happens to human beings, and I have been convinced of that all my life. A man need only extend that brief, heavenly moment of peace and unity to the span of a whole human life. Then everything would become different. Do you understand?"

For a time he waited for my answer, but when none came, he went on. Now he was speaking quickly and angrily.

"My father, the finest of men, the leader of the Taichiud, was poisoned by his enemies. After his death my relatives took everything from my mother and me. The two of us wandered as vagabonds and went hungry. We caught fish to eat, and in the steppe not even the lowliest pauper stoops to that. When I tried to stand up for my mother, my uncle had me put in the stocks. Then our enemies abducted my wife, a woman I had loved since childhood, and brought her to their home and got her with child – but I recognized the bastard child as my own blood, that is my son, Juchi. Then my adopted brother waged war against me. And then I was thrown into a pit, and I spent fourteen years there! Fourteen years... Could you survive that long sitting in your own feces? But after I climbed out of that pit, I did not harbor the slightest drop of anger at anyone. I decided to help people, I decided to improve their lives at the root, and it was for the sake of this that I raised up the entire steppe. Only small minds would think that I was getting revenge, revenge for my father, mother, wife, the stocks, and that I was unable to stop. Do you know what it is that I live for?"

　　　　　　　　　　　　　　　　　ALEXANDER GRIGORENKO

He talked about himself as if he had not actually died.

"So that a beautiful maiden in clothes embroidered with all the colors of the steppe in springtime, could bear a golden tray from the Yellow Sea to the Red Sea without having to fear for her clothing, or her tray, or her honor. All men would live as I said. Then they would stop saying preposterous things about me."

Even as he was still speaking, the riddle fell away and I no longer felt any burning curiosity at all.

I saw in him something familiar, something I had already known: the stout man, only one who had enjoyed some success in his life. Just like Yabto, he feared life, he feared everything that was not tamed and lived by its own accord. Even halfway through his speech I wondered whether I should tell him that his grandsons, to whom he had made presents of little swords, were already at each other's throats. I suddenly felt very sorry for him, a man who had deceived himself and no longer resembled a god in the least.

"What is your name?" I asked.

He seethed – clearly that was the only question that the man who had become the ruler of the world, could not bear to hear. Without hiding his discomposure, he said:

"What do you need to know that for?"

"You're right, I don't," I said aloud, and he vanished.

I did not call him to me again.

***

After that exchange, I stopped seeking within the Void.

I found no cause there, no new god, and though I had totally forgotten about being part of that joint entity, I was still Sewsi-Khasi, Deaf-and-Blind, and that gave me comfort. I did not even consider the return of my hearing a miracle. What was it, then? I do not know. It sometimes happens that a person's illness subsides, and that happened to me, too...

I introduced myself to people with my real name, Ilget, but they transformed that into Ilhan, which in the local language meant "prince", and they chuckled whenever they called me. It was fortune's way of mocking me.

Few words were said as I lay on the salt-treated beam, and many years passed. I spent them all with a hoe in my hands, or working with clay and stones. I became no different to those people, I wore the same clothes and spoke several local languages as many of them did. Perhaps the only thing that set me apart was that the local people dreamed of packed bazaars, while I dreamed of the cold breath of the Yenisei and the look that the big perch – the *kaygus* of my river – had given me. Sometimes I would think about going back. It made little difference whether I died here, under a foreign sun with a hoe in my hands, or on the journey. Making that journey at least offered a ghost of a chance at happiness. I would smile and dream about doing it, but then I would snap out of it and feel embarrassed at indulging the fantasy. What would I go back for? To bow to a god who was weak? To see people dear to me, when in fact they had been gone for a long time, never to return?

***

What also set me apart from the people here was that I did not pray as they did. I did not pray at all. Initially, when the stench that came from Afrasiyab was still oppressive, and many were dying from hunger and grief, no one paid any attention to this. Strong arms – and I was undoubtedly stronger than many, though I was short in stature – meant more than a man's religious beliefs.

But time passed, and the people here recalled their god. They began to bring stones and mud into the middle of the settlement, so that they could build a house of prayer. One of the local rich men – and any person who had enough to

ALEXANDER GRIGORENKO

eat was considered rich – promised everyone who helped in construction a flatbread and some gruel. I took part in this labor, too. As we sat around in a circle and ate, one of the men who knew me said loud enough for everyone to hear:

"You're helping to build a mosque, but you're an infidel yourself. That's not good. Why don't you become a Muslim?"

I asked what that would entail.

"Get on your knees and say 'There is no god but Allah, and Mohammed is his prophet.'"

"Is that all?"

"And say it with sincerity."

He was a kindly man, and I did not want to offend him, so I said that it was better that I build the mosque – that meant more than words.

When he heard that, he stopped chewing.

"Look," they suggested a second time, "don't turn this down. Otherwise things will turn out badly for you. In the end, every soul will be judged by Allah. All infidels will be sent to eternal torment, and the righteous will go to the gardens of paradise, where they will dwell in bliss among angels and houri. Come to the mosque, Ilhan. I'll tell you about paradise, and you'll understand that our religion is the true one."

These words pained my heart, and I replied, "No need for me to visit the mosque. I am already in paradise."

The good man looked at me with astonishment and, without saying anything, he resumed eating.

The caravan

We did not finish building the mosque that year. The winter –
when rain alternates with quickly melting snow and work comes
to a standstill – I spent as I always did, supported by the people
I had helped in the fields. I had become a strong worker.

Things became different in the spring. Everything
changed that spring, both in my own life and for what remained of Samarkand.

A rich man arrived in the settlement, along with wives,
children, camels, and goods. His name was Ali. Where exactly he came from, no one could say. They said that he was a
friend of Amid al-Mulk, once the richest merchant in the city,
whom the Mongols had kept alive so that he could collect the
tribute from what remained of the local people. The tribute
was great, but the remaining population were few and poor,
and the fields had been overrun, the irrigation channels filled
with sand and corpses. No longer did caravans come by, nor
was paper produced, silk woven, leather tanned, or iron and
gold forged, and one could take no more from Samarkand
than from a dead man.

What saved us in those first years was the Mongols'
prudence: they took little and would put off the deadlines
for payment. The city remained lifeless, and its debts mul-
tiplied.

Then Amid al-Mulk died, and people said that the rich
man had gone to Allah as a pauper, for he had saved his own
life and the lives of his people by handing over money that he
had hidden away. The Mongols were merciful to other local
rich men, albeit to a lesser degree, and their wealth flowed to
the headman of our settlement, and from him to the Mongols. After a few years had passed, the local magnates turned

into men who merely had enough to eat and decent houses, and some of them began doing manual labor themselves.

People also said that the most important man in Bukhara, whose name was Mahmud Yalavach, won the favor of the rulers of the world by paying them in full, and then some. To do this, however, he took the people that he had authority over and turned them into a *khashar*, only one that served to work the fields and dig irrigation instead of to wage war.

While Amid al-Mulk had lived, the people in our settlement knew hunger, but not the lash – there was no one who would have wielded a lash. After he died, they realized that the Mongols' patience would sooner or later come to an end, and a detachment of warriors would be sent to us with weapons and a cruel man at their head. The people therefore prepared to suffer the same fate as Bukhara.

However, before the rich man turned pauper went to his grave, he had sought out Ali, and entrusted him with not only his debts but also the lives of his sons, widows, and what remained of the local people. Some old men in the settlement had known Amid al-Mulk's friend, so everybody came out to meet the caravan and got down on their knees before it, tears in their eyes. The caravan was like some apparition of a bygone life. It arrived at midday, and already by that evening the settlement was calling Ali "a generous man" and "a savior".

His camels bore a whole life on their backs: foodstuffs, vessels, fabrics, tools for artisans, women with faces uncovered and covered, suckling infants and feeble elderly – it was said that the latter were wise men whom the generous man had found among the rubble of other towns and taken in. Men walked alongside the caravan, their clothes were gray from the dust of their long journey, but they walked confidently and so they possessed strength and endurance. Those were master craftsmen that Ali had gathered to replace Samarkand's own, who had either died or been driven away into the steppe.

He was not exceedingly generous – just as Amid al-Mulk had done, he gave his workers a piece of flatbread and a bowl of barley gruel. But he attracted everyone who had at least a little strength in their arms, and the work was buzzing in the settlement from the crack of dawn. The first thing to be finished was the mosque with its low minaret, and one of Ali's wise men climbed up it and then announced the sunrise with a long, drawn-out wail: "Allah is great, Allah is great! Get up! Prayer is better than sleep." His call reached even my solitary dwelling, I got up and hurried to begin my work of carrying stones and kneading clay for bricks.

The mosque was followed by artisans' workshops, as well as a house for Ali himself which resembled a city in miniature surrounded by walls. His wives, children, and servants lived within those walls. Stables were also built there.

My life remained unchanged, only I now carried stones instead of a hoe, and the other people went on living in nearly the same way, but I could see a change had occurred: they no longer looked towards Afrasiyab. Ali brought craftsmanship back to this area, he paid the Mongols with what those craftsmen made, and though there were few such goods, Ali's quick wit sufficed to ensure that no new hardships came upon our settlement. In that year I saw many new faces – artisans from neighboring regions who had escaped death and servitude, were drawn to our new leader. Some came with women they had picked up on the devastated steppe and they built homes for their families. The women became wives and no longer left the home with their faces uncovered.

This all brought joy to people.

After the mosque, artisans' workshops, and the headman's house, a marketplace appeared. At first it was occupied by a few old men who set out some items they had saved from the city. No one bought them. However, for the local people a bazaar meant the same thing that Ali's caravan had: it was a vision of their former way of life, and the place soon grew crowded. They brought fabrics, leather, clothing, baked goods, decorative items, goat's milk, and sheep bones, without even knowing if they would manage to sell their goods or simply barter with them. Few people then had any actual money.

Those old men became the first tradesmen, while I – a manual laborer who owned nothing more than the ragged clothes I wore – became the first pauper at this market. Though I already knew the local language and customs, I did not understand money, and so it was with a pure heart that I would come and beg the sellers for a bit of bread, whenever I was not needed for kneading clay, carrying stones, or hoeing the earth. Sometimes they gave me some, sometimes they sent me away.

One kindly man, Murtaz, laughed and told me, "Ilhan, if you're going to beg, then sit over there." He pointed to a place by the gate leading into the marketplace, where a stunted tree grew. "The place for beggars is at the entrance. Take your robe off and show them your wounds, put on a suffering face, then they'll be more likely to give you something. That's what all beggars do if they're smart, I know that for a fact."

I sat by the wall, under that tree, and wailed. I wallowed on the ground, stirring up a gray cloud of dust. As it settled Murtaz laughed.

The place was a sea of dust, as warm and fine as down. My legs were covered in dust up to my knees. I liked that place by the wall, it shielded both me and the warm, gray expanse of dust from the wind. Granted, people did not give me much, and after I had sat long enough to feel a cramp in my legs, I went to the tradesmen to ask them for some work to do, and I got a flatbread for carrying something heavy or driving the dogs away. After that, the tradesmen began to call on me themselves. There were no other poor men around, and I concluded that this is how things should be.

But one day I saw someone at my spot next to the wall, it was a hunched, immobile figure covered entirely by a blanket, and I shouted, "Hey, this is my place, go away!" I had already bent down to drag the stranger away from my gray patch of earth, but people came running up to me from behind. They grabbed me by the arm and whispered apprehensively into my ear that this man was no beggar, but rather one of the wise men whom generous Ali had brought along. He preached a contempt for worldly things and therefore he always chose to establish himself in the lowliest spot around.

"You don't want to upset Allah, now, so don't bother the wise man," they told me. "Find a place farther away, or better just leave here. People are going to tell you to leave."

Yet I could not leave – I stood some distance away and waited for people to give me something or hire me for some job. However, I was hired less and less often, and the crowds in the market thinned as winter approached.

While grass had still not grown over the mound of Afrasiyab, I did not notice how special this time was. The houses that were often missing a part of their walls or roof, were open, and though the remnants of the local population went hungry themselves, they shared what they had with me, knowing that my strong arms would be useful. Time passed, however, the houses were renovated, the dead fields came back to life, shepherds brought herds of sheep, and the less hunger was a problem, the more I saw doors locked from the inside. After the new leader arrived for the community, there were more strong arms around, and no longer did anyone feed me thinking of what I could contribute in the future.

When the marketplace was entirely deserted, I knocked at the artisans' workshops and asked for whatever work I was capable of doing. Yet the craftsmen already had their own people for that work, and sometimes I was simply given something out of pity. Moreover, I found that I was not the only person begging there, and soon the craftsmen's pity ran out.

The people begging were elderly or handicapped, who were still hanging on when they might have been better off dead. Hunger had not yet made them indifferent to life, instead it made them brazen. They said that along with abundance, evil had returned to men's hearts, and we had no choice but to go to Ali's house.

We headed for the home of that generous man, sat in a semicircle at its gates, and waited. It was a sunny but cold day, an icy wind blew at us, and finally one of the poor people could bear it no longer:

"Sir, give us some bread!"

Then another spoke up. "Have pity on us, sir!" he shouted.

The two of them shouted until the gates opened and a tall man came out. He wore a long robe of red felt, and without saying a word he flung two flatbreads down on the ground and then brandished his whip. We rushed toward the bread and tore it apart like dogs.

The next day, however, there was only the whip.

Then one of the beggars, who had a withered arm like a bird's leg, said that obviously Ali himself was not at home, but he had heard that the man's wives, especially the senior one, had good hearts. So, we ought to hide, lest we anger the watchman, and wait for his wives to be taken to the dressmaker or somewhere else, and then we could throw ourselves at their feet.

"We might get a beating for it," he said, "but we'll get some bread, too."

Yet Ali's wives remained inside the home. After many days spent waiting, the hunger and cold had taken most of the beggars away, and when the gates finally opened, it was only myself and the man with the withered arm who met the wives.

There were three of them, they were covered from head to toe and only by their differing heights could one tell them apart. The women were accompanied by the same watchman in red felt. He saw us and brandished the whip.

"Merciful lady, for Allah's sake," the man with the withered arm managed to get out, then he cried out and buried his face in his hands. He was crawling on his knees while I stood.

"Don't let us die, wives of Ali," I said. "There were once many of us, now only two are left."

The watchman then took a step towards me, but one of the women stopped him. She walked up to me, her hand flashed from under her gown, and a coin fell to the ground.

The other beggar rushed at the money before the woman had barely managed to step back. He grabbed the coin in his teeth and then rushed off. I ran after him. He seemed to vanish without a trace, and I spent a long time looking for him among the buildings before I finally found him. He was lying on his back in the mud and writhing, his eyes bulging from their sockets – while running with the coin in his mouth, he had accidentally swallowed it. I grabbed him by his clothes, put his chest over my knee, and thumped him on the back until the coin came back up.

He breathed in deeply, flung his hands around my leg, and said, "You saved me from death once, now do it again. That's a dirham, a whole dirham… It can buy a lot of bread…"

That day we ate bread and porridge. Once we had eaten our fill, I told the man with the withered arm not to come with me to Ali's house. He looked dejected and left without saying anything in reply.

I went back and waited for some charity, without any sense of shame and without fear of a beating.

A cold rain whipped me. No one emerged from the house, except that one day the gates opened and the man in red felt briefly looked out. Cold assailed me from the inside, but then my body yielded to it and began to grow soft. I seemed to be falling asleep, and perhaps I would have never woken up again had someone not shaken me by my shoulder. It was night, only yellow firelight flickered within the walls around Ali's home. I opened my eyes and first saw the gates open and the watchman look out, and then only a woman with a veiled face.

"Better not sit here. The master will be back tomorrow. He hates people just loafing around." After she said that, she dropped a bag on the ground – it contained bread and meat – and then she disappeared.

***

Ali arrived the next day. He was tall and thin, and had a short gray beard. He wore a round white hat and a robe of several colors. He rode up to his house on a shining, thin-legged horse, accompanied by three other riders. Before the gates opened to welcome the master home, I ran up and grabbed his stirrup.

"Sir, buy me," I said.

"From who?" Ali asked.

"From myself."

"What do you know how to do?"

"Carry stones, knead clay, hoe."

"Then wait for the warm weather to come."

"I can also watch the door."

"I already have a man at the door. I need skilled workers. Do you know some craft?"

What could I tell him? That I knew how to line skis with animal skins, make sleds, carve arrows from larch wood? The language here did not even possess the words I needed to tell him that.

"I've got strong arms, sir."

"Wait for the warm weather."

"Look, I won't survive until the warm weather comes. You arrived, and now no one wants to help me eat during this cold and rainy time."

Ali called out to his men, "Give him some food and get him out of here!"

"I want to earn my own food. In this town is there really no opportunity for one man?"

"Wait for the warm weather, beggar."

Two men rushed up, tore me away from the stirrup, and flung me to the ground.

"Your wives are merciful, but you are not!" I cried as he rode on.

The gates closed and I waited for the promised food to be brought out, but it never came.

***

Along the wall, to the right of the gates, a tall, bare tree grew. When it grew dark, I lay at a low place next to its roots and waited for the gates to creak open, so that I could tell the servants, "You did not carry out what your master had ordered and bring me bread…"

Instead, my last words had proved prophetic: the next morning, a sunny and cold one, the wives – two of them – appeared. One of them had plunged her hand into her clothing in order to take out some alms. Suddenly the man with the withered arm crawled up and shouted:

"Ladies, he's an infidel! Why are you giving alms to an infidel and driving a believer away? A Muslim is going to die, while that idol-worshiper lives. Where is the justice in that?"

The coin had already fallen nearby, I picked it up and walked away, lest I face the lash of the fellow who was accompanying the wives. The man with the withered arm came up next to me.

I turned – and what I saw struck me like a heavy, iron-tipped arrow.

***

The gates had been flung open, servants were beginning to carry out carpets and hang them from wooden beams next to the walls around the compound. Then lengths of white fabric and articles of clothing were hung up – so the people of this land were accustomed to doing in wintertime, so that the wind would blow any musty smell out of the things.

The gates remained open, and I saw a large pot boiling over a fire in the middle of the courtyard. A rich steam rose from it. One of Ali's men was carving a slab of mutton while other broke branches and laid them on the fire. Women ran through the courtyard. They were caught up in their tasks and shouted, laughing, to one another. Then I saw the man whom they called generous.

Ali walked forth from the gates carrying two children in his arms. They were little girls with braids like black ribbons. A third child, a boy, walked next to his father and held on to the latter's robe. Ali was smiling and talking to them. Then one of the wives appeared, she had not considered that outsiders might see her, and so she emerged without her veil, and I could see her fresh face and enormous black eyes, as well as the colorful fabric that had been woven into her braids and the shining necklace that hung over her breast. The woman took one of the children from Ali, set her down on the ground, and led her away by the hand – her daughter had only just learned how to walk. Ali said something to her and laughed.

The wives returned to the gate. The watchman walked behind them, he led a donkey loaded with two sacks and carried a third sack over his shoulder.

"The rich man is generous," the man with the withered arm said. "Dried melon from Bukhara, apricots, meat…"

"Come on," I told him. "I'll give you some bread…"

We walked away from the spectacle of those opened gates that had been too much to bear.

***

In my hand was a coin that would keep me going for a day, or perhaps several, but I felt no gratitude inside my heart. Instead, my soul writhed in anguish and anger.

In those opened gates I saw the answer I had been seeking all those years. The answer to the question of what fated wanted from me. Just as other people had given their lives for me, so that I could live and live happily, so my life ought to bring happiness to other people. I, an unassuming little man, and the only survivor after we had bashed our heads against the walls of many cities, ought to now disappear so that I would not disturb the happiness of that rich man, his wives, and his children. I had survived while death carried off hosts of other people, and now, when the people around me were beginning to forget all they had suffered, death was coming ever closer, it was calling out my name, and life was pushing me towards the exit like a guest who had overstayed his welcome.

Most importantly, however, this was simply how things ought to be, for the same had happened in my case: the happiness of some people arises from the misfortune of others, just as a tree might grow from the dust and ashes of earlier trees. I had received my due, and now it was my turn – this is what the opened gates of Ali's home told me.

Perhaps, with a coin in my hand and another day on earth granted to me, I should have rejoiced and lived in hope that tomorrow would not let me down – every beggar lives like that. But a thought, a simple and terrifying one, came over me, and I was unable to shake it off. From hunger there is escape, even if it is fleeting; but not from one's thoughts.

Fate was staring me in the face – and I decided to stop it.

***

I went into a building and exchanged the coin for two flat-breads, and I gave one to my companion.

"Wow, they are really generous to you," he said. "Let's live together, I've got my own house."

"You're willing to live with an infidel?"

He answered without a second thought. "It's not me talking right now, it's the hunger. Earlier my father supported me, but he died a year ago." After a silence he went on. "I want to thank you for this bread, only I don't know how."

After we had eaten half of the bread, I knew exactly what to do.

"Steal one of the big skins for carrying water for me."

"What do you need that for?"

"I'll go to the shepherds and beg them for some sheep's milk."

"Ugh," the man with the withered arm sighed. "You really are an infidel. What milk are you going to get in the winter?"

"Steal the skin, and I'll beg for some food for you."

"No reason to steal it, I've already got one."

We went to his home, bare walls and no door, and I got what I needed.

"You'll come back?" he asked. "I was planning to trade that skin for bread once things got really bad."

"You already traded it," I replied and went to my own place.

There were only two things in my own home: a flint that had been given to me years before by some kind person, and the leather bucket with the long, half-rotten leather strap that had once joined the creature called Sewsi-Khasi.

I took the flint, water skin, and leather strap, and went to that far-off hill, at the foot of which the black, flammable liquid oozed up from the ground. I dug a hole in the cold mud with my bare hands and then spent the rest of the day filling the skin until the sun set.

***

I arrived back at Ali's house when it was already completely dark. I kept my distance from the gate and made my way to the tree under which I had slept before. I climbed up into the branches, then lifted what I had brought along by the leather strap tied to it. Back at the source of the black liquid, I had cut a small bit of the strap off, soaked it in the rock oil, and stuffed the opening of the skin with it.

The courtyard was illuminated by a few dim lamps. In front of me and slightly below was the flat roof of a house, the largest in this compound and undoubtedly the place where Ali and his wives and children lived. Everyone was asleep – even the watchman. There was no need for him to be vigilant by night, for no one, whether among his own people or outside the household, would lift a finger against the man who paid the rulers of the world their tribute and whom the remaining population here called their savior. The watchman's job was to accompany the master's wives to the dressmaker or the bazaar. Rich Ali did not even keep guard dogs.

I laid the skin over a fork in the branches, felt around for the wet strap, and began to strike sparks. Fire came at the very first call; it awoke and began to snake its way along the strap. I took my heavy burden, threw it down on the roof of the house, and then I jumped down from the tree.

I stood back up and went up to the gates. The glow over the walls of the compound grew increasingly brighter, and then a fierce flame shot up through the darkness. This was followed by people's cries. My own words now flew towards the shouting and the roaring fire:

"O generous man, it looks like the warm season has come. Are you warm, Ali?"

The gates opened and servants came running out, followed by the master of the house and the watchman carrying the children. When the watchman saw me, he set the little girl down on the ground and reached for his weapon.

His master put an arm up to prevent him from striking. "Stop," Ali said, panting. "Put that sword away."

The watchman spoke through his own panting. "Forgive me, sir… an easy death… I wasn't thinking… Forgive me."

People ran fleeing.

The generous man

The blaze that shone over the settlement woke people up. In the morning, they all knew that the man who had saved what remained of Samarkand from the Mongols' wrath, had barely escaped death at the hands of a destitute idol-worshiper whom he had refused a chunk of bread. If I had been set in front of the crowd, they would have torn me apart. Ali however came out and said that the matter would be judged by his own tribunal, and he ordered the gates closed. The crowd began to thin. Someone shouted, "Pity that Mahmud the Red isn't here" – he had been Samarkand's chief executioner. A number of people remained standing in front of the generous man's house all the same.

Ali's wives, children, and servants had remained unscathed like the man himself – the water from the well in the courtyard had saved them. The roof of the house, where I had set the fire, collapsed, and probably at least some of the man's household had suffered injury. People continued to bustle around the place, albeit no longer so frantically. They carried water, some cloths, and I heard shouting behind the door. Ali himself then stepped forth from the door.

Two of his servants bound me and held me by my hair. Ali now spoke without any rancor or threat:

"You weren't given any bread?"

"I was. By your wife."

"And this is how you decided to show your gratitude…"

I said nothing.

"As you can see, I'm still alive and even speaking to you, you dog."

"I set fire to your home, and now you praise me: among my people, not every man is worthy of being compared to a dog."

Ali's kindly expression vanished. "Who sent you?" he shouted. "Ata-Melik? The merchants of Khujand? Rahim of Kashgar? Mahmud Yalavach? Who?"

"You want to know the truth?"

"You have no other choice but to say it."

"Once my household was just as nice as yours: two sons, two daughters, a beautiful wife like a prince would have. Now they are all gone. That was how fate ordained it. Why can't I treat fate the same way it has treated me? At least then I would feel like I exist. If I hadn't set fire to your home, would you be talking to me now? Would you or anyone else notice if I just died like other beggars have? Now I'm the talk of the town."

Ali stared at me for a long time. "You'll confess. I'll have you hung up on a pillar until your tongue starts telling me what it should instead of nonsense. But we can avoid all that or whatever else could get the truth out of you. Who sent you?"

"I told you about fate…"

Ali spoke now to the watchman in the red felt. "Go, prepare the tongs, the funnel, whatever is needed…"

The watchman left.

"If I was the man you were taking me for, I wouldn't have sat outside your gate waiting for you and shouting."

Ali laughed. "Is the khan unhappy with me? Take out your paiza and I will fall on my knees before you."

"I don't know any khan."

He got down on one knee and then quietly said, as if confiding a secret, "For thirty years I have been leading caravans, from Turfan to the sea. I know every caravanserai, every water well, every moneychanger, every innkeeper. I have a lot of friends and a lot of enemies. You set fire to my home, and then you didn't run away, but you think I haven't seen something like that before? Merchants negotiate with the sheikhs of the assassins, they send their murids out and those kill whoever needs to be killed, but if ultimately an executioner gets involved, they enjoy the pain like melon wine. After all, first you wanted to get into my home, but you couldn't manage…"

A servant came up and whispered something into his master's ear. Ali's expression changed. He looked at me and said, "You'll talk." Then he went into his home.

I did not see him for a long time. Ultimately, he did not emerge but rather I was led, pushed down towards the ground, to him. Those several steps to the doors of his house seemed interminable. I knew that on the other side of those doors, pain awaited, great pain. I felt a strange pleasure, however, from the thought that I myself, through my own strength of will, was putting an end to the senseless path I was on.

Only instead of fire and other implements of torture, it was a bed I saw behind the door, and a woman lay on that bed under a colorful blanket. Ali sat next to her, his hand on the edge of the bed.

"Greetings, my prince," the woman said. "Now I see that it's really you."

At the time it was as if the very air had uttered those words, for they were Ostyak words, and the woman who said them was Nara. She was Ali's fourth wife.

***

I looked at her, but at first it was not her face I saw but time, an abyss of time.

She smiled and tears rolled down her cheek.

"Don't you have anything to say, Ilget? Say something. So that Ali would understand, because he must think I've lost my mind."

"Hello, Nara," I said and then burst into tears. I cried like I had cried on the day when the smooth waters of the Bountiful River swept me away from Yabto's encampment.

ALEXANDER GRIGORENKO

She went on, "I saw you already last autumn, at the bazaar. I saw you and I almost died from happiness, you were still alive. Or it was grief that pained me – I didn't know how to tell my husband about you, for after all, you were once my husband."

She drew her hand from under the blanket and wiped a tear away. "You looked at me, but you couldn't recognize me under my chador. But look, you found a reason that we could meet."

"Why aren't you getting out of bed?"

"The flaming roof fell right next to me. But don't you worry about that, I'll get up… Ali brought some wise men, they know physic. Let's just talk now."

"Where have you been all this time?"

"We were forced to go to the Mongols' camp, it was big, on the banks of some river. Then merchants came, there was a marketplace there and they put us up for sale, me and our daughters. Ali came with his caravan and brought me. After all, I was beautiful, wasn't I, Ali? He bought me and our daughters, because I told him that I couldn't live without them, and he generously agreed and immediately took out the money. How often does that happen, that the first thing a bought concubine asks for is granted? He made me his wife, his senior wife, because he liked me so much. Right, Ali? Only Allah took the children I bore him away as soon as they were born – obviously Allah needed angels more than people, so he took them away…"

Ali said nothing.

"He knows – earlier, another man had wanted to buy me, he served the Mongols. You know him, it was Yando. He was smart, he always managed to survive when others didn't. When everybody else from the taiga had perished, he became a member of the Mongol calvary. But things turned out badly for him: he stole money so that he could buy us, but the Mongols found out and broke his back. Yando had eyes for me since we were little kids, the poor soul, let him rest in peace…"

She sat up on the bed and I could see that even this action brought her pain, but Nara smiled and went on. "What do I care about the fire, these burns, when Allah has showered me with gifts that a person could only acknowledge with faith and joy? And joy that you're still alive. Look at Ali, he's the man that everyone calls generous. His caravan flowed into this dead city like a river of living water – and you weren't forgotten either, Ilget, my sweet prince. You weren't. But you didn't have faith, you wanted to set fire to Ali's…"

What could I say in response to all this?

"He raised our daughters, now they are married to merchants, and the Mongols don't trouble merchants. Now their names aren't Etl and Kyogl but Leyla and Zeynab…"

"Maybe you know something about our sons, Togot and Balna?"

"A Mongol in lavish armor took them away, there in the camp. They are probably serving him now. Wherever they go, the Mongols take strong young men… For some reason my heart doesn't ache for them, so that must mean they're alive."

While she spoke, the smile had never disappeared from her face.

There was a knock at the door and the watchman's head appeared. "Sir, the wise men are here."

Ali indicated some mats in the far corner of the house and said, "Go sit over there." He was not forcing me away, however, and when the wise men entered, he came and sat down next to me.

The wise men were two of the elderly that his caravan had brought. They unrolled a colorful carpet and from far off I could see that her body, the living streams of which I had once listened to, had turned into one large, moist wound.

The wise men conferred about something, then one of them came up and sat down across from Ali. He told the rich man that the fire had burned deep into her skin, and the only thing that would help was mandragora leaves, which were not available in these parts.

"What else might help?" Ali asked.

"Fat, though it is a weak substitute."

"Then go get some. And bring every potion there is. She must live, otherwise you'll both answer for it with your heads."

"I'm a philosopher," one of the wise men said, "and I know a physician's art as well as any philosopher knows it."

The wise men gave Nara some kind of tincture and she immediately fell asleep. They then left.

"There's no need for you to threaten those men," I said. "It's me you should be threatening."

"Be quiet. Everyone will get his due, and you will, too."

***

It grew quiet in the house. I could hear the crowd bustling outside the gates. People expected that vengeance was now falling upon me, but Ali and I sat opposite one another and said nothing.

The Ali suddenly spoke. "In Khotan I saw a young lady, the daughter of a Uyghur dyer, but she looked nothing like her father. I had never seen a face like hers among the Uyghurs. Nor among the Chinese, Persians, or Kipchaks. It was hard to figure out what people she came from. I was used to everything and everyone being easily categorized, but she didn't belong anywhere, and that intrigued me. The dyer demanded a high price, however. I didn't have that kind of money then, because this was a long time ago. So, I went off, but I thought about her for a long time, and then many years later I found her in the steppe, at a market there, and now she had kids and strange clothing. I readily spent my money to buy that apparition that had never left me. A year later she began to speak, and gain mastery over me. She ruled over me sweetly. I say this with no embarrassment, because I didn't even notice myself how I turned from an ordinary caravan trader, who saw danger and deceit lurking everywhere, into Ali the Generous, though I still think I'm the same old person. She directed my caravans, she brought me into this dead city where no reasonable merchant would ever set foot. Amid al-Mulk invited me here before he died, but I could have chosen not to come…"

He fell silent, then looked up at me and whispered, "Who will tell me what to do? If you know, say it."

I had no answer to that.

Ali himself answered. "People believe in Allah, but they don't want what he wills, they don't like it and they fear it. People say 'It's Allah's will' when they lose another person or they suffer from something themselves. But when you lose someone who is dearer to you than your own self, then only a saint could sincerely say 'It's Allah's will.' I'm no saint. I tell you now: you're still alive because that is what she wants. If she orders you to be dressed in the finest clothing and called my brother, I will dress you in those clothes and call you that. And I will hate you. It doesn't matter to me that you hold some grievances against how your life turned out."

I spoke then. "My life was her life, too. You took my life when you took Nara. You simply forgot about that, Ali."

He truly had forgotten that – he backed away from me as if I had struck him. I suddenly recalled the man with the withered arm who said it wasn't him talking, it was hunger. Now it wasn't Ali talking but grief. It was here next to him, because for many years Nara had been next to him. But what came over me, I could not call grief. Like an animal stunned with a club, I felt only a pain and buzzing in my head, but not resentment, guilt, or fear – that would all come later. And then I could see my own thoughts as if they were objects there in front of me, and the most terrible of them was the thought that I had burned Nara – it was my doing.

The wise men brought potions. They silently waited for Nara to wake up. Once she did, they rubbed her with some ointment, stuck dry leaves to her body, and had her drink from a small bowl.

Then we went up to her and sat down at her side. Ali held her hand. We said nothing.

Springtime Girl looked at me and smiled. "What are you thinking about, Ilget?"

"I don't know."

"Sit over there." She motioned with her eyes to the other side of the bed. "Hold my other hand like Ali. You don't want to?"

I did what she requested.

"There," she said, and then quietly laughed, "now I've got two husbands. Where could you ever find a woman as fortunate as me? Have you ever seen such a thing before?"

I looked at Ali. He was stroking his wet beard as if he wanted to wipe something from his face.

"Do you remember the Yenisei? Our river, do you remember it?"

"No," I lied.

"I had a dream of it…"

"Let's talk in Ostyak," I suddenly begged her.

"Ali is the master of this house, ask him."

"Go ahead," the man they called generous said, then he got up and left. The two of us were left alone.

"Are you in bad shape?" I asked.

"I'm okay…"

"Are you in pain?"

"No, not at all."

"Tell me, how could I ever live with myself after what I have done?"

"Allah gave us the ability to forget things, otherwise every man with a conscience would die of guilt eventually. You too will forget this in time. Just don't ever forget me, then it'll be easier for me to wait for you."

"Wait for me where?"

"Where all human beings eventually go."

My heart began to pound, I jumped to my feet and cried, "Those men with the potions said that they would help you!"

She replied calmly, without the same smile. "The wise men don't matter. A person knows when her time has come. I know. No leaves or ointments are going to help."

Then I felt – perhaps even saw – the ceiling falling down on me. My guilt was crushing. I put my head in my hands and rocked back and forth like a man insane.

"What's wrong with you?"

"Where am I to go, Nara?"

"Wherever your heart calls you to."

"It called me here, to you…"

"There's still time. Live here. I'll ask Ali…"

"He'll never forgive me."

Nara was silent for a moment – she realized that I was right. "You've got your own river. Where else should you go? Go home, Ilget."

"How could I? I don't know the way. I could spent the rest of my life and never reach it."

"Don't be afraid, just go… Look back at how things have gone so far: what other miracle do you need to happen, what other encounter with a person do you need so that you stop doubting in yourself? Go, my dear, go…"

She squeezed my hand, slowly pulled me towards her, and laid my head on her breast. I heard something that I had completely forgotten, but simultaneously had carried with me always: the sound of her breathing. Only it was no longer the gentle sound, as deep and warm as soft moss, that would lull me to sleep. I now heard in it a distant howling of wind that augured a blizzard. Then I realized that this was what pain sounded like, for after all, my head lay right on her wounds.

I sat back up, tears in my eyes.

"Don't cry. You know one of my lives, and I told you the other – there was nothing else. Know what I realized? Life only happens as one single thing, and you think about that as you die. If someone came along and said that he had seen a great many things in life, I wouldn't believe him. I could no longer believe that. Tell me about your life."

What could I tell her then as she lay dying? How I had battered down the walls of cities? About Samarkand's moat? About Yekha? About how I alone of the entire taiga had survived?

"Are you scared?" I asked, almost inaudibly.

"Yes," she whispered and closed her eyes. "Only it's a different fear," she whispered without opening her eyes. "Not the same kind of fear I always experienced before. It's… like the trepidation before a wedding. Probably the very same kind…"

***

The door opened and servants entered. They carried large trays and laid them down on the carpet. Ali was the last to enter. He had not said a single word to me since we last met, but he did everything as if I was a welcome guest in his home.

We spent three days talking. Sometimes she asked me to tell her about my subsequent life, and I told her about how the joint creature called Sewsi-Khasi danced, about how Yekha would ask me about ants, about the horn trumpet that the Mongol named Boorchu had given me, or how kind people had wanted to make me a Muslim or teach me the art of begging. While I sat there looking at her, I was unable to recall the *khashar* or the moat.

Nara smiled. "Now tell him, Ali," she asked him, "Tell him about our lives."

"He already knows everything," Ali replied, again stroking his wet beard.

She wore a smile those three days, and then she passed away with the same smile.

We took shovels and began digging a grave in the courtyard. Ali did not permit the servants to join us in doing so. Those servants and the three other young wives with the children were sitting some distance away and mourning their beloved lady, sweet Fatima – that was Springtime Woman's last name.

Then the watchman came up. "Sir…"

"Say it."

"The crowd is getting restless, they want to know when the trial and execution will be held."

"Tell them that I still need the man for something. He's still in the stocks, waiting."

"I said that three days ago. Now they are saying that you are being too merciful, that you are sheltering an idol-worshiper…"

"Let them say that."

"And they are refusing to leave," the watchman insisted. After a pause, he went on, "Someone is executed in Samarkand every week. People come out to see it, in all their finery, and they bring food. They won't go away, sir."

Then I told Ali, "You did say that we can find a solution without having me tortured."

The man they called generous thrust his shovel into the earth. "We can," he said and ordered that the gates be opened.

The crowd spotted me standing behind Ali – I was still alive, on my own two feet, and not hanging from a post. They realized they had been deceived and began to murmur.

Ali walked out to address the crowd. "What are you waiting for?"

"Retribution."

"You're getting bored without some execution to watch?"

There was silence.

"Isn't that moat filled with bones enough for you?"

Again silence.

"Go home. That is my verdict."

People remained where they stood. A voice in the crowd shouted, "If you forgive him for what he did to your home, who will defend our homes?! Any vagabond could burn them down."

Then another shout came. "Have you become an infidel yourself, Ali?"

"You'll get your justice," he said. "Just wait."

The servants shut the gates.

***

He told me about what he had seen, that the crowd outside his house did not consist only of what remained of Samarkand's population, but also the men who had arrived with him: the master craftsmen, their apprentices and journeymen, camel drivers, and some of the turbaned wise men. Ali had also seen that they would not stay gripped by fear for much longer that they had no other way to buy off the Mongols.

He, like everyone else, was well aware that the great khan had ordered that the residents of his conquered lands be regarded as his subjects and not killed, so that they could pay tribute as long as they lived. Though some had counseled the great khan to wipe cities and populations from the face of the earth, and turn the land into pasture for the Mongols' herds, the great khan ignored those voices and sent them away from him. The stench rising from Afrasiyab had long since vanished, homes had now been rebuilt, and people no longer pined for the way they formerly lived but had, in fact, returned to it.

"I'm no longer their savior but merely a wealthy man," he said. After a pause, he went on. "If I give you up to the crowd, what will I tell her later, when my time comes?" He walked over to the wall. "You can't stay here. The world is big, and *insh'allah* you will find a place where you can live. I'll give you money, clothing, and get you out of town safely. Let's go inside."

I said I would not accept any money or clothing. "Just give me some keepsake of her."

"As you wish."

He disappeared into the house, then brought out a small, richly embroidered bag. "These are her prayer beads," he said. "When she began to pray, she did so constantly. Perhaps it was for you she was praying."

I hid the token of remembrance under my shirt.

"Saïd, Rahman, Kutuz!" he shouted. "Bring out the horses, and bring your swords along."

***

The gates were opened for a third time, and now I went forth escorted by three armed men on horseback. Ali himself emerged on foot alongside them.

The man they called generous told the crowd that he had come up with a just punishment for the infidel: the arsonist would be exiled, and abandoned to Allah's will and to those who served as the instruments of Allah's wrath. The servants would take him far away and then ensure that he did not return.

The crowd had expected something different and they said nothing, but now a turbaned man came forth and said, "This man is wise and, as always, he had chosen the best possible solution, for there is no punishment more just and, at the same time, more terrible."

The crowd murmured, and it was hard to tell whether the sound denoted approval or discontent.

The rider behind me nudged me in the back and we set off for the edge of town. I gripped the rider's stirrup and my legs could barely keep up with his horse.

The pike's tail

We moved quickly past the bazaar. It was deserted, only the wise man who preached contempt for the world was still sitting at the spot he had driven me away from, there among the dust, under the bare tree by the wall.

There were no more buildings after the bazaar, instead the flat, pale-yellow expanse began. The mounted men brought me as far as the nearest hill and then stopped. From here I could see the entire settlement, I saw Afrasiyab and the tiny speck that was my dwelling opposite the Prayer Gate.

"Do you understand where you need to go now, or do we have to whip you?" they asked.

"I understand."

Ali's servants turned their horses around. I was left alone and all that I could hear was the wind and the dwindling sound of their horses' hooves. Then there was only the wind.

I took out the embroidered bag, undid the thin silk lacing and took out that accessory for counting one's prayers that had belonged to Nara. The beads made from black wood alternated with the birds made of now-yellowed bone that I had carved in my childhood – Nara had kept them all this time. When I saw the prayer beads, I realized that for Nara my life had gone on even when I myself believed it over. The prayer beads revealed that in the suffering I had lived through, which I called the Void, there had been a plan, a will that I was not aware of. How could I recognize it? Who would reveal it to me? This burning curiosity grew stronger than my fear, stronger than anything else on earth.

The dead were close to me, as close as my home and the salt-treated beam. But anything the dead could have told me, I had already heard. And of the living, there was only one who could have told me something: the wise man at the bazaar. I waited for darkness to fall and then ran to find him.

He was sitting there at his usual place.

"Hey, wise man," I whispered.

The man under the blanket said nothing, but I suddenly heard, as if the wind itself spoke, "Sit down here in the dust, next to me."

I sat down in the warm dust and waited, but the wise man said nothing to me. I could hear only the wind, and then I began to speak myself:

"There were boundless rivers of human beings, they flowed into one another, spread out all across the earth, raised cities up from their bottoms, and what significance did I have, just one drop in these rivers? What did my desires mean, my love? My dreams of happiness and a quiet old age, my dreams of having enough to eat and nothing to worry about? How small I am, how small and tiny my life is, but it keeps going on… Perhaps tomorrow, or even sooner, everything will be over – hunger will come for me, or a man with a weapon. What awaits me? Why aren't you saying anything? Tell me, why do you sit here and bother people? If you really are a wise man, say something. Say something, you fish shit, you wolverine, you hollow bone!"

From under the blanket I heard, "Are you that Ilhan the beggar?"

I was still seething with anger and I did not recognize the voice.

"No, I am Sewsi-Khasi, Deaf-and-Blind."

"An apt name," the voice said. It was like the creaking of a dead tree. "Every person is Deaf-and-Blind and unless he goes all the way, breaks his skull on the stone that lies at the world's end, he sees nothing, hears nothing, and does not understood what he is needed for. That is the only thing that I have come to understand all my life. That is why I'm sitting here in the dust. It may be that you understand more than I do… But how could you, you're a weakling who was too afraid to rip my heart out and burn it."

The dead tree creaked with a familiar laugh, and with all my strength I reached out and ripped the blanket away. In the moonlight I saw Man-Effigy sitting there. Besides the blanket he had no other clothing. I wanted to say something to him, but now the wind howled and beat at me, and something flew at my face, covered my eyes, and penetrated through my clothing…

Ali's caravan had found him somewhere on the earth, where my river had ultimately bore him off to, and then they carried him in a basket hanging from a camel's side. Here, in this village, he had reached the end of his span that, by some whim of the spirits, had been measured out in pike bones, he had reached the very tail of the pike and now he had become dust – all that had kept him together was his frozen pose. What now flew at me was not sand or dust, it was his withered flesh, and I wiped it from my face in an attempt to open my eyes. Not just his heart but his entire body came washing over me. I saw this once I was able to see anything again: instead of Man-Effigy, all that lay in front of me were his inert bones, and his larynx through which he had uttered those last words.

I ran. My legs swept me towards the house in which I had lived all these years. The sky was growing brighter now.

***

Dawn had already broken, but I still ran on, and I wiped the dust from my face as I did. When I had nearly reached the dwelling, I heard people's voices.

That house stood on open ground, people could easily see me. The voices were coming closer… I had no choice but to run towards Afrasiyab, where what remained of the gate called Namazgokh towered like a broken cliff. I hid under the gate, yet I was still noticed and I heard, "The infidel is here! Come on, catch the infidel!" Through the dense, dry grass I could see people coming towards me.

They were prevented from reaching me, however. The earth shook and was plunged into a chaos of rumbling, people's cries, and darkness.

Then it was quiet. The stillness lasted a long time, it seemed endless. I lay there and did not even think of what would happen to me next. A far-off shout broke the silence:

"Look, the Namazgokh gate collapsed!"

I did not hear any further voices after that.

I crawled out from under a heap of rubble and dust. The earth from which the gate had been constructed lay around me in massive clods – not a single one had come down on top of me. I walked up to higher ground and saw that there were no longer any people around, they had all fled towards town. The words "Go home, Ilget" rang within me.

So I did. Later, along the way, I heard that an earthquake had struck Samarkand – such things happened sometimes. But I know that it was no earthquake, that the Sleeping One had awoken and sent one sign after another, patiently forgiving my foolishness, pride, and cowardice.

I was in no danger of dying, and how long this condition might last, I did not know. When a man has no fear of death, he becomes a solitary figure; over time he finds it harder and harder to understand other people's cares. But I know that this solitariness was not the same kind that I had already experienced, that in this solitariness there was Someone alongside me...

I know that living without fear is a great blessing, and that I had received it undeservingly, and only so that I would understand how good it is to live and not be afraid. I will tell this to everyone with whom fate brings me together, and I myself will closely examine other people's lives, too, so that I might find therein some wisdom and something similar to the miracle that was granted to me, a small man, Deaf-and-Blind.

I also know for certain that the Tree of the Yenisei is not a lie. It led me to my own river with remarkable persistence and patience, because my little river flows across the whole world. Though I see steppe, mountains, desert, other lakes and rivers, I know that I am really wandering along its banks. I secretly hope that one day, the Great Perch, the spirit of my native land, will look out at me from the waves. I would be happy to see it, but I will walk on. I must walk and walk, because the road is long, and those who wander are blessed.

Look around: maybe I am somewhere here, among you.

October 2011 – April 2013

- *A History of Belarus* by Lubov Bazan
- *Children's Fashion of the Russian Empire* by Alexander Vasiliev
- *Empire of Corruption: The Russian National Pastime* by Vladimir Soloviev
- *Heroes of the 90s: People and Money. The Modern History of Russian Capitalism* by Alexander Solovev, Vladislav Dorofeev and Valeria Bashkirova
- *Fifty Highlights from the Russian Literature* (Dutch Edition) by Maarten Tengbergen
- *Bajesvolk* (Dutch Edition) by Michail Chodorkovsky
- *Dagboek van Keizerin Alexandra* (Dutch Edition)
- *Myths about Russia* by Vladimir Medinskiy
- *Boris Yeltsin: The Decade that Shook the World* by Boris Minaev
- *A Man Of Change: A study of the political life of Boris Yeltsin*
- *Sberbank: The Rebirth of Russia's Financial Giant* by Evgeny Karasyuk
- *To Get Ukraine* by Oleksandr Shyshko
- *Asystole* by Oleg Pavlov
- *Gnedich* by Maria Rybakova
- *Marina Tsvetaeva: The Essential Poetry*
- *Multiple Personalities* by Tatyana Shcherbina
- *The Investigator* by Margarita Khemlin
- *The Exile* by Zinaida Tulub
- *Leo Tolstoy: Flight from Paradise* by Pavel Basinsky
- *Moscow in the 1930* by Natalia Gromova
- *Laurus* (Dutch edition) by Evgenij Vodolazkin
- *Prisoner* by Anna Nemzer
- *The Crime of Chernobyl: The Nuclear Goulag* by Wladimir Tchertkoff
- *Alpine Ballad* by Vasil Bykau
- *The Complete Correspondence of Hryhory Skovoroda*
- *The Tale of Aypi* by Ak Welsapar
- *Selected Poems* by Lydia Grigorieva
- *The Fantastic Worlds of Yuri Vynnychuk*
- *The Garden of Divine Songs and Collected Poetry of Hryhory Skovoroda*
- *Adventures in the Slavic Kitchen: A Book of Essays with Recipes* by Igor Klekh
- *Seven Signs of the Lion* by Michael M. Naydan

- *Forefathers' Eve* by Adam Mickiewicz
- *One-Two* by Igor Eliseev
- *Girls, be Good* by Bojan Babić
- *Time of the Octopus* by Anatoly Kucherena
- *The Grand Harmony* by Bohdan Ihor Antonych
- *The Selected Lyric Poetry Of Maksym Rylsky*
- *The Shining Light* by Galymkair Mutanov
- *The Frontier: 28 Contemporary Ukrainian Poets - An Anthology*
- *Acropolis: The Wawel Plays* by Stanisław Wyspiański
- *Contours of the City* by Attyla Mohylny
- *Conversations Before Silence: The Selected Poetry of Oles Ilchenko*
- *The Secret History of my Sojourn in Russia* by Jaroslav Hašek
- *Mirror Sand: An Anthology of Russian Short Poems*
- *Maybe We're Leaving* by Jan Balaban
- *Death of the Snake Catcher* by Ak Welsapar
- *A Brown Man in Russia* by Vijay Menon
- *Hard Times* by Ostap Vyshnia
- *The Flying Dutchman* by Anatoly Kudryavitsky
- *Nikolai Gumilev's Africa* by Nikolai Gumilev
- *Combustions* by Srđan Srdić
- *The Sonnets* by Adam Mickiewicz
- *Dramatic Works* by Zygmunt Krasiński
- *Four Plays* by Juliusz Słowacki
- *Little Zinnobers* by Elena Chizhova
- *We Are Building Capitalism! Moscow in Transition 1992-1997* by Robert Stephenson
- *The Nuremberg Trials* by Alexander Zvyagintsev
- *The Hemingway Game* by Evgeni Grishkovets
- *A Flame Out at Sea* by Dmitry Novikov
- *Jesus' Cat* by Grig
- *Want a Baby and Other Plays* by Sergei Tretyakov
- *Mikhail Bulgakov: The Life and Times* by Marietta Chudakova
- *Leonardo's Handwriting* by Dina Rubina
- *A Burglar of the Better Sort* by Tytus Czyżewski
- *The Mouseiad and other Mock Epics* by Ignacy Krasicki

- *Ravens before Noah* by Susanna Harutyunyan
- *An English Queen and Stalingrad* by Natalia Kulishenko
- *Point Zero* by Narek Malian
- *Absolute Zero* by Artem Chekh
- *Olanda* by Rafał Wojasiński
- *Robinsons* by Aram Pachyan
- *The Monastery* by Zakhar Prilepin
- *The Selected Poetry of Bohdan Rubchak: Songs of Love, Songs of Death, Songs of the Moon*
- *Mebet* by Alexander Grigorenko
- *The Orchestra* by Vladimir Gonik
- *Everyday Stories* by Mima Mihajlović
- *Slavdom* by Ľudovít Štúr
- *The Code of Civilization* by Vyacheslav Nikonov
- *Where Was the Angel Going?* by Jan Balaban
- *De Zwarte Kip* (Dutch Edition) by Antoni Pogorelski
- *Głosy / Voices* by Jan Polkowski
- *Sergei Tretyakov: A Revolutionary Writer in Stalin's Russia* by Robert Leach
- *Opstand* (Dutch Edition) by Władysław Reymont
- *Dramatic Works* by Cyprian Kamil Norwid
- *Children's First Book of Chess* by Natalie Shevando and Matthew McMillion
- *Precursor* by Vasyl Shevchuk
- *The Vow: A Requiem for the Fifties* by Jiří Kratochvil
- *De Bibliothecaris* (Dutch edition) by Mikhail Jelizarov
- *Subterranean Fire* by Natalka Bilotserkivets
- *Vladimir Vysotsky: Selected Works*
- *Behind the Silk Curtain* by Gulistan Khamzayeva
- *The Village Teacher and Other Stories* by Theodore Odrach
- *Duel* by Borys Antonenko-Davydovych
- *War Poems* by Alexander Korotko
- *Ballads and Romances* by Adam Mickiewicz
- *The Revolt of the Animals* by Wladyslaw Reymont
- *Poems about my Psychiatrist* by Andrzej Kotański
- *Someone Else's Life* by Elena Dolgopyat

- *Selected Works: Poetry, Drama, Prose* by Jan Kochanowski
- *The Riven Heart of Moscow (Sivtsev Vrazhek)* by Mikhail Osorgin
- *Bera and Cucumber* by Alexander Korotko
- *The Big Fellow* by Anastasiia Marsiz
- *Ilget* by Alexander Grigorenko
- *Liza's Waterfall: The hidden story of a Russian feminist* by Pavel Basinsky
- *Biography of Sergei Prokofiev* by Igor Vishnevetsky
- *A City drawn from Memory* by Elena Chizhova
- *The Food Block* by Alexey Ivanov
- *Guide to M. Bulgakov's The Master and Margarita* by Ksenia Atarova and Georgy Lesskis

And more forthcoming . . .

www.ingramcontent.com/pod-product-compliance
Lightning Source LLC
Chambersburg PA
CBHW061537190726
48289CB00004B/1077